I0588027

UNDERNEATH THE WHISKEY
Copyright © 2017 by Chelsea Lauren

All rights reserved. This book, or parts thereof, may not be reproduced in any form without permission.

No part of this publication may be reproduced or transmitted in any form or by any means, mechanical or electronic, including photocopying or recording, or by any information storage and retrieval system, or transmitted by email without permission in writing from the author.

Neither the author nor the publisher assumes any responsibility for errors, omissions, or contrary interpretations of the subject matter herein. Any perceived slight of any individual or organization is purely unintentional.

Brand and product names are trademarks or registered trademarks of their respective owners.

ISBN 978-1-7324643-6-0
First printed, 2017. Second edition, 2021.

Represent
Publishing

Edited by Chelsea Lauren and Rebecca Ebert

Cover Design by Chelsea Lauren

Cover photographs by Gage Walker

For Mackenzie and Mia,
I love you both more than you know. Promise me, you'll always follow
your dreams.

Be honest.
Be true.
Learn to love you.

NOTE FROM AUTHOR

This story heavily deals with alcoholism, mental illness, conversion therapy, and attempted suicide.

I would not recommend reading this if any of those situations are triggering.

Underneath

the

Whiskey

Underneath the Whiskey

Chelsea Lauren

PROLOGUE

DECEMBER 2011

"I FOUND A THERAPIST." The words slice through frozen, relatively uncharted territory.

We already agreed to have a calm evening. An evening to reconnect and spend quality time together. This statement is cyclic.

"Sophia," I warn. My pizza slice flops in mid-air, never reaching my mouth.

"He's about an hour out, but he specializes in mental illness with married men," She calmly says.

My pizza drops to my plate, my hand frozen in the air. 'Mental illness with married men' … the fuck is she talking about. We've spoken about therapy countless times. Her demanding, me continuously saying no. I'm not the only one who needs therapy here, and I refuse to go unless she does. But this is something new.

"What are you talking about?" I ask slowly.

My mind gets to work, placing brick on brick, ready to desert the kitchen at a moment's notice.

"We have a newborn and a toddler, Ben. We're in this for the long haul. You're not happy, but you need to be. This therapist is trained to deal with these situations."

She has the audacity to ever-so-delicately sip some wine like she envisioned this conversation being peaceful.

"What *situations?*" I spit. I grip my wine glass, taking a few quick gulps, allowing the liquid to coat my throat before glazing over my thoughts.

"Reparative therapy."

I shove myself away from the table, the screeching of the wooden chair causing me to pause and listen. No cries start on the second floor before I walk over to the kitchen sink.

With a deep breath in, I pour myself a glass of water, but the idea of drinking it is nauseating. Instead, I lean over the sink, allowing my head to dip as my breaths are shallow.

Reparative therapy … gay conversion therapy. Sophia has never been so extreme with her therapy suggestions.

Pushing myself away from the kitchen sink, I ignore the dizziness and walk straight toward the island where the wine decanter sits. I pour myself another glass of wine, placing the decanter on the table between us.

Taking my glass, I pace the kitchen. We coated over my sexuality, claiming depression. She never wanted to speak of the affair. So, why now, after years, are we talking about the elephant in the room.

"Ben, if you love us … if you love Isabella—"

I pause. My back is to her. I take a sip of wine.

"If you love Isabella, you'd do this for her."

I spin toward her, narrowing my eyes. "How dare you manipulate me with her." My voice is low as I try to keep my free hand from clenching. Isabella may not have been the reason I initially stayed, but the newborn sleeping above us is the only reason I stay now.

"Ben," she breathes—calm and collected—like it was rehearsed. "I'm sure that Joshua was just a fluke. You fell for his personality, but not for *him*." Chills run down my spine as her tone changes with his name on her tongue. "I get that. I accept that. He was a wonderful guy. But if you are gay, you would have dated more than just him. You wouldn't have stayed with me. We wouldn't have a family."

"Soph, I—" I start, remembering the night in college when she broke the news she was pregnant. I came back to our apartment to end things with her. I had made the decision to come out. But then— "Sophia, I stayed because of Noah."

"So, then you are going to leave us?"

I stare at her, confused. We are a part of two very different conversations. I made my vows and my promise to her. We may not be religious, and I understand divorces happen, but I'm not that person. I'm doing the right thing, the mature thing. I'm supporting my wife and two children; what more could she possibly ask for?

"No, Sophia. I'm not leaving my family. That's the promise I made."

"Then it's settled. You need to love us if you are staying. I'll call Dr. Matthews tomorrow." She gives me a smug, satisfied smile as I down my entire glass of wine.

ONE

TODAY'S THE DAY. The day that I start interviewing managers to open my third coffee shop. In 2011, I opened up the first Isabella's Coffee, right after the birth of Isabella. She became the inspiration to fully dedicate me to my dream. Just four years later, I am going to have a shop right on Mackenzie Promenade, the main tourist strip in Cyan City.

All of the cafes are located in Cyan City. It is the perfect location, home to skyscrapers, the hustle and bustle of business workers, and a serene lake just a few blocks away. The city capitalizes on Lake Mackenzie, one of the greatest lakes on the east coast—complete with a pier that divides the city's lakefront. On one side, there is a park (where Sophia and I married), and on the other side lay a sandy beach. But even better than the park or the beach is the Mackenzie Promenade. It is lined with the best shops and restaurants, and naturally, it brings in all of the summer tourism. From every position along the street, you can look out and see the bright, cyan-shaded lake.

"Why are you so nervous?" Sophia asks, kneeling beside the bathtub. Isabella demanded a bath before daycare this morning.

I try to knot my tie one more time before sighing. I don't normally wear ties. It's not part of the uniform for either the barista or the managers. Today though, I wanted to look nice.

"I always get nervous hiring managers. So many have more experience under their belt than I do. And this *is* for an important location. This can't fail."

She raises her brow before standing up and drying her hands on Isabella's towel. "If it fails, it fails. You've got a loyal customer base, we'll get through it." Sophia stands in front of me, taking the tie between her hands and tying it for me. "However, if you plan to change your dress code, you need to learn how to tie this." She taps the tie before kneeling back down next to the tub.

"Thank you." I smile.

Glancing in the mirror, the tie is perfectly knotted. I take a deep breath in and exhale before smoothing my brown hair back. I should have gotten a haircut over the weekend. One restless night's sleep causes the strands to stand at attention.

Sophia didn't understand. Failing isn't an option, and there is only one prime candidate.

"Daddy!" Noah, our five-year-old, screams down the hall.

"Be right there!" I yell back.

Brushing away Sophia's golden hair from her face, I place a kiss on her lips before I lean down and kiss Isabella's damp face. She has a stunning resemblance to Sophia as her green eyes crinkle with a giggle.

"I love you both."

"We love you too," Sophia says.

Isabella frantically waves her hand. "Bye, Daddy!" she squeaks.

Blowing her a kiss, I leave the bathroom and then our bedroom before I hear Noah call out again down the hall.

He's standing in his bedroom with a blue sweater stuck on the curve of his head, his belly showing—though he has successfully put on a pair of brown corduroys.

Laughing, I kneel down and shimmy the sweater over his head.

"Thanks, Daddy!" He grins, showing off his new gap in his front teeth.

Both of his front teeth fell out over the weekend, and he couldn't be more excited to head to school.

"You're welcome, bud." I smooth his static platinum blonde hair before pressing a kiss to the top of his head. "You're looking very handsome this morning."

"Just like you?" His green eyes shine up at mine as I stand.

Neither of my children resemble me with my muddy brown eyes and sometimes horrid bedhead.

"Do you think I'm handsome?" I ask as I grab socks out of his dresser. Tossing them toward him, he sits on the carpet, placing them over his small toes.

"Mommy thinks so, and Mommy is always right. She always says, 'Noah, you're handsome just like your Daddy.'" He tries to mimic her voice, making it a slightly higher pitch.

Laughing, I grab him a pair of sneakers as he starts to giggle. He's our little jokester, the one that helps keep me on my toes and laugh even when our life starts to suffocate me.

I sit down on the floor across from him, placing his shoes next to him.

"Breakfast is ready downstairs. I have to go to work, okay? Be good for Mommy, and I'll see you at dinner?"

He nods, smiling wide. "And ice cream for dessert?"

"And ice cream for dessert, only if you're good today, alright?"

Noah shakes his head, giggling. "Daddy, I'm *always* good."

Laughing, I press a kiss to his forehead before standing up. He had said that exact sentence just the other day right before he got angry and grabbed Isabella's favorite toy from her.

"I love you, bud."

He shouts he loves me as I leave his room and run down the stairs. I pour cereal into two bowls and cut up strawberries and a banana, dispersing the fruit evenly into the bowls. I place the milk on the table and pour two glasses of orange juice. After preparing my coffee traveler and grabbing a banana, I pick up my briefcase from the island and head out the door.

———

ISABELLA'S COFFEE is not only a coffee shop but also a bookstore in a sense. We mainly serve coffee but there is a nook filled with at least two shelves of used books in both locations. It wasn't until everyone in high school started hanging out at the coffee chain, Beanery, that my fascination with coffee developed. Ever since I always wanted to open up my own business.

The obsession started off small. I would get all of the sugar-laden drinks, like my friends. We would all head there after school or even on the weekends. Eventually, my lack of sleep due to school pushed me to seek less of a sugar-high and more of a caffeine buzz. Thereafter, my addiction and dream took on a new shape.

It became an adventure for Sophia and me. At first, we would go on dates to different shops in the area, but then we started taking weekend trips throughout New England. The excursions were a thrill, but ultimately we were scoping out the optimal setup for my future shop. At sixteen, I was hired by our local Beanery. It was a perfect position, considering, but it also was a means to fund our road trips.

While my dream stemmed from a love of coffee, Sophia's was born via her love of reading. Her dream was to be an editor in the publishing field (which she had successfully become as of a few months ago). As I was busy admiring the cafes, she would be looking for a quiet spot to take her drink and book. Unfortunately, many of the shops we visited lacked that simple element.

When final exams became too much during college, and the library was too silent, I would seek refuge in coffee shops near campus. I loved the hum of the espresso machine and constant chatter from strangers' conversations. I did some of my best work in that setting—the free refills offered by Beanery helped too.

For my thesis, I had to develop a business idea that I would want to start in the future. We were required to plan every single detail and conduct interviews with business owners for research. That final assignment before graduation was the birth of Isabella's Coffee.

But those last few months at university caused our post-graduation plans to go askew. The plans to travel the country were squashed and replaced with preparing for Noah's birth. So while I continued planning and completing my thesis, the actual idea and process of opening a coffee shop were put on pause until four years ago, before we knew we were pregnant with Isabella. Luckily, the plans were already put in place that, with the surprise pregnancy, we couldn't back down.

Now, business is thriving, and I need to hire a manager for the newest shop. At the start of it all, I was responsible for both the managerial and accounting aspects, but with the addition of a third cafe (and a family to care for), the operations are growing beyond my capable hands, and I need the extra help.

When I arrive at the first Isabella's Coffee, my main working location, there is a line of customers wrapped around inside and almost making their way out the door. Every single table is already taken, and we are just nearing eight in the morning. I search in hope for my prime candidate, Caden, to already be here, so we have a space to talk. My eyes catch his at a table in the corner, the sunlight streaming in just right to bounce off his golden skin.

I wave before heading toward the backroom. I greet some of the staff as I beeline it to my desk. I'm not late, but I hate the idea of someone waiting on me, particularly Caden, someone who I've been intrigued by over the past few weeks. He's been coming into Isabella's Coffee for as long as I can remember, but it wasn't until a few weeks ago that I got his name.

At the beginning of December, I was interviewed by the city's newspaper concerning Isabella's Coffee. Although I had been featured in other local publications prior, this one was different. The *Cyan City Times* wanted to know more about me as a person. They reported on the history of "Benjamin Jacobson" and how Isabella's Coffee came to be, while the previous articles were more so reviews and forms of publicity.

The week it published, Caden and a friend of his were reading the article in Isabella's. I eavesdropped on the conversation, hearing Caden tell his friend how he'd love to sit down and get to know me better. I couldn't help myself and interrupted, causing him to turn a deep shade of red; he had the cutest face of embarrassment I have yet to forget. Since that interaction, I haven't seen him and have been worried that my forwardness was a step too far. But he is here and just as magnificent as I recalled.

Once I have my paperwork and his resume, I head back out to the lobby. The assistant manager hands me a cup of black coffee before nodding toward Caden as if I didn't know he was there.

As I walk toward Caden, his hands grasp his coffee cup, and his legs shake beneath the table. He's glancing out the window, his recently stubbled profile is completely clean-shaven.

Clearing my throat, I put on my most professional smile. "Caden Benson?" I place my coffee and papers on the table.

His chair screeches slightly as he jumps, and he forces it into action, standing up.

"Yes." He offers his hand. "Nice to officially meet you."

"Benjamin Jacobson," I greet, shaking his firm grip. "Please have a seat." I pull a chair out to sit and glance back up at him. "You're the gentleman from a couple weeks ago? My future competition?"

The same blush he wore that day softens his cheekbones.

"Yes," he laughs. "It's a pleasure to be here. When I found out you were hiring, I was ecstatic."

"Ecstatic, huh?" I smirk, an unknown confidence exuding. Ecstatic about working for Isabella's Coffee or about meeting me?

His blush deepens. "I, well, I'm a fan. I have a degree in business as well, and it's always been my dream to open a coffee shop. You seem to have done so well," he rambles. "I'm overwhelmed by your success, and here I am, still at Beanery."

"I believe everything happens for a reason." I offer him a comforting smile.

He takes a sip of his drink, and I take a moment to browse through my papers, despite knowing his resume like the back of my hand.

I blow steam off of my coffee. "Tell me about yourself. Your resume says you went to the University of Arizona? What brought you all the way out there?" I take a moment to take a few sips of my coffee.

According to his cover letter, he is a native of Cyan City but lived in Arizona for four years.

His brows furrow slightly. "I was in love." He huffs out a laugh. "That's the responsible thing to do, right?"

I want to laugh, but I know all too well what one does for love. My attempt comes out as a cough.

"But," he's quick to continue, "it is a great university, and I'm glad I went. Of course, me and my boyfriend broke up two months in, you know, college dating, but I'm just glad the school we chose wasn't a bad one."

I feel my mouth grow dry at his confession.

Dr. Matthews' words come filtering through my mind: *You are not gay, Benjamin. Being gay is a sin.*

Shuffling the papers before me, I shift in my seat. I try to steer the conversation elsewhere. "So, uh, University of Arizona?"

"Yeah, it's a fantastic school. I ended up meeting another guy and eventually graduated from there." He holds my eyes for a moment before studying the cup, his finger playing with the plastic lid. "Though that may make me seem boy crazy, I promise I'm not." He chuckles before adjusting the cardboard sleeve on his cup up and down. "I swear to you, I'm a mature, responsible employee."

I force out a laugh. My legs tense as I try to keep them from shaking beneath the table. It's a foreign feeling, my blood growing warm beneath my skin. Every once in a while, I'd come across someone who would have me catching my breath or stumbling in a conversation. But no one I ever knew by name nor someone I've had an active conversation with.

A lump forms in my throat as I swallow down Dr. Matthews' voice.

Caden's hazel eyes turn a shade darker as he narrows them. An uncontrollable jolt of excitement dances through my veins at his intensity. What if there is potential—no.

This isn't you, Benjamin.

I break our eye contact, staring down at his resume as my hands grow clammy. I need to say something, anything for him to know I'm not an asshole or a homophobic piece of shit.

"So, Isabella's Coffee is named after your daughter?" he asks. Caden's hands are now knotted together, resting in front of his cup. His shoulders shake just slightly as I'm sure his legs bounce rapidly.

I nod my head and gaze back at the papers in front of me. I have to stop my mind from chastising itself. I need to get through this interview, but my mind is out of sorts. Subconsciously, I am already comparing him to Joshua: his smile is different, his so full and white (Joshua's a crooked grin), he bears zero resemblance with his dark, wavy hair and hazel eyes (Joshua's blonde, pin-straight, and blue eyes), and in such a short time span I can already tell their personalities are worlds apart.

Taking a deep breath, I turn my focus to professional concerns. We talk about his references and how he has been offered a district manager position at Beanery, but desires this position more. We discuss his skills, strengths, weaknesses, and likes and dislikes in working at Beanery as I try desperately not to think about his sexual orientation. Under no circumstance could that alter my decision to hire him.

When I can jump the hurdle of being an unprofessional idiot, I find he's easy to talk to. In all honesty, he *is* an excellent fit for Isabella's, but would it be the wisest decision—considering his potential to threaten what I have worked so hard to maintain?

"Well, Caden, I think I've asked everything I needed to, but I believe you mentioned wanting to get to know me better?"

He grins, running a hand through his thick hair. God, his hair is amazing. It falls perfectly into place.

"How do you do it? Wife, kids, work?" Caden repositions himself, elbows on the table as his body leans forward.

"Very little sleep for many, many years. It's finally paying off, though I'm still not getting much sleep."

"Is it just you who handles everything? Or do you have a team?"

"I'm looking to eventually hire a partner."

His brows raise, his eyes never leaving mine. Only seeming to grow more amused.

"With opening the third cafe, the operations are becoming borderline unbearable for just myself. I do have an accountant and a social media assistant, but all of the behind the scenes is completed by me."

"A partner? That's a big step." He lifts his coffee and takes a sip.

I want to keep talking. Telling him everything he wants to know. The idea of him walking out without knowing when I'd see him again is unacceptable.

"Maybe if it all works out over the next couple of weeks, we could talk about you becoming a partner?

He swallows hard before clearing his throat and placing the cup back down on the table.

"Wait, what? How could I?" His brows furrow before he covers his face laughing while I grin. "You're giving me the position?" Through separated fingers, his eyes connect with mine. "I can't believe this is happening. Are you ... are you sure?"

Aside from personal reasons, I am sure. I need someone like him in my work environment: someone who is passionate and dedicated. Someone who has a reason for doing what they do—and he is actually qualified for the position—one of the only people who applied with his qualifications.

"Yes, I think you'd be perfect for the position."

Before parting ways, we talk over the logistics of when he will begin (tomorrow morning) and how to schedule him: He is still working at Beanery for another two to three weeks while they find a new manager. But he is quick to suggest working double shifts; one with me at Isabella's and one at Beanery.

As he exits the cafe, something unsettling jostles in the pit of my stomach. Something tells me that this is more than a new hire.

"HE'S AMAZING," I say as I chop up carrots and a cucumber for our dinner salad. "He's about four years younger than us and has a degree from the University of Arizona."

"We already knew this," Sophia mumbles, finishing the eggplant parmesan.

"Right. I'm just excited." I laugh softly, throwing the cut-up vegetables into the bowl. "He said he was really interested in co-owning Isabella's too."

She drops the tongs in her hand against the granite countertop. "Co-own? Ben, you're not handing over half your company."

I shrug at her concern. It *is* a massive deal and a slip of the tongue during the interview, but I want a business partner and have spoken about it before.

"I really can't believe you offered him the job on the spot. Shouldn't you have at least waited until you interviewed the other candidates tomorrow?"

"Well, I'll still hold the interviews tomorrow. I mean, I need supervisors." I sigh as I toss the knife and cutting board into the sink. "I don't know why, but I'm confident in Caden's ability to be a successful manager. Just his references alone. Plus, a partnership would be a conversation for later. I still need to figure it all out, but you and I have spoken about it."

She nods despite her shoulders dropping at the admission.

"Besides, I need to see how he actually performs first."

"Okay. I trust you." Her expression is skeptical, but she lacks the business knowledge to know what would and wouldn't be good for Isabella's.

Sophia walks toward me, holding the frying pan of eggplant, and kisses my cheek. "I can't wait to meet this amazing Caden you speak of."

A wave of guilt washes over me. I'm not telling her every reason I offered Caden the job on the spot or addressing the elephant *I* am placing in the room. Old feelings and distractions are coming back, but it isn't the time nor the place to address it. In this household, it will never be the right time or place.

Sophia yells to the kids in the next room over, "Noah and Isabella, dinner is ready!"

Grabbing the salad bowl and the dressing from the fridge, I place them both on the table.

"Daddy, did Mommy show you what I did today?" Noah asks excitedly as he climbs up and onto his chair, hurriedly grabbing cucumbers out of the salad bowl.

I help Isabella up into her booster seat. "No, bud. What did you do?"

He vacates his chair and runs to the refrigerator.

As I start preparing a plate for Isabella, he shoves a piece of paper into my arm that must be new amongst the other artwork he's placed on the fridge.

"Look! It's us!"

He shows me a picture he has drawn of the family. Sophia and I are holding stick hands while he holds hands with his sister. There is a dog on a leash too.

"Noah, we don't have a dog," I say, focusing on cutting up Isabella's eggplant into bite-size pieces.

"No, but now it's in a picture. We need to get one."

I glance over at Sophia. She tries her best not to laugh— a welcomed expression from her straight face through dinner prep. Noah goes back to his seat without another word and begins assembling a plate of food with Sophia's help.

"That isn't how it works. Just because you drew a picture of us with a dog doesn't mean we will get one."

He looks up with sad eyes and a familiar pout.

I ruffle his hair before sitting down between him and Isabella.

"I want doggy!" Isabella exclaims.

Sophia pushes Noah's plated food toward him. "Your father and I will discuss it."

Grabbing more cucumbers from the salad bowl, Noah settles and begins to eat.

———————

IT'S a difficult night of getting the kids to sleep—by the time they pass out, Sophia and I head straight to bed.

As Sophia changes her clothes a few feet away, the day's events filter through my head. Interviewing Caden, hiring Caden, Caden's red and embarrassed face—

"Caden's gay," I blurt.

Sophia looks over at me as her head comes through the loose t-shirt she is pulling on. I watch as fear passes over her face.

"Should I be concerned?" She pulls her bra off from under the shirt.

"What?" I shake my head. "No, definitely not."

She loosens her hair from the ponytail and brushes her golden locks.

"So why did you mention it? If it's not going to be an issue?"

I look her up and down. She's flawless, as she tended to be. Her face is free of makeup and holding a small amount of exhaustion from the day. Her nipples poke against the cotton of her t-shirt, and I can see her black lace underwear beneath her shirt that makes her ass look so tempting. Yet, here I am thinking and talking about someone else, instead of pulling my wife close to me and making love to her.

"I don't know," I answer. In all honesty, I do know why. I am *supposed* to be straight.

"How'd you even find that out?"

"He said he moved to Arizona for university with his boyfriend," I explained. "I don't even know why I keep thinking about it."

"Ben, we are in a really great place right now." Her

dismay is evident with a wrinkle right above her right brow and the way she inhales slightly deeper. "This year has been the first year in a long while that I'm confident in us." She climbs onto her side of the bed, snuggling into my side. "Our children are wonderful, our careers are blossoming, and I feel like we are both finally happy. Please, don't go and fuck this up."

I swallow at her vulgarity, wrapping my arms around her and kissing the top of her head.

"I won't, love. I won't."

Still, I can't help thinking about what it would be like to get to know Caden. Maybe I can take him out on a date if he is interested in me? Would he be worth the risk?

"So, about this dog?" She lets out a giggle, changing the subject as her body relaxes against me.

TWO

A WEEK into working with Caden, he has already proved to be exactly as I hoped. While his days are long and it's challenging to schedule seamlessly with Beanery, his dedication makes it work. Most mornings, he is free, which allows him to assist me in the remainder of the hiring process. Therefore, we can hire and go through training without me working double shifts, and this allows me to pick Noah and Isabella up from their respective schools and be home in time for dinner. A lot of work ends up following me home as I try to maintain the other two stores, but spending the evening with my family is a priority.

"God, everyone is awful today." Caden laughs, burying his head in his hands. "There is no amount of coffee that can fix this."

Today we are hoping to finalize the new hires for the third shop. We already selected an assistant manager and two baristas, but we are far from being finished. There is an open fair going on from 9:00 a.m. to 4:00 p.m.—and it is only noon.

I place my hand on his back, about to offer sympathy, but quickly pull away when he looks over at me. Straight guys can touch the backs of other men, right?

My cheeks redden as I clear my throat. "Wanna grab some lunch?"

"Oh yes, please." He laughs. My lapse in judgment going unnoticed.

After leaving a note and informing the store staff that we'll be back, Caden and I head out of Isabella's.

"Can I take you to my favorite place?" Caden asks once we take a right out of Isabella's and head down the street.

I nod with a smile, and he starts a half a step in front of me to lead the way.

When we aren't talking about work, it's like my brain stops functioning. I don't know how people speak or communicate despite me doing it with every other person in my life aside from Caden. Instead, my mind overthinks, and my hands get clammy, and my heart starts to race, all over thinking about asking him about something in his life.

"You okay?" His arm nudges mine as we bypass a couple walking toward us. Caden's hand accidentally grazes my own causing me to stumble on my feet, falling a few steps behind him.

"Ye-yeah. Just a ... a lot on my mind." Blinking rapidly, I try to focus on my footing and coming up with a better excuse —one that explains my stuttering.

"Anything I can help with?"

"Tell me about yourself," I blurt.

Caden's eyes crinkle in laughter. Once I'm standing next to him again, we start to walk.

"That's what is on your mind?"

"Yes." I swallow. Obviously, as the owner, I'd be curious to know more about my employees than just their resumes. *Right?*

Perspiration gathers in my palms in his silence, but his eyes remain amused. Suddenly, he stops short, reaching out for my arm.

"Sorry! Right here." He apologizes, gesturing to Bread and Co., a sandwich and soup cafe.

Sophia always mentions her job often provides lunch from here, but the two of us have never gone together.

We seat ourselves, and before I can try to resume a conversation, a waitress strolls over with menus and water. After all the coffee we had this morning, water is greatly appreciated.

"You seem off today," Caden says, resting his hands on top of the menu. "Like you're really nervous for some reason."

I lift the menu from the table and bow my head to read it better. "I'm sorry," I mutter, scanning all the options. It seems they have every sandwich and wrap combination under the sun.

He doesn't push, just sits and sips water as I continue to mull my options. When the waitress returns, we both ask for buffalo chicken wraps, and she takes the menu back as I feel my face warm.

"Can I be honest with you?"

Remain calm, act confident. You're a successful business owner, and this guy barely knows you.

"Of course." I smile.

"I feel like whenever we aren't talking about Isabella's, and we are alone, you get ... weird?" He squints his eyes slightly as if 'weird' tastes bad on his tongue. "Have I done something wrong?"

I wave my hands. "No, no, no." I let out a fake laugh. "Definitely not.

"Then, what is it?" He interlocks his fingers, placing them on the table.

"I'm fascinated by the fact that you're gay." My hands fly to cover my mouth in an instant.

FUCK.

"I'm sorry, but did you just say *fascinated?*" His face pales, and he leans back in his chair, crossing his arms.

"No! Yes ... goddamnit." I tug at my hair, resting my elbows on the table before massaging my eyes with my palms.

"What I meant to say is I think it's awesome you're comfortable with who you are."

"And you're not?" The edge to his voice is unsettling.

"Maybe not," I snap.

There is no reason to snap at him, considering I'm the one who made a comment in the first place. Maybe it's due to the fact that it's been an exhausting day, and we are only halfway through interviews, but I don't snap—at least not to those I don't know.

I take a deep breath, ready to apologize when he pulls his phone out and begins to scroll through his Instagram feed. Breathing out, I let my shoulders sink back into the seat.

When our food arrives, I take him setting his phone down as my opportunity to speak.

"Look, I'm …" I exhale. I had so many minutes to think of an apology.

"Let's just forget about it, okay?" His eyes are on his wrap the entire time before he takes a massive bite.

"No, I don't want you to feel uncomfortable around me," I say. "I'm cool with who you like. I just—I just wish I was more comfortable in my own skin."

He finishes chewing before he looks me in the eye. His hazel eyes are a shade darker than they were just outside when he laughed.

"You seem to have it figured out, Ben. Business, wife, and kids by the age of twenty-nine." There seems to be a hint of jealousy at his words.

"My life is a bit more complicated, but I apologize for my behavior."

Despite my sincerity, he doesn't seem phased.

He sighs. "Look, it took me a long time to get to where I am today. I'm at a point in my life where I can stand up for myself. I know exactly who I am and who I want to be," he explains. "I don't want to be put in a position where I feel uncomfortable or disrespected. You say that you don't mean it to come off as if you don't have a problem with me, and maybe you don't, but I have no problem walking away if I need to."

And just like that, he finalized the conversation, taking to eating his wrap, leaving me questioning how the hell I was going to control my overactive brain around him.

LATER THAT EVENING, after the kids are asleep, Sophia pours us two glasses of red wine before we settle in the living room.

"How were the interviews?" she asks, scrolling through the channels as she leans into my side.

"Everything was pretty shitty."

She sits up a bit, intent on hearing more.

"The interviews were terrible, and I'm messing things up with Caden."

She's quick to make space between us on the couch. "How so?"

"I'm making it awkward, him being gay and all. For some reason, it won't leave my mind. It was never an issue with Joshua, so I don't understand why it's an issue with Caden."

Sophia takes a sip of wine before placing her feet flat on the ground. "You need to focus on opening up Isabella's. Whoever Caden likes has nothing to do with you." She shuts off the television before standing. "You have far more important things to worry about."

With her wine in hand, she leaves the living room, padding up the stairs.

THREE

THE FOLLOWING morning is the last day of the hiring fair. All I need is for today to run smoothly and for Caden to hopefully forgive me for yesterday. Except, Sophia ignores the alarm because she doesn't feel well, leaving our usual duel parenting team solely up to me. We had a perfected system; Sophia gets Isabella ready while I oversee Noah's process and prepare breakfast.

Isabella isn't thrilled by the change of routine, making it more complicated to get her situated. And Noah isn't satisfied by the shape of his toast. In the meantime, I spill coffee on my shirt, not only staining it but burning my skin in the process.

By the time I drop both kids off at school—not only are they late, but so am I. I rush through the doors, my eyes immediately searching for Caden. A few people look up from their tables alone, most likely awaiting an interview.

I spot Caden at the same table we were at yesterday with our paperwork and two coffees in front of him.

"Good morning." He smiles.

I sigh in relief. At least someone has a smiling face this morning.

"Rough morning? I got you some coffee."

"Morning." I take the coffee from him, taking a sip of the thankfully still warm liquid. Naturally, I left my travel mug at home after I spilled coffee.

I excuse myself to get situated in the backroom before I rejoin Caden, ready to call upon the first interview: a young girl fresh out of high school.

The interviews are turning out better than they were yesterday. I intended to ask Caden to lunch again to make up for the day before, but Caden leaves with a friend once our break comes. Instead, I spend my lunch working on paperwork produced by the new shop, but I keep getting distracted by thoughts of Caden.

We will only be working side by side for another two weeks, but I can't allow there to be any awkwardness between us. I don't need to build a friendship, but I do need to be professional and friendly. I refuse to run a business where my employees aren't happy working for me or Isabella's, and Caden won't be the first one.

A few hours and many interviews later, we finally are done for the day. After getting a text from Sophia that she picked the kids up from school and was feeling a little better, I make the executive decision to not go home immediately. The day was so hectic that we haven't had a moment to even discuss potential employees.

"Hey Caden, do you want to go out for a drink before we call it a day?" I ask. "Maybe we can make a final decision on your staff and just relax a little?"

He sits up straight and checks his watch. While his schedule at Beanery is to work nights until his two weeks are complete, he managed to get both of our hiring fairs off since they were longer shifts.

"Don't you have to head home for dinner?"

I shrug my shoulders, picking up the resumes we received. "Usually, but I figure interviewing can be a bit mind-numbing."

He eyes me, collecting his belongings before he clicks on his phone, reading through a few messages he received.

"Give me one reason we should hang out."

I smile, which causes him to lift his brow. This always worked with Joshua when we'd get into disagreements: "I'm buying; you choose the place."

He lifts his messenger bag onto his shoulder before smirking. "Follow me then."

Caden is out the door before I can comprehend him agreeing. I jog to catch up, taking a left outside of the coffee shop. About 500 feet from the cafe, we turn down a lane that's foreign to me. It always seemed so desolate that I never felt the need to check it out.

To be fair, my assumptions are correct. All we head toward is a garbage bin. Behind it leads to the next street.

"Prepare for your life to change, Benjamin." Caden grins, opening a plain, unassuming door to his right.

Cautiously, I walk in.

It's a small place, filled with velvet chairs and tiny, two-person wooden tables. The dark wood and mythological paintings on the walls give it an antique, mystical feel.

A bartender greets Caden before we take a seat off to the side of the bar.

"What is this place?" It's beautiful and … quiet.

Caden hands me a menu that reads "Gin and Grin" in bold, gold letters. I chuckle at the name and open it, noticing it's strictly a gin-only bar.

"I hope you like gin."

I nod, trying to disguise how overwhelmed I feel. The menu is roughly ten pages long. I never knew there were so many different types of gin.

"It's a friend's bar," Caden says, again his menu closed. "It's dead now, but around eight every night, it's packed. I hated gin before he opened this place, and now I'm in love.

It's perfect to come and unwind here because even when it's packed, it's not a raging pub, you know?"

"This place is beautiful. I can't believe I've never heard of it before."

"He isn't into advertising. There's a small sign on the door with two G's, but other than that, it's all been word of mouth. And shit, it's worked well for him."

"That's amazing, but I'll be honest, I know nothing about gin." I look up sheepishly. "I'm more of a whiskey guy. What's your favorite?"

He grins, taking the menu out of my hands. He places it in the menu holder before walking up to the bar.

I watch as he visibly relaxes, talking to his friend. His face lights up in a way I hope one day I can be the reason for. They talk a bit longer than necessary as both drinks are mixed far before their conversation ends, but I'm not bothered, nor in a rush. It's almost comforting admiring him in a new element.

Caden comes back to the table with two cloudy glasses. He hands me one, raising his glass in a toast.

"To you," he cheers.

"To *you!*" I follow, clinking his glass before taking a sip.

Savoring the moment—the coolness on my tongue, the goosebumps on my forearms, his smile directed toward me. I close my eyes, taking a snapshot of the time we are on equal footing.

"So, why are we toasting to me?" I ask.

His smile glows in the dim light.

Taking another sip of liquid, I let it coat and burn the back of my throat before swallowing. It's been a few years since I last had hard liquor.

"Because without you, I'd still be at Beanery. Now, in a couple of days, that will be history. So, thank you. I'm sorry we got off on the wrong foot."

"Don't be. It is my fault," I say, waving him off. "I'm an awkward idiot, and my marriage has been rocky lately. So, it was a breath of fresh air to see you so upfront about who you are."

There's a shift in my head, questioning why I'd offer information that isn't true. My marriage is stable.

"I may be comfortable with myself now, but that doesn't mean that my relationship life is great," he offers, tilting his head slightly.

I take another sip, sinking further into my chair. He has phenomenal taste in liquor.

"So, the interviews today were much better than yesterday. Anyone catch your eye in particular? There are a few people I really—"

"Ben," he sighs, cutting me off. "You seem like you could really use a friend. Can I be that friend right now?"

My fingers grip the condensing glass as they start to slip. I'm grateful for the low light of the bar as my face grows warm, my pits sweat underneath my layers. Of course, I want him to be a friend. But I'm not ready. I'm not comfortable enough.

"I appreciate the offer, I really do." This time, I take a gulp, blinking through the burn. "But if I let you in my life, it'll not only ruin mine but yours also."

"I don't understand." He leans forward, giving me a puzzled look that releases butterflies in my stomach.

"Caden, you seem like a wonderful person." I down the rest of my gin, knowing I have only mere minutes to desert the area before I make a mistake. "I want nothing more than to have you in my life, but I'm just not strong enough."

I stand, tossing forty dollars on the table to cover the drinks.

He tries to protest, but he doesn't follow me. He just remains at the table as I walk out the door. The cool winter air sobers me quick. Another minute in the warmth and I could have damaged my marriage. I can't let my guard down. I can't go back to therapy. I sure as hell can't trust that Caden wouldn't file a harassment case against me.

Everything in me fights to go back to Caden and explain. Each step just a step too far. It takes me two circles around town to convince myself that instead of going back to the bar that I need to pick something up for Sophia to make her smile.

By the time I make it home, I pop a mint and head inside —dinner is just about ready. Noah is sitting on the living room floor attempting to solve math problems while Isabella is lying next to him, scribbling in her *Frozen* coloring book. I kiss them both on the head as I walk toward the kitchen.

The table is already set, and Sophia is taking a pasta bake out of the oven.

"How lovely of you to join us," she comments without looking in my direction.

I place the orchid I bought for her on the table before I wrap my arms around her from behind.

"I'm sorry. The interviews ran a bit late." I place a kiss on her cheek, another on the side of her neck. "Good news is that it's over. I think we found the right baristas. Caden just has to call and offer them jobs tomorrow."

She leans back against my chest with a sigh.

"I'm sorry if last night upset you. I am committed to this family. I hope you know that."

Sophia turns in my arms, leaning her forehead against mine before pressing a kiss to my lips.

"I'm sorry. I just … worry sometimes," she says, "and if you're worrying, then it makes me worry more. I just—I love you so much. The thought of losing you terrifies me."

It's an overplayed argument, one we're dusting off from years ago.

"I love you, Sophia. Only you." I tighten my grip and press a kiss onto her hair.

Noah bounds into the kitchen. "Mommy, I'm starving!"

Sophia chuckles against me, and my heart warms. "Go get

Isabella. Dinner's ready," she says, her words muffled by my chest.

"Yes!" Noah screams and then yells for Isabella from where he is standing.

With one more kiss on Sophia's forehead, I let go. She brings the pasta bake over to the table as I pour us both a glass of wine. When plates are filled with food, we all sit down to eat, Noah, the most eager of all.

"Careful, buddy. It's still hot."

Noah chugs water, shoving another heap into his mouth. "Did he eat today?" I laugh, blowing on my own fork of food.

"Yeah, all of the lunch you packed and three snacks after school," Sophia says in disbelief.

"I'm a growing boy, Daddy," he explains, "and I learned how to subtract today."

"I saw that. I'm so proud of you!"

"Ms. Reynolds says I'm the best!" A fork full of pasta misses his mouth as he grins.

"He got student of the month today," Sophia clarifies. "So, dessert tonight is cookies n' cream ice cream."

Noah flashes a smile with bits of pasta and sauce seeping through.

"Noah, that's wonderful. I'm really proud of you."

These are the times that everything I work for becomes so important. If I let down my family, I'll be sacrificing moments like these.

FOUR

A FRESH COAT of snow on the ground and a school cancellation is a blessing in disguise. I often work from home on snow days, not only having more flexibility than Sophia, but I also bask in a day spent with the kids where I have less responsibilities.

Thankfully, Caden and I are in the position to take a day off. He just worked his last shift at Beanery, and deserves a day to relax before we start training the baristas. So, after canceling our scheduled day, I take the kids on a sled-riding trip.

We have a massive hill that is popular near the city that all the children (even adults) love going to in the winter. In the past, we try to all get together as a family with our best friends, Luke and Annabelle, to take advantage of the winter, but this year our schedules are too chaotic to coordinate.

Often, Noah rides on a sled alone, claiming to be a big kid, while Isabella goes down with Sophia or me.

"Daddy!" Noah screams, already having run ahead in the snow. "Can we race?"

There are only a few families at the hill today, giving us plenty of space to ride as often as we please.

"Of course!"

We get on our sleds; Isabella snuggled between my legs before I count down from three.

The three of us fly down the hill, Isabella and I going faster than Noah with my added weight. Isabella screams in excitement, and I can hear Noah's laughing behind us. As we near the end of the hill, his sled flips over, igniting a fit of giggles from him.

"That was awesome!" he exclaims.

"Again, again!" Isabella giggles.

Isabella is out of my grasp, running after Noah before I can even stand up. As I head up the hill after them, I hear his infectious laugh. Turning toward it, I see Caden rolling off his sled, shaking the snow from his snow pants, and grinning as he watches two other people come down the hill.

"Caden!" I call out.

As his friends reach his feet, he glances my way. Beaming, he walks over to me.

"Hey! Couldn't get away from me, huh?" He laughs.

"Perfect day for sledding," I say.

I keep my gaze on Noah and Isabella, who have forgotten about me, and are now at the top of the hill. Noah is helping Isabella onto the sled in front of him so they can go down together.

"Definitely!" Caden's friends say they are going back up, but he doesn't move. I look over at him, giving him a smile before he continues, "I used to come here as a kid. My friend and her boyfriend were heading here for the day, so I, of course, had to join."

"Daddy!" Isabella yells.

Caden and I both look toward the two of them, flying down the hill. Isabella is gigging, and Noah holds her tight while he tries to guide the sled. They fly past where Caden and I are, and Noah flips them, so they stop.

"Daddy! Did you see that?" Noah exclaims. The two of

them come rushing toward us, both with rose-colored cheeks, covered in snow.

"Amazing!" I say.

"You were going so fast!" Caden says. "How'd you do that?"

Noah gives his star-studded smile, rambling into a whole explanation about how it's important to sit in a certain position and how the snow has to be just perfect.

Caden's amused smile grows as he holds in a chuckle. Noah is very serious about the science of sled-riding.

"Wow. You seem to know your stuff. I always lose when I race my friends down the hill. Maybe I have to take your advice."

Noah's eyes widen at Caden's response. "I always lose to Daddy and Izzy!"

I'm about to introduce them to who Caden is, but the light in Noah's eyes takes over as he declares an idea.

"What if we race Daddy and Izzy? We could win!"

The child in Caden comes out immediately. "We so could!" His eyes glisten when he looks at me. "Can we?"

Between Caden's hopeful expression and Noah's pouting face, all I can do is grab Izzy's hand and race up the hill.

"We'll beat you there!"

Glancing behind me, I see Noah take Caden's hand, and the two run to catch up to us. At the top of the hill, Caden and I situate ourselves on the sleds—Noah claims that Caden's is better—so we ditch Noah's at the top of the hill for a moment. Noah sits between Caden's legs and Isabella between mine.

"So Noah, you have to steer, okay? I'll adjust the weight properly." Noah nods, his competitive side thriving, and Caden wraps his arms around Noah.

Caden smirks over at me, an amusement glued to my face. The two of them are instantly best friends.

I count down to one, and we race down the hill, Caden

and Noah beating us by a long shot. When we get to the bottom, Caden and Noah are high-fiving each other.

"That was so awesome! Can we do that again?" Noah's pleading eyes work their magic on Caden. I watch as he glances behind us before kneeling down to Noah's level. I follow his gaze and see his friends not paying any mind to us.

"Yes! You're a great partner." Noah hugs him before dragging Caden up the hill.

As he passes me, I whisper, "I'm sorry."

Caden just replicates Noah's cheeky grin.

Isabella and I opt out of sledding not much longer after that. We have about five races down the hill with the two of them before Izzy grows tired. So, the two of us sit at the bottom of the hill on our sled, watching Caden and Noah. Now, they are racing each other, both of their competitive sides have elevated.

It's a side of Caden I didn't anticipate. Things have always been so serious between us, leaving very few moments where our guards could come down. When we get into light-hearted conversations, they are usually cut short by handling something important.

He never questioned my disappearance from the gin bar only a couple of days ago. He chose to drop the subject, and we picked up the next day like nothing happened. Now, after a few highly stressful days on his end, he can let go as he hangs out with Noah. Happiness suits him.

After a while, Noah runs up to me, and Isabella, who has fallen asleep in my arms.

"Daddy, can we get lunch? I'm starving!"

"Of course, bud."

Caden, who was lagging behind, makes it up to us.

"Can Caden come? He's fun!"

I look up to Caden. There seems to be a permanent smile on his lips. "If he wants to, of course. But no puppy dog eyes, Noah. Let him decide."

Noah gives me a thumbs up and turns, shocked to see Caden right behind him.

"Wanna come to lunch?" Instead of his pleading eyes, he gives Caden a toothy grin. "Daddy says I can't beg, but please?"

Caden burst out laughing, and butterflies erupt in my gut. Noah's impatience has his eyes blinking rapidly.

"Noah!" I laugh, and he immediately stops his adorable eyes but shows just another tooth or two.

Caden kneels down next to Noah. "I'd love to."

Shortly after, the four of us pile in my car. We strip off our snow gear, and Caden says goodbye to his friends. Noah controls the conversation, telling me everything about Caden that he's learned as we head to Noah's favorite cafe. Like how Caden isn't sporty, instead he's artistic. He loved drawing as a kid, and when Caden was young, he and his sister would sled-ride down the same hill. Isabella, bless her heart, sleeps through the entire thing.

When we get to the cafe, we sit at a booth, Caden and Noah on one side, and I on the other with Isabella in my arms. My energy starts to dwindle despite my body constantly reminding me of my proximity to Caden. I'm not sure how Caden still has as much enthusiasm in his face as he speaks with Noah. Aside from us both ordering coffee, his energy seems to thrive with children.

Noah eventually asks Caden how he knows me and grows even more excited when I mention we work together. He then takes to telling Caden all about his special hot chocolate and the cinnamon buns that he gets to eat only when he's a really good boy. Noah then takes Isabella's placemat and the crayons we were given and pushes them to Caden. I become invisible as the two of them color together—Noah wanting to learn how talented Caden is—until our food comes. Even with him eating, Noah continues his picture while Caden teaches him how to draw different things better.

Isabella, half-asleep, eats her food in my lap as we both watch them. Caden's admiration for Noah is almost equivalent to Noah's for Caden.

"You're a natural," I comment.

"He makes it easy." Caden grins down to Noah. "You're a great father."

I flush at the compliment. "They make it easy." I smile, running my hands through Isabella's hair.

"Daddy!" Noah exclaims.

My eyes grow heavy just at his exhilaration. The coffee needs to kick in soon.

"Can we go to a movie after this?"

"How about we go home and watch a movie? Daddy has to get some work done."

"Caden can take us to a movie!"

"No, Noah, it's time to head home soon. We promised Mommy we would make some delicious treats for dessert tonight, didn't we?"

"Brownies!" Isabella suddenly wakes up.

Noah's face drops a little, looking toward Caden before back at me. "Can we draw a little while longer then?"

I eye Caden, his childish excitement giving me a slight nod. "Of course," I say.

Noah and Caden high-five.

When we get home, the kids and I make dessert like initially planned, before I pop them in front of a movie so I can get work done. The plan is to butter Sophia up with dessert because I know Noah will talk about his exciting day. She plays her part of excitement before dropping the act in front of me, only commenting on how exhausted she is and how it shouldn't happen again.

Yet, as I fall asleep, my dreams are filled with a video reel of Caden as my other half, and we raise Noah and Isabella together.

FIVE

WE ARE EARLY. Only mere minutes from when my staff will arrive, but long enough for us to see the brand new deserted store. Sophia parks the car alongside the snow-banked street. We both get out, helping Noah and Isabella from the back seat. They stand hand in hand, Noah grabbing Sophia's hand.

I hesitate to cross the road. I'm not ready to step foot into the new shop yet. As with the other two, we stand facing the store in complete silence, admiring how the sign is dusted with a coat of snow and how the shop fits perfectly between two of the busiest businesses on Mackenzie Promenade.

Isabella is confused by our pause, having been too young to remember our tradition. Noah, being more familiar with the concept, gently whispers to Isabella that it's some weird thing our parents do.

Sophia laces her hand with mine, leaning her head on my shoulder.

"You did it," she congratulates. "You have a store right on Mackenzie Promenade."

The new staff and I have been busy working in the new location for the past week, but the store will still be a sight to see. We cleaned every nook and cranny from leftover construction and set up the tables and interior in preparation for tomorrow's opening, but also tonight's Family and Friend's event.

Although it is a Thursday night, the restaurant closest to us is notably packed with customers. To our right is Angeline's Bookstore, which is closing up for the day. We watch as pedestrians stroll by the vacant coffee shop, glancing at the signs and peering in with curiosity. There is a sign in the front window that announces our "Grand Opening" scheduled for tomorrow, starting at six in the morning.

Angeline's Bookstore has given out vouchers all week that offer a free drink of choice with a book purchase.

With the first two shops, book donations fill the shelves, but I teamed up with Angeline this time. Though we will still carry pre-owned books, available free of charge, I'll also carry new books that will profit Angeline.

"Are you ready?" Sophia questions, breaking me from my thoughts.

"Yes, but we are missing just one more thing."

She lifts her head from my shoulder, looking up, and puckers her lips.

I laugh—our good luck ritual—and kiss her to celebrate a new beginning. I place both of my hands on her rosy cheeks, deepening the kiss.

"Thank you," I whisper against her lips. "I could not do this without you."

"I love you."

"I love you too." I peck her lips once more for good measure.

While the month has taken a toll on our relationship, we are working through it. Days have been longer than usual, family time few and far between, particularly in the last week, but I have done my best to be present when needed.

I let go of Sophia and turn back to the coffee shop to find

Caden standing in front of the door with a handful of our employees. Everyone stares back at us, smiling. I scoop Isabella up, and Sophia tightens her hand on Noah as we make our way across the street.

Once at the door, Caden pulls a red ribbon from behind his back, and he stretches across the door with the help of Audrey, our barista. Marsha, another barista, offers me a pair of scissors.

"Ready to open your third Isabella's Coffee?" Caden asks, beaming.

Everyone is patient, despite visibly shivering from the cold. I'm so grateful. This opening is special, and I have enough credibility now that my staff shows an investment in the shop opening here versus just another business opening.

With the scissors in hand, I look down at Isabella. "Want to help Daddy cut the ribbon?"

"Yes!"

I help her guide the scissors to the center of the ribbon as the staff begins to count down from three. On one, I let her grip the blades together and cut the fabric.

"You did it!" I exclaim, kissing her cheek. She giggles, burying her head in my neck.

"Now, let's make some coffee!" Caden announces, a grin plastered on his face.

I fish the key out of my pocket and take a deep breath before unlocking the door. As I make my way past the bar to turn on the lights, I stop in my tracks, seeing a cake, a small bamboo tree, and a poster that reads 'Congratulations, Ben!' Next to the poster, there is a card. Opening it, it's filled with well wishes from the staff and photos taken during the setup and training. I flip through the pictures; there are some of just me and Caden that I know I'll pocket for safekeeping. The last one is a group shot of us standing outside the shop last night.

By the time I am done looking through the gifts, the lights I forgot about are turned on.

"Daddy, I want cake!" It's Isabella, looking up with pleading eyes.

"Soon, sweetheart. Maybe we can get you a hot chocolate first?"

She gives me a wide smile and wiggles to get out of my arms. Placing her down, I turn to see the staff all huddled together.

"Thank you, guys! Congratulations on making this happen. Now, as Caden said, let's get brewing!"

Everyone cheers and turns to Caden for direction.

A 'Family and Friend's' night is something I started with the first store. It's a small gathering for the employees to show their family and friends where they are working. I find it creates a stronger sense of community, and it's the first time the staff gets to know each other without the distraction of training. It's even influenced their family and friends to informally promote the cafe.

Though mainly a night of celebration, they still have work to do. The guests are invited to try new drinks made by their loved ones—and baked goods from a local bakery that we will be selling regularly.

Once Caden delegates tasks to his staff, they dart off in varying directions. Samantha, one of my oldest staff members who came to work as a supervisor in the new shop, takes position behind the bar.

"Two extra special hot chocolates coming right up!" She smiles, winking down at Isabella.

Isabella shies away, hiding behind me, though her excitement is bubbling. The hot chocolates, for Noah and Isabella, are caramel mocha with whole milk, whipped cream, and caramel drizzle. They rave about it constantly.

Samantha, with her years of experience, whips the drinks up in an instant. After handing one to Isabella, she takes the second over to Noah. His face lights up as he shows his drink to Sophia.

By the time we place the pastries out on a table, agree on a song playlist, and make ourselves drinks, a half-hour has passed. Guests start to collect outside, and as I'm about to open the doors to let everyone in, Sophia clears her throat.

"Hey, can I get everyone's attention?"

The crew stops what they are doing, turning toward Sophia. I have no idea what she has planned, but my eyes are drawn to her.

"For those of you who don't know me, I'm Sophia, Ben's wife. There are so many new faces in this room that I can't wait to meet properly, but I just wanted to take a moment to thank you all for being a part of this. In high school, when Ben and I started dating, we spent so much of our time in different cafes, imagining the perfect one—one that would be located right here along the promenade." She takes a deep breath before continuing, "this dream hasn't been easy. We've had a rough few years." Her eyes brim with tears, but her voice remains strong. "But I am so excited after years of hard work and dedication to see that Ben now has a cafe on Mackenzie Promenade. It's unbelievable he was able to be so successful with one cafe, nonetheless three. So, thank you to each and every one of you."

I blink the tears away as my gut twists. She deserves the world, and I'm barely giving her enough.

Everyone raises their coffee cup to cheer before she raises her own glass.

"And to Caden," Sophia continues, looking toward him, "thank you for all your hard work. I've heard only positive things about you, and I have full trust in your ability. So, with that, let's toast to Isabella's!"

I watch as everyone lets out a universal cheer. I raise my own glass too. Whether she mentioned Caden specifically as a warning to him or as a peace offering to us, I'll never know.

"To me!" Isabella yells, interrupting my thoughts. She turns their cheers to laughter.

I squat down, gathering her into a hug as I lift her off the ground and head to Sophia.

"I love you both so much," I say to Sophia and Isabella, giving them both kisses on the cheek.

I have to remember that Sophia knows what these cafes mean to me. Despite having issues, I genuinely hope she recognizes that Caden is a positive addition to my dream.

"Thank you for everything," I say, extending my free arm to Sophia, giving her a hug. I press a kiss to her lips as a flash goes off in the corner of my eye.

"Sorry," Samantha says with a smile and a shrug, camera in hand. "It was too beautiful not to capture."

SOPHIA, Caden, and I stand at the front of the cafe, greeting people as they enter. It's encouraging to see the faces of regular customers from the other shops, as well as a few fresh faces. Sophia's face lights up as Luke and Annabelle, our best friends, stroll in. She follows them into the cafe and starts to show them around while Caden and I continue our greetings.

"Hey, can I introduce you to my parents?" Caden asks once there's a lull at the doorway.

"Of course." I smile.

He leads us over to a group of four people, each with a drink in hand, browsing the assortment of pastries. They stop talking as soon as they see us approaching.

"Caden, this place is beautiful," an older woman says. She's the spitting image of Caden, with her dark brown, wavy hair, hazel eyes, and warm, welcoming smile.

"Guys, this is Benjamin, the man behind Isabella's Coffee."

I can't help but blush at the introduction. I've never had another manager of mine beam with such pride over my shop.

"Ben, this is my father, Richard, my mother Susan, my

sister, Kaley, and my best friend, Bethany." He introduces, gesturing accordingly.

"It's wonderful to meet you all." I smile. "Caden has told me so much about you four. Richard and Susan, you couldn't have raised a better person or the perfect guy for this job."

"Oh, stop." Caden laughs, his face turning pink.

"I remember Caden telling me how nervous he was to meet you. He couldn't stop raving about the job, the fact that you were opening a new store, and how amazing it'd be to work for you," Bethany says, the friend he was with the first time I met him. "He was so shocked when he got the job on the spot."

Caden hits Bethany playfully, shuffling his feet.

"She makes me sound obsessed, which I wasn't," he clarifies, his face now resembling a ripened tomato.

"Well." I smirk, allowing my confidence of the night to take over for once. "If I do recall, you were interested in getting to know me better."

He buries his face in his hands. I love this. Today it's not me being embarrassed or fumbling over my words. We have grown more comfortable together since the sled-riding day, but it seems the ease of his family being around helps to break some of our awkwardness.

"I do believe Isabella's Coffee is a better fit for someone as talented as Caden." I offer, taking one step further to win his parents over. I've only ever spoken greetings to other manager's parents. But Caden's I felt the need to impress, even though it should be reversed.

"Beanery helped Caden. A lot." His father's tone is slightly defensive, my brain taking a step back.

"They helped me too." I give his father my award-winning smile that won most parents over. "I started with Beanery when I was in high school. They inspired my love of coffee— but they are becoming too much of a corporation that doesn't care for its employees."

"We sort of have a personal connection to Beanery. It's a touchy subject," Caden warns.

"Daddy and Caden!" I hear from behind us. My shoulders drop in relief from the interruption. Turning, Noah and Isabella are bounding toward us. "Can we cut the cake?" Noah asks with his damn puppy-dog eyes.

"I think this sounds like a great idea!" Caden says, taking both of their hands, walking them over to the cake.

Noah and Isabella haven't seen Caden since the snow day, but they easily relax in step with him. I can't help the thoughts that begin to brew at how natural he looks with them. Caden starts to slice the cake, and Sophia joins in, helping Noah hand out the slices to guests. The real kicker is how wide Noah's eyes grow with each slice in his hands, but his patience is impeccable. Isabella sits just off to the side, a slice in front of her, waiting for Noah.

Eventually, I'm handed a slice, and the conversations in the room resume. Sophia goes back to chat with Annabelle. Luke is helping with Noah and Isabella, laughing at their antics as Isabella, while she was patient, is now shoving cake down her throat. The only people missing from the room are mine and Sophia's parents, but they both live an hour away.

"I can't get over how wonderful Noah and Isabella are," Caden says, joining me where I moved up against a side wall to observe.

"Me either." I smile. Truth is, I have no idea how my children have turned out so well-behaved with our unplanned pregnancies and marital issues. If, through all this, it's the only thing we've done right, then I feel like we've succeeded. "It's going to be a long night." I laugh, watching my kids with chocolate icing smeared across their faces.

"I'm not jealous in the slightest." Caden smiles, shaking his head. "Hey, I wanted to apologize for my father. I should have warned you."

My brows raise, trying to figure out why he'd be apologizing.

"It's not necessarily something you just bring up in conversation. But I went through a difficult time, and Beanery ended up being my light at the end of the tunnel. Everyone's still sensitive on the subject. My father didn't want me to leave. He feels like it's disrespectful after everything they've done. He doesn't understand that it was the people I worked with versus the corporation that did anything. Hopefully, I'll prove to them that this is the right decision."

I glance over at him. It's the most honest he's ever been, and he isn't even telling me anything. At the ages we've both worked at Beanery, there's no doubt we both went through some difficult stuff. But each time I'd joke about Beanery, he'd grow silent, and our conversation would change. For his dad to say something it must mean it was pretty serious.

"I hope this is the right decision too," I say. "I pride myself in having a supportive management team as well. If you ever need anything, the other two store managers will be more than happy to help."

"Can I not come directly to you?"

My jaw drops, and I grip the paper plate in my hand.

"I—I just assume that you might not feel comfortable." The thought of him wanting to open up to me warms my chest. "But of c-course. If you ever need anything, I'm here."

"Ben, we may have gotten off on the wrong foot, but I feel comfortable with you. I don't know why exactly, but I want to open up to you."

He gives my arm a squeeze, his presence lingering a few seconds too long before he walks away. With a glance back, he winks in my direction.

My heart races as my mind goes into overdrive. What the hell just happened.

"Everything okay?" I jump at the sound of Sophia's voice.

Immediately, I throw my arm around her shoulders. I give her a peck along her temple—no need to be suspicious.

"Everything is perfect, love." We smile at each other. "Exactly as I had hoped."

I keep my arm wrapped around her as I attempt to watch Caden from afar. He's now talking to Luke, which feels a bit too close to home. I never introduced them, though. It's a friendly encounter on their own. I can't help but wonder how Luke would react if he knew Caden's gay … or that I even liked him.

Would he support me?

SIX

THE STORE IS PROVING to be an overwhelming success. Within the first week of being open, the cafe on Mackenzie Promenade has doubled the other two stores' sales. I underestimated the amount of extra work running a third store would involve. I'm an overachiever, always have been, but it's becoming more evident that I can't handle everything on my own. While Sophia's been understanding and supportive, the only dinner I was home for was yesterday, Sunday night, the tenth day open.

On Monday, I walk into Isabella's Coffee on the promenade, carrying two subs. Caden's sitting at a table in the corner with two coffees in front of him. We have an unofficial agreement that every day at lunchtime, we take a break and eat together. It's become the calm in the mayhem we're consumed in.

"Hey you," he greets, happily unwrapping his sub the moment I hand it to him. "Everything okay?"

My brows furrow. There is no way that Caden can tell something is off. Frankly, I think I look just as stressed as I should be—considering I opened up a cafe, hired an attractive store manager, and am running by the seat of my pants.

Besides, Caden is similarly stressed. I essentially abandoned him. The only support I've provided him has been our lunch break because I learned over our first weekend with the cafe open that he proved to be quite a distraction, and I was falling behind on my own job.

"Your tie is crooked, you're a few minutes late, and your smile isn't reaching your eyes."

"You're good," I joke, but dread washes over me. I can't be read like a goddamn book.

"I'm all ears. What's going on?" He presses, taking a bite of his sub, while mine remains wrapped.

I take a deep breath and exhale. There are two directions to take. Only one direction would cross a line.

"I have everything I've always wanted, yet I'm not completely happy. Here I am, sitting in my dream cafe, but something isn't right."

"Do you feel like you're sacrificing something?"

His eyes are calm but focused on me. His sub is now back on the table.

"Yes," I whisper. "I'm elated with the success of Isabella's, I am. I'm blessed to have these opportunities, but—I don't think I'm happy with myself."

The volcano within me is bubbling over. The sub in front of me looks like a brick, and the acid of the coffee feels like it'll set off a bomb. I press my lips together as one more word will disrupt the lava.

"Do you feel like your own needs are taking a backseat?"

I lean back against the chair, trying to create whatever sort of distance I can. My jaw tightens as I give a slight nod.

Caden takes a sip of his coffee. His hesitation makes me want to brush it all off. Grab my sub and dash out the door. I don't know what's going on in his head, but I have to switch the conversation. Sophia and my ex-therapist are the only two people in the world who know about me.

But why do I have the sudden urge to tell him everything?

His fingers rest on my wrist—goosebumps rise along my skin as his thumb brushes across my veins. I force myself to keep his eye contact. If I falter, it shows my weakness.

I'm not gay.

My body shivers at the voice inside my head—one so seemingly foreign. As Caden's boss, I need to shut down his advances. As Benjamin, I can't find the words.

"Ben, I know there is something you're struggling to say. Coming from someone who felt lost and alone not too long ago, I want to help you. If it's something involving your family, I can be a neutral person. In the short time I've known you, I know you'll bend over backward for the people you love. You work nonstop to provide for your family." His grip tightens.

I realize my eyes lost focus, clouding over, but with a blink, I'm back to his eyes.

"I admire you, Ben." His words are soft. "From the day I started coming to Isabella's, I gravitated toward your strength. You know why Isabella's is so popular? It's not just the great coffee; it's the fact that each person who works for you is genuine and loving. That you, despite having the weight of the world on your shoulders, still come and greet people. You always make people feel welcome and important like you want to be their friend. To outsiders, you're like Superman. It's okay to be lost. It's okay to let your guard down in front of me. You don't have to carry whatever is bothering you by yourself."

I use my free hand to brush away the tears threatening to spill over. With each word, he chips away at the walls, allowing air to enter my lungs just a little easier.

He continues to rub my wrist with his thumb. But I want more. I want his arms embracing me. If just a tiny touch brings me this much comfort, I want to feel the relief his arms would have. I want to believe he can solve all my problems. But there's a demon inside of me, one repetitively telling me that there's no way that my secrets can come out.

"There is something that's upsetting you at home," he

continues. "I've noticed you haven't been yourself, but it's incredible, really. You refuse to allow what's happening at home to disrupt your workflow. You compartmentalize. It's amazing to an extent, but it's really toxic. You've reached your limit, I think, and if I can't be that person for you, Ben, you need to find someone else."

This time I look down, breaking our eye contact for the first time since we started talking because I don't have it in me anymore. He's already knocked down some walls that between building them back up and his continuous speech, I can't seem to recover.

"What about Luke?" He suggests.

Luke and I have been best friends since we were toddlers. We used to be like twins, always in sync, until I started hiding more and more of myself. Then, when I got married and had kids, the connection suffered further. I never told him I was gay, and a part of me resented him for not realizing something was different on his own. I wish he had cornered me sometime throughout our friendship and asked me, like Caden seems to be doing now. Not even a month of friendship, and Caden's questioning my entire being.

"He's too invested," I say. My hand shakes as I lift it, placing it on top of his. "I …" I pause, swallowing the voice in me. "Caden, I'm—"

Caden rips his hands from beneath mine in an instant.

"Good afternoon, Sophia."

My breath catches in my throat, my body swaying just slightly. I shift to face Sophia, who is now directly behind me —a fake smile plastered on her face.

"Hi honey," I greet, standing up to meet her, gripping the back of my chair to steady myself. The warmth in my body has turned cool, the untouched sub going unnoticed in my empty stomach.

Her smile grows thin, but her eyes remain friendly as she glances at Caden. It's a wildly terrifying talent. "You said you had a lot of work to do. I figured you'd be in your office." Her arms cross on her chest.

"I do, but I was having lunch with Caden. Just wanted to check in and see how he is doing with the cafe."

"May I talk to you?" She asks, her voice like honey. "Excuse us." She smiles at Caden.

I place my hand on her lower back, not daring to look at Caden. I walk her out of the cafe and onto the sidewalk, making sure we're out of sight from the windows. No one needs to witness whatever she has to say.

"What are you doing here?" I question.

Her arms tighten as her brows lift. I should have remained silent. "I was getting coffee for my co-workers, you know, supporting my husband, but it seems like I walked in on something. Care to explain?"

"Nothing is going on, Soph. Caden and I have been meeting for lunch. It's completely professional. I've been feeling stressed, and he's only trying to help." I wrap my arms around her, her arms falling to her sides. "I love you, okay? I would tell you if anything was going on. Caden just understands the nitty-gritty aspects of the business. It's easier to unload on him and leave work at work, so I can come home to you and the kids and be present."

She nods against me. There's no way she's convinced because while that's great in theory, I haven't seen the kids after work since the Family and Friend's night. Our time together has been strictly our morning routine, where I even run off before they go to school.

Sophia doesn't remove herself from my arms, though. She takes a deep breath in, and I interlace our fingers, kissing her temple. It doesn't seem like she noticed Caden's hand. The interrogation would have been more. If Caden didn't notice her when he had ... a shiver runs down my spine.

"Let's go get those drinks for your co-workers. I'll be home for dinner tonight. Maybe I'll bring home take-out? We can have a family movie night?"

She steps back to argue, we *never* have a weekday movie night. We decided it would be a bad precedent to start even if the kids are still young.

I press a kiss to her lips, silencing her. Her shoulders drop when she leans it.

"We need this, Soph. I love you."

"I love you, too." She concedes.

When Sophia leaves the cafe, coffees in hand, I go back to the table where Caden is still sitting. Whatever just happened to us needs to stop immediately.

"Hey, sorry lunch got interrupted. I have to head back to the office. Are we still on for Friday night?"

Friday night is his celebratory managerial dinner. It's a tradition I started, allowing the store managers to have a night out to either just get to know each other or have time to connect about the pros and cons of the cafe. I find it creates a better work environment for everyone. Now, I meet with the store managers, usually on lunch breaks, similar to what I have been doing with Caden.

This Friday feels like it is going to be way more difficult. Except, I can't cancel on him because canceling means that something is wrong.

"Yeah, I'm free. But Ben?" He grabs my wrist again as I pick up my untouched sub.

Swallowing, my body grows stiff. I need to get the hell out of here.

"Can you sit down and talk to me? We were actually getting somewhere."

"I can't." I shake off his arm, grab my luke-warm coffee, and walk away, feeling more off-kilter than I did upon entering the cafe.

SEVEN

SOPHIA ANALYZES my every move while I get ready for my dinner with Caden. I shave off my facial scruff, put gel in my hair, pick out my nicest pair of black jeans, and even put on a tie. (I had watched a video on how to tie a tie earlier as a means to avoid asking her for help.) She hasn't questioned my efforts, but her smart remarks say enough. It's easily the most effort I've made in over a week.

I'm anxious to see Caden. I spent most of this week avoiding him after our incident at lunch, and I know I can't hide behind work at dinner. It will just be the two of us in a fancy, dimly-lit restaurant, talking one-on-one. Often, these dinners take place in more casual settings, like a chain restaurant, but the decision is always up to the new manager. Caden's choice feels like he's trying to put me on the spot.

Caden chose a seafood restaurant down in the inlet of Cyan City. It is a wealthier area, home to fancier fish and chips and classy bars that white-collar workers frequent due to its close proximity to the business district. Luke has mentioned going to this restaurant numerous times with his colleagues from work, but Sophia and I never thought the kids would enjoy it, and date nights are hard to come by.

When I pull into the parking lot, Caden is already waiting outside. He's dressed in a button-up and tie. I will myself to find the professional person who hired him. The ball is my court. I can't continue to be a love-sick schoolboy fumbling on my words and blushing at everything he says.

He looks in my direction, recognizing my car. I had managed to calm myself on the thirty-minute drive here, but now the nerves are making me sweat. I force myself out of the car, walking toward him. Caden catches my eye, and excitement dances across his face as he scans me up and down. His smile doubles in size.

"Hi, I was afraid you weren't going to show."

Stay professional.

"I'm sorry. This got hectic at home, but I'm here now."

I open the door to the restaurant, ushering him in. His side grazes my hand as he passes, but it's like he's unphased, walking straight up to the hostess.

We are led to a small booth, and though the restaurant is busy, the atmosphere remains quiet and intimate. A waiter comes over almost immediately to pour us both a glass of red wine without request.

I raise my brow at Caden, who gives me a smirk back in return.

"I hope you don't mind. I took it upon myself to order the drinks and meal ahead of time. When you said you'd never been here, I had to make sure your experience was perfect. So, dinner is ordered, and this," he says, picking up his long-stemmed glass, "is my favorite wine."

"Wow. Thank you." I'm startled by the relief that washes over me from not having to make any decision, allowing me to just remain present.

We lift our glasses and toast to the new cafe and the success it is having.

I compliment his taste in wine, as it's the best red wine I have ever tasted. Despite the low light, I can make out the blush on his cheeks. My heart swells at the idea that he may feel something more for me.

"Now that you've made your ultimate dream come true, what's next in the life of Benjamin Jacobson?"

There's no way I can tell him that the cafe is far from my ultimate dream. In terms of my career, yes. But personal life? No way.

"I haven't thought much about it." I shrug, taking another sip.

"You're kidding!" In his shock, he puts his wine glass down. "You don't have an ongoing list of dreams?"

"Well, Caden Benson, what is on your list?" My quick rebuttal fails to throw him off.

"My ultimate dream is to have a big family." He smiles to himself as he pauses, deep in thought. "I'd love to have my own cafe one day, or at least help run an already established one." He winks.

Before I can react, the waiter returns to our table with a bread basket and olive oil, pesto dip.

Caden's quick to snatch a steaming slice from the basket before eyeing me. I'm not an idiot. I know he is referring to Isabella's. But beyond that confession, what the hell did the wink mean? Or even the last time he winked at me?

"So, what about children? Are you and Sophia trying for more?"

I furrow my brows at the switch in conversation, taking the opportunity to grab a piece of bread.

"I mean, if your cafe dreams are accomplished, what about your family life? I know things aren't perfect, but it's just a rough patch, yeah?"

Why is Caden the only person who remembers every conversation we have?

"Can I ask you a question as a friend and not as your boss?"

He nods, sitting up and taking another sip of wine.

"When did you become comfortable, you know, with being gay?"

Caden chokes on his wine, his eyes growing glossy as he searches for air.

This question has been stirring in my head since the moment I met him. I shouldn't be doing this, but I need to. If he up and walks away thinking I am being discriminatory, then so be it. I can handle the consequences. But I can't keep walking on eggshells around him. I'm not in the place to handle the added stress. He said he even wanted to help me, so if that's the case, then I need to get to know him.

"Well," he takes another sip of wine before continuing, "I believe around middle school when everyone started to hit puberty. I quickly realized I was more interested in naked guys than girls." His response is so matter-of-fact. "I actually dated Bethany for a couple of months. When I realized I wasn't attracted to her, I knew something was up. She was the first person I told. I kept it a secret until this guy in the tenth grade started hitting on me. My first boyfriend actually; the one I moved to Arizona with."

He was certain from such a young age, and here I sat: stressed, anxious, and confused, almost wishing someone could tell me the path I need to take.

"Were you always so comfortable, though?" I press.

"I suppose during my first relationship. My first boyfriend was confident and encouraged me to tell my parents. They never even batted an eye. And, in college, I just surrounded myself with people who supported me. It was certainly easier the older I got."

I take a few more sips of wine, keeping my eye contact with him. I try to gauge his mood as he speaks. I already crossed the line, so how much longer will he humor me for?

"That's why," he continues, "when I felt like you were judging me, I was ready to walk away. I don't have time for people who think differently of me just because I'm gay."

"I promise I'm not judging. I'm sorry if it came across that way." He only nods, so I let myself continue. "I've only ever been with two people," I admit. "I started dating Sophia in high school. In college, I ... experimented."

"Experimented, how so? Was it with a guy?"

I swirl my wine around in my glass. Laser-focused on how the red coats the clear glass. "Yeah. I dated one of my best friends. We ... well, we were in love." I smile to myself.

"So, why did you marry Sophia?"

"We got pregnant."

I know he's being careful, thinking of what to say next as he drinks his wine, but I can't help fidgeting in my chair, shoving pieces of bread down my throat. It feels like he's judging my life decisions.

I look away from him, grazing the restaurant as my anxiety starts to bubble. There's a familiar figure by the hostess that causes me to narrow my focus.

"Is that what is going on at home? Does Sophia knows you're gay or maybe bi?"

I barely hear his question as I cough up pieces of bread onto the table. The familiar sensation I tried so hard to forget resurfaces just at his presence.

Joshua is here, in the same restaurant, looking stunning in a fitted black suit.

You don't love him.

I watch, ignoring Caden's question, as the hostess leads him and his husband to a table in our vicinity. As they pass, our eyes connect briefly before his dart toward Caden. His wedding ring catches an overhead light, blinding me.

"I'm sorry. It's incredibly disrespectful of me to be so blunt about something this sensitive," Caden says.

I focus back on him, attempting to break through the muddled fog consuming me.

"Benjamin, repeat after me. You're not gay. Being gay is a sin."

"I'm not ... I'm not ...."

I need to talk to Joshua.

"I uh, will you excuse me?"

"Ben, I'm sorry. If I insulted you … I—"

I shake my head, placing my napkin on the table. "No, no. I just need to talk to someone."

Standing up from the booth, I turn in the direction Joshua went. He's only two booths down from us, Joshua facing our direction. Part of me wonders if he is intrigued, wanting to scope out Caden. Perhaps he's jealous?

Joshua is quick to notice my approach, holding my eye contact while speaking to his husband.

"J-Joshua," I force out.

My hands are coated with perspiration now. I need to remain strong, but just his name feels thick against my lips. Dr. Matthews walked me through potential encounters like this multiple times. Just by standing up, I disregarded everything I was taught.

"Hello, Benjamin. With all due respect, I really would appreciate it if I could enjoy my meal without being interrupted."

His voice is full of dominance. This isn't the same Joshua I had come to know; the carefree, no worries kind of guy.

Sweat pools around my brows as I try to swallow the bile that's burning the back of my throat.

"I'm sorry. I was just coming to say hi. It's been so long."

"Yes, it has. If I do recall correctly, it wasn't on my account. Now, will you excuse me and my husband?"

I flinch at his tone. I want to glance over at his husband, see him up close. I imagine he knows about me, but it's taking everything in me to keep eye contact with Joshua.

"I'm sure you need to get back to your wife and kids, am I right?"

Sophia is well aware of tonight, and I have no reason to feel guilty, yet Joshua still has this effect on me. Making me feel small and weak, judging me for my actions instead of helping.

I do my best to keep my head up as I walk back to Caden, who is staring at me. He most likely watched the entire ordeal.

"Everything okay?"

I grip the wine glass that got refilled in my absence, taking a sip. The liquid coats my throat, and a few more walls collapse by my added exhaustion. I had imagined what that moment might look like. In my imagination (disregarding what therapy said), the end always resulted in something better than dismissing me for his husband.

"Everything's fine." I give him a tight lip smile.

My stomach lurches at the lie. Nothing is fine.

"Ben, may I ask again?"

"Ask what?" I snap.

Blinking, I sit back in the booth and sigh.

"If you're gay."

"It's not that simple."

Almost a decade later and I still can't formulate an answer to that question. When I was young, I was aware that I was different than other kids, but it wasn't really until I started dating Joshua that I admitted to myself that maybe I was gay or bi. But after physically and emotionally being abused into believing I was straight, I honestly don't know who the hell I am. Now, everything is unraveling. I'm not even sure how I am sitting upright.

"Okay," he says slowly. "It's not all or nothing, but you are married with children."

"I know," I snap. I take a gulp of wine as he recoils. "I know," I whisper.

Grabbing a piece of bread, I contemplate whether to try eating it or just pick off crumbs to keep myself occupied. I take a deep breath in the silence. Maybe Caden isn't the person I need him to be. I can't have another person judging my every move.

Looking up, his eyes are on me. He's not angry, though. There is no trace of judgment.

"How are you not sure?"

He's unapologetically blunt, and it takes everything in me to not snap again. It's not fair to him, even though him asking me directly isn't fair to me.

"It doesn't matter what I felt then nor what I feel now. What happened is in the past. You have no idea the kind of shit I've gone through to be where I am. What's important is taking care of my family. So, can we please drop it?" I drop the bread on my plate, lifting my fingers to meet my eyelids. I press against my closed lids, trying to calm myself.

"Ben, I'm not naive. This has bothered you since I told you I was gay. If you're gay or identify within the community, you can't pretend you're not. It'll eat you alive. If you didn't want it to come out, you would have been better at hiding it. So, what is going on with you?"

I take a few deep breaths, downing the last bit of wine in my glass.

There was a time when I was certain Joshua and I were soulmates. We had made plans for a future that seemed easy and flawless. When I walked away, I didn't believe I would feel that way again. And after reparative therapy—when everything I believed was stripped from me—I barely remembered what love felt like. But with Joshua's presence, even through his frustration, bits and pieces of what that love was, is coming back to me. I can feel the fog begin to lift. I am allowed to feel blissful love again … and I am in the beginning stages with Caden.

"You." My voice betrays me.

He puts the bread he's nibbling on down and proceeds to drink from his wine glass. I grab mine only to remember that it's in need of a refill.

"Me? You're attracted to me or?"

I exhale and run with my thoughts. I'm already in the deep end.

"Yes. I mean, I think so. When I first saw you, I felt the same way I had around Joshua. At least, that is what I suspected. And then Joshua comes in here tonight—the guy I went to talk to—and it hit me. It hit me that everything I've been feeling is real. More real than anything I've felt in a long while."

"So, was I just hired to be your eye candy? Because you thought I was attractive?" His voice starts to rise. "Ben, that's—"

"No!" I rush out. My cheeks are warming at my volume. "Caden, you're more than qualified for the job. Sure, usually I would have given it more thought when hiring someone, but I don't regret hiring you."

He eyes me for a few moments before his shoulders drop. "Have you told any of this to Sophia?"

"Yeah," I say. "She felt threatened, but I told her there is nothing to worry about."

"Does she ... have anything to worry about?"

We hold eye contact, and I allow myself to imagine what it would be like to look at him romantically—as a partner. Someone who is looking at me because they love me versus someone who wants to know what to do next.

"I don't know," I whisper.

He switches to the water glass and takes a sip.

"That's why Sophia looked suspicious the other day at the cafe. You were about to tell me you were gay or—"

"Gay," I confirm, interrupting him. "Yeah, you almost had me confessing."

A long stretch of silence fills the gap between us. He devours the rest of the bread on his plate as I swirl my empty wine glass.

The tension is sliced when our appetizers arrive, and Caden dives into his plate, another thing for him to fiddle with.

"I'm sorry. I should have never said anything."

He looks up, fork filled with salad just hanging in the air.

His gaze sends shivers down my spine. It isn't a look he's ever given me before.

"I don't support cheating," he says.

"Sorry, I um …" *What.*

"I just want you to know that if you're interested in me, I'm not willing to be the other person."

Almost immediately, he chooses to switch the conversation to what he loves about the salad and this restaurant. Either saving me from this black hole or saving himself.

I try to keep up with the conversation, but my mind keeps going over what just happened. It's irreversible. Caden knows my biggest secret that's allowed my family to survive. I can't focus on the fact that if he wanted, he could ruin my marriage by having a simple conversation with Sophia. All that flashes through my mind is the fact that he just didn't want to cheat … which means he felt something too. Or, it could be a setup. All Caden has to do is report this because I disregarded all work boundaries.

And then there is Joshua, just a few feet away, burning a hole through the booths separating us—or it feels like it. I'm grateful I'm not sitting in Caden's spot. I don't want to see Joshua's face. Is he happy? Does he still have that bright crooked smile? Is he laughing at his husband's jokes like he did with mine? Do they develop their own discreet language like we once had?

Our main meal comes shortly after Caden finishes his salad, and I toss mine around. It's salmon, steak, risotto, and steamed broccoli. Though my appetite has all but vanished, I try to eat a good portion of the entree. With our meals, our glasses are refilled as well, finishing off the bottle Caden had ordered. I wish I wasn't driving home, so I could order another.

Caden continues to persevere through the dinner, single-handedly holding up the conversation about work. Once he gets to his concerns, my brain can get back into professional mode.

When we finish our meal, I say no to dessert, even though Caden doesn't seem in a rush. Maybe I'm the only one feeling uncomfortable, but the tension is suffocating. So, I pay for the meal, double what I usually spent on these dinners.

Outside, Caden and I pause in front of my car.

"Look, I don't know your family situation or why you are hiding your sexuality. Nor do I understand what went on with that guy in there. I won't get involved if you don't want me to, but I know hiding your feelings isn't easy. Just know that I am here if you need me. I do still want to be that person for you, Ben."

"Thank you."

I wish I could turn back time to the day of hiring Caden and hire someone else. I'm not sure my marriage can survive another one of these situations.

Caden leans forward, gripping my hand in his, and my heart all but stops. With a thank you, he kisses my cheek before walking away.

Sweat breaks out across the back of my night despite the cool winter breeze. My hand grips my car door handle, holding me steady as I watch him climb into his car.

I am fucked.

"HOW WAS DINNER?" Sophia asks as I walk through the front door and into the living room. She's sprawled out on the couch, reading her newest manuscript with a glass of wine.

I walk over to the couch and lift her feet as I sit down on the other end.

"It was delicious. Expensive, but worth it. I'll have to take you sometime."

She smiles up at me, placing the manuscript on our coffee table.

"I'd love to. We haven't had a date night in a while. I'm actually pretty jealous that you take your managers out more than me." She laughs, taking a sip of wine. I wish she was joking. "You can, however, make it up to me."

"Oh really?" I smirk, inching forward to place my hand on her hips, pulling her forward. "And where should I make it up to you? In the bedroom? On this couch?" I kiss her cheek. "In the kitchen, perhaps?" I kiss the other cheek.

"Right here," she whispers against my lips, her hands trailing down my chest.

I tug her down the length of the couch, positioning myself above her. "You're beautiful," I say before kissing the curve of her neck.

After tonight, the least I can do is tell her and show her how wonderful she is. Despite the back and forth happening internally, I have to put everything into this moment. We undress each other as I struggle to find the passion and love I still have for her. Once naked, we cover ourselves with a nearby blanket, cautious of the two children sleeping upstairs. The look of pure ecstasy across her face motivates me to continue as I fail to feel much of anything. Images of Joshua's face flash through my mind, but I'm quick to will them away, trying not to ruin the mood for her. But as I come, I envision Caden beneath me, not the mother of my children.

I jump off the couch, pulling my boxers on, and sprint to the bathroom. Closing the door, I dash to the toilet just as my stomach reaches my throat. I empty the contents in the bowl, retching a few times. After, I flush the toilet and stand in front of the mirror.

I recognize myself as the same person I was just a month ago—before meeting Caden. It feels like my entire world flipped, but on the outside, no one noticed.

I splash cold water on my color-drained face, trying to

think of an excuse as to why I abandoned my naked wife on the couch. Looking once more, I see a glimpse of the lost man from a few years ago. My hair is now longer, breaking the gelled look I had meticulously styled for Caden. My eyes are no longer sunken into my skull like they used to be. The man in front of me looks healthier. I've gained weight, drink less, and eat better, but there are hints of bags reappearing, and the crease in my forehead is deepening.

You are straight. You were not born gay. Being gay is a sin.

I repeat the phrase I haven't spoken out loud in years: "You are straight. You were not born gay. Being gay is a sin."

After a few repetitions, I dry off my face and exit the bathroom. I walk back to the living room in search of Sophia but come up empty. I can see her shadow shifting in the kitchen. As I enter the kitchen, I find her washing the remaining dishes from dinner.

"I'm sorry, love." I slide my body up against hers, placing my hands on her hip bones. "I started to feel sick. I think the seafood got to me."

"Maybe we shouldn't go to that restaurant then," she replies, turning around to face me.

I nod and kiss her forehead. "How about we head to bed, and I'll clean the kitchen in the morning?"

She smiles, taking my hand in hers.

As we lay in bed, I cuddle her, trying to remind myself of all the reasons I love her.

EIGHT

ONLY A WEEK HAS PASSED since my dinner with Caden. It was long, treacherous, and tiresome. Each day, I fell deeper into a vicious hole—one I created myself. The secret of running into Joshua eats away at me the longer I keep it from Sophia. The act of compartmentalizing has become more difficult.

Seeing Joshua at the restaurant has broken a three-year drought of new information. Although he unfriended me immediately on Facebook following our college breakup, I was able to keep tabs on him for quite some time via our mutual friends. They would post pictures and tag him. That is how I found out about his new boyfriend (September 9th, 2008), engagement (January 15th, 2011), and his dream destination wedding—that we had originally planned—in California (June 18th, 2011). I witnessed each major event through a computer screen, each job promotion, and every birthday I kept track of. Every single one only pushed me further into a depression. It was bad enough that I was living a lie, but it felt like he was shoving it in my face.

When I had shared the news of Joshua's wedding with Sophia, I instantly regretted it. With the stress of Isabella coming, my own internal battle with my sexuality, and the cafe on the verge of opening, we didn't need the added drama. Nevertheless, I was honest with her.

The day before Isabella was born, I hit rock bottom. From that moment on, I deleted my social media and swore to never speak his name under our roof again.

When Isabella was a month old, Sophia decided it would be best for the family if I started reparative therapy to work through my depression. And it was. While we weren't really religious, we had religious backgrounds, and Dr. Matthews convinced me that being gay is a sin. No one is born gay; we just chose the wrong path. I learned in therapy how to be the best husband to Sophia and father to my children.

Now, all I have worked against is resurfacing. All due to Caden Benson.

The idea of exposing Sophia to this side of my life again is unnerving. We may be living ignorantly, but we've found a sense of happiness together. It's a happy-go-lucky lie, for me at least, so why shouldn't I have another lie that'll keep her safe and blissful? Sure, it's uncomfortable knowing that we could run into Joshua at any moment, considering he isn't out west like I originally suspected, but the chances of it happening seemed slim.

But then, there's that kiss. The kiss on the cheek from Caden; and the way his fingers interlaced seamlessly with mine as if they were made for each other. I can still feel the warmth of his lips grazing my cheek.

For the entire week, I ignored Caden. I didn't know how to act after dinner, now that he had far too many secrets. Despite Caden being mature about the situation and telling me he'd be there for me, I had to create distance.

I've been diligent in working out every kink to make sure I'm not at the new cafe when Caden is working. It isn't easy, considering it's new and there are issues to sort out, but I did my best. Only speaking with him through email and text—

never once answering my phone when he called. I fear hearing his voice will be enough to disrupt the walls I'm reconstructing.

All the while, I am attempting to give everything I possibly can to Sophia. She needs me to be the perfect man she wishes she married—the perfect husband in her fairytale. Every night I come home early to make dinner, I play with the kids while she finishes up work, and then after we put the children to bed, I remind her of all the ways I love her. But each night, when we climax, I imagine Caden is in her place. Each night the fantasies grow stronger until they turn into nightmares as Dr. Matthews' words seep through.

Night six is turning out to be no different as I guide Sophia up to the bedroom and effortlessly strip her. It's become so routine, but it's given her a pep in her step each morning. Tonight the act of turning myself on becomes a chore. I have a laundry list of things to do at work. The kitchen is still a mess from our "make your own pizza" night. Sophia has a manuscript to read, and all I want is to curl up and sleep for an eternity.

Still, I manage to focus enough to enter her because the haunting begins. Snapshots I was shown during shock therapy mingle with each other. I can't remember if I'm supposed to be happy or sad with the picture of Sophia or the picture of Joshua. The hairs on my skin stand straight with each thrust that soon results in pseudo shocks. Squinting my eyes, I try to regain clarity. I try to listen to Sophia beneath me instead of Caden's angelic voice telling me he'll be there for me.

Benjamin, you're not gay. This is just a phase.

"Fuck!" I scream, rolling off of Sophia and sitting up on my side of the bed. I dig my fingers into my eyelids, trying to stop the tears of exhaustion sliding down my cheeks.

"Are you okay?" Sophia's voice is soft and tentative as her fingertips graze my shoulder.

"Don't touch me!" I yell, standing up. "Fuck." I kick

through my clothes, bending to find my boxers. "Just—" I look up at her as I pull my boxers on.

The color drains from her face. She grabs the comforter, wrapping it around her naked body.

"Please, just … just leave me alone."

I spin toward the door, slamming it as I exit. I wince, holding my breath in hopes the children remain asleep. Without another sound, I shuffle down the stairs and curl up on the couch.

CHAOS ERUPTS the next morning as Sophia yells at the children to get ready while I cover my face with a blanket, remaining in fetal position on the couch. I pretend to be asleep when Sophia tries to wake me up with coffee. It isn't until I know the coast is clear and the fact that my phone is constantly ringing that I attempt to move.

A voicemail from Caden demands that I meet him at the store immediately. From the tone of his voice, it sounds urgent but okay enough that it can wait until I wash the regrets off of me.

Walking into the cafe, I'm thrilled to find tables occupied with pleased customers. The baristas greet me, informing me Caden is in the backroom. From the first glance, nothing seems out of order. With each second, it's becoming more evident that this visit is a plot.

Anger starts to rise in me. Whatever is happening can happen over email. I push open the door and immediately stop in my tracks as I catch sight of him. Caden's sitting at his desk, eyebrows furrowed, staring at the computer screen. My shoulders relax, and my mind drifts off as I take in his black uniform, wondering what lays underneath his button- up stretching across his shoulders. My gaze travels up, taking in his disheveled hair and his one too many bags under his eyes.

My anger is replaced with guilt as the man in my fantasies reveals an overworked Caden.

"Hey stranger," he greets, a soft smile on his face. Even though he looks exhausted, the smile is genuine, and his hazel eyes shine.

I walk toward him, running a hand through my untamed hair. "Everything okay?"

He motions toward a chair as he finishes something on the computer. Once I'm seated, he turns toward me.

"So, the problem is," he starts, "I have this friend, and things have become awkward. He's avoiding me, at least I assume so, but there is something I want to tell him. But now I don't know how. Do you have any advice?"

Heat rises up my neck, and I lean back in the chair. Lying to Sophia is easy. Caden, on the other hand, seems to know my actions before me.

"I'm sorry." I sigh. "I was humiliated."

Goosebumps climb up my skin as he rests his hand on my knee. I breathe in a shiver when his fingertips squeeze my kneecap.

"I'm going to be blunt," he inhales before continuing, "the truth is, I've been attracted to you for a while, and now that I know you, it's been really difficult to get you out of my head."

Every nerve in my body comes to life at each word. I sit up taller, leaning forward to catch all the hope being released.

"Honestly, there is nothing that would make me happier than to date you, Ben. But, you're married."

In one swift motion, my spine curves as I exhale—having to force myself to breathe in again.

"Y-you like me?" I stammer.

There is a lump at the back of my throat, making it hard to swallow. Sweat collects on my skin. I can feel the urge to switch moods—react negatively instead of focusing on this glimmer of hope he's offering.

Caden lifts his hand, turning it palm up atop my knee.

Tentatively, I place my hand in his. His fingers weave between mine, and he squeezes. All I can do is close my eyes. In just a moment, all of my spackled walls will shatter.

"I do, Ben. Isabella's Coffee, to me, is far more than just coffee or a job. Your first store popped up right when I needed it most. I found comfort reading in the nook. I don't know if you remember me coming in, but I was there often. The more I learned about you and the coffee shop itself, the more I wanted to get to know you.

"You could have just asked me."

His thumb caresses the top of my hand, a smile gracing his lips. "I could have, yes, but it seemed so far out of my element at the time. I wasn't in a great place back then, and I refused to do anything to ruin the safe haven I created. I was happier admiring you from a distance." His eyes dance, watching me. "Never in a million years would I have assumed you were gay. But I wanted to get to know you no matter what."

With a deep breath in, he straightens his spine, looking directly at me. "But, I've been cheated on before. Honestly, I don't think I have the strength to be the other man. And well, you're my boss."

It's as though I've been sucker-punched in the gut. Here I am learning that Caden—the guy that's knocked my world on its side—has been admiring me for years, but it can't go forward?

"Give me one date," I blurt.

He holds my gaze, eyes narrowing, as he pauses. His prolonged silence grows uncomfortable, but I can't look away from his contemplating eyes.

"Please, just one chance," I beg softly, squeezing his hand.

"One date."

I let out a breath I didn't know I was holding, and a smile overcomes me. "Thank you, Caden." A nervous smirk makes its way to his face. "I promise you won't regret this."

THAT NIGHT, when I arrive home, Sophia doesn't make any remarks on the night before. She eyes me cautiously as we carry on our normal routine. During bath time, I decide I need to make it up to her, so when we say goodnight to the kids, I start for the bedroom, but she goes to the stairs.

Doubling back, I follow her downstairs. She's pouring two glasses of wine by the time I reach the kitchen.

"I need to get some work done tonight," she says, glancing over her shoulder.

I move behind her, looping my arms around her torso, placing my lips on the base of her neck.

"Are you sure you don't want to come upstairs?" I stretch my fingers across her hips, inching toward the top of her thighs.

"Ben," she breathes. "Every night we've had sex—mediocre sex, mind you—I can't tonight. I really need to get work done."

Mediocre? *Fuck.* My acting skills are diminishing.

She turns around in my arm, cupping my cheek, her eyes laced with concern.

"There's something bothering you, and I know it's something you'll talk about when you're ready, but I can't help feeling like you're forcing intimacy at this point. Last night," she sighs, "last night you exploded. What the hell happened?"

I step away from her, leaning myself up against the island for support.

"Do you know how that makes me feel? Out of nowhere, my husband decides in the middle of sex that I have to leave him alone. What the hell, Ben?"

"I'm sorry," I whisper.

"Does this have something to do with Caden?"

My hands grip the island behind me, but I try to remain

straight-faced. "What does Caden have to do with our sex life?"

"You tell me," she says, handing me a full wine glass as she exits the kitchen with her own.

I make a failed attempt at collecting myself before meeting her in the living room. She's already on the couch, paging through documents in her briefcase. I sit down next to her, trying to find any plausible explanation for my outburst.

"I ran into Joshua ... and his husband." The words are out before I can swallow them.

She freezes, her grip crumbling the papers in her hand. "W-when?" She drops the papers on her lap, reaching for her wine, the liquid vibrating in her hand.

"Last week when I had dinner with Caden. I went over and said hi, but he told me to fuck off."

She takes a sip of wine before closing her eyes, placing pressure between her brows with the tips of her fingers.

"Ben," she huffs, regaining eye contact. "Of course he did. It's been seven goddamn years. Think of everything we've done and been through. Same goes for him. He was a lifetime ago, Ben."

I nod, rubbing over the skin that Caden's thumb had grazed only hours before. We sit in silence as I allow her to process the information. The unexpected weight of her hand on my knee ignites the memory of Caden's hand: how the weight of his feels different, bigger and stronger, protective in a way. Hers ... hers is condescending—dominating even.

"I love you," she whispers. "Remember what it is you're fighting for, Ben."

Just like that, the topic of Joshua is locked away once again. The next morning, I allow Sophia to control our situation. She leads the conversations and intimacy. Each night, instead of making love, we sit on opposite ends of the couch and catch up on our respective work. Conversation only flows when the children are around.

As the days pass, Caden and I struggle to find time for our date. We discuss options constantly in person and text throughout the night, getting to know each other better. But with my household being too fragile to introduce a new lie, I hesitate to commit.

NINE

TWO WEEKS LATER, with tension still thick at home, I make plans with Luke for breakfast, hoping to catch some sort of break. Prior to the third cafe, we had weekly breakfasts. But he got a promotion around the time that the promenade store opened, so our traditional Friday morning meet-ups were pushed aside. I lucked out when Luke said he was available. We used to go to the first Isabella's Coffee, but now the promenade store is right next to his office, so we meet there instead.

As we wait in the long line of morning commuters, my eyes drift to Caden standing behind the register, greeting each customer warmly. It's unusual to see him at the register, he's rarely behind the counter, but he's a pro at customer interactions, each one genuine and personalized to the morning regular.

Luke is up next in line, and Caden's eyes brighten in recognition.

"Morning, Luke! You're earlier than normal."

My brows furrow. Luke has a normal time?

"Morning, Caden," Luke greets with a smile. He begins to

fish out his wallet. "Ben and I are having breakfast this morning."

Caden looks behind him, his eyes catching mine. It'd be lying if I said my body didn't warm at the instant change in his demeanor. His shoulders relaxing and his face twitching, trying not to smile too wide.

"Hey Ben," he manages to get out before growing flustered. "D-do, you both, want your regular orders?"

"Mind adding two everything bagels with butter?" Luke asks.

Caden nods, seeming a bit uneasy, but he focuses on typing onto the iPad.

"You have a regular order?" I laugh, looking at Luke, who shrugs. "Please comp it, Caden," I add as Luke tries to hand over cash.

"Of course." His smile is a little easier now as he hands over our place card with our order number. "I'll bring everything over soon."

Luke and I walk away from the register and manage to get the last free table.

"How often do you come here?" I question as we sit.

"Usually every morning. I try to come on my first break to grab drinks and food for my co-workers. It's really busy here at this time, congrats dude!" He smiles, twirling the place card on the table. "Caden's doing a wonderful job. He usually takes care of me."

I never realized how much time Caden spent behind the bar. Most managers prefer the backroom. The information only solidifies my decision to hire him. I like that he's actively involved with the customers, meaning he also sees what his employees are dealing with. It's strange to know he and Luke are friendly. Feels a little too close to home.

"He's been a great choice," I compliment. "So how's work? It feels like it's been months."

The last time I saw him was the family and friend's night.

Before that, Sophia, the children, and I all had Christmas and New Year celebrations with Luke and Annabelle. All of us dropped the ball after the holidays. We used to be able to get together once or twice a week.

Our coffees are delivered by a barista as Luke starts to tell me about his promotion. More stable hours, a great staff, better pay. He's really excited that he can give Annabelle the wedding of her dreams with the promotion. They started dating after Sophia and I got married, and then it took another seven years for them to get engaged. Far from the arrangement Sophia and I had.

Shortly after, Caden approaches with our bagels. I can't control the natural smile that graces my face in his presence. Over the past two weeks, he seems to be carrying less stress, now having me step up as a boss and our friendship growing, he has less on his plate.

"Sorry for the wait," he says, putting the bagels on the table. "I don't mean to interrupt, I know you're not working." He shifts foot to foot. "But Ben, do you think we could touch base at some point today? I have a few questions."

It's endearing to see him out of his element when it isn't just the two of us. He's rarely nervous, but usually, I'm alone when he talks to me.

"Of course, we can touch base before I leave."

He flashes a smile, giving me a quick wink, before rushing away. My face reddens, and I keep my eyes on him until he's out of sight.

My trance is broken when Luke clears his throat, eyebrows raising.

What was that?" He laughs.

He couldn't possibly have seen the wink. I need to play dumb, so I grab my bagel and furrow my brows.

"Ben, Caden just had you blushing."

My stomach flips and my mind races. I need a reason in record speed. I shake my head, rolling up my sleeves.

"No, no. I'm just hot. It's warm in here."

"I think he has a crush on you."

I study Luke, trying to figure out his logic. "He doesn't. I promise that." I take to buttering my bagel despite no longer being hungry. I need a topic change immediately.

"Do you not see the way he looks at you?" He starts to butter his own bagel as if this conversation is no big deal. "He's definitely gay." My eyes shoot up toward him. "And he's very clearly infatuated. It's cute."

I take a sip of my too-hot coffee but try to use it to dislodge the saliva in my throat.

"Any ideas for a wedding date? Maybe next summer? I ask.

As I change the topic that he luckily is excited to talk about, I can't help but wonder how Luke is so confident that Caden is gay, but never once has questioned my sexuality.

Following breakfast, once Luke leaves for work, I head into the backroom to find Caden. The morning rush has signifi- cantly slowed, so he's now back at the computer.

"Hey, sorry. I'm sure you're busy. I appreciate you taking the time,'" he says, eyes still on the computer as he types away.

I take an empty seat next to his desk. "No worries. I always have time for you." I take hold of his hand underneath the desk, but he pulls away. "What's going on?"

He takes a deep breath before turning away from the computer to look at me. "I've been thinking ...."

Shit.

I open my mouth to interrupt, but he holds his hands up. "I want nothing more than to go out with you, Ben."

There's a catch. There's always a catch. He's about to end this before it even begins.

"Obviously, in an ideal world, you would be single. I know I already agreed on a date, but Ben, I can't be toyed around with any longer. I understand you're busy, but you're busy for the exact reasons we shouldn't do this. I won't—I refuse to be someone you only come to when you need a break."

"I don't—"

"Please, Ben." His confidence visibly diminishes as he begs. "I need to protect myself."

"Tonight?" It's time to do everything in my power to show him he's worth it, regardless of the consequences.

"Just like that? Tonight? You don't have to clear it with your family?" There's an edge to his voice as he straightens in his seat.

Holding out my hand, I watch as he peers behind me to check on the staff before placing his hand in mine.

"Yes, tonight. Your place? You can show me how amazing your culinary skills are?"

Caden had mentioned his love of cooking and how he wanted me to be his taste tester. The suggestion is just a brilliant way for us to spend time in the privacy of his apartment.

His face contorts as he tries to process my offer. It's obvious he woke up this morning and made a decision to end things today. I squeeze his hand in mine and glance behind me before I give him a quick kiss on the cheek.

"Send me your address. I'll be there at six."

When I get to the door, I turn to see his eyes still on me. There's a hint of a smile, so I give him a wink that sends him into a full smile.

IN ORDER for the date to happen, I tell Sophia there's an emergency at one of the stores, and I need to cover the night shift. As a compromise, I pick Noah and Isabella up from their respective schools, making it clear I have to be out by five that evening. I rarely need to cover for any of the cafes, but it has happened once or twice.

In the short amount of time I do have at home, I make

sure to prep dinner, sit Noah down with homework, and pack my briefcase with a change of clothes while I get dressed in something I'd wear behind the bar. All before rushing out as soon as Sophia walks through the door.

Recently, I started renting office space to have a dedicated location to work, and now it's coming in handy as a place to get dressed at before heading to Caden's. Dressed in one of my nicer sweaters and a tighter pair of jeans, I remind myself that I can't ruin whatever Caden and I have. I have one chance to prove this could be something.

Driving up to his address, I am greeted by a wall-to-wall windowed complex. As a person currently signing off on Caden's checks, it seems unlikely he could afford this place. With one quick glance in my car mirror, I take a deep breath and smooth my hair before walking across the street to the front door.

There is a doorman in the entryway who seems to double as a receptionist and security guard. The lobby I've walked into isn't large but quite similar to a hotel lobby, with couches and a coffee bar. With the doorman's assistance, I'm ushered to an elevator, traveling up three stories. The elevator dings and I follow Caden's previous instruction to head to the end of the hallway.

As I near his door, the smell of dinner consumes me. Soft music seeps through the walls, and I hesitate. Perspiration starts to gather under my arms, my sweater suddenly feeling like the wrong choice. I take a moment to collect myself before I knock three times. Immediately the music lowers, and his footsteps pad across the apartment. I'm greeted with a smile as soon as the door opens.

"Hi," he says, moving aside to let me in.

Shuffling awkwardly, I offer a small smile in return.

His apartment has more character than the rest of the building—a quirky home vibe instead of sleek perfection.

"This place is amazing." His kitchen, living room, and

dining area are all an open concept, just an island in the kitchen creating some separation. There's a narrow hallway attached to the living room on the left that presumably leads to the bathroom and bedroom.

He blushes and mumbles thanks. Walking over to a sliding glass door behind the dining room table, he points outside. "There's a balcony here, but the view isn't really great. It's definitely pushing my budget, but I love it."

"How many rooms?" I ask as he walks back to the kitchen. I follow him.

"They say two, but the second is small. I use it as an office."

I nod, surveying the kitchen once there. Expecting no less, all his appliances are stainless steel, his countertops granite. On the counter, there are already two long-stemmed glasses of red wine aerating.

"I remember this complex being built. How'd you snatch up an apartment here?"

This complex was one of the most sought-after places in the area when it was under construction.

"When I saw construction began, I jumped at the chance to rent. I needed to get out of my parents' home, and my choices were slim. I was on the wait-list for six months."

At first glance, I'm astounded by how spotless someone can keep their home without children running around with paint and crayons. We have stainless steel too, but his aren't caked in fingerprints of unknown particles.

Sophia and I lucked out when we married. Her parents are pretty well off, and they bought our home. They wanted to make sure Noah was raised in a good, safe neighborhood. It's a blessing to not have to worry about a mortgage, but our once pristine residence no longer exists.

"Dinner is almost ready. I also hope you actually liked the wine from the restaurant because I bought a bottle for us to share."

"I did." I smile at the thoughtful gesture. "Anything I can help you with?"

He shakes his head, so my head drifts to the dining room table, already set with plates and silverware, two lit candles decorating the middle. Glancing back at Caden, he's moving rhythmically around the kitchen and bubbling pots.

"If you want, you can bring the wine glasses and bottle to the table? You're more than welcome to take a seat."

I nod, doing as he asks, taking my time before sitting down. I feel bad. I know I can't really help but sitting around waiting only increases my nerves. He comes over to grab our plates from the table a few minutes later. He serves us each, continuing to add seasoning. It's obvious he's a natural. Caden has always seemed fairly confident, but seeing him outside of work, emitting the same happiness and concentration, it makes me want to get to know him even more.

He places the steaming plates on the table before bending over to kiss my cheek. My face warms as he sits next to me.

"I apologize for my hasty hello. When I cook, I tend to zone out. So, hello." He looks over at me, chuckling a little. "You're adorable when you blush."

My face only reddens further. "Thanks," I mumble, peering down at the meal. "This looks absolutely delicious."

He served chicken breast, cooked in what smells like a lemon garlic sauce, with roasted sweet potatoes and broccoli.

"I hope you enjoy it. I mostly cook for myself, so most dishes only have my taste in mind."

With just a bite, my assumptions are confirmed: Caden is an amazing cook.

We eat in silence for quite some time; only the scraping of our silverware is heard, leaving my mind space to overthink. The setup is perfect, exactly what I want, but I can't have this life; it isn't that easy. I have a family at home, a wife who is most likely finishing up dinner right now. I like the idea of starting a new relationship, though. Something fresh and organic; it's exciting. My relationship with Sophia feels old, too familiar, and dull.

"Hey, everything okay?" Caden asks, reaching across the table to touch my hand. "You look pale."

"Yeah. Yeah, sorry." I offer a smile. "Just lost in my thoughts for a second. It's really amazing to be here tonight. Thank you for giving me this chance." I interlace our fingers. "I know it's early, but this feels right. I'm nervous but completely comfortable at the same time."

He returns my smile and squeezes our hands. His hesitation is evident, though. His mind must also be playing games. While he can play the confident card in some places, this is a situation that could crumble everything.

The rest of our meal is met with small talk, seemingly hesitant to open up much more than we already have. What if tonight leads to nothing more, forcing us back into a strictly professional relationship?

When we finish, I take the initiative and bring the plates to the kitchen sink, helping with the dishes. He refills our glasses, finishing off the bottle, and meets me in the kitchen.

"Would you like to watch a movie?" he asks.

Throughout dinner, I honestly wasn't sure if there would be more than just eating and leaving. "I would love to." I smile, leaning back against his island.

I can feel the buzz start to kick it with my movements. Caden steps in front of me, resting his hands on my hips, hooking his fingers in my belt loops, tugging me close. My breath catches as our hips connect, and my mouth becomes the Sahara. His hands start to trace the sides of my body, roaming over my arms before they still to cup my cheeks.

"May I?" he whispers, his breath sending chills across my skin.

I nod slightly, not trusting my voice.

His moist lips come to rest against my parted lips. He deepens the kiss as my body relaxes toward him. I wrap my arms around the small of his back, leaning against the counter and pulling him with me. I can't help but notice that my arms don't overlap like they do with Sophia. Instead, my hands are perfectly interlaced. Even though Caden is broad compared to Sophia's petite frame, he seems far more delicate.

Caden's tongue teases my lips, sending a spark to the tip of my toes. The fireworks I have yet to experience in my life are being set off with just one kiss. The heart-racing, sweat-inducing, mind-blowing kiss everyone speaks about in the movies is happening, and I never want it to end.

I refuse to let my hands drop as he leans back. His clouded eyes and parted lips beg me for more, but it seems he's searching for a yes. My right hand cups the back of his head, pushing his lips against mine again.

"Don't stop," I mumble against him.

At my words, he surges forward, gripping my hair between his fingers. His tongue pushes its way into my mouth, no longer asking for permission. I've accepted his challenge, tangling one of my hands into his wavy hair, the other grasping his neck. I'm eager to fight for dominance here.

This isn't like kissing Sophia. And now, after kissing Caden, it's clear that kissing Sophia will feel like kissing a friend. Currently, and what feels like forevermore, Caden Benson is stealing my heart.

The wine tastes even better on his lips. His scent—his *flawless* scent of espresso and aftershave—fills my nose. I bury both of my hands in his hair, feeling his leg fall between mine. He presses forward, a soft moan escaping between our lips.

I know if we don't stop now, I will never. These are the fantasies that have me cursing out my wife. I pull away at that, though.

"Too fast?" he breathes, leaning his forehead against mine. He licks his lips, his own clouded eyes blinking at me.

"Too fast," I force out.

I want to take it back, let go completely and be irresponsible—even more than I already was. But I'm not ready, not yet.

"Let's watch a movie." He steps away, a sudden rush of cold air chilling my bones.

We grab our wine glasses, and I follow him to the living room, sinking down into the cushions.

"God, your couch is amazing."

"I fall asleep on it way too often." He laughs as he turns on the television.

Still high from the kiss, I grab his wine glass and place both of ours on the coffee table. Without hesitation, I wrap my arm around him. His frame cuddles effortlessly into mine, his head resting on my shoulder, feet up on the couch.

"Comedy to break the sexual tension?" He says it as a joke, but there's no hiding what happened in the kitchen.

We decide to watch *21 Jump Street*, a film neither of us are familiar with. As the movie starts, Caden snatches a blanket, spreading it over us. His hand rests on my thigh when I pull him closer to me. It all feels so normal. The night before, I was cuddling Sophia in bed, and we struggled to find a comfortable position. But here? Here it all fell into place.

It's easy to forget what is beyond Caden's apartment and that I have a family to go home to. Yet, I can't shake the fear that this isn't enough. It isn't fair for Caden to handle my baggage. Even if he claims he'd be patient, it isn't fair. He deserves to be treated like royalty with complete commitment and selflessness. And I have every intention to do all that, but my obligations will always demand that I put my children first.

Every so often, he shifts or squeezes my hand, reminding me how close he actually is. Being here in this room with him, I feel like I've found the missing piece that's been haunting me. It's all so simple.

His hand caresses my thigh casually, yet it reawakens my nerves. How far would we have gone if I hadn't stopped us? I'm eager, but this is way too fragile to rush. Whatever is happening isn't a silly fling—for either of us. My feelings are far too concrete, and that's fucking terrifying.

I inhale, only to have my exhale betray me, forcing its way out louder than intended.

"Hey, you okay?" Caden lifts his head from my shoulder.

I squeeze his hand to try to tell him I'm fine, but he just shifts to see my face better, tilting his head.

"I haven't felt this way about someone in ages. My brain just won't relax." He just sits there, nodding for me to continue. "I want to go all in. I want to be present. I want to feel everything. I *want* to lead you back to your bedroom and see where this takes us. You've invaded my every thought. I've imagined what your kiss may be like, and it only exceeded my expectations. I've wondered how your body would feel wrapped up in mine. Every touch sends shivers down my spine, and you turn me into a foolish schoolboy." I drop my eyes as silence consumes us.

He doesn't say a word, only moves the blanket slowly off our laps. My nerves spike as my heart accelerates. A smirk threatens his lips as he straddles my lap. I can hardly breathe when his face is mere centimeters from my own. My eyes close when he tangles his fingers in my hair. I *am* present in this moment, hyperaware of every single movement, praying I can control myself beneath him.

"Benjamin," he whispers against my ear. The tease knows exactly what he is doing to me. His voice—low and husky— saying my name like a musical masterpiece. "Keep your eyes closed. Be here with me. Be present. Take in every touch, every breath, every kiss." His lips graze the skin behind my earlobe.

Snaking my arms around his torso, I let them rest danger- ously close to his ass, doing as he asked. I take a deep breath in, focusing on this moment.

His kisses are delicate, making their way from my forehead to my eyelids, nose, cheeks, and ears. A soft, almost inaudible moan escapes me when his tongue glides down the crevice of my ear. His hands tightening in my hair at the sound.

He conveniently passes over my lips, focusing the attention on my neck. The last time I received this much attention, I was tangled up with Joshua. Sophia never took an interest, even though it made me lose control. The sensitivity isn't lost on Caden, as he relishes the fact that he has complete control.

I twitch, feeling warmth spread throughout my body. All he is doing is kissing me, fully clothed, and he's going to make me lose control. I want him beneath me. I want him to be mine.

I groan as he presses his hips forward. "Caden." I open my eyes, half-lidded. His have darkened and clouded over. "Kiss me."

And there it is, the taste I've dreamed about, his antagonizing lips consuming my own. His teeth nip at my bottom lip, causing me to jut my hips forward.

A blaring noise rips us apart in surprise. My cell phone is ringing in my back pocket.

Caden pulls away, his face void of our previous affections. A terrifying transition from lust to frustration.

"You should get that." His voice monotone, he climbs off my lap, storming off toward the kitchen with our forgotten wine glasses in hand.

A wave of emotion rushes through me, hitting me like a break. Unexpected tears prick my eyes—the all too familiar feeling of being alone. Everything outside of the apartment feels so foreign and distant.

My phone stopped ringing by the time I retrieved it from my pocket. I had a missed call and two text messages from Sophia. I read the messages asking me to pick up Tylenol on the way home because Noah has gotten a fever. I look at the time, and it's nearing ten. Regardless of the texts, I need to head home. All the cafes close at nine, so my lie only holds out for a few more minutes.

Standing up, my legs shake as I adjust my sweater before walking into the kitchen—Caden's leaning against the counter with his back to me. One wine glass is now empty by the sink. His shoulders shudder before he breathes in again. This isn't fair to him. There is no way I can protect him from my family.

I walk to stand in front of him, placing my hands on his shoulders. He looks up, his face guarded and pale. He blinks away the moisture collecting in his eyes.

"Do you need to head out?" he asks, his hands pinned to his sides.

"Yeah, Noah is sick. I need to go get medicine."

Despite his frustration, a sense of concern crosses his features.

"Is he okay?"

"Yeah, just a fever. Tylenol should do the trick."

In a flash, Caden straightens his shirt, standing taller. "Okay, keep me updated. Let me know if you need any help with work."

So, that is it. Back to boss and manager. This is all a big mistake, mixing business with pleasure. It's unprofessional, for starters, one disappointment, and Caden could report me. Not that I think he would, but I don't have any leg to stand on as a cheating husband and father.

"Thank you for tonight." I take his hand, but he doesn't return the grip. It was better than I ever could have imagined."

Without a word, he shakes my hand away and leads me to the door. Before my own mind locks up, I place a hand on his cheek, forcing him to look at me.

"I'm sorry," I whisper. "Tonight was amazing, and I hope I get another opportunity to get to know you better."

His cheeks redden, but he puffs his chest out just slightly. He seems just a few seconds away from losing his cool. Whoever hurt him in the past is the last person he truly let in, and my personal life can't give him something steady and safe.

"I'm afraid of getting hurt," he admits.

I pull him into a hug, my grip strong and hopefully protective. We both know inevitably he will get hurt. It just comes down to how much pain we are both willing to endure.

"I do like you, Ben."

I smile down at him and press my lips against his. He kisses me back, but it lacks the enthusiasm from only moments before.

"I like you too, Caden."

With the close of the door, my stomach fills with dread.

TEN

NEVER IN MY life have I sped so fast to the drug store and then home to try and make up time to reduce any questions asked. Noah had called on my drive to tell me that he ended up getting sick and needed me immediately.

I couldn't have predicted that tonight would be the night he'd get ill, but if it were any other night, I would have been home with him. Of course, Sophia didn't mind me going to work. Sometimes it did have to happen, but I didn't have to take advantage of that flexibility and trust. Noah is a daddy's boy, and he always clings to me when I'm sick.

I dash into the house, kicking off my shoes and throwing my work bag before jogging up the staircase. Sophia meets me at the top of the stairs, a small smile on her face. I give her a closed-lip kiss, trying to hold back the smell of wine, hoping Caden's aftershave hasn't lingered.

"Thank god you're here." She sighs. "He's been asking for you all night."

I hold up the plastic bag, and she takes it, quickly grabbing the Tylenol out.

"How is he?" I ask as we both walk to the hallway bathroom so she can pour the Tylenol and store it.

"He's thrown up twice since he called. He's miserable and won't stop crying. He's just devastated that he's sick."

Noah prides himself on being the tough one, loves when he doesn't cry after getting hurt. Despite Sophia and I telling him countless times he's allowed to cry and release his emotions, he says he's setting an example for Isabella. So, when he does cry, it's only that much harder to bear.

"How's Izzy?" I ask as Sophia fills Noah's water cup up from the tap, mixing it with Pedialyte that is also in the shopping bag.

"She's asleep. She was cranky tonight but tired herself out and hasn't woken up."

With the medicine ready, we head to Noah's room, where he is bundled in his *Despicable Me* comforter. His skin pale, tears still streaming down his face. When he notices me, he lifts his head off the pillow, blinking his sad green eyes.

"Hi, Daddy."

"Hey, bud." I walk over to him, pulling him into a hug. "I'm sorry I wasn't here." I grab the cup from Sophia's hand, and Sophia gives Noah the medicine. "We need you to take this medicine, but we have some yummy juice for afterward, okay?"

He nods, snuggling into me more as he swallows the bright, red liquid. His face scrunches, and he coughs a little.

I hand him the Pedialyte, and he downs the entire cup before looking back at us.

"That was gross." He frowns, snuggling his head into my chest.

Sophia and I laugh. I press a kiss to the top of his head, my eyes welling up.

"We know, bud. Good job, though." Noah hands the cup to Sophia. "I can take it from here. Get some rest," I tell her, moving Noah and me back against his bed frame.

After some hesitation, she nods and leans down to kiss Noah goodnight. She tells him she loves him before leaving the room. I reach to grab *Cloudy with a Chance of Meatballs* from Noah's nightstand.

"Try and fall asleep, Noah. Tomorrow it'll just be the two of us, and we can watch movies all day."

Instead of his normal excited reaction to spending the day together, he snuggles further into me. We lucked out with him getting sick on a Friday night with no chance of him having to miss school.

I read the book in its entirety even though he falls asleep a few pages in. I figure the longer I keep reading, the longer I can stay in the safety of his room. The way his body is clutching mine reminds me of when he was an infant, and he would struggle to settle down unless I was holding him. He still needed me as he was getting older. Just another reminder that it's something I cannot threaten.

I bathe in the solitude for a few more minutes before placing him carefully down on his bed. Flipping the light switch, I leave the door cracked just in case he wakes up. After I peek into Isabella's room and kiss her cheek, I crack her door open too.

When I exit her room, Sophia comes out of the bathroom, showered, and walks into our bedroom with just a towel. She really is beautiful. Her long golden hair lays damp against her back, and her toned legs stretch out from the edge of the short towel. A few weeks ago, I would have walked in, trying to seduce her, but tonight, I snap into work mode.

Once downstairs, I grab my laptop and situate myself on the couch. I load up the spreadsheets I should be working on, but I find myself staring blankly at the screen. The date with Caden and the events here in my home seem miles away.

In a single evening, I became the man who cheats on his wife. It was bad enough when I was just her boyfriend, but to have now added vows and kids into the mix? I always chastised men who did this, wondering how they could be so thickheaded, and here I am doing the same.

After spending tonight with Caden, though, I understand the mindset. I can sympathize with their need to be with someone other than their partner. The need to be with a person who makes them feel alive again. Sacrifice their seemingly perfect lives for the chance at a relationship full of passion and renewed excitement.

Sure, when I was a young and hormonal teenager, I felt that sexual excitement with Sophia. But then I met Joshua and discovered the repressed part of myself. I was convinced and trained that those feelings were wrong until Caden broke the dam that me, Sophia, and my therapist created. A dam, I am certain, can never be rebuilt. No amount of therapy can reverse the way I'm currently feeling.

I jump as Sophia's hand rests on my shoulder.

"Everything okay?" she asks, coming around the couch to sit beside me.

My face warms, my stomach bubbling again as I replay the last night I was with Caden.

"Sorry if I startled you. It seemed like you were in a trance."

I suppress the urge to snap at her. If I'm in a trance, I prefer to not be interrupted. Instead, I look over at her, giving her a weak smile. It's like I'm transported back in time, being greeted by a younger Sophia, sans makeup and the wear and tear of daytime. The shower has washed away the years of motherhood and a foolish husband. Instead, it's given me my best friend back—the young girl sitting before me who I used to be able to tell everything to.

When did it all change? What moment defined when I couldn't trust her with my secrets?

"Ben, what's wrong?"

I shake my head, refocusing on my laptop, moving the cursor aimlessly.

"Where are your work clothes?" I glance back at her—

hidden exhaustion surfaces on her face, a small crease forming between her brows.

"Ben." Her voice wavers. "You don't smell like stale coffee. Where have you been?"

I try to keep my eyes from widening, swallowing the saliva building up in my throat. "I'm sorry," I blurt, my voice working faster than my mind. "I went out with a few guys from work. I've just been working a lot, and I wanted a break, but I didn't know how to ask you."

Her eyes take in my appearance. Despite my heavy sweater and jeans, I feel entirely exposed, as if "I cheated" is written all over me.

"Why did you lie? You have nothing to gain from lying."

I have *everything* to gain from lying.

"I'm sorry," I say softly, opening my arms to her. She climbs into the cuddle, her head resting on my shoulder, her damp hair soaking through the fabric of my sweater. "I just feel like I haven't had any time for myself, you know?"

It's a terrible excuse. If anything, she is the one who needs a break.

"I know. Life has been non-stop since college. We have sacrificed a lot, but we can't start lying about needing space. You know you can always go spend time with Luke and have a guy's night."

The idea that my guy's night can only consist of Luke is what tangles my insides and causes my fingers to involuntarily clench. I should be able to have other guy friends without her constantly worrying I'm going to fuck one of them.

"Luke is great, but sometimes I—I need to go out with people who don't know our family."

She pulls away in an instant. The dampness on my sweater growing cold. Sophia crosses her arms and shifts to the other side of the couch.

"What are you hiding?"

Squeezing my eyes closed, I take a deep breath, running my hands over my face. I'm digging the hole too deep.

"I just," I sigh, "I just need some space and time to take care of myself."

"What, and I don't?" Her voice slices like a razor blade. "Don't you think I can use a break too?"

I open my eyes, and she's already standing, gripping the edge of the couch.

"Here you are bitching about needing time to yourself when you spend most of your time at work away from your own family. I'm here working, cleaning, cooking, and being a damn good mother and wife. And you're telling me that *you* need space?"

My hands are up in surrender. "I know, love. I'm sorry. Forget I said anything. You deserve some alone time too. We will make that happen."

She nods, but her body remains stiff, her fingers white from her grip that won't loosen.

"You remember I—"

"I remember," I interrupt, offering her a smile. "You have a book launch party tomorrow."

Sophia's face twitches, refusing to smile. I've shocked her by taking note.

"Do you think Annabelle can watch Izzy tomorrow? I want to focus on Noah getting better."

Her shoulders relax, and she lets go of the couch. "Yeah, I'll ask. Make sure to take Noah's temperature regularly, and if he gets worse, he needs to go to the doctor immediately."

"Of course." I reach my hand out, a peace offering.

She sits back down on the couch, taking my hand, but there's still a cushion between us.

"Do you really mean it when you say we'll find time for me?" I nod and squeeze her hand as she relaxes into the cushion. "It feels like everything is revolving around the cafes."

"I know. It'll get better. I think it might be time to admit I can't do everything on my own. You remember how I told you about Caden moving up?"

Her hand disappears from mine.

"It's either me away from home, or it's Caden learning more," I tell her as she looks away from me. It's not exactly an ultimatum. No one else on my team is skilled enough to take on more work without me having to train them for weeks.

Caden is smart and is dedicated to learning new things. He's already operated the new cafe different from the first two, upping sales goals. It may be selfish to have him help me, knowing he can easily spend more time in my private office space. But it is either Caden's help or no help at this point.

"Okay. Don't fuck up this time," is all Sophia says before she disappears upstairs.

ELEVEN

I END up sleeping in Noah's bedroom when I finally make it to bed around three. It isn't because I'm actively avoiding Sophia. It just happened to be Noah cried out before I could make it to the bedroom.

By the time the sun starts to shine into his bedroom, Noah is getting sick again. After cleaning him up and letting him rest some more, I force myself to stay out of bed despite the pain itching its way between my brows. I had no choice but to help Sophia this morning.

"Good morning," she greets as if our conversation last night didn't happen. "I heard you upstairs with Noah. I thought you might want this." She hands me a full cup of black coffee.

I nod gratefully. "Thank you." Taking a sip, I walk over to Isabella, who is devouring a plate of strawberries. "Good morning, beautiful."

"Hi Daddy!" She giggles, holding a strawberry for me to see. "Look! Mommy got strawberries."

I smile, snatching a berry, tossing it in my mouth. "Delicious!" Isabella nods, taking another bite. "Can I help you with anything, Soph?"

She's already dressed, wearing a fitted red dress that reaches her knees with a black blazer. Her hair is curled at the ends, and she's sporting a red lip that used to be her signature. Despite it being past midnight when she went to bed, you can barely see her distress. I imagine most husbands would be nervous about sending their wife out of the house looking as beautiful as she does, but in my exhausted state, I can't help but hope someone flatters her.

"Isabella just needs to get dressed, but there's time. How's Noah?"

I update her on Noah's night before she encourages me to finish my coffee and get some more work done before he wakes up. For a millisecond, I wonder if it's a trap, but I'm reminded I was in the middle of doing something last night when I started to fall asleep.

Once in the living room, I find my abandoned phone, already having a missed call. It was from Caden a few minutes ago. Taking another gulp of coffee, I hit the call button.

"Hey Ben," he greets after a handful of rings. While his tone is professional, I can't stop the smile forming on my face. I'd be lying if I say I wasn't fearful things would be awkward.

"Hey, what's up?" There's rustling in the background. Despite it being Saturday, he's working, bright and early.

"Good, good. How are you? How's Noah?"

"I'm tired." I laugh. "I was up most of the night with him." I lean back against the couch, taking another sip of coffee. "It'll just be him and me for the day, though, so he can rest up."

"I hope he gets better. I do have to go, it's busy this morning. I just wanted to check in and let you know I had a good time last night." I let out a breath I wasn't aware I was holding. A blush creeps up on my cheeks as his tone falters.

"Me too. I'll call you later?" I question. I don't know when or how, but I need to talk to him again soon.

"Sure, sounds good."

Hearing Sophia's heels, I throw the phone back on the coffee table.

"Who was that?" She rounds the corner, handing me toast with peanut butter and bananas with strawberries on the side.

"Oh, uh, it was Caden. Just some work issues."

"On a Saturday?" Her eyebrow raises, and I shrug my shoulders, lifting the plate up in thanks before I focus on my computer until Sophia and Isabella leave the house.

Noah wakes up around nine, feeling better. He's drowsy from the interrupted sleep, but he manages to eat and keep everything down. While I had an uneventful day planned for us, Noah keeps requesting a special hot chocolate. After he keeps his breakfast and snack down and rests for a few hours, I finally cave. Although it's the farthest from our house, we make the trek to Caden's store.

The cafe is still bustling, even in our slower sales period. I can't even fathom what summer tourism will bring to the business. It's hard to imagine sometimes that these cafes are all mind versus working for someone else.

Samantha spots us before we reach the bar. "Let me guess, you want your special hot chocolate?" She grins at Noah.

"Yes, please!"

"And I'll have a triple latte today," I say, and Samantha gives me a knowing look. I rarely drink espresso, I save it for the days I really need it; nonetheless, add an extra shot.

After processing the orders, Samantha comes around the bar to give Noah a hug. "Caden's in the back if you need to speak with him. I can watch Noah."

I take her up on her offer and head into the back office. Caden doesn't look up from his desk, so I take advantage of his ignorance and stroll over, kissing his head quickly.

His hand reaches to touch my arm before he looks up and behind me. "Hey, where's Noah?"

"Out with Samantha. She's excited to see him." I pull up a

chair next to him. With the desk coverage, I place my hand on his knee. "So, when can I see you again?"

His eyes grow wide for a moment before he looks down at my hand. With a sigh, he interlaces our fingers. "Whenever you can manage to be free."

"Right." I nod. "I'll have to see what my schedule at home looks like. Sophia needs some extra help."

He gives a curt nod and tries to turn back toward the computer, but I squeeze his hand, asking if he's okay.

"It's just hard to hear about your family after our date. This is becoming more real." He looks back at his computer and starts to scroll through his email. "I'm not rushing. I know you're in a difficult place, but hearing you talk about your wife and kids so nonchalant is difficult for me."

He doesn't look back at me, just opens and closes emails as we sit in silence. I know I need to reassure him, but I can't lie to his face.

"Daddy!" I hear and instantly slip my hand out from under Caden's, moving it to my own knee.

Turning my head, Noah wobbles as he balances our drinks in his tiny hands.

"Daddy, can I have a cinnamon bun with my hot chocolate?" He hands me my latte with a hopeful expression. "Please?"

I glance at Caden, who let out a soft laugh. He's looked away from the computer, drawn into Noah's pouty lips and pleading green eyes. Despite what he's said, he adores my children.

"Sure, but only if you share." Noah's face lights up, and I know I probably made a mistake that Sophia will yell at me for later, but I need someone who isn't frustrated with me.

Noah waves at Caden before he runs out of the office, his hot chocolate spilling over the edge of the cup.

"I should go." I stand up, placing my hand on his shoulder. "I'm sorry this isn't easier." I give his shoulder a squeeze, grab a rag from the shelf next to him and clean up Noah's mess before I leave the office.

NOAH and I are just waking up from a nap on the couch when Sophia and Isabella come through the door with a pizza. Noah ends up ratting us out when he mentions the hot chocolate and cinnamon bun because he can't contain his excitement. Luckily, Isabella is too excited about pizza to be upset she didn't get to go to the cafe. Sophia gives me a stern look but chooses not to say a word.

After dinner, she tells me to head to my office to get work done because she doesn't want our Sunday to be interrupted by work or me stressing about everything I still have on my plate. She said she wants to spend the day together as a family, so instead of admitting I don't have too much left to do, I take advantage of the high she's on from her day at work and head to Caden's to discuss a promotion. Naturally, I stop at the store to pick up some mint chocolate chip ice cream in celebration.

Caden opens his door, confused, after a few minutes of me knocking. He's only wearing a white t-shirt, boxer shorts, and thick black-framed glasses.

"Ben?" He clears his throat, adjusting his glasses. "What are you doing here?" He glances down at what he's wearing, pulling his shirt further down.

"I thought maybe we could hang out?" I lift the plastic bag in my hand. "I brought ice cream."

His eyes flutter toward mine, a smile forming. He opens the door wide, letting me in. "Let me change. The bowls are above the sink." He turns away, and I drop the bag.

Sidestepping him, I rest my hands on his hips, kissing his forehead.

"Don't you dare," I whisper.

"But, I—" he protests as I kiss his temple. "I feel weird in my boxers. You *are* my boss." He melts into my touch, though, as my thumbs caress his hips.

"Your boss who is kissing you. I think the whole theory goes out the window, right?" I raise my brow in question. He relaxes, leaning into my touch. My lips brush against his as I speak, "you should wear glasses more often, by the way."

With my grip still on his hips, I walk him up against the wall, loving the way he bites his lip. My left hand cups the curve of his neck, lifting his lips to meet mine, taking his bottom lip between my teeth. I give him a hungry kiss as his hands nestle in my hair, tugging gently on the ends. He arches forward when I thrust my hips against him, pinning him to the door.

My hands move to his hair, gripping the waves to keep him close to me. I swallow his moan, releasing one of my own. He trails his hands down to my cheekbones, cupping my face and pulling our lips apart. His clouded eyes try to find mine as our breath fogs up his glasses.

"God, Benjamin. What am I going to do with you?" His voice is deep with lust, a thumb moving to outline my lips. "I haven't felt this way in …" he trails off, an almost fearful realization overcoming him.

I loosen my grip on his hair, taking to combing through it gently with my fingers. I kiss his forehead before searching his eyes.

"Me too, Caden." I breathe.

There's a vague flash of recognition in his eyes. Things aren't optimal, but we are in sync. This isn't about choosing to have an affair. It's about two people understanding each other like no one else can.

He swallows and blinks, the moment gone for a new one. He shifts to look at the neglected bag behind me.

"So, what flavor did you buy?"

"Mint chocolate chip. My favorite."

"Mine too." He grins, skirting around me.

I let my hands fall limp at my sides. I watch in earnest as he grabs the bag and heads to dish out the ice cream.

I allow the silence to take over, trying not to interrupt whatever is happening in his mind. He's content distracting himself by scooping before he leads us to the couch with bowls.

"How did you manage to get away tonight?" he asks, shoveling ice cream into his mouth.

I place my hand on his cheek, smiling as he shivers from my cold fingertips.

"Please don't put your guard up. Be with me right now. Don't worry about the rest."

I kiss his cold closed lips before pulling away, scooping a bite of ice cream. "Besides, I was told to go work, and though I should be at my office, I wanted to spend time with you. I don't want to talk about my family, though. I want to talk about you."

"What about me?" He gets settled back in the cushion as if relaxing from Sophia's permission.

I eat a bite of ice cream before it melts. "First, why have you never told me you wear glasses? You look adorable."

His cheeks redden, and he pulls his knees to his chest. "I hate them. They remind me of the past when I was weak and vulnerable. I feel unprofessional in them."

"Glasses don't make you look unprofessional. It's how you carry yourself."

He cocks a brow at me, laughing. "You basically salivated when you saw the glasses. Admit it, I look like easy prey."

I laugh. "Well, they don't make me rethink my work-related offer."

"What offer?"

"Well, you see, a couple months ago, I offered this outstanding guy an opportunity to move up in my company.

Now I'm wondering if he feels like he's ready for the challenge?"

His mouth spreads into a huge smile as he takes in my words. He releases his cramped legs, leaning forward.

"Are you offering me a profit share in Isabella's?" I nod, smiling, and suddenly his face drops. "You're serious? I thought you may have been joking during the interview because you seemed so nervous, and now I understand why and I told myself to forget about the offer because it was ridiculous—"

"Caden." I laugh, placing my hand on his thigh. "Breathe." He takes a deep breath in and out. "That would have been terrible to joke about. I am serious. It wouldn't be immediate, but we would start taking steps to see if it would be a good fit."

"Wow." He eats another few spoonfuls of ice cream, his face contorting as his brain processes. "Am I even qualified? You aren't offering me this because we are seeing each other?"

"You are qualified. We have identical business degrees. I've been waiting to find a manager who I feel comfortable starting this venture with. Caden, you're overqualified for the position you're in now. Right now, I want to give you a share of the profits we make during a trial period. If all goes well, and we agree to make it a partnership, then we can."

"Ben, I don't know if this—"

I sigh. My exhaustion starts to set in. It's not that I'm frustrated with him, it's just I thrive off his excitement, and his skepticism about this … and about us adds another layer of stress. After the past twenty-four hours, I had hoped tonight would be full of celebration.

"I feel like an idiot. I shouldn't be offering this." I place my feet on the ground, putting my ice cream bowl on the coffee table.

"Wait, stop." Caden reaches out, placing his bowl next to mine before taking my hand. "I want to, Ben. It's just, I'm nervous, okay? A partnership into Isabella's would be a dream, but the timing is ironic, isn't it?"

"Everything I do isn't controlled by my dick." I groan, standing up, walking a few feet away. Sophia and Caden are wildly different but operating on the same track.

"I didn't say you were," Caden says softly.

"Then, why are you assuming I'm choosing favoritism because I like you?" I massage my temples as I pace.

"Does Sophia think that's the case?" He's standing in front of me when I turn back around to pace in his direction. His hands grip my shoulders, halting me.

"It's not like that. You're qualified. We will draw up a contract we agree on, one that benefits us both. If you choose to walk away, I'll still own Isabella's, but you'll get a fair share. No matter what, you'll always have an outstanding recommendation from me."

"As long as I'm not given special favors or feel pressured into doing something just because I want to keep my job. We can start training, but I want to decide when I will become a partner—when I feel like I've earned it, okay?"

I sigh, allowing my body to cave just slightly. "That sounds fine. My cafes are too important to take detrimental risks. There's a reason my other managers haven't been offered a profit share. But with you on my team, I'm confident we'd be able to crush the goals I have."

"Perfect." Caden leans forward. "However," his voice drops, a smirk across his lips, "during training, I will exercise my right to kiss you whenever I please." He giggles, crashing his lips into mine, washing away the frustration lodged in my muscles.

We kiss, and he massages my shoulders until I wrap him tightly in my arms. "Welcome to Isabella's partner-in-training." I lead him back to the couch, sitting down, and pulling on me, his legs straddling my own.

Just as I am about to kiss him again, he sighs, sitting back on my legs.

"How can something feel so right but so wrong at the same time?"

I do my best to not let out a groan or let my head drop back on the coach. I just want more than a few minutes of peace. More than a few minutes of uninterrupted happiness—that I anticipate getting with him versus my home.

"This all feels so easy and natural," he continues. "I don't want to stop doing this … doing us, yet I can't help but dwell on the fact that I'm the other guy."

We keep going in goddamn circles.

"I don't want you to be the other guy. But how am I supposed to let you go?"

He climbs off my lap, settling into the other side of the couch. He leans his head against the couch cushion, tugging a blanket off the back, spreading it over himself.

"I don't want you to. It's just, I thought I was over my past, but it's starting to creep its way back in. I went through hell, and I managed to come out on top. I graduated top of my class, paid my dues at Beanery, and then you offer me this job. I want this. I want it so bad, but I didn't plan on an affair being a part of the deal."

The word 'deal' settles into the pit of my stomach. Am I pressuring him?

"You're the guy I've fantasized about being with." He reaches over and gives my hand a squeeze as he admits this. "I said I would never put myself through this again, and yet, here I am. How am I supposed to commit to this without losing respect for myself? I would be committing to sleeping alone every night, knowing I'm not the only lips you kiss, the only person you think of and love each day. I want to be the only one, Ben. I need to believe I am worth that love."

I lean back into the couch cushions, pulling him back onto my lap, and give him a tight hug.

"Caden, you are worth so much more than I can give you right now. You deserve everything you want in life, and I can't promise you right at this moment I can give you that. I can promise if you endure these obstacles with me that one day I will give you all that and more."

He remains silent, but he cuddles further into me. I start to trail my fingers up and down his back, my smile growing as his muscles loosen.

"Can you tell me about your past? Maybe talking would—"

"Not yet," he whispers.

"Caden, you have to trust me if this is going to work."

"Don't." His voice is stern, but he doesn't pull away. "Don't push. I'll tell you when I'm ready."

We fall into a thick, awkward silence. He breathes steadily against me, no push to move out of my arms, but it feels like we crossed into unspoken territory.

"Can I ask a question?" he whispers. "You can say no too."

"Go for it," I say, kissing his head.

"In college, when you dated that guy, were you and Sophia broken up at the time?"

I try to remain still, fearful this is a trap. There isn't a right answer because I'm an asshole of a person. I did outright cheat on Sophia. She forgave me, but it doesn't make it okay.

"Promise to hear me out?"

He nods, but his fingers dig into my back. Caden, it seems, is the one person I can't seem to hide a secret from.

I take a deep breath and explain almost everything to him. Recalling the drunken night Joshua and I went back to his dorm, and a few beers turned into a night of honesty. A night I truly felt alive. I explain in-depth how that one time morphed into unintended months. Joshua and I were in love and planning a future together. I tell Caden of the plan I had to end it with Sophia over winter break, but how I was a coward. When we returned to school, Joshua mentioned marriage, so that night, I went to end things with Sophia. But before I could speak up, she told me she was pregnant. There was no debate. Regardless of what I had with Joshua, I had to end it. I gave myself to Sophia and our future family. I confess that my decision to leave Joshua and remain with Sophia was the hardest decision I ever had to make. A decision that haunts me daily.

Throughout the confession, he doesn't move away. Never even flinches. My concrete walls start to shatter at how easy that felt with Caden. The idea of telling anyone else in my life drives me into a spiral, but Caden? It feels natural.

The silence between us hums in the air as I start to feel myself close up again. He repositions himself in my lap, backing away just slightly so he can look into my eyes. Caden caresses my temple.

"Can I be honest?" he asks.

I nod, swallowing the tension in my throat, resting my hands on the waistband of his boxers.

"I think this facade you two have created is harming everyone involved."

My brows furrow. I remove my hands so I don't grip his waist. "Sophia never asked for this. I'm giving her the love that she needs and deserves. It was never a question whether or not I'd be a father to my children."

"You're cheating on your wife, Ben. This is the second time. If this doesn't work with me, it won't be the last time. I don't know Sophia, but I do know she deserves someone who can love her the way you aren't able to."

I gently nudge him off me, standing up from the couch.

"We all do," he mutters as I stalk off to the kitchen with the melted bowls of ice cream. I keep myself from tossing the bowls in the sink and just place them down to avoid breaking them. When I turn around, Caden's leaning against the island.

"You don't get it. You can't understand," I tell him. The

barricades are haphazardly being rebuilt. "I shouldn't have told you." I try to slide past him to the front door, but he grabs my wrist, twisting me toward him.

"Your kids are going to grow up thinking being gay is unacceptable. You're denying Sophia real, legitimate love. I don't care what lie you two think you're living, but you need to step away and realize how messed up this all is."

My blood is boiling as he strikes the core nerve of the issue.

"Fuck you, Caden." I spit, shaking off his arm. "Fuck. You." I storm past him, opening the door and slamming it behind me.

Instead of driving to work to actually get something accomplished, I stop at the corner store for a bouquet of cheap flowers and a bottle of wine. I'd prove Caden wrong and be the husband Sophia needs. I'm a damn good father to my children, and I went to therapy to be a better husband. No employee of mine can tell me different.

When I make it home, Sophia's upstairs reading. I rest my weight against the doorframe, rapping the wood.

"How would my beautiful wife like to join me for some wine?" I walk in, revealing the flowers, wine, and glasses from behind my back.

She grins, closing her book and tossing it on her bedside table. "Can that wine be served in bed?"

"Of course, love." I hand her the flowers I already put in a vase.

She smells them before putting them next to her book, eagerly taking the glasses. I pour wine in each glass and strip down to my boxers before climbing into bed.

"And why are we celebrating?" she asks as we cheer.

"Well, I have this amazing wife who does so much for me. Even after her own strenuous day, she offered to take care of everything. She bends over backward, and frankly, I think she deserves this more often."

"Thank you, Ben." She exhales, blinking away some tears.

I kiss her lips before we take a few sips of wine. In only moments, I have her straddling me like Caden had, and I capture her lips between mine.

Fuck Caden.

TWELVE

"WAKE UP!"

I groan at Noah's screaming voice as the bedroom door swings open. Curling closer to Sophia, I bury my face in the crook of her neck.

She hugs me back, laughing.

"Can we go to the park today? Please!" Noah exclaims, jumping up onto our bed.

Reluctantly, I lean up on my elbows to find Isabella wandering into our room. She's carrying her blanket, and her arms stretch up when she reaches my side of the bed. I lift her up as Noah bounces in front of us.

"We have to check the weather first, honey." Sophia rubs her eyes, sitting up against the headboard. She made the right decision to get dressed again in her pajamas.

"Mommy, the sun is big today! Look!" Noah grins, pointing out the windows.

The sun isn't exactly shining into our room just yet, but there's no mistaking the clear sky.

"How about we throw around a baseball today? Maybe we can sign you up for tee-ball in a few weeks?"

"What's tee-ball?" Noah scrunches his face.

"It's beginners baseball. The ball is on a stand called a tee, and you swing the bat at it. Some of your friends from school may be doing it this year."

"Yes! I want to."

"Ben." Sophia laughs. "Have you forgotten that we don't own baseball stuff?"

I shrug. She wants a family day. We'll have an all-American family day. "A quick run to the store can fix that." I give Sophia a cheeky smile and hug a quiet Isabella to my chest. "Let's go eat a big breakfast, then we will head to the park, and maybe go out for lunch?"

Noah nods enthusiastically. Practically already jumping off the bed.

"Perfect plan." Sophia's smile warms my chest, and I quickly give her a kiss.

"No kissing! Pancake time!" Noah giggles.

Sophia and I chuckle with our lips pressed together but continue to kiss as we feel the kids climb off the bed. It isn't until Noah yells from downstairs that we make our moves.

After far too many pancakes and a trip to the store to get new gear, we make it to our favorite park right near Lake Mackenzie. It's far busier than other parks in our area, but this one is special to our family. The afternoon unfolds just as I hope. Noah nor I have any natural athletic ability, but his passion and determination cannot be mistaken. Sophia and Isabella ended up ditching us to go feed the noisy ducks after a while.

I throw the ball a tad farther than intended, but Noah darts after it, weaving between some people walking. I glance over at Sophia and Isabella. Izzy is talking to another little girl.

"Caden!" I hear him yell.

My eyes focus on the direction Noah is in. Caden is walking toward him with a baseball in hand. He's with

Bethany and another guy. Caden kneels down in front of Noah and says something, but I'm too far to hear, yet Noah laughs.

I jog toward them as Noah is still giggling. "Daddy, Caden thinks you need more practice." He's covering his mouth with his hand as he giggles.

"Oh, is that so?" I raise my brow at Caden.

"Yeah, you're terrible." Caden laughs, but it's easily forced. Luckily, Noah can't tell.

"Noah, I think it's almost lunchtime. Maybe you should go back to Mommy and Isabella and see if they want to head out?"

Noah nods and hugs Caden goodbye. I keep my eyes on Noah until he reaches Sophia. When I look back at Caden, Bethany and the other guy have given us some space. It crosses my mind that Caden has told someone, and that's one too many people.

"I'm sorry," he says, but I'm not quite sure what he's apologizing for. "I was giving my opinion where it doesn't belong. You were right. I don't know you well, and I don't understand why you live the way you do. But you don't know me either, so you can't criticize my thoughts on the subject."

I look over to Sophia, and she's now watching me and Caden.

"I'm … I'm sorry I didn't hear you out." I sigh. "How about you come by the office tomorrow morning. We can clear the air and start your training?" He always gives himself Sunday and Monday off, so it's an ask for him to take on more of a workload without having coverage for him yet.

"I'll be there—but Ben," he hesitates, "why should I expect you to give me the world if you don't believe you deserve it yourself?"

I stand there dumbfounded. He offers me a face full of sympathy before he heads back to his friends. Of course, I know how to give the world to someone; that's all I know how to do sometimes. It's the reason I stayed with Sophia. Does he think I settled? There's no way I deserve to put my feelings before my family's. The therapist made it clear that I was doing the right thing by not acting on those desires.

A hand rests on my back, and Noah and Isabella's chatting breaks me from my stance. Interlacing my fingers with Sophia, I lead my family out of the park. The day started off as a family affair and will remain that way.

After we went out to lunch at a cafe in the city, we stopped by the original Isabella's Coffee for coffee and hot chocolate before trekking back to our neighborhood. We decided to watch movies the rest of the afternoon. We are on our third film, *Finding Nemo*, by the time the kids pass out on the couch, fully stuffed with Chinese takeout.

I offer to clean up and put the kids to bed, so by the time I reach her, she's already lying down with a book.

"Soph?" I ask, laying down next to her. She closes the book, giving me her full attention. "Do you think I give too much to others and not enough to myself?"

She sits up in bed, gripping her book. "Where is this coming from?"

"Luke." It terrifies me how smooth his name flies off my tongue. "Luke told me I don't give myself enough."

"Babe, you gave yourself three cafes."

"I mean," I swallow, "in my personal life."

"Do the kids and I not give you enough?" Her tone bordering on snide.

"No, no, you guys are everything. It's just—"

"Honestly," she interrupts, "I think you could be giving us more."

I suck in air, shutting my mouth so I don't start coughing. My immediate reaction is to excuse myself to get some work done, just as an excuse to sleep on the couch. But I remember our agreement. Today is a "no work day," and I can't mess up a perfectly good Sunday.

Instead, I turn on my side and flick off my light. She shuffles next to me, reopening her book, keeping her lamp on. There's an uneasiness in my stomach as reality sets in. I don't have anyone to confide in.

THIRTEEN

A RESTLESS NIGHT has me waking up before my alarm, preparing breakfast, packing lunches, and driving the kids to school. If I need to give more to my family, I can take control. But being in control also means making the executive decision that instead of starting Caden's training in my office, that I have to show him the world he's meant to have as well.

My brain already can barely function on the lack of sleep I've had this weekend, that my lack of focus on work won't be beneficial to Caden. After a quick text telling him to stay at his apartment, I detour from my office to the grocery store. I rush through the aisles, buying prepared fruits, some cheese, a baguette, Lindt chocolate, some water, and a single red rose before I head to the newest cafe, nearly around the corner from his building. After picking up coffee, I head to his place.

Outside of his door, I take a few calming breaths, trying to mask my accelerated heartbeat. He answers the door after I knock, a smile gracing his lips. He's dressed in his work uniform.

"Ben, what's going on?"

I left everything but the rose in my car. Revealing the rose to him, his body leans against the door, his smile widening.

"I want to give you the world, Caden." I take a step closer, placing a hand on his cheek. "If you'll have me."

His hand grasps my bicep, and he pecks my lips.

"I'm sorry," I start. "There's a lot in my life you can't understand because I haven't allowed you in. But I'd like to start today. Let's take a break from work, and I'll take you out."

He nods, taking the rose from my hand, drawing it up to his nose. He breathes in, closing his eyes. "Let's go."

Mother Nature works in my favor as the sun blazes in the sky, and the temperature is unseasonably warm for the beginning of March. I drive us through the city and down toward the beach on Mackenzie Promenade. I'm hoping it's relatively empty, considering it's Monday morning and only fifty degrees. When we arrive, we are only accompanied by a man playing fetch with his dog.

I grab the food and Caden's hand as we head to the beach. His sideways glance is enough to bring a smile to my face. A gust of wind knocks us back a step as we get to the sand. We create some distance between the dog owner and us before settling down.

"So, I brought snacks, but I forgot a blanket." I laugh as I realize my mistake. Having a picnic on the beach without something to sit on is less than ideal.

Caden just laughs, gazing out at the water. I take my jacket off and decide to use that for a surface. I lay it flat on the ground, placing the food on top so it doesn't blow away.

"We can go over to the park if you want? It may be warmer?" Caden suggests, but our date cannot take place there.

I place both of our coffees in the sand before I wrap my arms around his waist. His eyes dart around, and his smile shrinks, but I pull him close, tucking my head in his neck, giving him butterfly kisses.

"You'll just have to keep me warm," I mumble.

Goosebumps rise where my lips touch his skin. I kiss my way up to his mouth, his hot breath coating mine. He pecks me softly before we part and takes a seat in the sand.

Over coffee and brie, I learn more about the man sitting with me, like how he went to a charter art school instead of a public school because his mother was a school teacher there. Instead of following art, he majored in business and draws only as a hobby now. Aside from owning a coffee shop, his biggest dream is to have at least three children, preferably five. Bethany has been his best friend since they were four years old. He's always dreamed of traveling the world but has only been to Mexico and Canada. Somehow we skirted completely around the biggest part of his life—college—on account of his smooth subject changes. I figure out the Mexico trip happened with the guy who cheated on him, but he's quick to shift to a different memory.

When we finish nibbling on the food, we clean up, and I put my jacket back on. Our conversation dulls to a comfortable silence when I lay back in the sand. His body curls against mine, his head resting on my chest, one of his legs over my own. Caden trails his fingertips up and down my side underneath my jacket.

With the wind calming and the sun finally beating down on us, it's hard to recall a time I've felt so at ease.

"Caden?"

"Hmm?" he mumbles, resting his chin on my chest to look up at me.

"Have you ever heard of reparative therapy?"

He goes rigid. In one fell swoop, he is out of my grasp, sitting in front of me. "Of course. You're not … you're not thinking of doing it, are you? Ben, you can't just change who you are. That's not how it works." His words stumble over one another as his hands start to tremble.

I sit up, squeezing his hands in mine.

"Caden, no," I whisper. "I'm not thinking about it … I've

done it." His face flushes, and his grip tightens. "Every Monday for two years. I'd be heading out right around this time."

"Ben," he whispers. He tries to steady his hands.

I swallow my fear and meet his glossy eyes. His thumb caresses my skin, and I breathe in.

"You asked me why I am staying with my family. Why I am doing this. Caden, I am doing this because ..." I look down at our interlaced fingers. "I'm afraid of what happens if I don't."

He opens his mouth to speak, but I shake my head. I can't have him interrupt, otherwise, I may never finish my confession.

"Sophia suggested reparative therapy after Isabella was born. We had a rocky pregnancy, and she convinced me that it's what the family needed. She doesn't believe I'm really gay. She thinks if I was, I would have dated more than just Joshua, that I wouldn't have stayed with her. When I agreed to therapy, I made it my mission to protect my family with everything I had. Including not informing Sophia about what the treatment actually included—like shock therapy." I bring our hands to my chest, increasing the pressure to try and stop his trembling. "I still remember where I've been shocked, but the images of right or wrong are becoming foggy. I made the decision to leave after two years, but it worked in the sense of me being repulsed by anyone who wasn't straight, including my own reflection. I grew angry at people who identified differently before I became completely numb to the world around me. It took a long while for me and Sophia to get back on our feet as well. The healthiest we've been in years was this holiday, right before you showed up. I don't know what changed. I don't know if enough time has passed or if I started growing more comfortable in my skin again, but it was difficult being in your presence for a while."

I blink away tears, tilting my head back in the slightest. Caden unlaces one hand, brushing a thumb beneath each eye.

"I'm falling for you, Caden. But this ... this isn't just me coming out." I let go of him and curl my knees to my chest. "It's not that simple." I rest my chin on my knees and shut my eyes.

"Benjamin, this is for your own good."

The room grows dark, and pictures of my family fill the screen in front of me.

"Being gay is a sin, Benjamin. Repeat after me: I am not gay."

A photo of Joshua appears, followed by a shock when I fail to repeat the phrase. My breathing becomes unsteady as I struggle to form words.

"Benjamin."

"I am not—" I choke.

Another photo of Joshua appears. I scream out as another shock is administered.

Caden's arms engulf me in a crushing embrace. His face buried in my hair, peppering kisses to my scalp.

My eyes are flooded with tears. He isn't running. He isn't angry.

"Benjamin, listen to me."

My body breaks into a sob, and Caden pulls me closer. His own tears pool in my hair as he continues to press his lips to my scalp. We fall back in the sand, and I curl further into him as his voice tries to soothe my convulsions, whispering words of reassurance. I want to believe him. I want to know he'll protect me.

We are interrupted by my phone's ringtone. My body twitches at the noise, and before Caden lets go, he gives me another squeeze. This time instead of running away, he releases me gently. Isabella's daycare flashes across the screen.

Catching sight, Caden's shoulders visibly relax, and he continues to wipe a few tears from my eyes as I answer the call. They are quick to inform me that Isabella seems to have a stomach bug and needs to be picked up immediately.

When I hang up, Caden is already dusting sand off his body and has the bag of trash from lunch in his hands.

"Can I do anything to help?" he questions while I clean myself off.

The air changes, and I'm suddenly drained and nauseous. My hands start to tremble as I shove them in my pockets. The pit of my stomach churns as the weight on my shoulders triples.

Caden steps forward, but I sidestep him as I grab my jacket to head back to the car. He tries to reach for my hand, but the thought of touching him after what I confessed is too much. No one knows what happened at therapy. Not even my wife.

I stalk back to the car, and he's quick to follow. Silence consumes us as I drop him off at his apartment before speeding toward Isabella's school.

FOURTEEN

THE WEEK STARTED off as a way to destroy me. That night, I trade sleep for another sick child and brainstorm ways to build new walls to keep Caden out.

He reports to training with me Tuesday afternoon, after his shift at the cafe. I'm strict with the schedule, barely leaving him an opportunity to kiss me hello or goodbye. Wednesday and Thursday are the same.

Come Friday, my exhaustion reaches the level of canceling Caden's training altogether. Instead, I plan to have a low-key night with my family, with hopes of being asleep by the time the kids are.

As I pack up my briefcase, my office door swings out, revealing Caden with his hands in fists.

"You and I are going to grab drinks," his voice shakes as he speaks, a vein slightly popping out of his neck. "I've had enough of this bullshit. Tell Sophia that some of the guys from work are taking you out. I don't care what excuse you make, but do it."

I stand frozen, mid-file going into my briefcase. I've never seen him unhinged. "Go home and change. Be at my place by seven."

I blink before closing up my briefcase. It's just after four. If I say yes, I can still make dinner and get the kids bathed for Sophia.

Caden walks across the room, stopping just mere centimeters from me. Two cold fingers lift my chin, forcing me to make eye contact.

"This isn't up for debate. If you don't show," he connects our lips with a gentle tug of my chin, "consider whatever this is, over."

"O-okay."

With a curt nod, he spins around and slams the door behind him.

Fumbling from Caden's outburst, I manage to make it home with a reel of excuses to use on Sophia. I'm not sure what got into Caden for him to be that worked up, but I have to see it through. I've gone the extra mile at home lately by always dropping the kids off at school, cooking each night, and cleaning the house each day, so hopefully, I have some leeway.

"Hey babe," I call out, walking through the front door. I hear the bath running upstairs.

"In the bathroom!"

I drop my bag on the floor and bound upstairs to find a naked Isabella dancing in the bathroom while she waits for the tub. Isabella screams my name and jumps into my arms when she sees me.

"Perfect timing. She's been asking for you. Mind giving her a bath while I start dinner?"

"Not at all." I smile. Sophia nods and switches places with me so I can place Isabella in the water. "Hey Soph, would it be okay if I went out with a few guys from work later tonight?"

"Oh," she says, pausing in the doorframe. "Actually, Annabelle and I thought she and Luke could come over tonight? We haven't hung out in a while."

"Can we reschedule for another night? Like tomorrow?"

Sophia sighs, brushing fallen hair from her vision.

"Please?" I don't want to grovel, but I will if it means I don't ever find out what Caden means by 'over.'

"I'll call her."

Fortunately for me, Luke is unable to hang out, forcing Annabelle and Sophia to agree with rescheduling for tomorrow evening at Luke and Annabelle's. By the time I have bathed Noah and Isabella, and we've eaten dinner at a lackluster pace set by Sophia, the clock reads seven.

I am going to be late, but at least I am going.

Caden is already outside of his apartment complex when I arrive. I can't help but be surprised by his welcoming kiss on the cheek and him immediately interlacing our fingers. After he stormed out earlier, I didn't know what to expect, but affection isn't one of them.

"Everything okay?" I question, leaning my frame toward his.

"Everything is perfect," he says matter of fact. He then tugs my hand a bit, and we head down the street.

We walk a couple of blocks in silence. I'm not sure what to make of his 180 nor what conversation I should bring up. Before I can try to say anything, we turn down a laneway dotted with a few hole-in-the-wall bars, similar to Gin and Grin.

"I promise no one we know will be here. It's a college bar, a much younger crowd."

"Are you calling us old?" I laugh, though I'm relieved to find out his promise rings true. The bar is packed with frat boys and fake IDs. It's louder than I like, but hopefully, the commotion eases whatever tension Caden and I have.

We start with a shot to set the mood, that by the time we sit to talk, we've downed two beers and three tequila shots. Instead of addressing the tension outright, we spend our time swapping old stories from college and how we both had gotten kicked out of places before we were legal.

We down another shot when Caden suggests going back to his place for some peace and quiet. In a haze, I send Sophia a text that says I may stay at a friend's for the night to avoid drinking and driving. I have no idea where the night will lead, but one thing is for sure, I want to wake up in Caden's bed tomorrow.

Hand in hand, Caden and I depart the bar. Along the walk back to his apartment, I steal a few sly kisses. The cool night air is failing to sober me up as each touch electrifies my nerves. I haven't felt this intoxicated in what feels like a lifetime, or really pre-therapy. I'm certain I'm drunk on the way Caden makes me feel.

As we approach the door to his apartment, I pull him in by his belt loops. I laugh as he squeals in surprise and smashes his lips onto mine. His hands grip my cheeks, intensifying the kiss. I snake my hands underneath his shirt, touching bare, warm skin, smiling as his flesh breaks out in goosebumps. Caden pulls us over the threshold, closing the door behind us by pressing my back up against it.

We break for air. His eyes sparkle with intoxication and passion. Our breathing remains uneven as I kiss his forehead, trailing my lips down his nose, both cheeks, and chin, only to return to his mouth.

I gasp when his knee slips between my legs, pressing up against my bulge, my hips jerking toward him.

"Bedroom?"

"Yes," I breathe.

Caden inhales and exhales before licking his lips, reattaching them to mine. We stumble into his bedroom, his hand reaching out to flick on the light. The room is only bathed in a glow, just enough to see one another. He gently pushes me back onto the bed, falling next to me, draping his legs over mine. I can feel his excitement against my thigh as I'm suddenly aware of how much I want this.

As much as I want it, I grow self-conscious. It's been years since I've been with another man. I turn my head to Caden, who is now watching me with a soft smile.

"You okay?" His hand caresses my cheek.

"Just nervous."

He repositions himself, so his body weight is entirely on top of me. A groan escapes my lips as we press into each other, but his pressure helps ground me.

Caden looks me in the eyes. "Do you want this, Ben?"

I gaze into his darkened eyes and blink, forcing away the negativity that brims. I *know* what's real versus what's in my head. Caden's real. His feelings are real. He's patient in my world of chaos. I'd be silly to say no to this when I've dreamt about it so many times.

"Yes."

He smiles, his eyes crinkling. "And do you trust me?" His thumb brushes my bottom lip, and I'm eager to kiss him again.

"Yes."

With a brisk peck, he removes himself from the bed to unbutton his jeans and kick them off before coming back to straddle my thighs. My eyes can only seem to focus on the bulge in his boxers as he leans forward, distracting me. Caden kisses just below my hairline and across my face before settling on my neck. He nibbles beneath my ear while his hands rub up and down my sides, my skin squirming with his touch. His hands grab the hem of my shirt, encouraging me to lift it up so he can remove it. Once my chest is exposed, his lips trail down the center of my body, stopping every so often to dip his tongue into the crevices of muscle and skin.

My mind actively fights against each moment of pleasure, the kisses, nips, and touches cloud my head. It isn't until his mouth hovers over my right nipple, the bud hardening to attention, that I let out an involuntary moan. His lips close around it, circling my nipple with his tongue. By the time he repeats the action to my left nipple, I'm aching and yearning for more.

When he reaches the base of my jeans, he looks up, his lips almost touching my trail of hair. "Are you sure?" he asks.

I hesitate. I should be the one to ask him that question. "Caden." I pull him up so our faces align. "You make me want to be the man I've always wanted to be. I want this, but this isn't about just me. Do you want this?"

He closes his eyes, and it seems the same hesitation crosses his face. I want to protect him. I want to love him. I squeeze his hand, and he opens his eyes before a goofy smile graces his lips.

"Yes." He exhales and dives into another kiss.

This time, there isn't hesitation on either side. His fingers unbutton my jeans, and together, we pull them off—boxers included—so I lay naked below him. His gaze takes me in as my dick pulses for him. Just as I'm about to pull him up for a kiss, he drops his head, pressing his lips near my base.

My hips arch as they follow his lips and licks and erratic breathing over the moist areas. He's doing everything but touching and sucking where I'm anticipating. His tongue flicks between my balls and asshole, eliciting a guttural moan as I grip his hair, directing his head over to my dick.

His breathy laugh cools my pre-cum before the warmth of his mouth has me seeing stars. Never, in the history of my sex life, have I ever this lightheaded, cloudy, soaring through the sky type of feeling that'll surely have me crashing to the ground.

His fingertips never leave my flesh, always attached in some way, pushing me closer to the edge. As his mouth sucks me deeper, his fingertips rim my hole, and my heart *and* dick feel like they are ready to burst. I pull his head off of me and guide him to my lips.

"Fuck me," I murmur.

I don't want to play silly games. With Joshua and me, it took a few months before we "graduated" to anal. At that time, we weren't sure we'd both like it. While my mind is clouded by lust, it's crystal clear on one thing: I like being fucked.

His fingertips dive through my hair, gripping the strands tight at my words as he lowers his body over mine, grinding our hips together. His own dick slides up and down mine, and the friction is almost unbearable.

When he pulls his swollen lips from my own, the intensity in his eyes gives me goosebumps. There is no going back. No leaving this bedroom and returning to what we had. As he reaches into his bedside table, he grabs the lube and a condom, and I know that without my control, I am irreversibly falling for Caden.

FIFTEEN

UNLIKE THE MOVIES where you wake up dazed and confused after a drunken night of sex, I am well aware of my surroundings. I relish in the warmth of Caden's body next to mine before opening my eyes. The hand resting on my stomach reminds me of my naked body. The last time Sophia and I fell asleep naked was when Noah was in a crib. It's incredible how free it feels to be in such a vulnerable state with someone again.

My eyes barely have time to adjust before lips latch to my neck. Caden kisses along my collarbone up to the base of my ear.

"Good morning," he says, his breath tickling my ear.

"Good morning." A smile graces my face, and within moments, he's hovering above me.

"How are you feeling?"

He squeezes my hand as I digest the question. I have a slight headache from the shots, but nothing can compete with my current state of calm.

"I haven't been this happy in ages." I sigh, embracing this unfamiliar feeling. My chest rises and falls easily. My skin feels reminiscent of the kisses, massaging, and fingertip trails. "How are you?"

"I'm unbelievably happy." He connects our lips before he hovers. "So happy, I think I'm falling hard for you, Benjamin Jacobson."

Whether due to the remnants of alcohol in my system or the overwhelming sense of happiness, I swallow the tears.

"I-I'm falling for you too," I smirk, "Caden Benson."

The sound of his giggle sends a vibration through my nerves. His breath tickles my collarbone as he nestles his head. Wrapping my arm around him, I hug him into my side, loving the feel of our skin meshing as one again.

"Hey," he asks a few moments later when his fingers stop trailing my arm. "What happened?" His fingertips trace the scar on my left forearm.

The scar had faded quite generously over time that some days I forgot it was there.

"A box cutter slipped while working at Beanery one day. Got a few stitches." I shrug, pulling the lie from my back pocket. Not many people noticed it, but it was handy when they did.

"Ouch." He leans down, pressing a kiss against the mark.

My heart constricts, and I clamp my eyes shut, bringing his head close to my chest so he can't see the tears in my eyes.

I'm startled from sleep by Caden yelling, "fuck." I push myself upward, and he's already out of bed, pacing the room.

"I wish we could continue, but I really need to go to work."

"What time is it?"

"Just after one."

My blood turns to ice as I process that it's one in the afternoon on Saturday. Never have I been away from my family for that long, unless it was a business trip. My last message to Sophia was saying I may be staying somewhere. Nothing confirmed.

Caden gathers fresh work clothes before he darts out of the room. The sound of the shower turning on has me jumping out of bed to gather myself—pausing momentarily as pain shoots through my body, a slight throb in my asshole reminding me of last night's events. My gut tightens as I find my cell phone in the pocket of my jeans at the foot of the bed. In addition to a reply to last night's text message, I have a dozen missed calls and about twenty text messages. They start annoyed and quickly turn to worry. Her last text came through just five minutes ago.

I find myself sitting back on Caden's bed as I grow light-headed. I never considered the kisses with Caden as a form of cheating per se. But there is no way back from what happened last night. I slept with Caden. It wasn't just sex either; it was making love with another man while my wife was at home with our children. The feelings of pure happiness I was feeling are now invaded by my reality.

With my shaking hands, I search the bedroom for my rumbled clothes. Once dressed, I dart out of Caden's apartment, foregoing the elevator and dashing down the stairs. It doesn't hit me until I'm nearly driving fifteen over the speed limit that there isn't a use in me rushing. The damage is done. I can't beat the clock anymore. But I am getting dangerously close to when we would usually get together with Luke and Annabelle. There's no way I can attend dinner tonight. I can do my best to fake it in front of Sophia, but maintaining my composure for a crowd is more than I can bear.

My stomach seizes at the idea of getting caught. It's possible to fake sick and get out of the whole ordeal. The stomach bug is going around. My entire family is hanging out in the front yard when I pull into the driveway. Noah yells my name and runs to the fence before I can put the car in park. He's fast to go inside, though, as Sophia yells at both kids to go in.

When the front door is closed, I exit the car. She doesn't

even give me a chance to walk through the fence before she starts.

"Where the hell have you been?" Her arms are crossed, her fingertips losing color by the grip on her arms.

"Sophia—please, not now." I wipe the sweat that is now forming on my forehead. I truly do feel sick.

"Not now? Are you kidding me?" She blocks my path to the front door. "You go out with friends and then don't arrive back until almost two the next day?"

I sigh, glancing around the neighborhood. The last thing we need is for our neighbors to talk.

"I woke up with a stomach bug. I didn't feel okay to drive home until now."

"Stomach bug?" Her laugh is menacing. I feel my throat lodging up. "I'd guess you're hungover."

Bile burns in the back of my throat as I lean over and puke into the bushes. Immediately, her hand is on my back. I have never gotten ill after a night of drinking.

"Ben, I thought … I'm sorry." She sighs.

Her guilt causes me to heave more, and I hate that this illness isn't a rouse.

"I should have called earlier. I'm sorry. I just need to go in and sleep. Is that okay?"

Sophia wraps her arms around me once I stand straight. "I just worry. Next time, can we go out on a date? This way, I don't have to worry about where you are?"

"Sure." I nod. "We can do that."

SLEEP IS hard to come by—honestly, I'm not tired despite drinking too much. Last night was the most well-rested I've been in years. Instead, I spend most of my afternoon in a war zone created in my mind. There are moments of pure bliss, where I cannot hide a smile from forming, but then it turns to shame and disgust of the man I am becoming, to the frightening memories of knowing where this could lead.

Sophia is nice enough to leave me alone for a few hours, even takes the kids out of the house for a bit. I remain curled in the fetal position, unable to stop the sobs that erupt at a moment's notice. I've lost control. My life turned into a web of lies overnight. In one single act, I disregarded thousands of dollars spent on maintaining this family. There is no coming back nor forgetting what Caden and I shared. Never, in my entire life, have I felt as cared for as I did with Caden.

I turn my phone off shortly after being left alone, ignoring messages from both Sophia and Caden. I don't need the constant reminder that there's been a shift. There's something that needs to change, and I'm not certain I have the strength for either direction.

The urge to drink starts to buzz beneath my skin, growing the more I allow myself to reminisce in Caden's touch. I can still feel his fingertips in my hair and his wet kisses on my skin … on my dick. I can smell sex around me, whether anyone else can, but I can't will myself to shower.

I'm still under the weather—if not more so—by the time Sophia comes home briefly, only to let me know that she and the kids are still going to Luke and Annabelle's. She apologizes for going without it, but her tone makes it clear that she believes my sickness, but she also needs space.

Twenty minutes after they leave—giving enough time for someone to forget something—I raid the liquor cabinet. The cabinet is mostly filled with wine, but there is a full bottle of whiskey in the back corner that we received as a gift years prior. I don't think Sophia or Luke know it's still there. It's been three years since I've had hard liquor. The last time drowned myself in golden liquid was right before Isabella's birth. Since then, Sophia and I stopped drinking all together, up until recently when we started bringing wine back in.

I park myself on the couch, flicking through the television

to find some mindless reality show. I pour myself a glass and take a nice full gulp, smiling as the liquid warms my insides, a sense of relief coursing through me. I down the glass I poured, savoring the slight burn in the back of my throat before I pour myself another whiskey neat, one I'll truly sip.

My mind grows foggy just in time for thoughts to reappear and soon start to vanish. I just need a moment of stillness.

"Stomach bug, my ass."

I jump, the whiskey splashing out of my glass, running down my arm. I turn to see Luke standing in my doorway.

"What-what are you doing here?" I place the glass on the coffee table, wiping my arm with my t-shirt. As the whiskey courses through me, I focus on the anger starting to rise. "Well? Why the hell are you here?"

I'm immediately aware of the way I look, dressed in my university sweats and a baggy t-shirt. I haven't showered; not only does sex invade my nose, but there's a mixture of body odor too.

"Are you serious?" he asks, inviting himself to sit on the couch. I lean further into my own side, desperately hoping he doesn't draw conclusions. "You barely make time to see us, and now you bail? Sophia told us earlier you were sick, but I knew that wasn't true."

"I didn't want to come. I need some alone time."

His skepticism turns to concern as he settles back on the cushions. "Why? What's going on?"

Grabbing my whiskey, I take another sip, eyeing the liquid instead of focusing on Luke's judgmental eyes. There's nothing to draw conclusions to. If I smell of sex, I have a wife.

"I'm fine. Just stressed from work."

"Me too." He shrugs, and it seems he really can connect with that. If possible, he also looks more stressed than at the cafe the last time I saw him. "How about I order a pizza, and we hang out like we used to? I could use some space too."

I've never told Luke no, which is how we end up with

pizza thirty minutes later. When he places it on the coffee table, I see him grab the whiskey bottle and place it by him. When he goes to grab a glass in the kitchen, I'm quick to refill my glass before he returns.

"So, how are you and Annabelle?" I ask, trying to sound interested as I muddle through my head on what he told me last time we hung out, but the memories get intertwined with my current situation.

There's no mistaking Luke's eyes on my glass or the sigh he expels. "We're great, Ben. Nothing's changed since last week when you distracted me with the same question."

I take another sip, hoping that in a sip or two, the numbness will wash over me, allowing us both to just chill for a bit.

"Question," he says, "when you first got engaged to Sophia, did you feel trapped or like you were rushing?"

Luke and I have spoken about this. He already knows how I felt. *Of course*, it was rushed. *Of course*, I felt trapped. While I said these statements verbatim, he wrote them off as pre-wedding jitters instead of asking why. It's his flaw—one I take advantage of every day.

"Luke, Sophia and I married right after college. Yes, it was rushed."

"Do you think if Sophia wasn't pregnant that you would have waited?"

He's giving me the prime opportunity to come clean, to tell him about Joshua and how I planned to end it with Sophia. He's my best friend, and I have his undivided attention, which should mean that I can say whatever I need to without judgment.

"Are you nervous you're making the wrong decision with Annabelle?" My shoulders sink further into the cushion, feeling like I shut the door right in my face.

"Maybe a little. I mean, we've been together for seven years, and I know she's the one, but the commitment feels scary." I hang on to his last word. I know what the vows mean, and I'm still here breaking them.

"You aren't second-guessing your love for Annabelle, are you?"

"Oh god, no." His response is instant, something I know I'd hesitate to answer if the roles were reversed.

"You're going to be fine then." I give him a smile that feels as genuine as I can muster.

We carry on with conversations about the family as we eat the pizza. He does his due diligence as an uncle, asking about Noah and Isabella since he is missing them tonight. As I tell him about Noah's new interest in tee-ball, I casually reach for the whiskey by him, but his hand grabs my wrist.

"Ben, stop." He lets go of my hand as he sighs, and I lean back against the couch. "I saw you last night."

My empty glass tumbles to my lap, my fingers twitching to get closer to the liquid.

"Where?" I try to maintain composure in my voice. It's possible he just meant leaving work.

"At the bar."

I close my eyes, clenching my hands into fists. He fucking swore no one would be around. We were supposed to be safe.

"I was with a few buddies from work—it used to be their favorite frat bar. We were at a table when I saw you walk in with Caden."

My hands shake by my sides, and I squint tighter, trying to keep the tears in. I was supposed to tell my truth. Instead, it was stripped away from me with a careless night in a disgusting bar. I had so many moments in my life that I could have talked to Luke. Each and every time flashes through my mind, stabbing my brain as a constant reminder of how much of my life I've withheld from Luke.

Now he knows.

He fucking knows, and I can't do a goddamn thing about it.

"I wanted to come over, but when I saw you with him ... I ... why didn't you tell me you were attracted to guys?"

I try to open my mouth to speak, but it's dry. There is no changing the subject here. My throat burns as my fears are stuck in my esophagus. When I open my eyes, they narrow in on the whiskey bottle. I yank it from the floor, taking a swig.

"Ben, what is going on?" I take another sip and jerk slightly when he reaches out to touch my shoulder. I don't want his sympathy, and I don't want him taking the bottle. It's my only vice as I've been stripped to my core. "You know I support you, right? If you like dudes, I'm not going to judge you."

I curl up on my side of the couch, the bottle resting against my chest. I can't contain the tears any longer. The floodgates open. Everything I worked so hard to maintain is crumbling; the fear of Luke hating me suddenly shatters. I had created perfection.

Luke moves to my side, wrapping his arm around me.

"I'm s-sorry," I choke.

"You don't need to apologize to me." His hand moves up and down my spine, helping me lean into his touch.

"I-I cheated."

"I take it she doesn't know?"

I sit up, creating a little space between us. My skin is on fire as my lungs keep constricting. I pick at the lettering on my university sweatpants, watching the worn material fall to the floor.

"I promise I won't judge. Can you just explain to me how this happened?"

I don't know where to start. How do you tell your childhood best friend that you've been into men? Where do I start to unravel the lies? Take him through the journey of how I felt when I realized? How I never anticipated dating Sophia until the pressure from everyone became too much? Or maybe how Joshua and I were only business partners in class to cover up the fact that we started dating? Or maybe how the night Luke saved my life wasn't because I had fallen into a depression from money and stress, but instead because Joshua had our dream wedding and the life we always planned?

Luke starts, "when do you plan on telling Sophia? I mean, this isn't a secret you can hide. I could barely keep myself from telling Annabelle that I saw you with Ca—"

"I don't know, okay?" I scream.

Between the rising anger and tears, I can't seem to focus on creating a sentence or processing that Luke now has to keep my secret and how fucking *awful* he became at keeping secrets when he started dating Annabelle. Before they dated, it was easier to connect with Luke without anything getting back to Sophia. But once they started dating, it seemed every frustration of my marriage that I shared seemed to get back to Sophia through the grapevine.

This is a goddamn nightmare.

"Ben, this is really serious." I grip my hair, glaring toward him. "This doesn't just involve Sophia; it affects Noah and Isabella too."

I jolt off the couch, creating space between us. "Don't you think I fucking know that?" I yell.

A vibration courses through my veins that makes me want to hit something, but that something can't be Luke. I've never yelled at Luke, no matter the countless drunken messes he's saved me in.

"I don't know what I am going to do. I don't know how I feel anymore about Sophia or Caden. I know you've been judging my drinking, do you understand now? This isn't simple, Luke. I can't just come out and hope everyone supports me. I tried once, and it fucking destroyed me." I gasp, trying to breathe—to center myself. Calm the pulsing in my forehead, clear my vision, but it only makes me feel more flustered. "Luke, I slept with him last night, and it was one of the most terrifying and incredible experiences of my life. I want to forget it and be Sophia's husband, we could have another kid and live the perfect life, but—"

"You slept with him?"

His tone has me backing up against the wall for support. I can't decipher if he's disgusted or curious, but his shaking hands and own gulp of whiskey make me think the former.

"Was this the first time, or have you slept with another guy before Caden?"

I slide down the wall, taking my own sip from the bottle. Everything is closing in on me. Black specks fill my vision as I desperately search for air.

"Please leave," I mumble.

"It was Joshua." He laughs, and my body goes rigid. "I can't believe I didn't see it. That's why you guys fell apart and stopped talking in college. That's why you were sick over Noah being born. You and Joshua were attached at the hip until Sophia announced she was pregnant. You never wanted to be with her." I watch as he leans forward, leaning his elbows on his thighs as he holds his head up. "The day … the day before Isabella's birth," his voice catches, and I squeeze my eyes shut, feeling the tears stream down my cheeks. I can't witness his destruction. "Joshua's wedding day was the same day … the day I found you? Ben, why did you never tell me? I would have been there for you."

I choke on the sob that wants to escape, but I can't break down anymore in front of him. I need to clean up the pizza and kick him out before my self-destruction 2.0 happens— only a few more minutes. I can do a few more minutes.

I push myself up, bringing the pizza and whiskey into the kitchen. I place the pizza on a plate with saran wrap and put it in the fridge before tossing the box. I take another gulp of whiskey before hiding it back in the liquor cabinet.

Luke is now standing by the couch when I enter the living room.

"Did I ever do anything to make you think I wouldn't support you?" Wet tears coat the dried tears on his cheeks.

"Get the hell out." My voice is grave as I side-step him to open the front door.

"Ben, I think I should stay."

"I don't need you to save me. I needed you then, but I don't need you now. Get the fuck out of my house."

SIXTEEN

THE ASSHOLE STOLE my bottle of whiskey. I had a free moment in the kitchen after breakfast where I could take a sip, and it was no longer there, along with the two travel-size rum bottles we got from weddings. He must have used his key after I kicked him out and locked the door.

Luke's left me walking on eggshells around my home while I try to be present with the kids and Sophia—not having that sense of calm that was reignited. Noah and Isabella have been in every direction this morning, which has stunted a few conversations Sophia's tried to start. Luke didn't tell her anything though; otherwise, I'd be kicked to the curb.

"So, I was thinking," Sophia starts as she wraps her arms around me from behind.

The children are set up doing crafts on the living room floor, a situation where I thought I'd find some silence to calm my hangover versus having a conversation.

"We should try for another kid."

My body jerks from her arms as I swivel to look at her. Her arms cross and her brows furrow.

"Don't seem so frightened. Annabelle and I were talking

last night about when she and Luke are going to start trying, and it got me thinking. Isabella is now three, and we always talked about a third."

"No." My hands start to shake, so I shove them in my sweatpants pockets. I did shower before heading to bed last night but still placed the same ratty sweatpants on.

"No? What do you mean by no?"

I roll my eyes as I try to find an escape route. I need something to dull the ache in my head, and the only good cure for that is drinking more golden liquid; it's the only way to navigate this conversation before I dive further into the hell hole of my life.

"I mean, I'm not having this conversation. Now isn't the time. We are too busy and can't focus on a newborn." I head to the foyer.

"Neither Noah or Isabella were at the perfect time."

I put on my jacket and sneakers, grabbing my car keys. "And look how those situations ended up."

"Where are you going?"

"Out." I slam the door behind me.

I hear Sophia question, but her voice doesn't rise, nor does she follow me. This isn't a discussion to have in front of our kids.

My mind drives me into the city, where I contemplate stopping by Caden's to see if he's home. But he's been blowing up my phone since yesterday, even more so this morning, that I don't have the energy. Instead, I swing by a liquor store, pick up a bottle of whiskey, and drive to the park. I take a few solid sips before leaving it in the car and walking along the sidewalk, trying to find an empty bench.

All I need is silence and the coat of alcohol.

And I do find it, despite the occasional screaming kid or the sound of music playing off someone's phone as they walk passed.

Suddenly, someone is sitting next to me, panting. "Hey."

His voice has me sitting straight, gripping my thighs as I turn toward Joshua. His skin glistens with sweat, his t-shirt a darker shade of grey. He smiles before he gulps down quite a bit of water from his bottle.

What the hell is he doing here? Next to me? Dripping with sweat in the forty-degree afternoon. He hated running in college, and now he must have run at least a mile or two.

"Are you still with Sophia?"

I blink, holding my breath at his bluntness. Just a few weeks ago, he wanted nothing to do with me, and now we can be friends?

"I haven't seen you in years. Why now do I keep finding you?"

"I've moved back to the area. You and I know how small this city can be—and you've always loved this park."

"Have you been looking for me?"

His shrug has me thinking he has, but the running is a good excuse.

"Now answer, are you still with Sophia?"

I sigh. I wanted to talk to him before, so I can't exactly walk away from this conversation. "Yes."

His eyes immediately become sympathetic, and I want to shove him off the bench.

"Why are you leading that guy on then, Ben?"

But I do have the choice to stand up and walk away, go back to my car and have another drink, get take-out for my family, and be a fucking husband.

"He reminds me of you" is what I confess.

"Ben, we had a pending engagement. You walked away. You gave us up."

"And you seem perfectly happy with that decision." I challenge him, but I know it's not fair. On the outside, my family looks beyond happy. Whether or not he is truly happy, there is no way for me to know.

"I really thought you were going to come back to me. But then Noah was born, and I had to move on," he admits, his voice wavers just slightly on Noah's name. "Now? I'm so happy. But are you?"

My fingertips turn white as my grip on my thighs tightens.

"You know what I think?" he continues, "I think you lost your light. It's rare to find your true smile in pictures anymore."

I open my mouth, crossing my arms. It never occurred to me that he would keep on top of my life.

"I'm still friends with Luke on Facebook," he says. "You may have deleted yours, but my timeline has been filled with your family from his page for years. I think I always wanted to find your happiness again."

I run my hands over my face. All the years I spent pining, he was always on the other end, doing the same. Luke didn't know my history with Joshua. I played it off as growing apart, so I guess he never felt the need to delete Joshua off social media.

"You're the one that got away, Ben. I still love you, but I'm not in love with you. We had our issues that maybe would have been resolved through marriage, but I don't think we would have ended up together in the end. When I let myself love again, I found my husband and realized what the two of us didn't have."

"I know what you mean." The words surprise me as I say them.

"Oh?" His face glows.

Excitement rumbles throughout me. There is happiness outside of Joshua.

"Caden." I give Joshua a small smile. "When I first met him, I knew I was falling for him, but I kept comparing you and Caden. Then, it became clear that he's the one I want to fight for. But it's far more complicated now. The kids are older, and Sophia and I created this entire fucking facade. If I couldn't leave for you, how can I leave now?"

"You're exhausted, Ben. You need to do this for yourself and for Sophia. Do you know why?"

I shake my head even though I'm imagining it's similar to what Caden was going on about.

"When you said Caden's name, the light in your eyes reappeared. Don't let that go out."

Heat rises up my neck, and I turn away from him. My life can't be controlled by his validation. I can't help but think how good it feels for him to be rooting for me again and be on my side.

"You've been given a second chance to make things right. Do everyone a favor, Ben. Set you and Sophia free. Allow your children to be raised by parents who honor someone's sexuality and support them. If you don't have the strength on your own, imagine if Noah or Isabella were to identify within the community, would you want them hiding like you are?"

With that, he's standing and squeezing my shoulder before he walks away.

Before I head home with take-out, to try and reconcile my shittiness, I text Caden that I am fine and that I had a wonderful night on Friday. I apologize for running out without a note, too. I don't answer any of his questions about the weekend. Instead, just ask him to meet me at the office for training the next day. Without waiting for a response, I turn my phone off again and head home.

Making sure to have a few more sips of whiskey and a couple of mints before walking inside. The rest of the day is consumed by the children and a nice thick tension between Sophia and me. We have a casual conversation over lunch and dinner, allowing Noah's energy to showcase throughout both meals. Sophia gets the kids bathed and put in bed while I pack lunches for all four of us for the next day. By the time I make it to bed, Sophia pretends to sleep, her brows creased. Bags are under her eyes that weren't there at the start of the week-end. I want to reach out and massage her pain away, give her anything I possibly can. She only wants this family, but by giving her that, I'll only lose myself.

SEVENTEEN

IT'S early afternoon on Monday when I'm trying to work my way through much-needed paperwork that I've let slip away. Having the silence of my office has been comforting after an intense morning of both Noah and Isabella being off. I love my kids to death, but they feed so heavily off the energy within our house. By the time I dropped them both off at school, I felt exhausted. The only thing keeping me going is the fact that Caden will be here shortly. I wanted him to come first thing in the morning, but because Monday is his day off from the cafe, he said he had plans in the morning.

I gave myself permission to reminisce the memories of Friday night throughout the day since I've been alone. Allowing myself to feel everything that's happened, hoping it brings some clarity. The only thing it brings is a few sips of liquor and me being incredibly turned on.

At two in the afternoon, a knock on the door has me throwing back another shot from my flask before stashing it in my desk drawer. He opens the door before I can, and my breath catches. Caden's dressed in his usual black button-up and skinny black jeans he likes to wear at work. The aroma of semi-stale coffee doesn't consumes the room today. He gives me a tentative smile, the two cups of coffee in his hands shaking slightly.

"Hi," I breathe, taking the coffee and placing them both on my desk. I hear him say hi, but once my hands are free, I turn around and pull him close to me, kicking the door shut behind him.

"What are you—"

Interrupting his question, I kiss him, cupping his cheeks. His hands easily rest on my hips, and I walk him backward, pushing him up against the wall. He tries to break the kiss, but I deepen it, sliding my tongue across his lips, asking for an entrance.

"Ben," he gasps, pulling my head away.

"Sorry, hi." I smile, resting my forehead against his.

"Hi. A little feisty, are we?"

"I missed you. I want you, Caden." I kiss his lips again. "I need you."

His eyes flutter closed, and I can feel him inhale and exhale. Shoving away from the wall, he forces me to take a few steps back and pulls me over to the desk. I take my seat, and he moves a chair around to my side of the desk.

"What's wrong?" I ask. Is it something I did the other night? Could it be that while that was life-changing for me, he only found the experience mediocre?

"Can we talk about this weekend? You left me in silence and then sent a basic text message before not responding again for 24 hours. What happened?"

The anticipation of what could have happened tonight dissipates as I sink back in my chair. It was too good to be true to think I'd have someone who wanted me.

"Nothing happened. Just a busy weekend."

He nods, but it's like he doesn't believe me. It *was* a busy weekend. However, there was a lot of downtime that I usually spent staring at my phone, and that didn't happen because it was off.

"Okay, but I think we need to talk about what happened."

I can't help but roll my eyes, turning toward the desk to organize some paperwork. "Look, if you don't want to hook up, that's fine. We can do work, but we don't need to discuss our feelings."

Caden's hands rest on my thighs. I curse the wave of shock that courses through me at his touch. "I want to kiss and have sex with you, Ben. But we also need to be on the same page. I'm afraid of moving too fast."

"I'm not ready to talk." His face drops when I turn back toward him. I cup his cheek, leaning forward. "But I know I want to be with you, and I want to repeat Friday. Can we still have that if I promise I'll talk when I'm ready?" My smile grows as his face warms.

I take my free hand, tracing up his thigh.

"Y-yes," he breathes.

"Let's go back to your place."

His eyes cloud at my suggestion, and he swallows hard.

I attempt to calm myself as we walk through the door of his apartment. My nerves are settled by the whiskey still coursing through me that it keeps everything in me to not jump him. Luckily, Caden makes a beeline to his bedroom, dragging me behind him. Once inside, I push Caden down on the bed, ready to take control this time. It may have been a few years since I've had sex with a man, but the mechanics are the same.

"I want to fuck you," I say. The bluntness has him laughing, but he immediately rips off his shirt. I follow suit before I gently push him down and drag us both up his bed.

His delicate fingertips trace my skin as I discover the areas of his neck and collarbone that cause him to shiver and squirm beneath me. Each moan or groan has me exploring further down his chest. My tongue swirls around his nipples, which don't seem to create as much stimulation as my own. I find his happy place, though, once I have him stark naked, my face buried between his thigh and balls. The slight tickling sensation has his hips thrusting, begging me to touch his dick. I tease him like he did for me, kissing and sucking, licking and breathing, every available space without giving any attention to his throbbing, leaking dick.

It isn't until my tongue swipes his asshole that he yells out a "fuck," jerking his hips up permanently, giving me more access. My right hand grips his base as my tongue slides inside of him, something I've never done with an asshole before, or I suppose a vagina. Sophia has never been into anal, and I've never been into eating her out. But holy hell does a Caden moaning at me rimming only intensify my want to give him more.

As I stroke him, my tongue darts in and out, with the occasional finger slipping in and out of him. Once he claims he's close, I pull away. The guttural groan has me grinning as I sidle my way back up him, devouring his lips. I'm determined to mark his entire body with kisses, but I have limited time with him, so I plan to spend every second I can in this position.

When he's lying in his own sweat, his breathing erratic, and his hips permanently lifted, I finally allow myself to enter him. There's no way to describe the feeling of how tight he is, how my heart clenches, and my lungs exhale every ounce of air they have. The way we thrust in time, how his nails dig into my back, the darkness between his neck and the bed as I kiss and suck the skin, trying desperately to breathe.

He warns me that he is about to cum, and my pace quickens. I kiss his lips, gripping his hair as I pound into him. His scream is muffled before I break the kiss, moaning his name. I thrust into him until my dick is soft within him; a whimper escapes his lips as I remove myself. Before I collapse, as I know I will, I quickly discard the condom.

When I go back over to the bed, Caden is sprawled across the sheets. His hair is matted to his face, his eyes half-lidded.

He's flushed, and a hickey is forming on his neck. My tired dick twitches at me marking my territory. I fall onto the bed next to him, but instead of pulling him into me, I curl into his arms.

"That was … holy fucking hell, Ben."

Silent tears fall from my eyes, so I bury my face into his hair. I've never once cried after sex, but I've never felt this sense of overwhelming peace. My shoulders shudder when I try to take a breath, and his grip tightens.

"I'm afraid to lose you, Caden."

Instead of speaking, thankfully not acknowledging the vulnerability that terrifies me to my core, he peppers me with kisses.

After a second round, not only are we shattered, our stomachs start growling.

"I'd say it's time we clean up and find something for dinner," Caden suggests.

I follow his lead as we both take a quick shower, curbing our wandering hands as Caden's stomach then growls. We eventually make it to the kitchen and put a frozen pizza in the oven. We relax on the couch as dinner cooks, both wearing a pair of Caden's sweats. His clothing is a tad too small, but it's better than my jeans and button-up. Caden opts to even wear his glasses, making it more difficult to convince myself that dinner is necessary.

"Thank you," I say, wrapping my arm around him.

"For what?"

"Everything. For the other night. For today. For your patience and understanding."

His hands come to my face, pressing a kiss to my lips. "You're worth far more than you believe."

With another kiss, I try to remind myself of his words. It's something I hope I can lock away for the harder days.

When the pizza finishes, I pick a bottle of wine from Caden's collection and pour two glasses as he dishes out pizza.

We reacquaint ourselves with the couch, and Caden hands me a slice.

"Thanks, love." I smile, taking a sip of wine.

He chokes, trying to cover it up with a cough. The words have slipped automatically, but I don't regret them. I'm certain whatever this is, it's enough to start using pet names.

"Is the wine bad?" I concede. I just chose the label.

"No-no." He takes another sip as if to prove a point, but he avoids looking at me, his shoulders suddenly tense.

"Caden, what's wrong?" I touch his knee, but he leaps off the couch, wine spilling onto his paper plate.

His glossy eyes blink, and he slowly takes a seat, creating more distance between us. Caden puts his plate and wine down, pulling his knees up to his chest.

"Love, what is going on?"

Tears fall from his lashes, and he swipes them away. "D-don't." He flinches away from my hand. "Please," he whispers.

My brows furrow at his immediate switch. I watch him as he tries to regulate his breathing, eyes cast on his knees. In one fell swoop, he grabs his wine glass and gulps the red liquid down. His fingers press against his lids, wiping away tears before he finally reconnects with me.

"Please don't call me that."

"Call you what? Love?" He flinches again.

"You don't love me, Ben."

"Caden, I didn't say I did. It's just a pet name. But hell—I am falling hard for you."

His eyes narrow as if he's critiquing my very being. "How can you fall for me when you know nothing about me?"

Maybe the high from the sex has gotten to me because I have no idea where this is coming from. I thought we would eat pizza and maybe fool around once more before I left, but now? Now it feels like he's actively pushing me away.

"What could you possibly be keeping from me that would stop me from wanting to be with you? What are you hiding?"

Can't be worse than me having a wife and kids.

He leaves the couch, coming back with the wine bottle. He tops off his empty glass before putting the bottle on the coffee table and taking another big sip.

"Can you explain to me what's going on?"

He inhales, his shoulders dropping. "Remember the last relationship in Arizona?" I nod, and he continues, "do you want the long version or short?"

"Long, I have time," I tell him, but honestly, I don't think I do. I haven't messaged Sophia since before Caden arrived at the office. Right now, it doesn't matter. What matters is the troubled look on Caden's face. I reach out and sigh in relief as he clasps my hand.

"After I moved to Arizona, my high school boyfriend, Mark, broke up with me. The transition to college was a lot, so we broke up in October of our freshman year. Four months later, I met William, a junior. I was so excited an upper-classman was interested in me." He shakes his head at his confession. "We got close so fast, and my grades suffered. He was so endearing and romantic, the boy everyone is jealous you're dating. That summer, I stayed in Arizona and ended up canceling room and board so I could live in William's apart-ment off-campus for the next semester. My parents thought it was just friends living together, so they approved."

He takes a deep breath and another sip of wine. A hand squeeze has him continuing.

"The first year together was amazing. He was supportive and kind and even got me a job at Beanery. When our anniversary rolled around, he took me to a fancy restaurant and gave me a promise ring. I was certain he was the one. But after he graduated college, he started disappearing. I assumed it was normal. He was in a different transitional phase than me, you know, searching for a job and whatnot. But then, he stopped coming home at night. I was lonely, but I didn't want to admit that. I knew he was stressed that the last thing I wanted was to put pressure on him."

I wait patiently as he pauses again. His eyes closing as his grip tightens the wine glass. He downs the remaining liquid again before looking past me.

"Year two comes along, and he's back to being the attentive man I fell for. He even bought us plane tickets so he could meet my family. Everyone adored him and understood my infatuation. During those two weeks home, he was the same man I met in my freshmen year. We toured all over New England, spending every moment together. But, we flew back to Arizona, and the same habits started again. This time, I called him out. I couldn't do the highs and lows anymore. His response was to bring his work home." He lets go of my hand, shoving both of his hands between his legs. "I found him in bed with another man."

I gasp, and his eyes dart to me as if he forgot I was there for a moment. I want to reach out again, but I can't tell what he needs. The only thing that I know would help is me running home to end things with Sophia, but it's not that simple.

"Before I could yell at him, he asked me to join. I tried to escape, but he stopped me. He threatened me, saying I'd never find another guy like him who would take care of me the way he did. He refused to let me leave and gave me an ultimatum: I could either join them or ignore it. If I left, he made it clear he'd ruin my life—and I believed him. People *loved* him. So, I didn't leave." He eyes the wine bottle before massaging his temples. "While he entertained men and women into the middle of the night, I would sleep on the couch. I tried to bury myself in work and school, but I was miserable.

"Months of me refusing to join him in bed started to anger him; he said he had enough of my moping and whining. I started picking up more hours at work just to avoid being home, but one night I came home, and he shoved me into the bedroom, forcing me on the bed."

He takes a shaky breath and reaches for the wine bottle. Caden doesn't take a sip though, just holds it tight against his chest. I know that feeling very well.

"A week before our third anniversary, he raped me."

His head jerks up at the sound of my sharp intake of air.

"I'm sorry. Take your time," I say softly. I lay my hand on the couch, and his shaking fingertips interlace with mine. "I'm not going anywhere."

He blinks back his tears as my words register. I know I have to either step up or completely let him go. He deserves the world, particularly now, I can't be the reason for his emotional relapse.

"I didn't know what to do. The man I thought loved me became a monster. He was so rough and forceful." His deliverance seems disconnected, and he takes another sip of wine. "For the next few days, I slept in the library and showered in the gym. I had enough money to support myself because William fronted everything—he gave me so much. Eventually, I had to go get my belongings. My courage only came the day of our anniversary, when I think a part of me hoped things changed. And to an extent, they did. There were fresh flowers in a vase and a brunch spread on the table; the apartment was even spotless. Now thinking about it, it makes my stomach churn to think how predictable he knew I was. He had strolled out of the bedroom as if nothing was wrong, but he did apologize. He begged for forgiveness and told me we were going to Mexico for my graduation and our anniversary. Of course, I fell for it.

"The same William I loved came back for a few months. I was so relieved. I convinced myself he had just fallen into a trap, and now he was better." Tears well up in his eyes again. "But it got worse. When he brought people back to our home, they then took advantage of me. When I threatened to call the police, he threatened my life."

He lifts his shirt, exposing a few scars on his ribcage. I had noticed them before but only ever when I had another motive.

"Oh, Caden," I whisper.

Tears fill my eyes, and I immediately pull him into his arms, shifting us so his back is against my chest, his wine bottle still clutched against him. He's rigid at the sudden contact but doesn't pull away as we sit in silence. I allow my hand to trace his arm up and down, kissing his temple.

"It happened for another month. I had become a victim of domestic abuse. I never understood how it could happen until it happened to me. He had brainwashed me into believing it would all be good. When things got bad, he then followed suit with good things. He still treated me to the world financially. By this point, I had fallen into a depression that when he refused to let me leave the apartment without him, I never wanted to anyway. My breaking point, the first time in weeks I could feel again, was the night one of his partners beat the shit out of me. William just stood by and laughed before they both raped me. It's hard to even admit they raped me because, at that point, I was just a shell of a person. I never even said no."

His voice turned to monotone the moment he mentioned he was beaten. As if his body reverted back to being a shell, his own defense mechanism. I press a few more kisses to the top of his head. He's still sitting rigid but he hasn't tried to remove himself.

"I escaped, somehow. I don't know how. I was severely injured, but my mind was able to recognize this was now life or death. I ended up bolting to my manager's house, the only person I felt I could still trust. My manager flew home with me back to Maine to make sure I got to my parents' house. He also set me up with an assistant manager position at Beanery. It took me about five months before I could start working again. I was severely depressed and going to therapy once, sometimes twice a week. My anxiety was so bad that I went out one day and was rushed to the hospital for having a panic attack because I thought William had found me."

Suddenly, he's pulling away slightly, turning toward me. His face is pale, his eyes dilated from the wine, and there are dried tears on his cheeks, but he gives me a sad smile.

"I started getting better, though. I ended up going back to work and found this coffee shop right across the street, Isabella's Coffee ... maybe you've heard of it?" His entire demeanor has changed, a soft glimmer in his eyes, but I can barely crack a smile.

"The first day I went into Isabella's, you greeted me with that stunning smile of yours, took my order, commented that it was the same as yours, and told me to make myself at home. There was something about your presence that made me feel safe, so I did make myself safe. For some reason, my brain told me that if William did ever show up, you'd do something to protect me, which seems silly now because you didn't know me." I shake my head, my smile heavy. I vaguely remember him coming in that day. He sat in the book nook for hours, and I had never seen him before.

"I came often. You weren't always there or behind the bar, but I knew when I was ready, I'd come talk to you about how you started Isabella's, and I'd tell you what it meant to me. It took me three years, but I would have never expected this."

I wish I could go back in time and make more of a connection with him. I only ever saw him as an attractive, loyal customer.

He places the wine bottle on the coffee table and curls into me. I want to tell him something about what he's sharing, but I don't have anything uplifting.

"D-did you ever press charges?" I curse myself for asking questions. He shared all of his trauma with me, and if he didn't feel like sharing, I shouldn't pry. I should change the subject and tell him how much he deserves.

"No. I just wanted to move on. Plus, two men in a relationship, one claiming rape? No one would have believed me." He shrugs. "It's taken me what feels like forever to stop looking over my shoulder, wondering if he would come here to find me, but he hasn't. I just can't seem to rid the pet name. He used it violently and condescendingly. It just makes me remember the violence more than anything."

I tighten my arms around him and bury my head in his silky hair, hoping his mop of brown hair can soak up my tears.

"I'm an asshole." My words muffle.

"Why?" His fingers grip my forearms. He knows why.

"Because I'm not faithful to you either."

Caden's entire being starts to shake, my words validating presumably his inner demons. I pull him further into my lap, and he curls his limps into a ball, his head burying in my chest, soaking the t-shirt I'm wearing.

"Caden, I'm so sorry." I kiss the top of his head. "You're incredible and strong and deserve more than I can give you."

His sobs grow louder, his grip tightening on the t-shirt. All I can do right at this moment is tell him that it will be okay. But I don't know if that's true.

Time passes in slow motion, my shirt now soaked with his cries that have turned into stray tears. I want to reach for the bottle to soothe my own nerves as my brain tries to come up with a solution. But I can't. He needs something stable right now, and ironically, that's me.

"My parents don't like you," he mumbles into the fabric.

The unexpected sound of his voice causes my heart to jump.

"Why even give me a chance?" I sigh. I'm trying to be strong, but I'm milliseconds away from my negativity consuming me.

His face tilts up. His cheeks are scattered with blotches of pink, and his bloodshot eyes only darken the bags underneath. Caden studies me for a few moments, taking the time to untangle his arms and place his hands upon my cheeks. The pads of his thumbs stroke the skin below my eyes, brushing away residue from my previous tears. He moves forward, connecting his chapped lips with my own. I peck him back, but he soon hovers, his hot breath hitting my damp lips.

"Ben, there is something about you that makes me believe, something I am willing to take a leap of faith for. You're capable of great things—things I don't know you're aware of, but I want to be there when you do."

I'm not sure what he's trying to convey. I, Benjamin Jacobson, am a fuck up. The ultimate fuck up. A man who continuously takes great situations and wonderful people and screws them over. What potential can he possibly see?

EIGHTEEN

THE HOUSE IS dark minus the porch light illuminating the front door. Our laneway is still, only a few homes with lights on. It's straight out of Pleasantville: a white picket fence to contain the children's toys scattered on our lawn, a garden bordering the stone pathway, even a wooden swing sits on the wrap-around porch that we wore out when the kids were infants.

Glancing in both directions, I admire the laneway inhabited by neighbors who accepted both Sophia and me with open arms; the older couples with grandchildren were eager to offer their babysitting services or bake up a casserole when we were trying to juggle our careers and raising Noah. The neighborhood had become a family of its own, holding block parties in the summer and Christmas caroling with snowman-building competitions in the winter.

My secret would be the first legitimate disruption within our pristine corner of Cyan City since we moved in when Sophia was pregnant. I will be the black sheep, receiving dirty looks as I drive by, everyone insisting on supporting Sophia and the children. While it will hurt to be disowned, it is relieving to know that my family will be looked after.

My world has shifted significantly. I'm coming home with a new outlook. The interior of my house is spotless. You would never know the kids munched on popcorn all evening or that a family meal was eaten. I don't know how Sophia's been doing it. She loves them, feeds them, and puts them to bed with very little evidence on her face. I can barely take care of myself at the moment.

In the kitchen, I open the fridge to find a plate of leftovers, a welcome surprise since all she texted me when I was with Caden was what time I'd be home for dinner. I never saw it, and she never pressed. I heat the plate in the microwave and pour myself a glass of whiskey.

I had promised to take Sophia out on a date tomorrow evening, but I had yet to formulate a game plan to right my wrongs with her about not wanting another baby and the fact that I'll be absent from the house on Wednesday. It's Caden's birthday, and while I wasn't invited to anything, I wanted to do something for him.

His confession weighs heavy on my shoulders as I sit at my kitchen table in silence.

I eat dinner, drinking three whiskey neats, trying to figure out how to unravel my mess. Everyone gets hurt, no matter the plan. But is there a good time to destroy lives around me?

The bedroom light is already off when I reach the top of the stairs, so I take my time checking in on Noah and Isabella, giving them each a hug and kiss. These moments feel so fragile. I'm walking a thin line between me confessing or making a mistake that outs me.

I brush my teeth twice, trying to get rid of the whiskey breath before heading to bed. Tossing Caden's sweats in the back of my closet so Sophia can't find them, I then climb into bed. The moment I settle, she spins toward me.

"I have to stay late at work tomorrow. I need you to take the kids to school in the morning, pick them up, make dinner, and give them baths. I may be home in time for bed, but I won't be able to go on our date."

Relief washes over me at the thought. I can toss everything aside to take care of the kids, but I can't stumble my way through a date yet.

"Okay. What's going on at work?" My tone seems interested.

"Deadline for a book due Wednesday. We are behind."

"What if we move our date to Thursday?"

"I was thinking Wednesday? Our deadline is 5 p.m."

"I have plans, remember?"

Frustration flashes over her eyes, and she turns away from me. "I'm leaving at 7 a.m."

We lay silently. I know she's not asleep yet, but I hesitate to pull her into my arms. It's probably what she wants, but I seem to be overthinking every interaction. Is that what I would do when she's frustrated with me? Or would I leave her alone? Regardless, I only want to remember the way Caden felt in my arms tonight.

NINETEEN

TUESDAY GOES AS PLANNED: the kids are dropped off, I work from home while they go to school, and I pick them up promptly. A trip to the park is made before we go home for the day; Noah and I throw around a baseball while Isabella struggles to conquer the jungle gym.

Back at home, Noah hides in his room, playing with Legos, while Isabella darts between the kitchen and the living room with her dolls in hand. After being on the receiving end of a few, "Mommy does it this way" comments, I focus on cooking the pot of pasta in front of me. It's hard not to take their innocent observations to heart, but it's obvious I haven't been around much.

My spirits are lifted at dinner, though, when a mini food fight breaks out, deeming me "Parent of the Night." I'm secretly happy to get a text from Sophia that says she will be home later than she originally thought, which gives me the chance to put the kids to bed solo. These one-on-one moments are what I cherish. This isn't what I want to lose out on.

After a second story, both kids are worn out and content to call it a night. Pride swells as I close their doors and head back to the kitchen. In a single day, I am reminded why I never strayed in the past. Not much can compare to the joy of my two children.

I work on dishing up a plate of food for Sophia and place it in the fridge with her favorite bottle of white wine to start chilling. A small gesture that I hope she can appreciate.

"Hey, you." I smile at her from the couch where I'm working when she walks past, juggling her briefcase, purse, and keys. Even after a twelve-hour workday, she looks flawless.

"Hey." She smiles back. "How did the kids do today?"

I place my laptop on the coffee table and follow her into the kitchen. While she pours herself a glass of water, I grab a wine glass from the cabinet.

"They were fantastic. Noah's teacher told me that he is doing wonderful. I guess he is offering to help students learn to read better." A grin spreads across her face. "You hungry?"

She nods, and I take out the plate from the fridge, grabbing the wine as well. I lift the bottle in question, and she nods again. Her exhaustion is starting to seep through as she allows her walls to drop.

"Noah was telling me the other day how much he loves his class. It's nice to hear he's doing so well."

I hate that I missed this conversation. Noah hasn't confided in me about school once today, even after congratulating him.

Sophia continues discussing Noah's class while I prep her dinner. The onset of information on how he's handling things and what he's learning—even Isabella—feels like we haven't connected in weeks. She moves on to talk about her day at work as we sit at the kitchen table, her taking bites of leftovers in between sentences. The ease of conversation feels strange but comforting. It's encouraging to know we can still have interactions that don't result in disappointment in one another.

DESPITE HEAVY EYES and the grogginess of a late night, I force myself out of bed the next morning to properly help Sophia with the kids. My efforts surprisingly go noticed; Sophia thanks me as she and the kids pile into her car and leave for school. While the thanks felt nice, the longer it sits in my mind, the more I'm reminded that I shouldn't be thanked for being a father to my children.

Most of my workday is spent at the computer, going through documents scattered on my desk. I try my hardest to focus on the tasks ahead of me, but I keep getting distracted by tonight's events: Caden's birthday.

I hadn't heard from him since Monday evening when I left his place, the both of us in tears, separated by his bedroom door. When I tried calling yesterday, his phone went straight to voicemail, and all of my text messages have remained unread. It's hard not to succumb to the worry and rush over to his place early, but there are far too many things to do prior to our night out. He is turning twenty-six, and I have planned a celebration for just the two of us. The agenda includes a walk along the river, a meal at the restaurant he introduced me to when we celebrated the cafe opening, and hopefully a glass of wine with a movie and/or sex at his place afterward.

Sophia knows I'm going out for his birthday, but she is convinced it involves all the managers and just a few drinks. It is her assumption of the night. She questioned why Caden would spend his actual birthday with co-workers, and I answered honestly, "I don't know," because I don't know why someone would.

Hours later, I'm changing into fresh clothes: a simple white button-up with a maroon tie and dark wash jeans. I'm greeted by the familiar doorman, who escorts me to the elevator. Knocking on his door, excitement bubbles up in me. I may have withheld information from Sophia, but I didn't have to lie to be out tonight.

Instead of Caden answering, Bethany does.

"Hi, Ben, nice to see you again."

"Y-yeah, hi," I greet, my confusion taking center stage. "Are you coming out with us tonight?"

Her smile falters, and she moves forward to close the door behind her, leaving us in the hallway together.

"I don't think it's best for you to be here right now."

"Why? What's going on?" Guilt and worry collect in the pit of my stomach as my mind whirls over everything that could have gone wrong since our talk. "Is Caden okay?"

"He told me you two talked about William the other night." I nod, but I don't understand the correlation. "He's a bit out of sorts and embarrassed, hence why he hasn't returned your calls or messages. I'm sorry. I told him he needed to let you know he is okay. I think he just wants to be alone."

"This is ridiculous. You're here. It's his birthday. Let me inside."

"Ben, please. It isn't a good idea," she says, holding out her hand to block me.

I dart around her and twist open the doorknob. "With all due respect, I need to see him." I make a beeline straight for his bedroom, where I find Caden in a fetal position, his comforter tangled around his body. In a hurry, I kick off my shoes and loosen my tie before climbing into bed.

"Caden," I whisper, hugging him from behind. To my relief, he doesn't shrug me off, but his body remains rigid. "I told you to call me if you needed anything." He leans his head back against my chest. "I know things aren't ideal right now, but please remember that I am not William. I would never hurt you like that. Caden, I want to be with you."

"A-are you sleeping with her?" he whimpers, his voice is raw.

"From today on, I promise I will only be with you. You're the only person I want to be with."

"Have you slept with her recently?"

"Not since you and I slept together."

He exhales, my arms going limp around him. Caden swivels in my arms. His red-rimmed and bloodshot eyes cause me to gasp. He looks utterly shattered. I run my hand through his hair, pressing his face against my chest, tightening my grip on him.

"I don't know when I'll be able to tell Sophia, but when I do, and she is out of the picture, you will be everything to me. I understand if you cannot wait for someday or if our talk on Monday night made you realize you can't be in a relationship like this again. But I just want you to know that my intentions are not to hurt you." I swallow the sharp pain coming to the surface. "I wish things could have been different when we met. I'd spoil you rotten and treat you like a king if I could."

His leg wraps around mine, and he unravels his hands to wrap them around me. "Do you want to officially meet my parents?"

My grip tightens just slightly.

"Turns out they made plans for my birthday. I know it's early, but my mom won't take no for an answer." He looks up at me again.

The pain coursing through them twists the guilt in my stomach. It doesn't matter if I have reservations or the entire night planned to show him how special he is. The only thing to show him is to swallow my pride and fear and go to dinner with his family.

"I wouldn't want to do anything else. Happy birthday, Caden." I whisper against his lips.

His lips press against mine for a few moments before he pulls away.

"I need to shower. Bethany should be in the living room if you want to hang out in there."

I nod, but I make no attempt to move. His bed is comfortable, and it smells just like him. As he exits the bedroom, I curl between the sheets and pull his comforter over top of me. I need to soak in the presence of Caden— here is where I feel calm and safe. If I could wake up in this bed every morning, I know I could be happy. I only wish that my wants and desires would only hurt Sophia, not Noah and Isabella. My beautiful children shouldn't have to be faced with a divorce and split household. I sink deep in Caden's bed and even deeper down the rabbit hole of guilt as I hide, waiting for my boyfriend to emerge from the shower.

"Ben, are you okay?" I peek out from beneath the covers to find Caden with a worried look, just a towel hanging from his hips.

"Yeah, I'm okay."

Caden bends over to grab a pair of boxers from the dresser and puts them on faster than the towel can drop before he crawls into bed.

"What's wrong?" The covers fold down, and he climbs in next to me.

"I don't think I should go tonight."

"Ben, they'll love you when they give you a chance."

I shake my head and sigh. "Caden, they already know I'm unfaithful. How can they ever like me?"

"I like you." Sadness and defeat weigh down his argument. "Just because you're still with Sophia doesn't make you a bad person. The person you are with me will be the same person when you are *just* with me. Plus, you've already met them before. You'll be fine."

I sigh, knowing I don't have a choice. "Should I bring something?"

"You could bring a bottle of wine if it would make you feel better about going," he says, shrugging. "We can stop at the store on the way there."

"That's okay. I'll walk down the block to the liquor store now while you get dressed."

"All right. Bethany's going to drive us there and back. I asked her to spend the night here."

"Why?" I blurt before taking a breath in. My intimate evening is turning into a family affair with a chaperone in the next room over.

"Honestly?" He raises his brow, and I nod. "Because when you leave tonight to go back to your other life, I don't want to be alone."

It would have hurt less for him to stomp on my heart than admit the reality.

"I'm sorry," I whisper, wiggling out of bed. I put my shoes on and straighten my tie. "I'll be back in a few.

Though only a five-minute walk away, the liquor store provides me with some alone time and a foolproof excuse. While there, I purchase a bottle of red and white wine and a personal helping of whiskey for the stroll back.

Knowing Caden wouldn't be quite ready yet, I turn down the first alleyway and lean against the brick building. I place the paper bag of wine on the pavement, taking out the whiskey. Unscrewing the top, I indulge in a few sips, the warmth coating my throat. The tension and stress slowly dissipate as I take a few more. Half of the bottle remains when I decide it is time to get moving again.

Caden nor Bethany are outside as I reach the front of the complex, so I elect to take another breather in the seclusion of my car. A couple more deep breaths and a handful of swigs have me feeling relaxed. I hide the almost empty bottle in my glove box and shove a stick of gum in my mouth before stepping out of the car. I hope the buzz will last until I can get my hands on a glass of wine at dinner.

I make it to the front door of the apartment building just as Caden and Bethany are walking out. I hold up the paper bag.

"Great! Perfect timing." Caden smiles.

His hand connects with mine; a dark blue button-up, grey cardigan, and jeans complement his slender form. You can barely tell he has been in bed crying for two days. The way he looks does not help curb the need to have him alone tonight.

"You look great," I comment, leaning in to kiss the crease in his forehead. "Thanks for driving, Bethany. And thank you for looking after Caden."

I glance at her, but there isn't a smile present.

"Get used to it. I'll probably be around more than you'd like."

My brows furrow, wondering if her statement infers that I will be around for a while or that she believes I will mess up.

"Are you sure it's okay with your parents that I'm coming?" I question Caden, sitting beside him in the backseat of Bethany's car.

"Believe me, everyone is eager to get to know you," Bethany chimes in from behind the wheel. Eager isn't a word I want to hear.

"It will be fine, Ben. I promise." His hand comes to my leg, stroking it. "Besides, you're bringing my family wine. Instant way to win them over." His laugh echos while his head comes to rest on my shoulder.

Despite the buzz of the whiskey and the support from Caden, nerves are gaining traction, and I am growing more and more uncomfortable.

I sit back and just listen to the conversation between Bethany and Caden. The ease of back and forth is familiar; Bethany is his Luke. I can't blame her for her concern. I am sure there will be an interrogation when Caden isn't around.

A half-hour passes when we turn onto a small, hidden neighborhood. A few lefts and rights have us pulling into a quaint ranch house; red with white shutters, sitting back on an acre or so of land, dotted with pine trees. The lights inside are visible as the sun is starting to set.

I interlace my fingers with Caden's as we walk up the driveway, tugging him to a halt.

"I'm nervous," I whisper, hoping Bethany can't hear me. The whiskey is all but gone from my bloodstream, and I feel unworthy of his family's time and consideration.

"Hey Bethany, would you go on in ahead of us?" Caden calls to her. She nods and heads inside.

Caden walks me over to the porch steps, urging me to sit down. I place the bag of wine on the step below.

"Listen to me, I wouldn't be introducing you to my family if I didn't believe in you. My family means everything to me. I've dated since William, but no one has ever been special enough to meet my family until you." He takes my hands in his, clasping them tightly. "I'm not going to lie, they don't approve of you still being with Sophia—and I understand that —but they also know how happy you make me. They're willing to give you a chance, so all you have to do is be yourself. And hey, at least you don't have to hide any secrets from them?" He brings my hands to his lips.

"Besides, how does a strong, smart, successful businessman like yourself get nervous like this?" he jokes, nudging my shoulders with his own. I give what I assume to be an unconvincing smile. "Come on, let's go inside. I'll pour us some drinks, calm your nerves a bit."

I try to stand and follow, but I fail, remaining seated. "W-wait a sec," I tell him, heaving in some air.

My stomach twists into knots. I let myself imagine how I'd feel if I was on the other side of the door, waiting for Noah or Isabella to bring home a cheating boyfriend or girlfriend. I know I would be furious at the person for disrespecting my child, yet, here I am, disrespecting their son, their baby boy, who has already been on the receiving end of a toxic relationship.

"I-I," I stumble over my words. "I can't do this, Caden." I drop my hands from his.

"What? What do you mean?" His face immediately pales.

"I can't walk into that house. I can't go in there and wonder what your parents are thinking. As a parent, I would never approve of my children doing any of this, and they shouldn't either. I don't deserve their approval." I stand up and descend the porch steps. "I should go. I don't want to ruin your birthday any further."

"Ben, stop. I want you here."

I shake my head and continue down the path toward the street. Caden follows, his hand reaching for mine as he catches up.

I pull my hand away before his grip can tighten. "I'm so sorry. Happy birthday."

"Ben!" he yells.

I turn around only once I've reached the sidewalk. "A-are you breaking up with me?" His shoulders drop—his expression helpless.

"You deserve better, Caden. I'll see you at work."

I watch him shift in place before I force myself to turn and walk down to the end of his street, despite his pleas.

My phone rings in the cab once I'm halfway back to Caden's apartment, where my car is parked.

"Hey, what's up?"

"Noah has been throwing a fit for the past half-hour because you aren't home. He keeps saying he misses you and that he never gets to spend time with you anymore."

I sigh. My stomach churns with the deepening sinking feeling. I can't be ignorant enough to believe yesterday would have been enough for Noah. I've been too preoccupied.

"Can I talk to him?"

There is muffled talking in the background before Noah's voice is on the phone. "Daddy, where are you?" His voice cracks.

"I'm working, bud. I'm sorry I'm so busy."

He sniffs heavily into the phone. "Do you still love me?"

Tears burn my eyes. Whether or not I leave Sophia, I am still harming my kids.

"Oh, Noah. Of course. I love you so much. I'm just busy. That doesn't mean I don't love you, okay?"

"Love means being here and playing with me."

"I know. And I'll be there to play soon. I just really need to take care of things at work right now." Though my evening is now free, I don't think I have the courage to face anyone at home.

"Isabella misses you too. I don't know if she even remembers who you are."

"Noah, I saw you both last night."

"But Isabella is small, she doesn't get—"

"Buddy, I miss you both so much."

"Then come home, Daddy," he pleads.

I blink back the tears as frustration begins to boil in me. "I c-can't."

"I hate you."

The line clicks, and I drop my phone into my lap. Within a second, the phone is ringing once more. This time Sophia must be calling.

"Hi." I hold back my sigh and look out the window.

"Are you really telling him you can't come home? I get that there is a party tonight, but he needs you. Your son, who never asks for anything, needs you."

"Sophia, I'm sorry. I can't."

"I really hope you're having a great time while you neglect your wife and children."

I rest my head back against the seat. I did the right thing by walking away from Caden. Somehow, doing the right thing by Sophia feels impossible.

"Do you love me?"

I grip the phone as her voice wavers. The pine trees are giving way to the city lights. I'll be back in my car soon. It's a simple decision, really. Just get in my car and go home to my family.

"I—" The phone disconnects before I have a chance to respond.

I could make it home for story-time. I could fall back into the routine I had before Caden. The secret isn't out. I could play it off as a rough few months. I could go home and have a third child with Sophia—relatively no questions asked.

But when the cab pulls in front of Caden's apartment complex, I find myself walking down the street to the dive bar, leaving my car behind.

In the mostly empty bar, I dedicate each drink to those I have hurt in a single week. The first for Luke, second for Sophia, third for disappointing my children, fourth for Caden, and the fifth goes to breaking up with Caden—my ultimate mistake.

TWENTY

A DRY MOUTH and nasty headache greet me when I wake up. Unwelcome sunlight prevents me from piecing together where I am or how I even got here. Moaning, I roll to my side, and my stomach lurches. I sit up, attempting to adjust my eyes to the daylight in search of a wastebasket. I gratefully take the can that is shoved into my hands and vomit; violent heaving that feels like this is the end.

"God Ben, what the hell did you do to yourself?" Caden's voice rings beside me.

My eyes dart up, locking with his. I cringe, imagining what I must look like with spit dangling from my mouth and a bucket of vomit in my hands.

"C-caden," I croak.

He hands me a paper towel and a glass of water.

"I'll be right back." He grabs the trash bin and walks out of the room.

Downing the water, I'm desperate to alleviate the bile lingering in my mouth. I curl into fetal position, hugging the blankets to my sweaty chest.

The sound of footsteps grows closer as Caden approaches the room. He places the can on the floor next to me. With my eyes closed, his shadow borders the bed, and he climbs in beside me.

"How did I get here?"

"The bartender called me from your phone last night. You were in rough shape and kept asking for me." My cheeks warm, my head tightening a little more. "Bethany and I got there as soon as we could and walked you back to the apartment. You blacked out before we made it to my floor."

"I'm sorry, Caden." I barely have any memory of walking into the bar.

"Ben, what's going on with you?" I open my eyes and see Caden's eyes are glossy. "I—Ben, I don't want to end things. Did you mean what you said yesterday?"

"You deserve more than I can give you." My voice is thick with saliva building up as I force away the tears.

His voice is now a whisper, "please, don't leave me."

I avert my gaze. If I don't look at him, I can maintain my composure.

"The minute you walked away last night, I crumbled. I sat outside stunned until Bethany came out to check on me. I was miserable the entire night without you there, without knowing if you were coming back to me." His thumb caresses my temple, soothing some of the pain. "I'm sorry for asking you to meet my family right now. It is too soon. I shouldn't have done that. I was just excited to include you in that aspect of my life."

"Caden, I—"

Tears spill over from his eyes, and soon they are accompanied by my own. He smashes his mouth against mine in desperation.

I cry for the pain I am in, for the loss of my family, for hurting Caden, for my cowardice; I cry for being gay.

Through every tear, Caden holds on, lips refusing to leave mine. He kisses me while steady streams of tears leave our eyes. He kisses me as snot leaks from our noses. He kisses me as the heavy breathing escapes my mouth, bricks weighing down my lungs.

I squeeze him against me, haphazardly trying to continue the kiss amidst our ragged breaths. Eventually, our mouths part, in need of oxygen, leaving us to press our foreheads and chests together as we try to gain stability. Though we don't attempt to move, the air is heavy between us, paralyzed by the sadness we've created.

THE SOUND of music blaring and banging pots and pans fills my ears. I place my belongings in the front foyer and wander toward the noises coming from the kitchen. Sophia has on an apron with a whisk in hand—the kitchen entirely destroyed. I reach to turn off the Bluetooth speaker. Her body stills, slowly turning, the liquid on the whisk dripping to the floor. Her face is frightened, but it flips to anger when she sees it's me.

The whisk soars through the air, missing me and landing on the floor with a clatter.

"Are you kidding me? Are you fucking kidding me?" she screams.

"Let me explain," I start, her hands raise up to stop me.

"No, Ben. I don't want your excuses. Your son hates you. He cried all night, and I finally got him to sleep by promising you would be home when he woke up." Her voice wavers. "But you weren't. It started all over again, Ben. He wouldn't stop screaming and yelling, calling me a liar. We didn't raise him to speak to us like that, but you hurt him. You hurt him worse than anyone else ever has."

"I-I'm sorry. I crashed at Caden's. We drank too much." We meaning me. I sigh; it's a shit-ass excuse. I used to go out to drinks with friends before Caden, but I remained sober. Old Ben would have gone home to see Noah.

"Everything you've worked for is going to come crashing down if you keep this up. You're their boss, and you're acting like a teenager out with his friends."

From her perspective, I'm irresponsible and unprofessional.

"I know, Soph."

"I don't think you do."

I sigh, moving toward her, cautious with my steps.

"I messed up, I get that," I say, my tone defeated, hands coming to rest on her forearms. "I'll spend extra time with Noah and Isabella, I promise. How about you go shower and get ready for our date tonight. I'll clean the kitchen."

With an aggressive shove away from me, she goes to pick up the forgotten whisk, throwing it in the sink. When she turns back to me, her eyes scan my body, head to toe.

"Are you wearing Caden's clothes?"

My head snaps at attention. I stand frozen, watching her eyes glaze over and her pale complexion grow red.

"Please tell me you aren't cheating on me, so help me, Benjamin."

This is it, my time to expose everything I have been hiding, an opportune time to come clean without the children around.

"There is nothing going on between Caden and me." The lie tumbles out involuntarily. "My clothes reeked of alcohol, so I borrowed some of his." There it is again, another lie.

Sophia isn't convinced. It's written in the creases of her forehead as her eyes give way to her mind overthinking.

"Why would it matter if you were coming straight home? Those clothes don't fit you."

"Well, I-I …" My brain sputters, stumped by her logic. I didn't think of that.

"Fuck you, Ben." She spins around to pour batter into the glass baking pan. Once full, she flings open the oven door and shoves the raw dessert inside. "I'm going to Annabelle's.

You're watching the kids tonight. Dinner is in the fridge; just heat it up. The brownies will be done in twenty-five minutes. Annabelle picked the kids up from school and will bring them home in a few." She rips off the apron, tossing it on the kitchen island amongst the mess. A pointed finger comes mere inches from my face before she continues her verbal assault. "I swear, Ben, if I find out you're cheating on me, prepare for hell. Don't you dare ruin this family."

I swallow, staring back into her eyes that brim with emotion. Her hand flies back to her side as she brushes past me and leaves the kitchen.

I release the breath I have been holding in my lungs.

The post-it note on the macaroni and cheese reads: preheat oven to 375, bake for 40 minutes. I wait for the brownies to finish baking, then turn up the heat. The kids will want dinner the moment Annabelle brings them home. I'm hoping an early dinner will give me time to warm Noah up by suggesting we watch a movie of his choice and snack on brownies. Though I had spent the majority of Tuesday by his side, I can't blame him for being upset by my absence. I need to be there for him always.

The sound of high heels clicking against the wooden stairs causes me to look up. Sophia is wearing a form-fitting black dress with a pair of red stilettos. Her hair is lightly curled, and that familiar red lipstick is painted on her pout. I gaze peacefully as she pays me no mind. I think about how I wish I could love her right, take her upstairs while the kids are still away, and make her late for her evening out. She would laugh at my desire, playfully arguing that she didn't have time to indulge—

"Ben," she says from in front of me. "The oven beeped."

The smell of her perfume greets my nose, the same eucalyptus lavender scent she loved to use in college. I let it take me back to memories of the two of us in her dorm room after class.

The oven door slams down, breaking me from my

daydream. Sophia slides the mac and cheese onto the grate and sets the timer.

"Sorry," I mumble.

"Get your shit together, Ben." The phrase feels like a bad case of deja vu.

"You look beautiful, Sophia."

My compliment hovers in the air as Sophia darts out of the kitchen to greet the kids. I stand, unmoving, not wanting to face anyone else's wrath just yet. I can hear Noah and Isabella retelling their day's events to Sophia. Footsteps grow louder, heading in my direction. Annabelle comes to stand before me, her face grim.

"I don't know what's going on, but you need to sort it out immediately. I just spent the last two hours trying to convince Noah that you loved him. If opening this third store is too much for you to handle, then you need to find help fast. I know Luke knows something that he won't tell me, and I understand that trust between best friends, but you better not make him hold onto it for too long. Figure your shit out, Ben."

I remain stone-faced as she spews her concerns. I want to argue that my family is none of her business, but I can't find the strength.

Her mouth opens to continue, "I'm taking Sophia out to try and forget this mess. She may not make it home tonight, but you know what that's like, don't you?"

She turns on her heel and leaves before I can respond. I reach for the handle on the liquor cabinet. Lucky for me, the whiskey possesses the same color as apple juice, which is easy to hide from the kids. After taking a swig, I walk out to the hallway where they are.

Isabella races toward me, hugging my legs between her petite arms. "Daddy, I missed you!" I kneel down, kissing her head.

"I missed you too, sweetie. Are you excited to spend the entire night together?"

"Yay!" she screeches.

"Mommy, I want to go with you! I don't want to stay home."

Sadness replaces the encouraging welcome that Isabella gave me. Noah doesn't even look in my direction as he pleads to Sophia.

"Noah, you have to stay home. Daddy's here and wants to play with you."

"Noah," I say, trying to get him to acknowledge me. "We have mac and cheese for dinner and brownies for dessert. I'll even let you stay up late to watch a movie." My own compromises make me sound like a babysitter instead of a parent.

"No, I hate you!" he screams, stomping away and upstairs.

Sophia and I glance at each other, exchanging a shared moment of fear and disbelief. Noah has never reacted like that.

"Just go," I say, shaking my head. "I've got this covered. Have a good time."

Sophia looks between me and the stairs, possibly contemplating if I know how to be a dad. "It'll be fine. I'm his parent too."

She nods and grabs her purse from the back of the couch. A quick peck and an "I love you" is given to a quiet and confused Isabella. "Tell him I love him. And fix whatever is going on," she says to me.

Without another word, she is out the door with Annabelle on her heels.

As dinner bakes, I'm set on convincing Noah to come downstairs. Fortunately, Isabella, oblivious to the tension, is distracted by the baby dolls I brought into the living room to try and keep her busy.

I push Noah's bedroom door open. He is sitting on the floor cross-legged, playing with Legos. Tears are streaming down his face, but he's focused on the toys before him. For the next half-hour, I sit next to him, rubbing his back and talking, but nothing seems to work. I'm convinced I'm doomed when I have to go check on dinner. Though, when I reach the stairs, I hear his tiny feet shuffle behind me.

Isabella carries most of the dinner conversation, recounting what the two of them did with Annabelle. Noah only contributes when Isabella tells the story wrong; otherwise, he eats in silence. I'm starting to fear what his teenage years will be like—particularly if our family is broken.

The two search for a movie to watch while I clean up our plates and place the leftovers in the fridge. My heart warms when they leave a space for me in the middle of the couch versus Noah refusing to sit next to me. I cuddle both kids into my sides as I press play on the movie.

Halfway through our viewing of *Monsters Inc,* Isabella asks if she can have a brownie, causing Noah's ears to perk up. I return shortly, balancing three bowls, each filled with a brownie and a scoop of vanilla ice cream. Their smiling faces and eager hands are enough to bring the first genuine smile to my face.

When the movie ends, their sugar-high selves ask to watch a cartoon. While it's nearing bedtime, I find myself unable to say no. Mostly, I don't want to face backlash from Noah.

Two episodes later, I'm ushering them upstairs to take a quick bath. While I scrub the shampoo into Noah's hair, Isabella playfully swats water at her brother. Before I can tell her to stop, an all-out water war is in full effect, my—Caden's clothes end up soaking wet. I let out a chuckle before I join in.

Once the kids are clean, dry, and dressed in their pajamas, I instruct them to pick out a book while I change into my own pajamas. I venture into Noah's room, where they both leave space on Noah's bed, so I can snuggle up to them. Isabella is fast asleep by the second book, and Noah has a pile of books ready and waiting.

I indulge him, reading a third story until he starts snoring.

Reaching over, I turn off the light, his nightlight the only thing illuminating the room.

I close my eyes and let the love of my children wash over me. I need this. I need them. Isabella has saved me once; they can both do it this time.

"I love you, Daddy."

Silent tears fall from my eyes as Noah's voice unexpectedly fills my ears. I pull his head against my chest and kiss his hair.

"I love you too," I choke out.

TWENTY-ONE

A SUSPICIOUS SILENCE fills the morning air. I open my eyes to an empty bed. Glancing at the Avenger's plastic clock, I shoot up out of bed. I fell asleep in Noah's bedroom without an alarm. The kids have to be off to school in less than thirty minutes.

My feet threaten to slip out from beneath me as I race downstairs and enter the kitchen to find Noah busy scribbling away at his homework and Isabella shoving dry Cheerios into her mouth straight from the box.

"Good morning! Why didn't either of you wake me?" Noah shrugs and continues to write. "Can I get you guys anything? Izzy, do you want milk? Juice?"

She smiles and reaches for another handful of cereal. I open the fridge, grabbing a package of blueberries, and two bananas from the fruit bowl. I cut up the fruit and place the plate in the middle of the table before pouring them both orange juice.

"You can't just have cereal. Please eat some fruit."

Isabella's already grabbing all the blueberries she can hold, popping a few into her mouth that still has chewed up cereal.

"I dressed me today, Daddy!" she exclaims.

I cringe as saliva dribbles down her chin and onto the white blouse she had picked out. I shake my head, mentally assessing what I could remember she had in her dresser drawers.

"Noah, I'm so proud of you for doing your homework. I'm sorry I forgot about it last night."

He grins at me and starts to eat some banana slices. Noah has also dressed himself, so I take the opportunity to run upstairs to put on work clothes and grab Isabella another top. In record time, I have packed lunch for Noah, thankfully Isabella's school provides lunch, and I've sorted through my briefcase.

We make it to school with only a minute to spare.

The promenade store is bustling, but I need coffee, and I hope to run into Caden. Much to my dismay, I'm told he is on the night shift. After getting my coffee, I go to my office and finally take my phone out. I haven't given it a single glance since I got home yesterday. To my surprise, there are numerous missed calls and a few unread text messages.

I scroll through the messages to find that Caden texted to make sure I was okay. Another is from a manager asking if I could meet him the next time I was free. As for the calls, every single one had been made by Sophia, all five complete with an attached voicemail. Her last call came just after midnight. Taking a deep breath, start with the first voicemail.

Her disgust and use of profanity grows with each voicemail. I reach for the whiskey stash in my desk as the fifth and final message starts to play. With the whiskey to calm my anxiety, I decide it's best to send Sophia a text and pretend the calls never happened. I hope her state of drunkenness might mean that she doesn't remember what she said.

I text her. *Noah is doing better. They are at school. Hope you had a good night with Annabelle. Love you.*

An hour later, she messages back. *Thanks. I'll pick up the kids. Dinner is at 6.*

For the remainder of the day, I do as I should, work diligently until my time is up, only breaking to shoot Caden a text to let him know I'm okay and that I'll be stopping in for an inspection that following Monday. Soon enough, it's time to pack up and head home.

Noah is at the coffee table working on homework, and Isabella is pressing a purple crayon into the pages of her princess coloring book on the carpet. Sophia is in the kitchen working on dinner.

"Hey." I force a smile, trying not to let the sour words on my voicemail deter me.

I shove the urge for a drink down and move toward her, placing my hands on her hips. She stirs the homemade tomato sauce, ignoring my touch. I press a kiss to the side of her head, and only then does she turn to acknowledge me.

I wrap my arms around her, grateful when she returns the embrace, burying her face in the crook of my neck. No words are spoken as tears fall from my eyes. Guilt consumes me. Sophia clutches me tighter, her own tears wetting a patch on my dress shirt. While she holds onto our marriage and the life we built, I try to grasp onto what little sanity I have left.

A faint sentence escapes her lips, "I'm scared, Ben."

I kiss her head and let out a muffled sob, unable to keep it down any longer.

"I'm going to believe you when you say there isn't anything going on. You were honest about Joshua, so I should believe you now—but I know you have feelings for him. There's been something since day one." She sighs. My body is frigid as I'm afraid to exhale. "I'm trying to be the bigger person by saying that I am at least happy you are trying to fight those feelings for the sake of your family. I know that isn't fair to ask you to stay, but I can't do this alone."

I attempt to maintain my equilibrium, taken aback by her

first admission that she is a part of the problem. My mind reels at the notion that maybe her degrading my emotions isn't something I should have accepted all those years ago. I have always trusted the fact that she is my wife and my best friend. For that, she must know what is best, and I should never question her judgment. Right?

I always used to believe she had my best interest at heart.

"I do love you, Soph." The phrase feels mechanical, almost bitter on my tongue. This isn't the time for me to dissect her confession or how it alters our history together.

It's her turn to release a sob. "I know," she whispers. "I love you too."

TWENTY-TWO

THEREAFTER, my days resemble one another with pristine similarities. In the morning, I drink a cup of coffee as usual, and by mid-morning, I jump into my first glass of whiskey with something minimal to eat. Somedays, it is necessary to opt out of the coffee and fill my trusty travel mug with liquor instead. By the time dinner comes around, I am ready to handle any duty, whether it's playing house with Sophia or entertaining Caden when I should have been playing house.

I find comfort in my small square office space. The solitude provides me with some of the only sanity and silence I see. The four plain white walls don't judge me or talk back.

As talks between me and Caden progress with him becoming a partner, I make sure Sophia is present with each meeting with the lawyer. While the cafes are mine in the event of a divorce, including her becomes a way to provide her with an additional role in my life. A means to ensure her suspicions about Caden are kept at bay.

At the start of every week, the two of us sit down and set an hour-by-hour schedule that solidifies clear communication of my priorities and where I'll be at any given moment. Now though, she is always aware of my locations, leaving me zero time to pursue a personal life outside of her or the family.

By week three, Caden's irritated with the stolen kisses and conversations that are limited to only the time I've spent training him on the clock.

Today is the three-month assessment for the promenade store. I scheduled it prior to the grand opening. It's an assessment where I sit down with the staff to discuss all feedback, positive or negative and work to secure a steady and efficient routine for the staff. Before I talk to the team, though, I get to have a one-on-one with Caden.

On my drive to the city, I suck down my first cup of coffee and munch on a banana. I take a pitstop to my office to prepare my briefcase, and before leaving, I snatch the bottle of whiskey hidden beneath the mess of papers in my desk drawer. Once my flask is refilled and stored in my briefcase, I rinse out my almost empty travel mug to top it off.

About a third of my mug is gone as I sip it, sitting inside my parked car outside of Caden's store. Nothing can give me the same relief as the initial burn against the back of my throat; a heat rises across my body. I let the calming sensation run through me a little longer before I head into Isabella's Coffee.

While the line in the front of the bar is congested, I'm pleased that the seating area is relatively deserted, giving me space to set up. I watch as the baristas and Caden work with impeccable pace to get the morning commuters in and out with care and speed. Taking a seat with a clear view of the bar, I allow myself to settle in, admiring the business I've created.

Though I'm still in competition with Beanery, it's reassuring to see how we can combine efficiency with a flare of personal touch, developing relationships with customers. Eyes shift, and mouths twitch down the line behind the bar as each barista is alerted of my arrival. When word reaches Caden, he pauses for a moment, looking over at me, smiling with a cheeky grin.

The only downside to working with Caden is his lack of fear; he doesn't see me as a boss anymore. There is rarely a filter to be found when he tells me what he does or doesn't like about Isabella's. Sure, honesty is an asset, but I worry his openness will create issues for me with my current and future employees as I try to hold on to his authority. This struggle is just another reason Caden needs to become a partner sooner rather than later.

Half of my traveler is cruising through my bloodstream when Caden slips away from the bar to greet me.

"Hey, you." He beams, eyes wild and cheerful.

"Good morning," I greet.

His smile falters slightly from my professional remark. He takes a seat, and his hands come forward to fold in front of him on the table, his back straight. The quick correction of his mannerisms is an important piece to this game we are trying to play. There isn't room for error on his part, nor mine.

For the next half-hour, we discuss sales and general goals for the upcoming month. We talk about hiring more staff for the impending peaks with summer and then the holidays. Fortunately, we are doing better than anticipated, which gives us the resources to hire more. From Caden's observations, he predicts most, if not all of the staff, will remain on their full-time schedules, but as a company that provides vacation time, we need enough staff to account for those.

I finish the whiskey by the end of our meeting, the tension of not having been alone with Caden starts to eat away at me. I try to keep my anger for Sophia and her anal weekly scheduling at bay with each sip. The hostility toward her and the desire for Caden's intimacy threatens to boil over, but the numbness of the whiskey paints a fog inside—a way to dilute my emotions.

Next in line for the day's meetings is a young, bubbly

college student. I wrack my heavy brain for her name, shuffling through my papers.

"H-hi Aubrey? How are you?"

"It's Audrey. I'm good. You?"

"Right. I'm so, so sorry." I shake my head, embarrassed as I find her file. "I'm great."

Offering a smile, I feel my mouth expand further than intended, the whiskey causing me to be a tad too relaxed. She looks nervous, almost unsure, causing me to grow flustered by my own actions.

I search for a sheet of questions I wrote up to ask each barista about their opinions on the cafe and their manager. As I kick off the questions, I'm quick to grab a pen and jot down her responses. It's difficult to keep the focus on her, as my whiskey brain clouds, and I spot Caden working behind the bar.

Halfway through the meetings, I excuse myself to use the bathroom, only to take some sips off the top of my flask. The meetings progress as such, employees even coming in on their days off. By the end, I chalk it up as a win when only Samantha becomes suspicious of my behavior, which I credit to being sleep-deprived.

Gathering my papers, I go to stand and pack up for the day. The sudden need to use my legs and support my own body weight poses a problem as my vision goes blurry and my face overheats. I grab onto the corner of the table for support, my weight tilts the table, and the papers atop go flying to the ground.

Flustered, I kneel to the floor and shove the papers back together. Audrey comes to offer a hand. I thank her and close my briefcase with shaky fingers. I shuffle my way to the back of the store to find Caden. Trish, another young barista, throws a concerned glance in my direction.

"Ben, are you okay?"

"I'm fine. I just haven't eaten much today. Just a little lightheaded." I brush her off with a smile and head into the backroom.

Caden looks up from the desk and smiles. "You finished with everyone?" he asks, standing up.

I move forward and crowd his space. "I want to be with you so bad," I blurt, moving to grab his hip, but his hand stops me.

"Ben, we're in public." His voice lowers to a volume only I can hear.

"Then let's go somewhere more private." I try to sound sexy, but my words only slur as I try to keep my hands at my sides.

"I have to work a few more hours. One of my shifts is running late. Besides, don't you still have work to do?" His logic is irritating when all I want to do is give into my desires.

"Yeah, but——" A stern look stops my arguments. "Fine, then as soon as you're finished … in my car or your apartment, or even my office." I smirk at my own suggestions, doing everything I can to not imagine him in each location.

Caden's hands reach out to latch onto my arms and guide me to sit in his computer chair. He pulls up a metal folding chair next to me.

"Not that I don't appreciate your enthusiasm, but what's going on today?" After a quick shift of his head to make sure we are alone, he rubs my thigh underneath the desk.

"What's wrong with me wanting to sleep with my boyfriend?"

"Am I your boyfriend?" Skepticism shrouds his face. I look back at him, confused by the sudden question. "I mean, you've basically been M-I-A since my birthday, and now, all of a sudden, you want to jump me? What gives?"

"Yes, you are my boyfriend," I state with confidence. "I'm ruining my relationship with my wife to date you exclusively. Aren't I your boyfriend? Or are you dating someone else too?"

A loathsome laugh fills my ears as Caden's face goes from concern to outright bitter.

"Unlike some people I know, I'm dedicated to only one person."

Chills run down my spine.

"I don't need this," I spit, standing up.

As I walk away, my leg tangles with the chair, and I tumble forward. I catch myself on the metal shelving unit, only knocking over a few plastic-wrapped paper cups.

"Neither do I." My heart stops. "Remember, Ben, you're the one who is cheating on your wife. You chose to do this, not me."

My chest deflates, his words puncturing my lungs. I want to face him, to show him just how wrong he is, but instead, I stumble away, leaving him without a response.

Back at my office, I make a whiskey neat and reluctantly snack on a bagel that Trish prepared for me. I need something in my stomach to right the loss of coordination, but I'm not interested in losing my buzz. Caden's words replayed in my head, sobering me up enough to drive back to my office.

A knock at the door startles me before I can do any damage to my office in my oncoming fit of rage. Removing my legs from the desk, I stand up, breathing through the struggle as pressure soars to my head. I run a hand through my sweaty hair and smooth out my shirt before opening the door.

Caden is standing in the doorframe, bag in hand. He pushes past me without permission.

"Did you change your mind?" I ask as I close the door and turn to face him.

"Nope. I came to talk to you over dinner, though."

I don't have the energy to argue, but I have the energy to change his mind. I move forward and wrap my arms around him.

"How about," I start, lowering my lips to his ear. "We work up an appetite."

I run my hand down to his ass and squeeze as my teeth nibble his earlobe. I'm willing to forgive and forget if he just lets me have this.

"Stop!" he yells, shoving my chest. "Sit your ass down now."

Stumbling backward, I try to grab onto something but hit the wall before I can. I slide down to the floor, my hand cradling the back of my skull.

"Fuck, Caden." The throbbing forces me to close my eyes. "I'm sitting. Are you fucking happy?" I blink up at him.

He's immediately kneeling in front of me. "Shit—I'm sorry." His anger disappears as concern settles in the crease of his brows. "I didn't think you were that drunk."

"I-I'm not … drunk."

His right hand runs through my hair as he gives me a small nod. With a kiss to the forehead, he then stands and takes two containers out of the bag he brought. My stomach growls at the scent. He opens up the first dinner to reveal a helping of lasagna—my favorite—before returning to help me up from the floor. His hands grip my frame, maneuvering my body until I'm situated at my desk with food in front of me.

"Eat," he says.

The two of us eat in silence, embarrassment battling with my primal hunger. My eyes flicker up, catching his glance. I dart my eyes back down, intently analyzing the food.

"I'm worried, Ben." It isn't the first time I've heard that, but it's enough to curb my hunger. "I feel like maybe I should just let you go. This is putting too much stress on you …," he pauses, "it's putting too much stress on me."

"No, Caden—" I could feel myself begin to sober up again. His words seem to have that instant effect. Caden looks at me, his eyes wet, already rimming red. "Please," I beg. "I— I need you."

A few tears fall from his eyes. I want to wipe them away, but I'm afraid to make any movements.

"I don't know how much longer I can do this. I want to be with you, but I can't take the circles. You say you care about me but then give me nothing for weeks. I can't even spend a night with you. You're always at work or at home doing god knows what with your wife," he says, eyes staring at the wall—blinking rapidly.

"I haven't slept with her since before your birthday like I promised."

"Ben, that isn't helping anymore. I—I need you to be with me. I can't be third best," he says, head shaking as his hand comes up to brush away the fallen tears.

I nod, wishing I could throw back the whiskey that sits only inches from my hand. Although he hasn't mentioned it, I'm positive it hasn't gone unnoticed.

Caden continues, "It's getting old. I feel like I don't even matter most of the time. You're too busy trying to balance both of these lives, and I'm getting walked on in the shuffle. I want to start a life with you, but you need to talk to Sophia."

My elbows rest on the desk, and I bury my face in my hands. Rubbing at my eyes, I wish everything would just pause for a moment. Anxiety claws at my insides as I digest what he is asking me to do. I already have a suspicious Sophia, an angered Annabelle, and an absent Luke to deal with. Soon enough, I'll be on my own.

I let out a deep sigh. "Our seven-year anniversary is coming up," I say softly, not even sure why I'm offering this information.

"Don't you think she deserves to know before then?"

"I'm scared," I whisper, peeling my hands from my face to look at him.

"May I?" He stands up, gesturing toward me.

I take a deep breath. I have to let him in. If I can't, I'll risk never seeing him again. Nodding, I open my arms. He's quick to fall into my open lap. As much as I want to push him away, I can't ignore the wave of relief that rushes through me with his touch.

His eyes peer into mine, his hand coming up to caress the side of my face. "What are you scared of, Ben?"

"Everything," I mumble. "I'm scared of you, of Sophia, of my kids. I'm scared of making the wrong decision and losing everything I love in the end. What if my kids end up hating me? I've been doing this for them, and if they ..." I trail off, looking up at Caden. He brushes away a few stray tears. "And losing Sophia—she's been my rock since I met her in middle school. If she ever hated me ..." I close my eyes. "I've been living this lie for over a decade, and I'm afraid—" I open my eyes, swallowing the fear. "I'm afraid of what freedom will feel like." I bow my head, letting my confession hang in what little air sits between us.

I have never been so honest.

"Caden," I sigh. "With you, there are no secrets. My entire life has been a lie. I've had to filter myself in every situation. But with you, it's different. I'm sorry you're getting the brunt of the issues. That genuinely isn't my intention."

His forehead is flush against mine, his lips ghosting over my mouth in a gentle kiss. Pulling back, he asks, "How do you feel when I kiss you?"

"Safe." I don't hesitate. "Like even after everything I've put you through, you will still bend over backward for me."

Caden's hands move to cup my cheeks, pulling my head back slightly.

"Ben, I want to be your boyfriend. I want a future with you. I want to fall asleep next to you and wake up next to you. I want to be able to kiss you no matter where we are or who's around. And if we make it through this—" he says, gesturing between us, "I'd like to build a life with you and meet your kids as their dad's boyfriend, not his work partner. But I need you to know that if you choose not to divorce Sophia, we can't be together. I don't want to give you an ultimatum, but I cannot do this anymore. If you decide to stay with your family, I won't judge you. I can try and support that, but then you need to let me go."

The alcohol coursing through my system is on the verge of disappearing; most of my nerves feeling the weight of sobering up. I want to cave in on myself and ignore the responsibility of choosing.

"I do."

"You do what?" His face scrunches up, puzzled by my comment.

"I do love Sophia," I breathe, reaching for his hands before he can recoil. "But I'm not in love with Sophia." His body relaxes back into my hold. "The truth is, I don't want to break her. Here's this woman who goes above and beyond to take care of her family, and I am going to ruin what she's working to hold together. I'm afraid if I do this to her, she'll never believe in love again."

Caden's hand wiggle out of my grasp to card through my hair.

"Ben, what happens to Sophia afterward isn't yours to worry about. Please don't take this the wrong way—I know it's sensitive—but lying to her and pretending to love her isn't protecting her either. If things stay the way they are, she's only being kept from finding the same real happiness you've found. And …" he hesitates, but I give him a slight nod to continue. "You keep saying she's this incredible person, but she knows your gay. She's been denying you your truth this entire time. That isn't love, Ben."

I blink away the tears in my eyes. I've know Sophia's denied me of my truth, but no one has told me that outright. It was easy to convince myself that *I* was in the wrong. Not her. But Joshua had said exactly what Caden did. Sophia and I are holding onto something that has always been laced with dishonesty. And maybe that is out of fear, fear that we will lose the security we have built around us. I've been lucky enough to find what I've been missing, and now I owe it to Sophia to let her find that pure happiness too.

Caden's hands are still in my hair as they tug my head forward, pressing my face to his chest.

"There is something about you, Ben. I've had conversations with myself, with Bethany, and my family, trying to talk sense, but I can't let you go. We have this connection. I know you feel it. We can be phenomenal together if given the chance."

"I'm sorry," I whisper into his chest. I let the tears fall as he continues petting my hair and pressing kisses to my head like a mother soothing her distraught child. "I'm so sorry."

"I know, Ben. I know."

And in my desperate need for comfort, I relax further, accepting his affections.

"I hate seeing you in so much pain. Come back to my place to sober up before you go home?"

I nod, allowing myself to let go of control.

Once back at his place, Caden accompanies me in the shower, wanting to steady my wobbling form as the beginning of a hangover kicks in. While drying off and redressing, he excuses himself to do something in the kitchen. I walk out of the bathroom and down the hall to find him carrying a cup of steaming coffee and a glass of water, filled to the brim.

As we settle on the living room couch, I take grateful sips of both, hoping to reverse my drowsiness and dehydration. Both lacking the emotional energy for much more, we spend the time talking about trivial matters. I'm glad about the unspoken understanding. Before I can even worry about contacting Sophia, Caden reaches for my phone and texts her that I'll be home a bit late and not to worry.

TWENTY-THREE

THE END of May comes in the blink of an eye. My life is still a hectic mess of balancing my duty to Sophia, spending time with the kids, and keeping Isabella's Coffee running smoothly. Training sessions with Caden are pushed off in favor of preschool recitals for Izzy, parent-teacher meetings for Noah, and a steady ritual of family time when I'm off the clock. The courage I had mustered to tell Sophia and take the plunge was stomped out in a flash. And though Caden's offer—telling me I can end it at any time—calms me, I still rely on the whiskey crutch whenever things get too heavy. I'm convinced the only thing keeping Caden around at this point is my honesty with him. While I can't be around as often in person over the past few weeks, I never lie to him about why. We still talk every day, almost all day, through text. It helps that most of my reason-ings for cancellations have involved the children and not Sophia.

It's now Sunday, and I sit at my office desk trying to complete the mounds of paperwork that has stacked up. In a desperate attempt to gain some ground, I compromised with Sophia earlier in the week. If she let me work on Sunday, she'd get a personal day of her choosing.

Anxiety rises in the back of my throat as I glance at the clock, realizing Caden will be here in mere minutes to train. After weeks of pushing it off, he cornered me, demanding that we find time to move things forward with his partnership. He had a good point. His promotion and our relationship shouldn't be intermingled.

My hands shake; the first few shots of whiskey from earlier have worn off. As footsteps pad down the hallway, growing closer, I reach into my desk drawer to take a couple of sloppy gulps from the bottle I have hidden. Excitement and arousal replace my nerves when the door handle turns, opening to reveal Caden carrying two cups of coffee.

He smiles bright. "Hey, I figured you might need this."

I accept the drink, taking a sip as my eyes linger on his lips; I can't wait to taste them.

"Thank you!" I put the cup down and stand, letting the wave of dizziness subside before moving my feet. I wrap my arms around his body, unapologetically inhaling his scent, letting the black coffee and peppermint fill my senses. "Mmm," I moan, pressing my lips to his. The contact has my body feeling electrified—the dry spell finally catching up to me. "I want you to strip for me."

He lets out a breathy laugh, nudging me away.

"What?" My brow cocks.

"You're joking, right?"

His amused smile makes my skin warm, slack growing tighter. I throw him a smirk, my fingertips grazing his belt.

"What? No, Ben, stop." He shies away, backing up. "We aren't here to play. I'm here to train."

Like a flip of the switch, the liquor has me focusing on one thing and one thing only: taking advantage of what is in front of me.

"Don't worry, I don't plan to play. We can get right to business." I move forward and crowd him against the wall, resuming my efforts of removing his pants. The palms of his hands come to press down on my shoulders, fingernails digging into my flesh.

"No, stop. I'm not in the mood. I'm exhausted, and you reek of alco—" I strip his pants down to his ankles. "Stop!"

"Turn around and show me that beautiful ass of yours."

"No!" he says, attempting to reach down and pull up his pants.

"C'mon." I laugh, grasping his wrists in my hands.

Using my weight, I push him around and pin his chest against the office wall. The groan I hear from him turns me on further.

"Ben, stop. Please."

Frustration rises, my blood beginning to boil. "Shut. Up." I need this fucking release.

Before I can crane my neck forward to suck on his neck, his body spins around, hands shoving me backward. I stumble, never losing my balance, watching in surprise as Caden falls to his hands and knees from the force. I bolt forward and flip him over, moving to straddle his waist. His head smacks against the cold hardwood with a thud. I race to unbutton my jeans.

"Why are you doing this? No means no!" His arms struggle against my form.

"William, stop!" he screams.

I recoil—the shock of his name is enough to throw me.

Caden scurries from beneath me, standing up as he pulls his pants up.

"Please don't leave," I beg, trying to blink away the fog.

"Do not put your fucking hands on me," he seethes, pointing a finger, looking me square in the face.

I snatch his hand, gripping it with force. My voice is grave as the anger consumes me, "You'll be sorry."

"No, Ben. You're going to be sorry," he says, shoving past me and slamming the office door behind him.

A SHOOTING PAIN sears through the back of my neck as I go to lift my head, a string of drool marking the desk in my office. My office? My eyes widen, realizing I'm still at work, a now empty whiskey bottle tipped over on a pile of paperwork I have yet to look over. I lean back in the computer chair, trying to avoid the irritating brightness of the sun seeping through the window, and reach forward to wiggle my mouse.

I cringe. The clock in the lower right hand corner reads 10:04 a.m. With Sophia at work and the kids at school, there is no way to right my wrongs. My neck and back protest as I go to move and gather my belongings. The sun bombards my vision when I slip out of the office building and into the parking lot.

Upon entering my car, I'm quick to plug my phone into the car charger, eager to see if Caden has tried contacting me. Only bits and pieces of our night filter through my exhaustion. After a few minutes, it powers up, blaring to life with missed calls from Sophia and Luke, but nothing from Caden. Fear bubbles in the pit of my stomach. How much permanent damage have I made?

With Luke contacting me, after having minimal contact in a couple months, I know things are serious. I create a game plan: visit Sophia at her office and then return Luke's call.

A half-hour later, I enter Sophia's workplace with a simple latte in hand. I catch her eyes as I approach her and her co-workers. She smiles kindly and excuses herself, cooing at the gesture of her husband visiting her at work with coffee.

I play the part, greeting her co-workers cheerfully, before following Sophia into her office. The door slam shuts and the window blinds shut with the twist of her wrist. She lunches forward and pulls me in by my collar.

"How dare you come to my work," she hisses. "Go ahead and fuck up your life, Benjamin. But don't you dare—" she tightens her grip, "mess up my career."

She snatches the latte from my hand, letting me go with a

push. She takes a deep breath and forces a smile back on her face before swinging open the office door. Standing in the doorframe, she ushers me forward, giving me public thanks for the coffee with a kiss on my cheek. A firm hand comes to my back, pushing me out. With a hesitant smile, I shuffle past her colleagues and leave the building.

Shaking off the anger boiling in me, I try to ring Luke from inside my car. He finally answers after the fifth call.

"I can't talk," his voice is short, and there is commotion in the background.

"I'm sorry," I sigh.

Despite the frustration in his voice, there is a relief to even hearing him speak.

"Look, Ben, I can't keep this secret. It's creating a strain on my relationship with Annabelle, and frankly, even you. If Sophia calls me again, asking where you are, I will tell her. Figure your shit out, man."

The line clinks and I let the phone drop onto the middle console. In order to rekindle a portion of any relationship, I have to gather all my energy and focus.

With a call to Isabella's Coffee on the promenade, I learn Caden has taken a sick day. I groan, putting the car in drive, and speed off to his apartment. The details are still muddled from yesterday, but I know I fucked up far worse than I did with Sophia. I'll probably be on the receiving end of a door slam.

I knock on his apartment door for a good ten minutes before he opens the door, just a sliver.

"Go away."

"Caden, please let me in."

"You still don't understand what 'no' means, do you?"

"I'm sorry, Caden. I am. I promise there is no alcohol in my system. I just want to talk to you. I have a peace offering," I say, holding up the flat white.

One eye peers through the crack, shifting downward to acknowledge the drink.

"If I let you in, do you swear not to touch me?"

"I promise," I whisper, shame churning in my stomach. How badly did I hurt him?

The door creaks open, but he quickly leaves the doorway, walking over to the kitchen table. I place the coffee on the table and take a seat opposite him. Hesitant fingers come forward, snatching the coffee and taking a sip.

"It's cold," he mutters.

"I know. I'm sorry." I had gotten his drink at the same time as I got Sophia's.

He scoffs at the apology, placing the cup back on the table. I sigh at the state he is in. Caden looks miserable, arguably the worst I have ever seen him. It's apparent he hasn't showered, his hair is greasy and flat, pajamas are still on—my zip-up hoodie hangs loosely off his shoulders—and bloodshot eyes beneath his glasses. He curls into himself, noticing my gaze.

"I don't even know how to apologize for the way I acted. I said I'm nothing like William, but yesterday didn't prove that."

He sits up straight, moving to the edge of his seat, suddenly not so shy.

"Do you even know how it feels, Ben? To start trusting someone again and let them in, only to have them start the same shit all over again?" His eyes zero in on me. I want to look away, but I can't. Before I form a response, he shouts, "Do you?"

"N-no. I don't." I speak softly, my eyes no longer able to withstand eye contact.

"Exactly. You don't know, Ben." He lets out an exasperated sigh. "I have stood up for you and made the same excuse for you as I did for him. I accepted that I was the other guy. I still do, dammit! But I won't take your behavior last night. I refuse."

I remain silent, trying to stop my lip from quivering.

"You acted just like him. You spoke the exact same words. Y-you were violent, Ben." His voice chokes on those words, eyes filling up with tears. "Out of everything, I never thought you would hurt me like that."

"I-I don't know what to say."

"Don't say anything, just listen. You need to grow up. Stop drinking and get a fucking grip on yourself. I need you to decide: either let me go or step up. Fuck," he groans, pulling at his hair. He reaches for the coffee cup again, his fingertips pushing the cardboard sleeve up and down the cup.

"You're turning into an alcoholic," he continues. "I hate that every time I'm with you, you're either drinking or already have alcohol in your system. And I've missed you—I've been missing your touch, but I will not sleep with you when you're too busy getting wasted trying to forget your problems. This isn't social drinking. You're literally drinking yourself to death."

I swallow around the lump in my throat, gripping my thighs underneath the table. "You deserve better. I know."

"I don't think you do," he answers, his voice raw and laced with hatred.

"I told you, I'm trying. I'm learning," I snap.

"Excuse me? Why are you angry with me?" His chair screeches on the hardwood as he comes to stand in front of me.

"You called out William's name yesterday."

"Don't you dare play the damn victim card on me," he shoots back. "You treated me like shit. For a moment, I really thought I was back with William. It terrified me—*you* terrified me. I tried to come home and sleep, but every time I started to drift off, I woke up in a panic, worried that someone would attack me. It has taken me three hard, long years to get to where I am now, and I'll be damned if I let you abuse me. I'll be damned if I let you *rape* me."

My heart stops. I grow lightheaded at his words. *Rape?* I

yearn for air to breathe. Tears stream down my face as the weight of his words settle. I've never mistreated someone in my entire life. I've been raised to respect and love. Yes, I am a cheater, but I've never physically harmed someone. I've never done something without consent.

"Caden, I'm so sorry," I force out through the mucus collecting.

His sobs break through, a shadow of his body collapses back onto the chair and into himself.

I don't know how to move forward, and neither does he— leaving us to sit in the silence of my mistakes. I can't bear to look at him, to look at what I destroyed. The Caden that had waltzed into my coffee shop five months ago had been so excited to have a chance to work with me. I was an unknown aid in his recovery. Now, that same confident, bright person is shattered. His light is all but gone, his confidence failing him.

I am the reason for all of it.

"Ben," he says, his cracked voice breaking through. "I thought we were making progress."

I look up at him, gazing into his hazel eyes that beg me for change.

"Caden," I sigh. "I can be the person you've always wanted and needed. I know I can. Please."

"How can I believe something I've never seen?" he questions from his curled-up position on the kitchen chair, his limbs a tangled mess.

"Let's make a deal."

His eyes roll. "Great," he mutters.

"Give me one more chance. I'll show you who I really can be, and I'll talk to Sophia by the end of the week. I won't drink either. If I don't do either of those, you can walk away, no questions."

He scans my face skeptically, taking a nonchalant drink from the edge of the to-go cup. His face cringes when he remembers the temperature.

"To be clear, I can walk away right now. You don't control me."

"Of course," I breathe, scolding myself internally for another fuck up. Caden doesn't owe me a god-damned thing.

A twinge of a smile graces his lips, but he quickly becomes stone-cold again. "You have until Sunday. If Sophia doesn't know by then, consider us over. Completely done. I'll go back to Beanery."

I nod, trying to hold back the cringe of the throb in my forehead.

One person down, two to go.

"Thank you," I whisper. An ounce of confidence consumes me as I latch onto his second, third, fucking fourth chance. "Caden, can I just hold you? Nothing more?"

I wait with a baited breath for him to respond.

"You swear you haven't had a single thing to drink today?"

"I swear on my children."

After some contemplation, I am led down the hall and into his bedroom. With some hesitation, his body relaxes against my form, accepting the comfort. As he begins to drift off, I press kisses to his hair, speaking soft apologies even though I know nothing I can say will completely fix this.

The sun is setting, and dinner is over back at home. I ignore the voice telling me to go home. I can't find it in myself to leave Caden. I need to fix my future and stop bandaging what's already broken. Slowly, I fall into a light sleep, dreaming of a day when I never have to leave him.

I wake to screams what feels like minutes later. Caden's arms and legs thrash, pushing me away as he yells for William to get off. His fist lands not once but twice as I pull him closer, trying to soothe him back to reality. It's my first of many throughout the night—each episode ending with an apology as he recognizes my face.

TWENTY-FOUR

THE SMELL of toast and coffee grounds fills my nostrils, awakening my exhausted senses. I open my eyes to find Caden standing before me, carrying a weighed-down tray with two cups of coffee and four slices of toast generously topped with peanut butter and raspberry jam, a comfort food of his.

I smile up at him, sitting my body upright, taking the tray from his grasp. He moves to the other side of the bed and climbs underneath the covers as I place our breakfast securely between us.

"Good morning," I say softly. I'm not sure where we stand with kissing, but my smile broadens as he leans in.

"It means a lot that you stayed last night," he mumbles against my chapped lips. His fingertips come to inspect the tender bruise near my eye. "H-how bad was I?"

I shake my head, cupping his cheek.

"I'm sorry," he whispers, burying his head in the crook of my shoulder.

"Me too."

We sit silently, munching on toast and gulping generous sips of coffee between each bite. I welcome the silence, allowing my mind to find peace in the conscious state for the first time in what feels like forever. Despite the unresolved complications between us, and the impending fight awaiting me at home, I am here—and I'm grateful. Every so often, Caden throws a shy glance my way, smiling each time I catch him in the act. Eventually, his head comes to rest on my shoulder. I close my eyes and let my head fall on top of his.

To our dismay, the morning in bed is forced to an end when Caden's alarm for work goes off. As he gets up, I reluctantly follow. In another world, I would have showered and gone to my office, knowing I'd be right back in this bed that night. Instead, I have damage control.

The house is empty when I get home and will be until about 3:00 p.m. By the time I make it home, I have approximately six hours to shower, clean the house, mow the lawn, trim the hedges, and thaw out ground turkey for dinner. I haven't been home in almost two full days, and Sophia's charade of the perfect wife with a pristinely clean house has dropped—thankfully.

Whether it helps or not, I need to put a visible effort in for Sophia to see, and with what's accumulated in my absence, the effort will be noticeable. I have just enough time to sneak in a whiskey neat and a shower before the kids come bursting through the door.

"Daddy!" Isabella screams as I stand in the kitchen, hair still damp.

I kneel to the ground and catch her with open arms. Looking up from the embrace, I see Sophia standing firm in the doorway.

"Noah, can you take Isabella upstairs for a bit? Mommy and I need to talk," I ask.

My once innocent six-year-old stands before me with a blank and unresponsive face. Void of all emotion, it seems like my little boy who wanted to play T-ball is now a hormonal teenager. Without making eye contact, he walks over to Izzy and takes her hand.

"Come on, Izzy. Let's go build something with my Legos."

"The superhero ones?" The hope in her heart crushes me, but not as much as Noah agreeing for the first time ever, that, of course, they can build with his Marvel legos that he has never let a soul touch.

Izzy's excitement has her darting out of the kitchen, Noah kicking his feet behind her.

Sophia places her bag, and Noah's lunchbox on the kitchen island before listening for Noah's bedroom door to shut.

"You think you can just come home, do some yard work, and be forgiven?" Her volume is low, but her tone is toxic.

"No, I—"

"What the hell is wrong with you? Gone for two days, embarrassing me at work only to not come home last night? What the fuck!" She's struggling to keep her voice down. "And your children. Don't even get me started on Noah and Izzy. The last two nights, I found Noah sleeping in Izzy's bed because he heard her crying in the middle of the night and got to her first because he wants to protect her from—from you. But of course, Izzy doesn't understand, so she'll be ignorantly happy when you do decide to show up."

She picks Izzy's bag up from the floor where Izzy dropped it, and she slams it on the island.

"You know what, Ben? Whatever you're going through, don't involve the kids. If this is something to do with me, then we can handle that, but don't you fucking dare involve those kids anymore."

I stumble over to the table, taking a seat before I fainted; the two slices of toast and whiskey render me unable to handle Sophia's words. I drop my head in my hands, trying to stabilize the dizziness.

"I-I never meant to hurt anyone," I say through the hands muffling my words.

Shoes clack against the kitchen floor. Lifting my head, I

find Sophia sitting beside me. "Ben, can you please talk to me? I'm so angry with you, but I really need you to talk to me. Are you getting depressed again?"

"Soph—"

"I noticed you're drinking more ... like you did a few years ago." Her concern startles me. I didn't expect her to even assume depression. "Listen, I understand that work has been difficult, and a lot to take on, and things haven't been great between us, but I worry about you. I worry that someday you won't come home. Where do you go, Ben?" Her hands come to mine, removing them from my face. "Where did you sleep the last two nights? Your office? I drove by and saw your car still there Monday morning. What's going on that you can't even come home?" Her voice trails off as she tries to blink back the tears.

I interlace our fingers, a foreign feeling tracing through me. I lift our hands, placing a kiss to the knuckle on her ring finger. Her diamond sparkles of broken promises.

"I'm not trying to end my life, Sophia."

Her eyes connect with mine. I'm taken aback by how uncharacteristically dull and sad her usually glossy, moss green eyes shine. Beyond the sadness, there is fear. I scan her face, noticing the stress wrinkles that crease her forehead and the way her body sits, slouched and tired.

"You promise? Because I can do a lot of things, Ben, but I cannot be a single mother. I cannot lose my best friend."

I move my chair out from the table and beckon her toward me. She sits on my lap, tentative, almost as though I'm a stranger. And in many ways, I am. I can't remember the last time we sat like this.

Wrapping my arms around her torso, I take a few deep breaths and feel her do the same. It's the closest contact we've had in a week. I allow myself to sink into the familiarity.

"I promise," I say. "I promise I'll stop drinking and be home more. I'm struggling at work and never wanted to bring that home with me. I'm still trying to figure out how to balance all of this."

She nods her head and hugs my arms to her chest, letting her tears fall. I hold on as she cries, overcome with the feeling that I'm holding on to the same girl I fell for a lifetime ago, the best friend I would comfort whenever something went wrong. I held her through silly breakups in high school after arguments with her parents and the night she found out she was pregnant. As she sobs, I wish more than anything that I can take away all the pain and heartbreak like I could when we were younger.

I can't protect my loved ones when I'm the one haunting them.

TWENTY-FIVE

FOLLOWING the heartfelt conversation with Sophia, we sit back down and go back to our detailed schedule. Sophia is convinced that my depression comes from my inability to focus and prioritize. While she isn't wrong, she also didn't factor in Caden. Nevertheless, the following morning I'm making my best effort to be a clear-headed family man. I go to work and directly home with only a few sips of whiskey, hoping it takes off just enough of an edge that it isn't noticeable.

The next day isn't as easy. I make an effort to get into work early, but everything I try to do fails me. I sleep through my first alarm. I left the car lights on overnight, forcing me to jump my car, causing the delayed trek to my office to be congested. By the time I make it in, I'm almost two hours later than anticipated. Frustration seeps in as I reach the seclusion of my space—my urge to pour a full glass of whiskey is too heavy to ignore.

One glass turns into two and then three, the morning passing at an excruciating pace. My distraction doubles as I wonder what the evening window of time I have set aside for

Caden will hold. The minutes on the clock barely move as if in spite of my anxious state.

Traffic is again backed up, this time due to an accident, only a few blocks from Caden's apartment. My impatience grows as I inch closer and closer. It's been about a month since Caden and I have been intimate. I'm hoping I can play my cards well tonight. I finish up the remnants of whiskey in my coffee traveler before I can park.

Then, I run through the double doors of his building and book it to the stairs, taking the steps two at a time until I reach the third floor. I pause to catch my breath, the exertion taking its toll on my tired lungs. I trudge the rest of the way to his door, knocking rapidly and throwing the little patience I have left away as my body hums with anticipation.

Seconds later, Caden opens the door with a smile. Before he can open his mouth, I urge us both inside and slam him against the wall with a kiss. Although his initial reaction is passion, I feel him pull back.

"Ben," he mumbles.

Ignoring his resistance, I grip the bottom of his t-shirt, letting our hips collide as I run a hand along the bare skin of his stomach. I moan, biting his lips when goosebumps rise along his abdomen. When he pulls away a second time, I move my mouth down to the base of his throat.

"Ben, stop."

I throw my head back with a groan, keeping my hands planted where they are. "What now?"

Caden scoffs, shoving me away from him. "You're drunk."

"I haven't drank today." Even in my drunken state, I can register my first lie to him.

Caden brushes past me, but not before I catch his eyes glaze over. "You told me you'd never lie to me. How fucking stupid am I to believe that? What else have you lied about, Ben?"

I spin around, ready to defend myself. Out of the corner

of my eye, I see Bethany, and her boyfriend, Jack standing in the living room.

"What the hell are they doing here?" My face warms as my blood begins to boil. Caden knows I have limited time. Why the hell wouldn't we spend it alone? Especially when it's been so long since we've slept together—tonight could have been the night.

"I thought it would be nice to have dinner with them. I want you to get to know them."

I glare toward Caden, crossing my arms. "You know how fucking hard it is for me to get here, and you can't even prioritize us? Send them home."

"Send them home? Are you trying to control me now?"

"Control you? I'm just trying to spend time with you, Caden."

"If you wanted to spend time with me, you wouldn't show up at my door drunk." Caden opens his apartment door. "And you wouldn't lie to me. You have a problem, Ben. That was the final straw, and you broke it."

"Are you fucking kidding me?" I stand in front of the door, slamming it. "I haven't drank today, Caden. Please, let's just hang out. We only have a couple of hours."

"And I want a couple of sober hours. We're done, Ben." Caden tries to reach around me to open the apartment door, but my hand involuntarily swings to push him back.

My arms are pulled behind me, making me stumble backward.

"He said, get out." I recognize Jack's voice spit in my ear.

I look at Caden, who seems genuinely as shocked by Jack's movements as me. But he doesn't ask Jack to stop.

Instead, Caden crosses his arms. "Get out."

"Fuck you, Caden."

I WIND up at Lake Mackenzie Park soon after leaving Caden's. I know I can't go home without letting my emotions take center stage. As I stroll through the trees and blissfully unaware people, I sip a fresh traveler of whiskey. I could stop drinking. I could end things with Sophia. Or I could numb it all for a few more hours.

My sips turn into gulps as the personal history in this park seems to creep up on me.

I stop and settle upon a family of rocks that dot the edge of the lake hidden behind a brick building—gentle waves lap just below where my feet dangle. This spot has become a sanctuary of sorts where strangers feel miles away, and my clarity thrives. The only other person I have ever shared this spot with is Luke.

We stumbled upon it in a drunken state during our high school years. After our first discovery, it morphed into a place where we shared our souls and found solutions to daunting problems. I tug at the damp grass as I recall the time Luke promised our friendship wouldn't change if I dated Sophia or the time Luke sobbed on my shoulder when he found out his parents were getting divorced. For all the times I shared the space with Luke, I find myself utilizing the small patch of solitude on my own just as often.

When Sophia revealed she was pregnant, I sobbed with my face to the sky, questioning God's existence. I wondered how something so life-altering could have happened while I struggled with my sexuality, astounded that the God who was supposed to love me was instead torturing me. But years later, after therapy and learning that being gay was a choice, I returned to the same spot to ask for forgiveness.

And now? Now, I feel defeated again, lost and alone, as the sun begins to set and the chill of the night emerges. Being gay isn't a choice. There is no amount of therapy to change that. If there is a God, why would he place me here and try to change me?

I sigh, taking another swig. I have three more days until Caden's deadline, which may not even exist anymore. Even if Caden walks away, I'm not sure I can walk away from myself this time. Imagining the look on Sophia's face or the devastation I can bring on the family makes me ill.

A rustling from behind breaks my thought process. I try to adjust my eyes to the oncoming night.

"Hey," Caden whispers.

I turn back to the water, remaining silent and still. I don't remember ever telling him about this place.

He takes a hesitant seat next to me, leaving a generous amount of grass between our bodies. I watch from the corner of my eye as he hugs his legs and gazes out across the lake.

I hate that my body relaxes next to him. He just kicked me out of his place, and I still want him. With him here, that must mean the deadline is still on. My whiskey brain allows me enough clarity to recognize I shouldn't speak, though.

He audibly swallows and lets out a sigh. "Luke told me about this place."

"What?" My tone is short, and I cringe as his body jerks. I'm not angry ... at least, I don't think. Just more so, confused.

"When you started drinking, I kind of started to talk to him more. We exchanged numbers one day when he came in for coffee."

My blood turns to ice. Luke has barely spoken to me since he learned about Caden, but now they are buddies? And how much are they confiding behind my back?

"I asked him tonight where I might find you when you weren't at your office. I know well enough that you didn't go home."

I shove my palms against my eyelids, bringing my knees up to rest my elbows. This was our secret spot, all destroyed in a simple message. The least he could have done was told Caden he'd handle it. Luke should be here. Not Caden.

"When did you start drinking today?" Caden's voice is the

strongest I've heard in days. I open my mouth to speak. "And if a lie comes out of your mouth, I will never speak to you again."

"Mid-morning. I'm not drunk, though." I was okay to drive from Caden's to the park, but after finishing half of this traveler, I know well enough that I can't drive.

"Please stop with the bullshit, Ben—"

"Why are you here if you're just going to judge me?" I interrupt him. "If you want me gone, stop finding me."

"I'm concerned. Do you have any idea how bad this has gotten?" Exhaustion riddles his voice. "Do you understand how awful you make me feel?"

I swallow around the lumps forming. I try to breathe through the sob brewing, but my lungs are restricted.

"I feel like I'm not good enough for you until you're intoxicated. Like you're repulsed by me. And maybe that's still my own work to deal with, but I know a drunken Ben more than a sober one."

My breath catches, and I suck in the air.

"I'm n-not repulsed by you. I'm falling in love with you." My body shakes as I lose control of the sob. "The thought of losing Sophia terrifies me, though. I b-barely know a time when she wasn't in my life. She's been my constant since I was eleven."

His face relaxes as if he understands better, like if he were to choose between me or Bethany.

"I'm losing my mind trying to sort all this out. I don't exactly have a neutral person to vent to."

"You can't rely on alcohol, though. Maybe you can get a therapist."

My body shivers as Dr. Matthew's face comes to mind. I will never see another therapist.

"I can sort it out. I promise. I won't get drunk anymore, okay?"

"You promised me that two days ago. And here you are

intoxicated, repeating the same bullshit." He looks out at the water, taking a few deep breaths. "I promised myself I wouldn't be in this situation again. Ben, without all this bullshit, I think you're an unbelievable person. Each time you let your guard down, and I see the real you, I fall harder. But I can't keep doing this. I'm not sleeping, I'm on my last leg at work, and I'm pretending I'm sick, so people don't get suspicious. This mess of a guy," he says, motioning to himself, "isn't who I have worked so goddamn hard to be. I can't allow you to have this control over me."

Tears fall from his eyes, and it takes everything in me to not brush them away. My chest tightens as a new onset of tears consumes me.

"Bethany told me I'm acting like I did when I was with William. Do you know how terrifying that is?"

Even out of all the times I've hurt Sophia, nothing compares to the pain I've actively placed on Caden.

"There isn't any reason you should stay with me." I hide the slight smile that appears when he gasps at my omission. "But you've asked me to tell you how this became my life, and I haven't been ready. So before you walk away completely, can you hear me out?"

He looks over at me, his eyes intent. I hand him the traveler as my own submission. With furrowed brows, he glances at it before opening the container. There is still some whiskey left. His shoulders sink as he closes the lid, but the wheels are spinning. He never knew my secret.

Caden places the traveler on the other side of him before he returns his attention to me.

I grip my hair between my fingers. I hope this works, but if it doesn't, it's one step closer to stopping the lies.

"I've always wanted kids, but I never knew how much they would mean to me until I became a father. I've gone above and beyond to try and protect Noah and Isabella, but now my life is destroying them. Noah won't speak to me, and Isabella cries at night. I truly believed I was protecting them, but the fact that I'm hurting them kills me. It isn't their fault that I'm in this position, but it would have been easier to leave Sophia without them. I never wanted a broken family. I saw how much Luke's parents divorcing hurt him as a kid. I swore I'd never do the same." I inhale, trying to calm myself before I proceed. "I-I never told you this, but the night before Isabella was born, I tried to kill myself."

My gaze is unfocused, my eyes are unable to blink, but I can see his arms release his legs from their grip as he turns completely toward me. I remain still. I can't look at him if I want to continue.

"I fell into a depressive state. This was a month before reparative therapy. Sophia and I were on and off after Noah was born. We had great months followed by bad months. We even saw a marriage counselor for a while. On a streak of doing well, I was getting the coffee shop up and running—I had just confirmed the business deal when Sophia announced we were pregnant again. The weight of the business, Sophia's pregnancy, and my own sexuality weighed heavily on me. I started drinking, and Sophia and I would fight almost every day. I was depressed, something Sophia knew about, but we were both too stubborn to do anything about it. I had a business trip in New York a few weeks before Isabella's due date. After a long day, Sophia and I got into the worst fight we ever had. Already intoxicated, I took it a step too far and let the depression drown me."

His hand gently reaches out to my left arm. He pulls my shirt sleeve up over the forearm and traces my scar.

"You didn't hurt yourself at Beanery."

I shake my head, finally finding his eyes. His index finger continues to trace up and down the scar as he glances between me and the scar. Solidifying my mistakes. Every single wall has broken down, and instead of feeling a rush of relief, I feel empty. I need more than just a trace of a finger. I need him to envelop me in a hug. I need to be protected.

Taking a deep breath, I continue.

"Luke called me, in the midst of it all, to tell me that Sophia was in labor. The next thing I remember is waking up in the hospital bed. He called reception and asked them to send an ambulance while he booked it to New York. He met me at the hospital and spent the night with me while I was under suicide watch. When they released me the next day, we flew home together to meet Isabella." I smile briefly, thinking about the first time I set eyes on her. "The first moment I held her, I questioned how I could have ever considered leaving this beautiful child. That's why the cafe is named after her. She saved my life and my family. After she was born, Sophia and I kept my suicide attempt under wraps; not even our parents found out. That's when I started reparative therapy. And things were getting better—then you came."

I stop his fingers on my wrist and interlace them with mine.

"Thank you for opening up to me. Thank you for trusting me." Caden squeezes our fingers, leaning toward me. His lips press ever so slightly to my own before he leans back.

My breath catches, and another onset of tears burns my eyes. There's finality in his voice. I've broken him. He's ending it all.

"You need to tell Sophia, Ben." His body turns back toward the water, his hands buried in his lap.

"All I need is time," I beg. I reach for his hand, but he shrugs me off.

The current stillness of the lake mirrors his silence, taunting me. The traveler of whiskey is in clear view on the other side of him. The rapidly growing emptiness is eating away at me from inside out.

I am not okay. I'm screaming out that I'm not okay. Can no one see the comparisons?

"You're out of time. If you need more time, take it. But I can't wait for you anymore."

Before I can react, he's walking away, disappearing into the shadow of the building. I lunge for the traveler he leaves behind and down the rest of the whiskey.

A strangled cry rips through my throat as the liquid courses through my body, not working fast enough to numb the pain. I have to get home and leave my wife. It's the only solution. Caden came into my life, and in less than five months, he's rearranged the way I see the world. I can't let him walk away. Losing him will be losing me all over again.

My phone rings in my pocket, and I rip it out, hoping to see Caden's name. Instead, Luke pops up.

"Hey," I breathe, trying to speak through my tears.

"Hey, Ben." His voice soothes me over the line. It isn't the hug I need, but it relaxes my muscles and starts to untangle my paths. "It's time to tell Sophia."

The phone almost falls to the ground as my grip falters.

"She came over with the kids because you didn't come home. I know where you are. I've talked with Caden. Sophia thinks you're depressed again, and while I think that's true, you also need to tell her why."

I find myself saying, "okay," before I comprehend the words.

There is silence on the other end with my response before he breathes out. "Thank you, Ben. The kids can stay here tonight, and we will bring them to school. Be honest with Sophia. Take this time to sort it out."

"Thank you," I whisper.

"Ben, I love you. It's going to be okay."

TWENTY-SIX

THERE ARE two whiskey glasses—one with coke and the other neat. Whiskey and coke had been Sophia's drink of choice during our college years. And though she hasn't requested it in years, I'm fairly certain she'll want something stronger than her red wine.

I place the bottle down close to me and reach for my glass before pacing the circumference of the living room. When the front door opens, I bolt for the bottle and pour another glass, quickly sitting on the couch to try and appear calm.

An easy, hopeful smile graces Sophia's face as she rounds the corner. Guilt fizzles up in my stomach. This isn't fair to her; it isn't fair that I have led her on for so many years, nor is it fair that our anniversary is less than a week away. Worst of all, she isn't going to be the only victim of my deceit.

I swallow a sigh, giving her a small smile.

"Hey you," she greets.

She shimmies off her jean jacket, draping it over the couch, revealing a black sleeveless maxi dress. Her hair remains wavy from the curling iron this morning, but her makeup is fading, revealing her heavy bags and fine lines. A trace of excitement dances across her face, though.

I stand up and hastily approach her, taking the time to contemplate how to proceed.

"Hey," I reply.

Gingerly, I place my hands on her hips, only to move them to wrap around her frame. She still feels safe—comfortable even.

I bury my head in her golden locks and pepper kisses on her scalp. I try to breathe in her familiar presence—wanting to be reminded of the love we shared one last time.

She untangles her body from my arms, her hand slipping into mine, and tugs me backward, heading to the stairs.

A part of me—most of me—screams for this to stop. The other begs to follow this through. One last time to solidify that our love wasn't a fluke. To remind Sophia that no matter what happens tonight, my love for her wasn't a complete lie.

The door to our bedroom remains open as she pushes me toward the bed. Her hands grasp my cheeks, thumbs caressing the skin under my eyes. She knows there is a secret, something so much bigger than she can even comprehend. It isn't lost on her that she is losing me.

"Make love to me like you used to. When nothing else mattered but us." Seduction and desperation laces the soft request.

I close the space between us and take her bottom lip between mine. My fingers tangle in her hair as I cradle her head. The rise and fall of our chests move as one.

I try to give her everything she wants while memorizing everything she is. The smell of vanilla and sweat. The sound of her whimpers and moans as she begs for me to love her, to go faster, to go slower. The rhythm of her hips and the way her face contorts in pleasure—eyes squeezing shut, head thrown back, mouth agape. I envelop her into my arms, sweat sticking our chests together as she comes undone.

As her heavy breaths lessen, I sigh in relief and lower her down to the mattress. I have no motivation to continue, content to stay connected while burying my face in the crevice of her neck, not ready to face the reality of our shattering marriage.

Sophia shivers as my fingers wander across the expanse of her body, ultimately drawn to her abdomen. I settle on the stretch marks that act as evidence for our family.

"Ben," her voice croaks, breaking the silence. "We're going to be okay, right?"

My chest tightens, suffocating me and trapping me in the confines of her embrace. I pull away and sit upright, crossing my legs. I tug the sheet over us, suddenly upset with how exposed we are.

The color drains from her face, glossy eyes overcome with worry as she watches me. She reaches for the comforter, hoping to bury her discomfort.

"B-ben—" Tears drain from her eyes, zigzagging unceremoniously down her cheeks.

I choke, forgetting momentarily how to breathe. I imagine how our situation might look from an outsider; a broken-hearted woman hanging on to a shred of hope while the man sits dumbfounded, silent as his web of lies strangles their lives.

"I-I …" My mouth is dry, the words lodged in my throat.

She clutches the blanket up to her neck, fidgeting.

"I-I'm cheating."

Her grip on the blanket drops as two open palms fly forward, shoving me backward and off the bed. She's quick to her feet, towering above me before I can right myself.

"I asked you!"

I close my eyes in frustration, struggling to untangle my limps and stand up.

"I fucking asked you!" A sharp slap to my face lands the moment I stand upright, her wedding ring scraping the top of my cheek.

"Soph—let's talk about this."

"No." The gravity of her voice is stifling.

I shift my eyes away from her.

"I'm done. I can't hang on anymore, Ben. The drinking, the lying, and now *cheating?*" Her hand pushes at my chest, emphasizing each wrongdoing. By the third shove, the back of my legs collide with the bed, and I'm forced to sit. "Here I am worried sick about you, working my goddamn ass off, and for what? So you can go screw Caden behind my back?"

My eyes shoot up at the mention of his name.

"You promised me—us—your family. Are we not good enough for you?" I blink back the tears from my eyes as she questions my reasoning. "You promised, Ben. After all that therapy, you promised you weren't gay anymore."

My face twists.

"I don't get to choose, Sophia!" I retort. "Don't you get it? I've been killing myself, bending over backward to keep this family together, to stay with you. But *I* can't anymore. Don't you get that? I tried for *you!*"

An obnoxious laugh rips free from her throat. "The only person you've bent over backward for is Caden," she spits, eyes darkening. "I hope he's fucked you hard because you deserve to get your ass beaten."

My body freezes. I have never heard her so volatile. A defensive heat rises up my neck, consuming my cheeks and forehead.

"If you really love us, you would have found a way to change."

I stand up from the bed and yank her arms into a feral grip. Fear and uncertainty wash over her face.

"Being gay isn't a choice, Sophia!"

Before I can rein in my rage, her back connects with the wooden dresser—the veins in my neck pulse as the sound of my heart pounding thuds in my ears. I glance down at my hands, still enclosing her wrists, betrayal and guilt replacing blind rage.

Her body grows slack in my grip, crumbling to the floor.

"G-get out," she says from the ground, arms and legs squeezing tight to her chest.

She recoils further as I move forward, looking to offer some explanation or apology. I watch helplessly as her body begins to shake with sobs.

Panic floods my mind. I rush past her, grabbing my clothes from the floor, and bolt out of the bedroom and down the stairs. I frantically dress in the living room, eager to snatch up the whiskey sitting on the coffee table from earlier. With the almost full bottle in my hand, I grab my phone and keys before booking it out the front door and onto the porch.

Sweat pours from my forehead, hands visibly trembling as I try to unscrew the cap of the whiskey bottle.

She had provoked me. She had started it. No matter how much I try to believe that it's the truth, I know I am the only one to blame for this. Once again.

There are only a few stars in the sky tonight as the almost full moon begs for attention. I trudge over to the wooden swing that hangs eerily still in the glow of the street lights. I lower my body onto the seat and let the swing begin to sway with the force of my weight. Goosebumps break out across my arms as my insides tingle with a swig of whiskey. When I go to stash the bottle between my thighs, my eyes latch onto the sight of my scar glistening in the moonlight.

Two inches below my wrist lay a five-inch-long scar, stark white and raised. I can still recall the feeling of the glass piercing the skin, blood oozing out in a steady stream. I have never stopped craving the sudden relief and relaxation I felt at that moment; it was euphoric.

Soon, the memory is replaced by the emptiness that travels from the pit of my stomach to the hollow of my throat. My shoulders tense as I try to focus on taking even and steady breaths. When a pain soars across my forehead, settling deep within my temples, I know my efforts were a waste.

Voices blare in my mind, each one contradicting the other,

always asking something different of me. Sophia, Caden, Luke, Annabelle, Noah, and Isabella shouting at one another —shouting at me.

I take another gulp of whiskey and somehow manage to stand up. Staggering, I descend the steps one at a time to the stone path toward my car.

There is no reason, no purpose left.

Sophia hates me.

My kids hate me.

Caden hates me.

I hate me.

I rifle through the glove box once in my car and find the personal-sized whiskey bottle I purchased on Caden's birthday. With a quick tip back, I down what remained and toss the empty bottle onto the concrete. A satisfaction fills me as the glass shatters, resembling the way my heart is breaking all at once.

A light flickers on in the foyer. I rush to put the keys in the ignition. The last thing I need is for her to call the police.

The tires screech as the car lurches backward and out of the driveway. I speed through the backroads, unsure of where I'm even driving to. So when the sign for our town park, Forestbrook, pops up, I veer to the left and into the parking lot.

I park my car and focus on my breathing. I inhale or at least try to before I choke on the stale air. I snatch the whiskey bottle from the passenger seat and unscrew the top, taking a generous chug. My system relaxes with the ritualistic crutch.

A single street lamp flickers in the rearview mirror while the park before me is shrouded in darkness. The familiar territory now appears frightening with nightfall. My instincts tell me to call someone—anyone—but there is no one left to reach out to. I pushed, cracked, and demolished every relationship in my life. The unsteady source of light behind me can barely even hold on.

I'm an asshole.

A shitty father.

A cheating husband.

A terrible boyfriend.

A lousy business owner.

Sobs overcome my body as the events of the day replay behind my eyes. The tug-o-war between staying above water and letting the tears fill up my lungs rage as visions of Sophia and Caden flood my mind.

I flip the visor down, blinking into the yellow light. Staring at my reflection, I feel lost. Never in my twenty-nine years have I laid a hand on someone. Yet, here I am with red-rimmed eyes, heavy bags, hollow cheeks, and a splotchy complexion. This isn't the Benjamin I have worked so hard to construct. This isn't the man that Sophia wants a family with. This isn't the coffee shop owner that Caden sees something extraordinary in.

The person in the mirror, sitting in his car in the dead of night with an open bottle of whiskey, resembles the broken and desperate guy who was sent to therapy. The guy who took all the verbal abuse, scrutiny, and brainwashing in hopes he could be "cured."

"You are straight. You were not born gay. Being gay is a sin." The words feel foreign and bitter. But through the mucus gathering in my throat, tears clouding my vision, and the burn of the whiskey, I force myself to repeat it.

"You are straight. You were not born gay. Being gay is a sin. You are—y-you are gay." I gag. "I-I'm gay." My face reddens at the admission as though it had been said by someone else within.

I want to help him. I want to find him. I want to reach out and give him a hug.

'Everything will be okay,' I would tell him.

But as soon as he is here, he disappears. I can't find him. I search. I run my hands over my face. I flip the visor. I scan the car. I open and close my eyes, but he is nowhere to be felt or seen. He is drowning in the whiskey that my inner demon continues to crave. There are two of me: the one who wants to honor himself and the one who thinks everything is a choice; the latter is in control. The Benjamin I need more than ever is being suffocated and gagged while the other coaxes me to reach for the bottle. And when the bottle doesn't suffice, he tells me to go one step further.

My hand searches through my car, opening compartments in a fury. I'm not inside my body; I'm on the outside looking in. This is no way to stop what has started, what *he* started.

Inside the glove box, beneath sunglasses, winter gloves, and a harmonica I took from Noah one day when I had a headache, I find an old box cutter—one I have casually taken from Isabella's. My fingertips pinch the metal, causing a wave of relief to rush through me.

He is gripping the bottle again, pouring the whiskey down my throat, letting the burn of the liquid coat my esophagus. The more that is consumed, the further he gains control.

He is laughing, laughing at my inability to fight back. Laughing at my mistakes, my fuck-ups, and my insecurities. Each and every mishap flashes through my mind. Every argument I caused, every regret.

The box cutter slides open, my thumb trailing along the edge of the blade. Lifting my arm, I trace the scar with the blade. The sensation of cold metal makes me smile. I line the blade up next to the scar and press down. My skin grows white with pressure.

I jolt in surprise when my phone blares, breaking the silence and piercing through the tension. The box cutter falls from my fingers and lands on the car floor. As I reach for my phone, an ounce of hope surges. The Benjamin I want to be is hoping it's Caden calling to save him from himself.

I look at the screen in disappointment. It is Luke.

Ignoring it, I steady my hand and pick up the blade again.

My eyelids flutter shut as the blade slices through the skin. Cool air hitting the warmth of the fresh blood—my shoulders grow lax.

Luke's name flashes again. This time I reach for it, the feeling of peace consumes me.

"Where the fuck are you?"

I shiver and smile down at the sight of blood seeping from the cut and falling onto my jeans, soaking through the fabric. The image is pure brilliance. *This* is freedom. *This* is a release.

"The park." I laugh with menace.

I grow dizzy from the combination of blood loss and alcohol. I roll down the window, hoping the night air will cool my overheating body and dry up the sweat on my tingling skin. I continue to twirl the blade between my fingers, taking sips from the half-empty bottle without much thought. As my eyes start to roll back, the first sign of life shines in the distance of the car's mirrors.

TWENTY-SEVEN

A SEARING PAIN lodges its way between my eyes as I go to open them; remnants of sleep are crusted within the inner corners. My eyes adjust to an unfamiliar room. The walls are beige, the lights much too bright.

My hand pounds, and my ears start to ring as if I have just attended a concert. I fight the desire to return to sleep. Looking around the space, I'm met with wall paintings and impersonalized furniture that resembles that of a hotel—I'm tucked into a hotel bed.

I spin my head to the side as a figure shifts on the other bed. Luke sits up, turning off the muted television, and moves to sit next to me. He is still dressed in what I assume to be yesterday's clothes, hair laying haphazardly atop a face full of sleep deprivation.

"Do you need anything?" His hand reaches out with a glass of water. My gaze flies past the glass and toward the blood that splattered his t-shirt.

I push his hand away and close my eyes. The idea of even drinking a single drop of liquid, water, or otherwise, sets my stomach churning. The movement causes my arm to seize up in pain. Looking down, white gauze engulfs the entirety of my forearm.

Deja vu hits me in the gut. Suddenly, the hotel room is now the hospital room, I woke up in three and a half years ago. I scared and hurt my family back then, and now, I'm here again. As if no time has passed at all. I'm right back to where I started.

"How are you feeling?"

My jaw clenches; I fear vomit will spew if I open it. I reach for Luke's hand, gripping it tight, and let my eyes slip shut.

I WEAVE in and out of consciousness for the rest of the day. Sips of water are forced down my throat as I remain caught between nightmares in my sleep and nightmares of my reality. The only thing I can remember for certain is that Luke will never leave my side.

"ANNABELLE, this is far more serious than him cheating. Baby, I know you don't understand, but you need to be there for Sophia and I need to be with Ben." Luke's voice drips with remorse. He walks the carpet along the window of the hotel room. "I'm sorry I didn't tell you but put yourself in my shoes. Just—just stay with Sophia and help her with the kids. I have some things to take care of on my end—I'm, I'm not sure."

Luke's eyes connect with mine, his face dropping in surprise and worry.

"Belle, I have to go. I'll call you later. I love you." Luke places his phone on the dark wooden desk and strides toward me with a competing mix of urgency and unease.

"H-hey. Feeling any better?" he asks, taking a seat on the edge of my bed again.

I inhale deeply, grateful that the pain in my head and weakness in my body has subsided a touch.

"Like a fucking truck—not once, but twice—barreled into me." The words come out thick and dry, dehydration evident.

Luke reaches for the glass of water and hands it over to me. This time, I am eager to accept.

"Tomorrow, we are going on a trip."

I raise my eyebrows at him as I sip from the glass. I am in no shape to travel. What the hell is he thinking?

"We are going to New Hampshire to see your parents. And then we are going to Vermont. There is a rehabilitation center there." The blood in my limbs goes cold. "It's already confirmed and taken care of. You'll be doing a detox program, followed by a stay for, at least, thirty—"

"I—"

"No." He places his hand on mine. "Let me finish. The center is on a ranch on the edge of a lake near the mountains. You'll be able to hike, ride horses, kayak, and just focus on yourself. At the end of the thirty days, you will move into a sober home back here in Maine with a therapist on call. Ben, none of this is up for debate. It's non-refundable. And after finding you on the edge of death twice, I'm allowing myself to make this decision for you."

My mouth drops at the unexpected information that I have silently prayed for but always tried to resist.

"N-no," I stutter.

"Ben, you don't have a choice. I refuse to let you hurt yourself anymore."

"N-no. Therapy will kill me. You don't understand," I say, shaking my head. His voice is coming back into my head.

You are straight. You were not born gay. Being gay is a sin.

"Ben, listen to me. Therapy is going to help you. It will be good for you. You don't need to worry about anyone else while you're there, and when you come back, you'll be better than ever."

I play with the edge of the fraying gauze, my anxiety causing me to shift uncomfortably on the bed.

"Stop." Luke's hand comes to grip my wrist, stopping my fingers from moving. "Talk to me. I don't understand why you won't give this a chance."

I stay silent for longer than necessary, eyes trained on his fingers that entrap my wrists.

"Who else knows about this?"

"No one. I wanted to leave that part up to you," he says, expression pleading. "Please just go, Ben. I know you're feeling lost, confused, and even scared, but I refuse to let you give up on my watch. I only want to help you."

"Then don't make me go. It'll be different this time. I'll make sure I get better on my own. I promise." I reach out my other hand so I can grip his. The contact with another man, even if it is platonic, makes me shiver.

You are straight. You were not born gay. Being gay is a sin.

I squeeze my eyes shut as the memory tightens in my chest. I tell myself to breathe, hoping the air will repress the thoughts.

"Ben, I—" he starts.

The air in my lungs comes out in short puffs, lungs clenching with what little oxygen I can provide them with.

"I-I, I was born straight! I am not gay! Being gay is a sin!" I yell. Tears sprout from the corners of my eyes. My hold on Luke remains as my body shakes in agony.

Luke moves to lay down on the bed, pulling me into his body in an all-encompassing embrace. His hand comes to rest at the base of my neck as I continue to sob into his chest. The overwhelming sense of comfort surprises me; Luke and I were never much for physical affection, but his concern is genuine.

"Ben, who told you that?"

"Dr. Matthews."

"Wait, you've been to therapy before?" he questions. "Was it after Isabella's birth?"

I simply nod. "R-reparative therapy. Luke, I can't go back."

"What is reparative therapy?" His face contorts.

I shut my eyes as the reel of memories begins to play. Images of Joshua, Caden, and the gay men I fantasized about in secret make my body seize up in shame.

"You are not gay, Benjamin. This is a life of sin," he says. "Your sexual relations with Joshua were repulsing and a disgrace to your family. You're better than this."

"Do you want to be better than this?" he demands.

I scream out as the excruciating pain from the shocks soar throughout my body; my skin crawls and aches. Each image, each desire I feel, is met with another shock, longer than the last.

The bed beneath me shifts, cold air rushing to my side as Luke slips away and leaves the bed. But my head stays stuck in the past.

"Do you want to be loved, Benjamin? Do you want your children to love you?"

"Ben," Luke's voice breaks through the memory. My eyes flutter open to his worrisome stare as he goes to sit beside me on the other side of the bed. "Ben," he says again, his voice soft as he yanks my body upward to rest against his, pressing my head into his chest. "I'm so sorry, Ben. I didn't know. I promise this place is different. There won't be anyone telling you you're wrong or need fixing."

The side of his face comes to rest against the top of my head. His hands move reassuringly up and down my back.

"This Dr. Matthews should be in jail. Those things he said to you are all lies, Ben."

I can see the glowing screen of his phone next to us. I lean forward to see his browser is open to a site describing the procedures that take place during reparative therapy. I twist my head away as the terms and descriptions take my breath away. Another sob rumbles through me.

"Ben, I need you to come back to me," Luke begs. "I promise I won't let anyone hurt you."

"Luke, I," I sniff, pulling away from him. "I just want to be happy." I sigh.

"I know. I do too. We *all* do."

"How … how's Sophia?"

"She'll be fine," he said, shaking his head. "You need to worry about yourself. We all want you to get better."

I raise my eyebrows. That sounds like bullshit.

"The truth is, you're royally messed up right now, but at the end of the day, we all love you—even Sophia. Everything is fragile and cracked, but we know it's more than just what's on the surface. We're all to blame, not just you," he says, eyes trained on the generic comforter. "Annabelle and I should have recognized that something more was going on. *I* should have fucking noticed something was going on. Sophia should have never asked you to stay, and you shouldn't have allowed yourself to live in such a state of denial. I really think you going to this place in Vermont and Sophia taking time to process is in everyone's best interest."

"What about Caden?" My voice is small, hesitant. Luke barely spoke to me when he found out about Caden. Is this even a safe place to talk about him freely? And what happens if I disappear? I can't lose Caden.

The way Luke's face drops tells me that he never once considered Caden in this equation. A rush of anger pushes through me. My sexuality is literally at the center of my attempted suicide, and still, my relationship with Caden isn't taken seriously.

"That's, uh, that's up to you."

I put space between myself and Luke and curl up in the blankets like a child. I appreciate the freedom of making at least one decision on my own, but the responsibility is suffocating.

"You're friends with Caden now. You told him of our

spot." Luke's eyes dart from mine as I speak. "And he still wasn't a part of your grand plan."

Luke sighs, resting his head against the headboard. "My priority was getting you safe. Sophia doesn't know you're in this position, so I sure as hell wasn't going to tell Caden."

Oh.

"All Sophia and Annabelle know is that I am taking care of you as someone who left your home absolutely trashed. They don't know about your arm. They don't know about rehab. Not yet. They will, but not yet."

I nod and allow my body to sink into the bed a little more.

"It's almost noon. Maybe Caden can come here to say goodbye? Someone should relieve him at Isabella's anyway."

"Isabella's—" I panic, trying to sit up.

Luke gently pushes me back down on the bed. "Isabella's is the least of your worries. You have a great team of people. Nothing is more important than your well-being right now. But Caden and I will make sure it stays afloat."

I snake my hand out from beneath the covers and reach for Luke's. Our hands stay connected until I fall into another sleep.

MINUTES OR HOURS LATER, I wake up to Luke placing another full glass of water and a plate of toast on the bedside table. I offer a weak smile. After prodding from Luke that my stomach would feel better with some food in it, I give in, eating just over half of the lightly buttered toast.

The weight of Luke's monitoring pushes me out of bed. I pad toward the bathroom in hopes of finding a moment of solitude. My balance wobbles as I sit on the toilet. I relieve myself and move to rest my frame against the vanity, hesitant to face my reflection in the mirror.

I wince at the sight: aside from a pair of boxers, my gaunt

frame, sunken face, and greasy hair are exposed. It is the first time I can recognize the physical effects of my lifestyle. But the visible weight loss and blood-stained gauze taped to my forearm are minor compared to what is going on underneath. I slouch forward, back bowing in defeat.

Luke knocks on the door.

Without a reply, he throws the door open, rushing in. His eyes are glossy, but his shoulders relax as he takes me in, his eyes darting to my bandage. A cry rips from my throat. I'm now the cause of Luke's pain too, I am his responsibility.

"I'm sorry, Luke. I'm so sorry."

He shakes his head, gathering me in his arms. "Don't be."

I clutch him back. In all our years as friends, I have never felt so loved and cared for. How mistaken I was to think that I couldn't have come to him in the first place. He is the true definition of a best friend, someone who would drop everything to protect you.

"I need you so much," I mutter.

He sighs, "I need you too."

I watch our embrace in the mirror, intent on witnessing this love from every perspective I can. I need to know that I am loved and deserving of love.

He pulls away, wiping his tears on his sleeve. "We're going to get through this."

I nod my head, blinking back a fresh set of tears.

"Do you want to call Caden?" Luke asks, both of us now laying back in one of the hotel beds.

I shook my head before he even said his name. "I fucked up with him too."

Luke doesn't bother to argue. He just turns the television on and lets his upper body sag against the headboard.

A VOICE TUGS me from a nightmare. But it isn't just any voice; it's *his* voice. I open my eyes, curious. Luke and Caden are sitting at the small table near the window. Food and coffee cups from Isabella's are set out before them. He is still in his work clothes, his casually cool appearance is now wracked with dark circles and worry lines.

"Caden," I breathe.

They go silent. He bolts upright and rushes to the bed, climbing in beside me. His arms find my body beneath the comforter and sheets.

His tears soak my neck as he buries his head in between my shoulder and neck. Panic sets in as my body grows stiff. I want to cry with him. I want to feel release from the pain I've caused, but I can't let go.

"D-don't. Don't love me," I whisper.

His breathing hitches in his throat, and he pulls away slightly.

"I …" I groan, frustrated by my inability to convey my emotions. "I cheated on you."

He sits up, letting the comforter fall from us, his brows furrowed. "What do you mean?"

"I slept with Sophia."

It takes him a minute to process my confession. I am positive there is a flash of disgust when he realizes what I mean. Another promise I've broken. His cries continue, but now for another reason.

Luke stands from the table and walks in the direction of the door. He motions his departure. Seconds later, his frame moves out into the hallway, the door clicking behind him.

Caden climbs off the bed, brushing his tears, and begins to pace the length of the room. I sit helpless and silent.

His pacing halts as he looks directly at me. "You're going to get help."

It isn't a question. Luke has already spoken to him.

I nod and lean up against the bed frame, hugging my

knees. The pressure on my wound acts as a reminder of my mistakes. I squeeze tighter, welcoming the pain.

"There's a Benjamin in there—somewhere—that I fell in love with. There's a Benjamin in there who is a good father, a good partner, and a wonderful friend. I know he's hidden right now, but I was lucky to get a glimpse of him."

He comes back to the bed and sits down on the edge, one leg hanging off. His eyes focus on the bedsheets, twisting them between his hands.

"I want to love and support you, Ben. I don't want to leave you here alone and afraid. I don't want to leave you here at your weakest. But—I think it's best. Take time away. Take all the time you need. When you get healthier, we can maybe try again. But I need to get help too. I think we could be great together, I do. But first, we need to be great by ourselves."

I try to tell him he is right, that I agree, but my voice is caught in the sorrow. I feel paralyzed by the reality of not seeing him until I work on myself. A time frame I have zero concept of.

Caden inches over, his mouth connecting with mine, disregarding the snot and salty tears. I press back with as much passion as I can muster. Breathing in through his nose, he keeps his lips connected, letting his own tears melt with mine.

I'm certain that I have reached absolute rock bottom the moment his lips disconnect from mine, leaving my lips wet, bound to chap in the dry air of the hotel room. When his body moves up and off the bed, I swear I can see disappointment flood the space between us.

"I love you, Ben."

I can't utter a word, so I settle for nodding as he walks toward the door. When the door closes, I collapse on the bed. My body shakes, hyperventilating as tears soak through the sheets, sending chills across my bare skin.

TWENTY-EIGHT

LUKE and I check out of the hotel the following morning. Our first stop is to tie up loose ends at my office.

As I cross the threshold, I'm met with the stale scent of whiskey. An open bottle rests atop an explosion of papers on my desk. So much has changed over the past few days, but the view in front of me is not a prideful blast from the past.

"Are you going to let Caden use your office?" I turn toward Luke, forgetting he followed me in.

I nod and make my way to the desk. I hate that he's seeing me like this.

"Then, let's tidy up a bit, shall we?" His eyes sweep over the room, a new wave of concern consuming him.

I don't blame him. The office is cramped to begin with, and I have turned it into a safety hazard. Before I can worry myself with spring cleaning, I rummage through the pile of papers. There is a specific set of paper-clipped documents that need my attention.

Once found, I stash them in my sweatshirt pocket and help Luke with the tidying efforts. I'm grateful each time he refrains from commenting when he finds an empty bottle of whiskey, more particularly when he comes across the stash in my bottom drawer—almost completely empty.

We finish with an exhale just before noon. Our stomachs are growling when we finish, both in desperate need of good coffee and substance.

Luke looks over at me, brows raised. "Isabella's on the promenade? You can talk business, and we can get bagels?"

I nod again, and Luke opens his mouth but closes it as I start the trek out the door.

Luke jumps in line when we enter the coffee shop while I venture toward the backroom. I keep my head down as I pass Samantha's prying eyes. She tries to move toward me before stopping herself short.

Just as anticipated, Caden is sitting in front of the computer, typing away. I stand in the doorway, thinking back to the first time I saw him in this spot. He was stressed over the pressure of being in charge of the new store, but now? All the stress and anxiety etched across his face is the consequence of knowing me. I can't help but notice his black t-shirt now sags on his frame.

"Hey."

"What are you doing here?" He doesn't look away from the computer as he replies.

I shake off the insecurities I have, pulling the papers out of my pocket. His curt tone has to be because I've reached his limit.

"I received these from the lawyer this week. With both of our signatures, we would officially be business partners." His face is unreadable as I pull up a chair next to him. He finally grants me his attention. "Look, I know this isn't the best time, nor have you said you're absolutely ready. So, I'm not asking you to sign right now. But, I want you to know that I would still love for it to happen in the future." I reach for his hand under the desk. "Caden, I still want you to be my business partner."

He goes to speak, but I shake my head, hushing him.

"I know a lot has happened between us, and I know I haven't given you enough training, but don't forget that owning your own coffee shop is still a dream of yours."

His fingers intertwine with mine.

"So, while I'm away, I want you to consider it. Also, I want to ask if you can take the reins on Isabella's during my leave. I know it's a lot to ask, but you already know what you're doing."

He grabs the papers from me, placing them on the desk. Looking back at me, there's a stern expression on his face.

"In a couple of months, we'll make the decision on the partnership. As for right now, of course, I'll take over Isabella's. Ben, just because things are rocky, it doesn't mean I love you any loss—" The declaration seems to roll off his tongue sans effort. "Nor, do I want this business to plummet."

"I owe you more than I could ever offer, Caden. Thank you for everything." I stand and tug him upward to mirror me. I pull his body into mine and let my head rest in the crook of his neck, pressing butterfly kisses to the skin. "I love you. One day I will prove that."

Leaning my head back, I give a small smile and press my forehead to his. It is time for me to leave, but I need to kiss him one more time. I tip my chin forward and latch onto his lips in a soft kiss; peppermint and coffee tingle on my tastebuds.

With reluctance, I take a step back and leave the embrace.

"Anyone's numbers you may need are in the top drawer of—"

Caden's hand comes to my shoulder. "Ben, go. I'll be fine." His hand trails down and grasps my hand again. "Please go and take care of yourself."

Closing my eyes, I nod, trying to keep the tears from spilling at his display of concern.

As Luke and I exit the cafe, I can't help but feel I'm

leaving behind a life and walking into a world of uncertainty. I set my entire world on fire and am now turning my head as the ashes gather.

WE ARE on the I-95 S heading to New Hampshire. The drive from Cyan City to Portsmouth will take us just under an hour and a half. My parents live on the outskirts, closer to the ocean. We let the music on Luke's playlist fill the car as we drive down the highway with the windows down.

There are so many questions I have, so many answers I crave, but I refrain. The want to reach for a drink buzzes beneath my skin, making the gauze still taped to my arm itch. I have yet to see just how bad the damage is. Luke had changed the gauze at the hotel earlier this morning, but I looked away.

My parents are standing outside their small, two-bedroom brick home by the time we pull in. They are expecting us, but Luke says they don't know why we are visiting. The friendly, excited smiles on their faces overpower the confusion as to why Luke organized the visit on my behalf without Sophia and their grandchildren.

I am engulfed in a hug from my mother the moment I step out of Luke's car. The scent of lavender wafts off her skin and into my nose, calming me instantly. While this isn't my child-hood home, I feel at peace in her embrace.

Luke carries in my belongings as my mom and I wander inside, attached at the hip. The smell of fresh-baked cookies and coffee greet us.

After placing our backpacks in the living room, we are ushered to the back patio. The picnic table is set with an array of raw vegetables, lunch meat, rolls, and condiments. I can't help but smile when I notice a steaming pot of coffee and homemade oatmeal cookies off to the side.

"Mom, you really didn't have to do all this," I say with a squeeze on her shoulder.

She takes a seat next to my father, and I smile to myself. The bagel from Isabella's did little to settle my stomach. I'm eager to dive in.

"Oh hush! It's nothing. Plus, your sweatshirt looks like it's two sizes too big. Have you been eating?" she questions.

"Yes, Mom." I laugh it off.

Sweat breaks out across my brow. The sun is beating down in the backyard, causing my skin to flush. I want to roll the sleeves of my sweatshirt up, but I need to keep the bandage concealed for the time being.

"Ben, aren't you warm in that? Would you like one of your father's t-shirts to wear instead?"

I look around helpless, noticing that everyone, including Luke, is dressed for the warm spring day.

"Uh, no. I'm fine." I squeak out, moving to busy myself with making a sandwich. The look of concern my mother flashes in my father's direction doesn't go unnoticed; Luke fidgets in the chair beside me.

"So, what do you boys think about them Red Sox?" asks my dad.

For the first two hours of our visit, I manage to avoid my pressing questions. But between the sun's rays and whiskey withdrawal, my body is growing restless. I scooch farther under the table, hoping to hide my jittery legs. Luke throws me a sideways glance but doesn't break the conversation he's having with my mother. When I can't bear to sit still any longer, I excuse myself to the bathroom.

I bypass the bathroom, though, and sneak down to my father's den. It's his safe haven, complete with a flat screen TV, leather couch, and mini bar. While Mom relaxes upstairs in the living room, my dad slinks away to the den to watch the baseball game with some of his friends.

Father like son, it isn't difficult to find a stash of whiskey.

Perhaps my love for it is partially to blame on genetics, I think, as I unscrew the cap with a twinge of resentment.

The first sip is thick and warms my body.

The second sip relaxes the tight muscles in my face.

With the third and fourth, a glaze coats my anxiety.

I return to the table without anyone batting an eye.

"So, Ben, what brings you two down to New Hampshire? Where are Sophia and the kids?" my mom asks. "I mean, I'm thrilled to see you both, but we are just surprised by the visit."

The whiskey helps, but I'm still not ready to partake in the discussion she is fishing for. I look to Luke for a lifeline, but he shakes his head, not knowing what to do. I clutch my injured arm and apply pressure, hoping the throbbing and itching will dissipate.

My mother's eyes narrow.

"Well, we … uh …" I clear my throat, digging my fingers into my skin.

"Benjamin, what's going on?" my dad questions. His face appears concerned, but his tone tells me he's irritated.

I fight the urge to curl into my frame as everyone's eyes narrow, anxiously awaiting my next move.

"I-is it okay if Luke and I spend the night here?"

"Of course, honey. You're always welcome. But—"

"And are you guys available tomorrow?"

"We can move our schedules arou—"

"Ben, spit it out," says my irritated dad, drowning out my mother's comfort. "Is everyone okay? Sophia? The children?"

I nod and absentmindedly rub at my arm. I acknowledge Luke again, even though I know he won't be able to save me at this point.

I sigh. "Tomorrow morning, I am going away for a little while."

"Going away where?" My mother reaches for my father's hand.

"Somerville Ranch."

Luke catches the disconnect on my parents' faces. "It's a rehabilitation center," he clarifies.

My mom releases an audible gasp and covers her mouth. My dad wraps an arm around her shoulders and turns back to me.

"What aren't you telling us?"

I don't want to tell them. If they didn't care to notice before, why should I tell them now? Anger bubbles in my throat. I roll up the sleeve of my sweatshirt under the tablet and start to peel back the gauze. Air hits the wound, causing my arm to seize up. I close my eyes and sit silently, breathing in and out.

"Ben?" My mother presses, her voice warm.

I shake my head, refusing to open my eyes or mouth.

Luke sighs. "Ben is an alcoholic," he states, cut and dry.

My head dips, my chin burrowing into my chest. At least that is the easiest of three bombs to drop.

"H-how long? Ben, honey, w-why?" My mother stumbles.

At the sound of her voice, I look up to find silent tears streaming down her cheeks. She's shocked, scared, and seemingly distraught that her only child has been keeping this secret from her.

The disappointed gazes are too much. I sit upright, knocking my chair back and shuffle into the house, ignoring Luke's plea to come back and sit down. I snatch our backpacks from the living room floor and bound up the stairs toward the guest bedroom. Two twin beds and an array of toys are crammed into the space for when Noah and Isabella come to visit. My eyes settle on the bed where Isabella sleeps when we make the rare trek out to Grandma and Grandpa's. Her face always lights up at the opportunity to sleep in a 'big girl bed.'

I toss the bags on the ground and strip off the constricting sweatshirt. The fabric peels from my sweaty and itchy skin. I throw it in the vicinity of our luggage before flopping onto

"Isabella's" bed, shimmying under the sheets. While the den housed whiskey, at least I could make an attempt at claiming innocence and helplessness if anyone finds me up here, hiding like the pathetic twenty-nine-year-old I am.

Laying on my right shoulder, I pick at the gauze. The medical tape is still attached on two sides of the bandage. I peel it back, wincing as the tape grips to hair and tugs at the raw skin. I exhale at the sight; Luke was right, it wouldn't need stitches, but it looked terrifying. A scab was at the beginning stages, and the depth isn't nearly as deep as the previous one that lay just a centimeter away.

How am I ever going to explain these marks to my children when they are older? How am I to tell them about a time when I thought their lives and my own would be better if I didn't exist anymore?

I let my mind wander, drifting in and out of sleep. I have no idea what time it is, but it's early enough that the sun continues to shine through the window, dust dancing in the beams that hit the bedroom floor.

The door creaks open. I shut my eyes and try to even my breathing. The bed dips, and the smell of lavender drifts up my nostrils. I pray my mother is here in comfort and not to wake me up to ask more questions. Her hands lift my head and place it gently in her lap as if hoping not to stir me awake. Her fingers card through my hair and massage, just as she had when I was a child.

"Honey, we are going to get you through this. Your dad and I still love you, dear."

I let go of my sleeping act and reach my arm up. She closes her hand around mine and brings our interlocked fingers up to my lips. A small gasp slips out when she notices the damage to my forearm.

She sighs. "I love you so much, Ben. You're not alone in this. I'm so sorry you ever felt that way."

I exhale and nuzzle further into her, taking comfort in the

warmth and love that oozes from her hands as she goes back to massage my scalp.

"Do you remember that night of your thirteenth birthday? When you, your father, and I curled up on the couch, but you refused to snuggle with me? You told me you were too old."

I remember that night in vivid detail. I fought the urge to accept my mother's love because I thought it was time for me to man up.

I nod against her legs.

"You cried to Dad that night because you thought I no longer needed you," I whisper. It had broken my heart that my mom was hurt, I had so easily linked the idea that it only made me less straight if I snuggled with my mom.

My mom curls her arms around me. "I felt like I'd lost a part of you that night. You suddenly seemed so distant," she says into my hair. "You were always so wonderful and loving, but after that, something just shifted."

I start to cry. "I'm sorry. I never meant to make you feel that way," I choke out.

The faint sound of baseball playing on the TV drifts upstairs; I imagine my father and Luke lounging on the couch with beers in their hands. The sun is now setting, and I know my mother and I aren't moving from the twin bed anytime soon.

"Ben, honey, can I ask you a question?" I nod. "Was there something your dad and I could have done differently?"

The words sit heavy in the air of the bedroom. Out of everything I've mulled over, I never once thought their parenting was the issue. To be honest, I never once considered that I could blame anyone else for mine and Sophia's mistakes.

Although I don't wish to break the comfort of her touch, I know I need to see her face-to-face. I sit cross-legged. Her back is leaning against the headboard, and I try my best not to slouch in front of her. Worry fills her soft wrinkles on her forehead. I hate the idea that she is nitpicking through all the years, searching for a mistake of her own.

"Mom," I reach for her hands. Her eyes shift down to the new wound and old scar. "There is nothing you could have done."

She nods, relief tangled with sadness.

I imagine that Luke unveiled my secrets to my parents after I left the back patio, but I need to say the words out loud. My mom deserves to hear it from me.

"Mom," I breathe. I shut my eyes briefly; his face flashing in my mind; his smile shined, bringing an involuntary grin to my face. My mom squeezes my arm in reassurance. I open my eyes to see nothing but love on her face. "Mom, I'm—" I feel a rock lodge in my throat. I suck in air. "Mom, I'm gay."

I hold my breath, awaiting her reaction. Her brown eyes glisten, and she smiles, nodding her head gently.

She swallows, "I love you, Ben. All of you." She pulls me into a crushing hug. "Your dad and I are here to support you every step of the way. Just tell us what you need, and we'll do it."

The amount of unconditional love a child can feel from his own mother shakes me to the core. I crave the support, yet I can't help but think of my own children. I haven't seen them in four days—that is a lifetime from their perspective. I whimper into her shoulder as I try to will the tears away. My chest tightens, and I push away my mother, curling into myself. If my children can't feel the love of both parents, I don't deserve hers. I'm weak and drowning in a headache that begs for a drink.

"Hey, it's okay. We'll get through this."

"No," I cry. " I ..."

He is coming back, seeping through my mind, ready to take over. The bubble of love and trust is threatened.

"Mom, I don't know what to do."

"I need you to talk to me. What's going through your head?"

I look up through clouded eyes. I feel pathetic and useless as I rock back and forth. I'm a sad excuse for a son—and an even worse father. My mom doesn't even know half of it.

I shake my head and run my hands down, pulling the dry skin over my hallowed face. I suddenly feel like just skin and bone. I'm deteriorating. So far from the man I strived to be.

"You don't want to know."

"Honey, I do. I need to know. I can't help you if I don't know what you're going through."

Anger surges through my bloodstream. I want to scream, throw something, destroy the bedroom that reminds me of my failed family. Their pictures fill the space, causing the room to appear smaller, taunting me the longer I remain.

I jump off the bed and pace. Anxious energy bubbles up in my throat.

"My kids hate me, I lost my wife, I'm abusive, I probably lost Caden and the company. I can't control *him!* He's poisoning me, and I don't know how to stop it. I don't know how to fix what he's done to me. What I've let him do to *me*. I just—" I collapse to the floor. "I just need some whiskey. Please. It's the only thing that makes it stop." I choke as an avalanche of tears release.

Her hand is on my shoulder in an instant, and I smack it away. The sound of my hand connecting makes guilt fizzle inside of me. I attempt to control the sobs that rock my entire body, but as I try to hold them back, my body shakes harder.

I hate myself.

"Your father and I will go up for a while and take care of Sophia and the kids, all right? I'm sure Sophia has thought of something to tell Noah and Isabella. It'll be okay. They'll be okay. You need to go to rehab and take care of yourself. Everything will still be here to figure out when you get better, okay?"

I'm afraid to speak, afraid to open my mouth and mutter words I don't mean.

"But Ben, tell me what you mean by 'abusive'?"

I avoid her distraught eyes by closing my own. But the memories of Caden and Sophia flash behind my eyelids, pressuring sex and shoving Sophia. And now my mother? I never even talked back to her as a high-strung teenager.

Her fingertips carefully touch my back, and my eyes shoot open. In a split second, disappointment morphs into anger.

"Don't touch me," I spit.

My body shivers at the harsh nature of my words. I soften in self-pity when her arm jerks away. I try to open my mouth to apologize.

"I'm going to brew some tea. We'll have dessert, and we can all watch a movie to take our minds off everything. You can collect yourself and meet me downstairs. Okay?"

The idea of being in a room next to my father, who I can't verbally speak my thoughts with, and Luke's knowing glances, makes my heart thud. I know my father supports me, but beneath the parental obligations, he's a critical man.

My answer comes in the form of my chest deflating as I attempt to regain control. My mom leans down and presses a hesitant kiss to my temple. When the door closes with a click, I crawl across the floor to my bag and search frantically for my phone.

Not a single person has tried to contact me. The damage I've done is now concrete and irreparable.

I find Caden's number and hit call. I lean up against the bed frame, wishing I still have my sweatshirt on to burrow into.

"Hey," he answers softly. "Everything okay?"

My skin dances at the sound of his voice. Gentle and warm.

I hiccup into the receiver, trying to regulate my breathing and not go through another onslaught of tears.

"Ben, it's going to be okay."

"I—I can't do this."

"You can. You're strong enough, Ben. You're amazing. And once you get healthy, you'll be able to be the incredible dad you are again and the loving boyfriend I know and I've seen you be. But first, you need to take care of yourself."

"What if these people are just like him? W-what if they tell me I'm wrong?"

"They won't. I researched them, Ben. They follow legal standards. I sent Luke a message about it, but I don't know if he's seen it. I called them today after work and clarified; they don't support reparative therapy. They even have a special community of LGBT patients who get together in a group a few times a week if that is something you're interested in."

I grip the phone. He never ceases to amaze me.

"Caden," I breathe. "I just—I'm sorry," I choke, forcing the words out. He deserves more than an apology.

"Thank you," his voice cracks through the phone.

I want to drive back and spend the night with him. I wish he was the one dropping me off at rehab instead of Luke. I want—no, I need his comfort and reassurance up until the very last moment.

"I'll be back soon," I whisper.

"Very soon. Before you know it."

I end the call and shove the phone back in my bag. Grabbing my sweatshirt from the floor, I shimmy back into it. The material rubs the barely forming scar, but I pull the sleeves over my hands and leave the bedroom. Before making my way to the living room, where the baseball game blares and the kettle whistles in the kitchen, I head to the den.

I reach for the whiskey bottle and take a few sips, more relaxed this time, feeling each drop tingle on my tongue. Catching my reflection on the television screen, I stare in disbelief at my figure. Broken, scrawny, and destroyed, holding the bottle of liquor up against my lips. I watch and suck down a few more sips, my Adam's apple bobbing as I swallow. It takes everything in me to not throw the glass bottle at the television. I want to destroy both: what is killing me and the man that stands before me.

Returning the whiskey back to its spot, I take a moment to breathe. My fingertips dance in my tousled hair before I trail down to massage my temples.

With a new wave of confidence and ease, I walk out of the den and to the living room. Everyone is facing the television with tea, the plate of cookies on the coffee table. Three pairs of eyes look up in my direction. My father and Luke are sitting on the two recliners, my mother is on the couch. Slouching my shoulders, I make my way to the couch and grab the blanket draped across its back. I unfold it and place half across my mom and half across me. I pick up the untouched mug of tea from the table and sit back.

"What are we watching?" I ask.

My father turns on *21 Jump Street*. Luke and my dad both comment on how they've never seen the film, and I relish in the memories of me and Caden. I take a sip of the tea and lean forward, placing it back on the coffee table before positioning myself to lay my head in my mother's lap. Her hands instantly rest in my hair, massaging me into a peaceful lull as the opening scene plays. My eyes flutter shut as the familiar dialogue fills my ears, and the memory of Caden's touch consumes my thoughts.

My mother wakes me as the closing credits roll across the screen. I had fallen asleep in only minutes. Half-conscious, I'm directed up stairs by my mom and helped into bed. Sitting on the edge, she caresses my cheek.

"I'll wake you up in the morning and we'll have breakfast, and you can shower before we leave, okay?" She leans down and presses a kiss to my forehead. "I love you, Ben."

My eyes shut, and I nod back to sleep, barely coherent enough to hear her close the door to the guest bedroom.

The rustling of bags stirs me awake. The room is pitch black aside from the flashlight on Luke's phone as he rummages through his belongings, clad in just a towel.

I wait patiently as he finds his boxers and steps into them. His flashlight shuts off, and he climbs into the other twin bed, but the glow of the screen illuminates his face. He sends a few text messages, presumably to Annabelle, before he shuts off his phone and curls on his side.

"Luke?" I whisper.

The sheets on his bed shift through the darkness. "Yeah?"

"Thank you."

The words travel through the air, but I'm not watching him anymore. I can't face him as I speak. Instead, I study the ceiling. The last time Noah was here, he asked if we could put up glow-in-the-dark stars—we've never gotten around to it.

"Of course," he breathes.

"I-I'm going to get better," I pause momentarily, turning on my side to face him.

He's staring at the ceiling now, oblivious to my movements.

"Can you tell Sophia I'm sorry?"

"He turns to face me, his features slowly coming into focus in the darkness. "Of course," he repeats.

"I have some money in savings that Sophia doesn't know about. I was going to surprise her and the kids with a trip to Disney this summer. I meant to book it months ago. But well—can you tell her to use it? I listed her name on the account. Tell her to take it all and treat the kids to a holiday."

"Ben, rehab isn't going to be cheap. I mean, insurance will probably cover some of it, but shouldn't you put your savings toward this now? Or a divorce lawyer?"

"No," I say, stern and loud. "Luke, there isn't much I can do to fix this, but I can do this. They need to go on that trip after everything I've done. I don't know what the future holds in terms of my family or Sophia, but at least I can give them something for the time being. Please."

"And if Sophia doesn't take the money?"

"Then at least I tried."

I turn away from Luke, ending the conversation. I close my ears, drifting into a sleep where my freedom isn't threatened.

TWENTY-NINE

FEELING MUTE, the morning remains silent as I shower and eat breakfast, each bite resting like a brick in the pit of my stomach. The conversation sputters as we all pile in the car like we are about to attend a funeral.

For the duration of the three-hour drive, I rest my head against the window and pick at the gauze my mother insisted on replacing over my injury again. My parents chat with Luke about his life, leaving me to stew in my own despair. At the mention of his and Annabelle's wedding, I question to myself what would happen. How will the pristine futures we envisioned for ourselves unfold now that I've shattered the mold?

We take the last turn around noon, down a long deserted road lined with tall pine trees. About a mile and a half down, we come across a sign that announces our arrival at the Somerville Ranch. We drive down the gravel path about another mile, the pine trees dwindling to reveal a serene, deep blue lake to our left. A stunning red barn appears in front of us with another sign announcing the name. Outside the car window on my side is a stable with a few horses roaming.

Sitting up straight, I look around. I never once checked

out the brochures Luke gave me, believing he honestly was up-selling the entire place.

"*This* is the rehab center?" I ask. The first words I've spoken all morning.

A smile appears on Luke's face. "I told you." He reaches into his bag and pulls out a brochure. "Ready to look at this yet?"

I snatch it, flipping through all the pages. The rooms, the hikes, the lakes, the horses. This is nothing like Dr. Matthews' small, damp building.

This is going to cost a fortune.

"How much is this place?" I ask.

"Son, don't worry about the cost. Worry about getting better. Your mother and I will take care of the bills."

I sink into the backseat, resting my head on the window as guilt erupts inside of me. I don't deserve the overwhelming support from the three people surrounding me. I deserve to be going to a run-down rehab center because *I*, single-handedly, am responsible for destroying my life.

We are greeted by a friendly, bubbly girl around my age as we walk through the front doors. The four of us stop in our tracks to admire the interior. It's almost like we left New England and drove South with the modern country decor. The walls are glossy, golden wood, decorated with photographs of horses galloping in untouched fields. Behind the main desk are two large horseshoes that I recognize from the brochure—their logo.

"Hi, my name is Serena. How is everyone today?" she asks with a smile, looking at each of us in succession.

Her cheerful tone already agitates me.

"Considering the circumstances …" I start.

"We're doing okay," my father interjects.

Luke throws me a glare, and her smile turns somber.

"Of course, my apologies." She offers a softer expression

this time before continuing, "I just want to assure you all that at Somerville Ranch we have some of the most talented and educated psychologists and top-of-the-line programs. We are also one of the very few centers that offer an extensive selection of activities. I'm sure you've noticed our love of horses," she says, gesturing to the pictures on the walls. "Through our experience and research, we've seen that horses can provide patients with therapeutic treatments. And if we don't offer something a patient enjoys, we will consider it and try to establish an activity tailored to them."

"Yes, we are very excited about everything you have to offer," my mom says.

"Now, I believe you are the Jacobson family, correct?"

I nod. "I'm Benjamin Jacobson. I am checking myself in." The words roll off my tongue easier than I anticipated.

"Okay. I have some paperwork that I need you to fill out. While I'm grabbing that, why don't you all have a seat in the waiting room and I'll take your suitcase. A staff member will deliver it to your room."

She points to the left, where the entryway breaks off into a room with chairs and a coffee table. My dad hands over my suitcase.

"Someone should tell her that no one is happy to be here," I mumble as I rest in a waiting room chair.

"Benjamin, please try and be open-minded about this." My mom gives me a stern look, sitting next to me.

"I think you'll really like it here. Maybe you can convince them to get an espresso machine, and you can make all the patients lattes," Luke jokes, bumping my right shoulder slightly when he sits on my other side.

"Ha-ha." I cross my arms over my chest. Truth is, I am intrigued. I'm in desperate need of taking a vacation, and while rehab isn't exactly the ideal vacation, it is a breather that'll lead me back to my kids.

"Try, okay?" Luke pleads. The tone of voice is a sound I need to lock away on days I want to give up. I need to get better for my kids, but I also need to be better for Luke. He's proven himself time and time again, and I cannot ask him to pick up more of the pieces.

"I appreciate you arranging everything. I'm sorry," I say, and he gives me a knowing look.

Serena comes back with a clipboard. There are numerous papers regarding my personal information, insurance information, a privacy disclosure, daily activity choices, and details on what exactly rehab will entail. I'm going to be placed in group and individual therapy that takes place every day but on the weekends. Aside from Sundays, each day begins at 7:15 a.m. and ends at 9:30 p.m. Lights out at 11 p.m.

It's all so structured. Everything scheduled to a T starting with breakfast, to showering, to counseling sessions. I'll be surrounded by people dealing with an array of addictions in group therapy, but I also have a daily AA meeting. There is time set aside for creative activities and exercises. With what little free time we do have, we can rest, read, or watch television.

"I suppose when I get out, I'll learn to be on a better schedule." I laugh. "Maybe I'll come home being able to knit and do yoga."

"Perfect, all your Christmas gifts will be sorted. We'll be looking forward to winter hats," Luke teases.

After a half-hour, I complete the paperwork. I chose a writing class (Sophia always told me I should get my thoughts out on paper), a cooking class (hoping that with some minor skills I can help Caden in the kitchen), and a kayaking course (hoping that the peace out on the lake will fend off feeling secluded).

"Luke, promise me that you'll keep an eye on Caden? You'll go into Isabella's every once in a while to make sure his head is still above water? Do whatever needs to be done to ensure that the company remains successful—whether it's giving raises or whatnot. And maybe, if you can, try to keep this under wraps?"

"I promise. I won't let this ruin everything you've worked for."

I give him a grateful nod and stand up. We all find Serena at the front desk, and I give her the paperwork. She has a folder and a lanyard with two keys on it.

"Are we ready for the tour?" We all nod. "Before I forget, do you have any electronics on you? Cell-phone, laptop, tablet?"

"Left them at home," I reply. Truth is, I felt loads lighter not having them on me.

"Wonderful." She gives my parents and Luke the spiel about how they cannot take any pictures with their devices, as it's a privacy violation. They only give tours at certain times of day when most of the patients are in other programs, so they don't jeopardize the privacy of the patients.

We walk out onto the grounds, and I notice a low wooden gate surrounding the entirety of the ranch. My eyes wander, barely listening to Serena. An area of log cabins comes into my field of vision as I follow her lead. They look like something out of a fairytale—rustic, but each one resembling the next. The wood is dark, forming a small, square living space that houses just two patients.

"There are a total of fourteen cabins. They are built to form a circle to help create community."

As we walk between the cabins, the grounds open up to a mammoth, stark white building that acts as the dining hall and common area. Two slightly more compact buildings, designated for activities, sit behind. Inside the commons building, there are both circular and rectangular tables with empty chairs. The setup is reminiscent of high school, but with a five-star touch, everything is polished, and the kitchen is hidden from view. Menus and plates are on each table, waiting for a rush of people that have yet to come.

My stomach growls as Serena guides us toward what she calls "the courts." Tennis, basketball, and volleyball courts are back to back with a soccer field and an outdoor pool to complete the outdoor sports complex. And while I'm enamored with the lake at the entrance of the center, there is another one, much larger, and somehow more serene lake parallel to the courts. A boathouse, much less glamorous, stands by the water.

As we near the back of the property, the Green Mountain range comes into full view. Depending upon the weather, Serena told us hikes are scheduled almost daily. To the right, the same horse stable from the front of the center has stretched to the very end. Every horse we passed was busy feeding and roaming.

I shake my head at the notion of living here. I can only imagine the culture shock of relocating back to a city after this stay.

By the time we make it back to the administrative building, it is almost two in the afternoon. Exhaustion and hunger are setting in.

"So Benjamin, because you are starting the detox process, you'll be in another building that we haven't seen yet. You'll remain in detox for a minimum of five days, but the duration will be determined by your intake. The detox center is slightly off-location to maintain more privacy. It's a five-minute trip up the road. Once you're finished with your intake, a member of the staff will take you there."

"We aren't able to see where he will be staying?" my mom asks, placing her hand on my arm.

We are all blown away by what we've seen, but there's hesitancy in her voice.

"Unfortunately, I am unable to show you the detox center because of the strict privacy policies. But I can show you pictures and walk you through the process?"

My mother nods.

A few more staff members are mulling around now, and someone else is manning the desk.

"I'll let you say goodbye. Ben, when you're ready, a staff member will direct you to the physician, and then I'll talk to your family about the detox center." She walks away, leaving us in the waiting area.

"Caden told me this place was safe … for you know …." I mutter, looking at Luke.

I refuse to tell my parents about reparative therapy. The suffering they have to deal with now is too much. The less they know, the better.

"It is. I checked and double-checked. If you have any problems at all, call me, okay?" He opens his arms, and I hug him tightly.

I'm uncertain how I'll ever repay him.

"Thank you. Take care of my family and send my apologies to Annabelle."

"Ben, don't worry. I love you, okay? Take care of yourself." I nod, and he gives me a pat on the back before pulling away.

"I love you too," I say before turning to my parents.

My father pulls me into his arms. "I love you, son. I don't —I don't understand everything, but I will eventually. Take care of yourself, and we'll sort everything out when you get home. It'll get better."

I mumble a quiet "I love you" in his arms, pulling away to look him in the eyes. Despite the awkwardness, I know he'll go home and study everything he can to understand me, my illness, and how he can support me in the future.

My mother is crying by the time I make it to her. After just a day of using her to keep me afloat, her body sags into mine. She buries her sobbing face into my chest.

"I love you, honey. Please take care of yourself. I need you to. You need to. And your children need you to." I nod and press a kiss against her head.

"I love you, Mom."

THIRTY

THE NEXT FEW days go by in a blur. The trip to the detox center was down a gravel path that follows the backside of the horse stables. The farther we drove into the woods, the more I felt as though I was going to be dropped off in the middle of nowhere and left to fend for myself. Fortunately, there was a one-story log cabin surrounded on three sides by enormous pine trees. It was the epitome of privacy.

With my arrival, the center had reached its maximum capacity of five occupants. We each had our own bedroom with an attached bathroom. In addition, there was a kitchen, a dining table to accompany patients and staff, and a living room filled with a stack of books, a record player, a television, and board games. The simplicity and family vibe reminded me of my grandparents' house.

The physician recommended six days of detox, depending on how my body and attitude adjusted. Though I preferred to keep to myself, the staff living with us tried to get us to stay together as a group, or at least prevent us from holing up in our rooms alone.

Although we were all detoxing—all unhappy—most of the other patients were friendly given the circumstances. Only one had checked in under their own free will, while the rest of us had been encouraged by family or friends. I'm the only father and patient over the age of twenty-five here.

By the middle of day two, I was suffering. My body burns and begged for relief. Headaches became permanent. I vomited following almost every meal, and if I felt like I was wasting away before, I'm a skeleton now.

At the start of day seven, I'm released from detox and driven back to the rehab center, where I'll be assigned a cabin and given more freedom and privileges. Six days down. Thirty to go.

Serena is waiting for me at the main entrance. The sun burns brightly in the cloudless sky. All I want to do is rest by the lake I keep seeing, but instead, I am directed to my cabin and instructed to prepare for my first day. By the time I reach my temporary home, the bell that signifies the start of a new day will be going off in fifteen minutes.

"Okay, Benjamin, this is your cabin." Serena stops in front of the fifth cabin on the left alongside the river. "Each cabin has its own mini kitchen, living room, bathroom, and there is a back porch. Yours overlooks the lake."

I can't stop the guilt that fills my chest. It's as though I'm being rewarded for my mistakes.

"Your roommate's name is Nicholas. He's halfway through his ninety-day stay, so if you have any questions, he can help you out." She knocks on the door. "Nicholas should be awake and expecting us."

Moments later, a blonde, tousled-hair, tattooed man, roughly around my age, opens the door in just his pajama bottoms. A tired smile appears on his scruffy face.

"Good morning, Serena."

"Good morning, Nicholas. This is your new roommate, Benjamin." His hand leaves the door handle and reaches out to me.

"Nice to meet you, Benjamin."

I shake his hand tentatively, giving him a small smile.

He opens the door wider, and I follow Serena inside and down the hall to the third door on the left. A bell rings out.

"That is the warning bell. Everyone should be up and awake, ready to start meditation in fifteen minutes. I'll give you a quick tour, and then Nicholas will lead you from here."

She gives me a tour that leaves us standing fairly still, considering the compact size of the cabin. Although it's small, the cabin contains everything one needs. The kitchen has a small fridge, microwave, three raised cabinets, and an electric kettle. Directly to my right is the living room with a forest green sofa and a matching sofa chair. A basic television is set up in the corner with a bookshelf to its immediate left. Nestled between the kitchen and living room is a square table with two wooden chairs tucked under each side. A sliding glass door extends off the kitchen and leads out to a porch that did indeed overlook the lake. While it doesn't compare to Lake Mackenzie, I know I'll be spending most of my free time in its company. A bathroom is situated between both of our bedrooms.

My bedroom is small, giving room to just a twin bed, small dresser, and desk. It has a single window as well. My suitcase that they picked up earlier is sitting beside the dresser. The comforter is navy blue with crisp white pillows. The wooden desk is entirely empty aside from a folder. I reach to open the drawers, expecting them to be empty, and come across a stack of paper, two pens, a book of stamps, and a handful of envelopes. I can't imagine needing them over the thirty days, but the gesture makes me feel less homesick.

"Benjamin, we do have inspections on Wednesdays to ensure that the apartment is being taken care of. Aside from that, the folder on your desk has a map, your schedule, ground rules, and names of the staff members you'll be reporting to. If you need anything else, please let us know."

"Thank you, Serena."

She hands me my keys before she walks out, saying goodbye to us both.

When the front door closes, I pick up my suitcase and place it on the bed. I dump the contents across the comforter. I strip off my now grimy sweatshirt that I refused to take off while in detox. I decided I should wear something cleaner and lighter on my first official day. With the last bit of clothing I shake out, Caden's favorite hoodie tumbles out. My breath catches in my throat. Picking it up from the pile, I bury my face in it, inhaling his scent.

My eyes fill with tears as I tug on the comforting material, disregarding the borderline summer temperatures outside. I need him to be with me in some way. I pick at the hem, noticing the once tight sweatshirt now hangs loose on my torso. I stuff my hands in the front pocket, my fingers stumbling upon a piece of paper that reads:

Be honest. Be true. Learn to Love you.
I love you, Ben.

"Ready to go?"

I jump at the sound of Nicholas' voice, quickly folding up the note and stuffing it into the back pocket of my jeans.

"Y-yeah," I stutter, wiping away any stray tears before turning to face him.

It will be okay. Caden is with me every step of the way.

"You okay, dude?" I look up at him and nod.

Without further questions, we walk out of the cabin and venture toward the meditation space.

Following a relatively weak attempt at meditation—thankfully, I'm not the only one who can't reach a state of zen—I follow Nicholas to the cafeteria. Though we aren't granted much time to eat, we are given a generous selection ranging from eggs to fresh fruit, vegetables, tea, and juice. I sigh as I realize that coffee isn't allowed in our diet. Not only am I subject to detox from alcohol, but also from my second drink of choice.

Nicholas and I occupy a table set for four and begin to dig in.

"So whatcha in for? Drugs, alcohol, both?" he asks with a mouth full of food.

I stare blankly, surprised by his forwardness. "Oh dude, I'm sorry. That was incredibly impolite of me. I've been working on that." He swallows what is in his mouth and gives me a half-grin. "I can be very blunt sometimes. Please don't feel the need to answer me whenever you're uncomfortable."

I nod, going back to picking at my scrambled eggs.

"Well, I'm Nick. I'm from the sunny coast of California. Been here fifty-five days so far," he says while still shoveling food in his mouth. "I had a severe drug and alcohol problem. Lost everything. But now I'm doing great. Got another thirty-five to go. Probably be dead if I wasn't here right now."

I struggle to keep my mouth from falling open. Do I really qualify for rehab? Surely my problems aren't nearly as severe as those surrounding me. Most of the people in the detox center have identified as alcoholics for multiple years.

"Um," I mumble, attempting to collect my thoughts. "W-what brought you from California to here?"

"I actually grew up in Vermont. My sister still lives here, but I moved to California in my twenties. Fell off the deep end from there. I checked in and out of centers in California but could never get myself to actually stay and commit," he says, taking a sip of his orange juice. "My sister eventually stepped in and made me move back here. I hadn't talked to her in over ten years, but she brought me back to Vermont, introduced me to my nieces and nephew, and showed me what a real family looks like. But gave me the ultimatum, I could only be a part of the family if I got clean. So now? Now I'm here for those little nuggets. I want to be the best uncle and brother I can. And well, I'd really like to give my sister some nieces and nephews of her own someday too." He shrugs and continues to eat.

I'm amazed by how comfortable he is telling a stranger his life story. Not to mention, his laidback, surfer appearance did not prepare me for such a heartfelt tale.

"How old are they?" I ask, happy to talk about him than my own story.

"Three, five, and eight. Two girls, and the boy is the oldest. They might be young, but they know when someone isn't right, and I don't want them to see me as the drunk, drugged-out Uncle Nick."

I nod, thinking of Isabella and Noah, hoping they are still young enough to forget my neglect and mistakes.

"I get it. I have a three-year-old daughter and a six-year-old son. I'm hoping I can come home healthy, and they won't remember the rest."

He nods in agreement but thankfully doesn't press for more information. The rest of breakfast consists of chewing and silence. Our schedules will soon be taking us in different directions.

I coast through journal writing by pretending to listen and jotting down bullshit about Isabella's Coffee. Apparently, the course runs with the instructor giving an emotion to touch on and then the class of six is asked to write about that emotion. Sharing our work at the end is encouraged, but fortunately, not mandatory. After listening to a few classmates read their pieces, all far more impressive than a new Isabella's Coffee concept design, I gather my belongings and trek toward my first therapy session.

My stomach lurches as the main building comes into view. Fellow patients are scattered across the grounds, either walking to their own appointments or busy with assigned activities. I can feel their eyes on me as I pass. It's obvious I am the newest addition to the facility, and everyone is interested in the new flesh and blood. I shy away from their kind smiles, not wanting any more interaction than necessary.

Once I make it to the second floor, I encounter a receptionist who instructs me to sit in the waiting room until my name is called. Two guys look up as I enter the area. I ignore their stares and pretend to read the motivational quotes on the wall before taking a seat.

My leg begins to shake in anticipation. I close my eyes and try to remind myself that this is a different place. Caden and Luke checked and double-checked.

"You're Nicholas' new roommate, right?"

My eyes shoot open. I nod, but I refuse to face the voice, eyes remaining downcast, focusing on the shine of my wedding band, my insides twisting tighter.

"Benjamin?" A woman calls from the doorway.

I am greeted by an elegant older woman with cherry red hair and deep hazel eyes magnified by sharp, rectangular frames. The freckles that dot her cheeks help to take years off her age.

"That's me," I say, raising my hand halfheartedly before standing up.

"Nice to meet you, Benjamin. I'm Dr. Morgan."

With a flash of her stark white smile, she turns on her heels and leads me down a hallway. As I follow behind awkwardly, nerves sputtering, I pull the wedding ring from my finger. Thoughts of Sophia and her persistent push for me to go to therapy flash through my mind. This time has to be different. This time I'm not going for her. This time, I'm going for me. I shove the band in the pocket of my jeans and exhale as though a burden has been removed.

She opens up the door to her office and waits for me to enter first. I walk across the threshold and into a gentle, cream-colored room with a mahogany desk that matches the molding. In one corner, a tiny table sits with two chairs made of the same wood; a jet black leather couch and matching chair are placed in the center of the office. There's already a vast difference between Dr. Morgan and Dr. Matthews.

"Please sit wherever you feel most comfortable."

I take a seat at the table. The couch seems too comfortable. I'm not ready to spill everything quite yet. Dr. Morgan follows suit and takes the chair across from me. I notice a manilla folder on the table, waiting ominously to be opened.

"Well, Benjamin, it's a pleasure to meet you. As I said, I'm Dr. Morgan, and I will be your leading therapist throughout your stay. There will be another therapist during group counseling, but I will be your point of contact. The plan is for us to see each other every day for an hour. If, for some reason, you don't feel as if it is working out between the two of us, you can request to switch therapists at the end of this week. I do hope you feel comfortable opening up to me. No one is here to blame you or to judge you. I am here to help you work through everything that is happening in your life and in your mind. Sometimes it can become overwhelming, and there is nothing wrong with asking for some help. I will be on call twenty-four hours a day, and while immediate medical emergencies will be dealt with by a physician or the local hospital, I am available to speak over the phone or on-campus if need be."

I give a curt nod and lace my fingers together on the table. I appreciate the assistance she is offering, but I have nothing to say. I was told something similar in my previous stint with Dr. Matthews. I remember being certain he would help me and know exactly what needed to be done in order to *fix* me. My skin itches as the similarities haunt me.

"So Benjamin, while today it may seem difficult to get through the first hour, I'd like us to try. How about we start with the basics, get to know you a little bit?"

"Don't you already know? Isn't that my file in front of you?" The emptiness inside me is filling with rage.

Dr. Morgan gives me a small smile and looks down at the file. She reaches for the documents, placing them on her lap.

"I do have a file, Benjamin. However, your file only contains the forms that you have filled out and the physician's report. I do know you are a business owner, but nothing too personal. And we don't even need to start off with that. Let's just talk, like friends, okay? Friends just getting to know each other." She keeps the folder on her lap and looks at me expectantly but continues when I don't respond. "How about I start with myself? I think it's only fair."

I nod at her suggestion but keep my eyes trained on my hands.

"I am a huge coffee drinker. I cannot function without a great cup of coffee." My lips twitch into a smile. I try to turn it back to a frown before she notices. "Can I assume you love coffee as well?" I peek up at her and raise my eyebrow. She laughs at my expression and shakes her head. "Okay, okay. Sorry, that was silly. I know you own Isabella's Coffee."

"Yeah, I own three stores."

"Impressive. Where does the name come from?"

"My daughter's name is Isabella." I smile as a memory of Isabella's laugh breaks through my fog.

She deserves a better father.

"She must be thrilled."

"She's only three. But I do hope one day she will want to take it over. Keep it in the family."

"Is Isabella your only child?"

I sigh, playing along with her act. "No. I have a son, Noah, who is six … going on sixteen." I close my eyes and shake my head. "He hates me."

"Oh?"

I hunch forward, detangling my fingers and resting my elbows on the table for support. My face falls into my hands, and I grip the hair at the edge of my forehead.

"I haven't been around as much as I should." I let my head hang, refusing to look up from the table.

"Ben, this program is designed to teach you how to forgive yourself and ask for forgiveness from your loved ones."

My chest tightens. There is no forgiveness to be given. I have destroyed almost everything. All because I can't stop myself from giving in to desire and selfishness.

"Look, I don't mean to be rude, but I've already done this. I've been promised happiness and forgiveness. I've been promised a better life if I continue therapy. I've hung onto every damn word, desperately hoping that my life would change. I believed the entire thing. And look where I am now. I'm right back in a similar seat, just in a different situation. Therapy didn't help me before; why should I believe it will help me now?"

She eyes me curiously. I fight the urge to stand up and leave.

"I don't make promises, Benjamin. Only you have the ability to truly help yourself. If you aren't ready for help, then this program may not work for you. If you are ready to accept help, then we are all here to help you succeed."

I stand up, walking over to the door.

"Please sit down. You still have forty-five minutes."

I twist the handle, revealing the hallway. Before exiting, I look toward Dr. Morgan. The energy in my body drains, eyes suddenly out of focus as my ears start to ring.

I walk out, slamming the door shut behind me.

THIRTY-ONE

THE CREAK of my bedroom door forces me to open my heavy eyes. My mind is clouded as I feel around for some familiar setting and attempt to blink the crust from my eyes. A searing pain swims through my temples, resting above my brows.

"Ben, can I talk to you?" Turning my head against the pillow, I see Nicholas peeking his head in.

Groaning, I shimmy myself up against the bed frame. Nausea sets in, and my stomach screams in agony. I had fallen into a restless sleep, tossing and turning all night. Each time my eyes closed, a reel of pictures, moments of distress and weakness, startled me awake.

Nicholas walks in and nudges me to move over. Sitting with our backs against the headboard, our feet stretch out in front of us. He is taller than me, his feet, at least, another foot length from my own. My body lets out a tremble as he positions himself comfortably on my bed, a defined bicep rubbing against my bony shoulder.

"When I first came to rehab, I spent ten days in detox. It wasn't nearly enough, but they needed to let other people in. They placed me in a cabin with another person who was pretty similar to me. He was on the ninety-day track as well and had been there for about fifty days when I arrived. He talked to me, comforted me, and accepted me. He wanted to make sure that I made it through just like his roommate had for him. One of the reasons I did so well, and am doing so well, is because someone actually cared. And I'm not saying I'm amazing or that I am going to change your rehab experience, but Ben, I want to try to do the same. I want to be there for you. I think I'm well enough to lend a hand or an ear."

In one swift motion, he twists and sits cross-legged. His eyes bore into my own, demanding attention. He leans his body forward, shoulders hunched, neck up, and his hands tentatively reach out. I quiver as his fingertips brush my knee. My voice vanishes.

"Right now, this may seem difficult. You probably think it's bullshit, and you want to reject all of it. It seems too happy-go-lucky, but let me tell you, shit gets real. The moment you open yourself up to accept help, the facade ends. Your therapist works with you. The two of you develop a routine that will benefit you and only you. And the progress that is made—man, it's incredible. Out of the ten rehabs I've been to, this is by far the best. It isn't until I got here and I met my therapist, did I realize that someone was truly concerned. He took the time to really care. I haven't met your therapist, but a few of my friends see Dr. Morgan, and they all say she is brilliant. One of the best there is." He sighs, applying slight pressure on my knee.

"You have another twenty-four hours before they kick you out for non-compliance. Just do yourself a favor and don't give up on her." He looks me dead in the eye. "Don't give up on yourself."

I curl the sleeve of Caden's sweatshirt into my palm and pull it up to my lips. My eyes cast downward to his hand resting on my knee. Swiftly, I pull my knees up to my chest and watch as Nicholas' hand pathetically drops to the bed.

"I assume you didn't decide to check yourself in? This was someone else's doing?"

I nod. My skin crawls beneath the scars on my forearm. I release the sweatshirt from my grip to put pressure on the wounds, hoping to relieve some of the phantom sensations.

"Attempted suicide. Twice." The words are out of my mouth before I can stop them.

In one fluid motion, Nicholas leans forward and covers my hand with his.

"I am so grateful that you're alive."

My eyes dart to his. I resist the urge to pull away, but I grow rigid.

He tightens his hold on my hand. "You deserve to get help. You deserve to get better. And you will. I care, Ben." He shakes my hand a little. "I care that you're here."

As if he has some force over me, I can't look away. My mind is sending mixed signals, refusing to remove contact but recoiling at each word spoken. His thumb caresses my hand, and his eyes crinkle—a smile forming on his lips.

Nicholas' hand moves from mine, coming toward my face. An elevated heart rate doesn't seem to be enough to signal my brain to put an end to this. *This* can't happen. His thumb presses right beneath my eye and swipes.

"Tears." He smiles.

I try to let the words sink into my thickened skull. While I thought I was hyperaware, I can't even recognize a single bodily function.

The bell blares through the property, shattering the moment. Suddenly, I feel lethargic.

Nicholas jumps off the bed, offering a hand out to me. "Come on, Warrior. Let's kick some ass today."

THE NEXT TWO weeks fly by as I attend my mandatory schedule, throwing the occasional pity party when in the company of my solitude. The idea of making friends seems intimidating and unnecessary, especially when Nicholas is enough to handle. He respected my need to wallow initially, but then he interfered, coercing me into playing basketball and tennis or watching television with his group of friends in the community center. He has never broken his promise, taking me under his wing completely.

Every morning and every night, he checks in with me. He begins the day with an energy and motivation that we will both kick our addiction, and each night, he makes sure we talk about our days—as if the individual and group counseling doesn't involve enough talking already. Eventually, it flows into conversations that leave us both satisfied at the end of every day.

When I returned to my sessions with Dr. Morgan, I swallowed my pride and apologized. We began with the basics but soon focused on the root of the problem. Once I gave her a fighting chance, it became evident that she is the complete opposite of Dr. Matthews. While I have opened up, I have never referred to Joshua by name or gender. She knows a story where a man cheated on his wife not once but twice. She has proven herself to be both decent and helpful, but I still fear the idea of coming out to her. Dr. Morgan knows something is missing, though, but she has failed to connect the dots, or is at least is not outing me before I'm ready.

I have yet to meet a single gay person on the premise. In fact, no one mentions the LGBT community sessions at all, the ones that Caden had researched. And while I know I need to come clean, I can't help but feel like I'd be ostracized if a single soul finds out my secret.

I continue to have nightmares and flashbacks, struggling to determine what is real and what my mind has made up on its own. There are nightmares in which I abuse both Caden and

Sophia in the state of drunkenness. There are nightmares of shock therapy. And nightmares where Noah and Isabella scream and cry, refusing to forgive me for being such a terrible dad. But the worst ones are the ones that play my ultimate mistakes with elevated intensity. It's on those nights that Nicholas comes to wake me up with a steaming mug of tea and stays by my side until I fall asleep.

Eventually, the rhythm gets easier, and the nightmares start to simmer. It's hard to not be infected with Nicholas' positive attitude. I find the activities I have without him are more difficult, but I see him enough throughout the day to brighten my mood. We have kayaking and cooking together, though. I'm certain that without him by my side, I wouldn't have made it another twenty-four hours.

THIRTY-TWO

A MUCH-NEEDED hour break comes just before dinner; a group of us huddle around the community center's television. Nick controls the remote, all of us trusting that he'll find something for us all to enjoy before we are called to our next activity. He seems to be the one that brings people together, the glue to the group. As he flicks past the news, I catch a headline about same-sex marriage.

"Wait!" I shout, placing my hand on his arm. "Turn that back."

The room grows quiet, confused by my outburst. Nick does as I ask without question. The CNN headline reads:

SUPREME COURT RULES IN FAVOR OF SAME-SEX MARRIAGE NATIONWIDE.

My inhale is sharp, mouth dropping. It had been legalized in Maine for two and a half years, but for the entire country to acknowledge it?

"Dude. That's amazing," Nick says. "I honestly didn't think the country had it in them."

The room blurs, and the excitement is reduced to a murmur as I sit frozen. My thoughts grow chaotic, my mind and body fighting for dominance over how to respond.

I am sitting in a room where I'm free. No one knows, nor do they seem bothered by the subject. I'm holding myself prisoner to my own accord.

"Ben, are you okay?" Nick's hand rests on my back as he turns to face me.

Shaking my head, I turn to him. Tears coat my cheeks.

There's a mixture of happiness and fear, excitement and terror.

I am free.

My eyes fly back to the television. News reporters are interviewing ecstatic gay and lesbian couples who are kissing on national television. Cheers and scattered confetti from earlier celebrations have been broadcasted to the general public. Marriages that would have been illegal hours beforehand are now being recognized as concrete unions.

"Ben?" I tear my eyes away and look into Nick's nervous ones.

"I …"

The room grows quiet again. I can feel everyone staring. The t-shirt I'm wearing grows cold and damp while my cheeks catch on fire. I let out a small laugh, an awkward laugh.

God, I'm so overcome with joy.

"I'm gay," I whisper. "I. Am. Gay," I say louder this time. I let out another laugh that refuses to stop. "I'm—I'm free."

Without hesitation, Nick pulls me into his arms. I let out a sob. My tears trailing down his neck. But just like every night following a nightmare, his hold maintains its strength. His chin rests on the top of my head, grounding me until my tears subside.

A sudden spark of motivation shoots through me.

"I uh, I have to go." I pull away from Nick. "Thank you," I blurt out before maneuvering my way to the door of the community lounge. I turn around to acknowledge the room. "Thank you," I repeat, slower this time. Connecting my eyes with Nick's, a smile drifts to my face. After holding his gaze for a moment, I spin and dart out the doorway.

Slightly out of breath, I ask Serena at the front desk if I can make a phone call. We are only allowed to make phone calls at certain hours of the day, free time being one of them. Thus far, I have only made two calls together: one to Luke and one to my parents, letting them know I was out of detox.

Serena nods and gestures to the unoccupied cordless phone sitting next to the couch. I sit and dial the number, fingers tapping the arm of the couch.

"Please. Please. Please," I whisper into the phone. My knees bounce nervously. I jump to my feet and begin to pace.

"Hello?" he questions.

At the sound of his confused tone, I remember that my parents said this number shows up as private. I swallow, preparing myself for what I am about to say.

"I love you. I want you. Only you. I want a life with you. I want to fall asleep next to you. I want to wake up next to you. Caden, I just want to love you."

The hand of the clock in the room screams each second that his silence ensues. Fifteen seconds pass, fifteen excruciating seconds before I hear his unsteady breathing on the other end.

"I have never been so certain of anything in my entire life, Caden. I need you. I want you. I love you."

My heart is begging to be released from my body. My shirt clings to me with sweat and anticipation.

"Do you mean that, Ben? Honestly?" The phone slips loose from my clammy palm as his haggard voice fills my ears.

Squatting, I fumble to retrieve the phone. "Yes," I breathe. "Caden, I've never been so sure. I am certain of three things. I am divorcing Sophia, I am going to be a better father to my children, and I am going to love you the way you deserve."

He unattractively sniffs, trying to compose himself. I can

picture him curled up on his couch, red face, puffy cheeks, hair distraught, and his hand frantically and unsuccessfully wiping the moisture from his nose.

"How are you? How are things going there?"

"Good. Okay. They'll be better. I am ready to be free, Caden." I want to unload everything on him. I want to tell him about Nicholas and Dr. Morgan and how well I am doing in my cooking classes.

"I love you," he says. "I do. I am seeing a therapist too. I want to believe everything you're saying, Ben. I just—"

"I know," I interrupt. "I've been an idiot. You shouldn't even be talking to me now. But I will prove to you that I am changing and growing. I want to be better. And, of course, you have every right to say no and walk away, but I'd love to be a better person with you."

"Okay, Ben. Okay." He sighs in what sounds like relief. "Good luck with the rest of rehab. I'll see you in two weeks, okay?"

"Okay," I whisper.

The phone clicks. I stare at it aimlessly. The urgency to speak with him is now replaced with uncertainty and disappointment. I know I should be happy that he is getting help, that we are both doing what we need to, but I can't stop the worry. The worry that Caden may never believe what I am trying to tell him.

On the walk back to the community center, I toy with every memory involving Caden. The more I force myself to acknowledge and remember, the more my mind grows weary. There is a bubble of guilt that solidifies in the pit of my stomach. I haven't shown Caden the man I truly can be, so how should I expect him to believe in my declarations?

Everyone is still seated, watching a familiar sitcom. I try to halt the memories, convinced I've tortured myself enough. I need to focus on what Caden *did* say. He said he loved me.

The spot next to Nicholas is still free. I make my way over

and plop down. Nicholas turns and puts his hand on my back as if I hadn't even left.

"I am proud of you, Ben." He pulls me into another hug before we settle back and watch the last ten minutes of the show.

I'm able to release my happiness and frustration as the two of us go kayaking after dinner. With every angry stroke of the oar, I try to focus on the positive. This isn't about Caden. It's now the realization that I've kept the biggest part of myself a secret and have just wasted two weeks here. I'm not certain if another two weeks will even be enough.

Once back at the cabin, Nick and I get ready for bed. He corners me in the bathroom as I brush my teeth.

"Ben, I know you're itching to get back to Dr. Morgan's office, but please know, if you ever want to talk, I am here to listen." He places his hand on my shoulder, and I pause my brushing. "But also know, if this isn't something you want to share with me, that's okay too. It won't change anything between the two of us."

He smiles into the mirror. I give a small nod, unable to speak with a mouthful of foaming toothpaste. With a squeeze of the shoulder, he walks out of the bathroom and retreats to his room for the night.

ON THE WEEKENDS, we are given a break from individual and group counseling. This gives us the ability to go horseback riding on longer trails, engage in more intense hikes, or get into a kayak and roam uncharted territories of the lake without worrying about restrictive time tables.

It wasn't until my first weekend here, when Nicholas asked me to go hiking that I began to embrace the center's activities. While we were on a trail with five other patients, the two of us were able to venture off on our own for a bit. I had fought going, wanting to wallow alone, but after the hike that killed my out-of-shape figure, I felt a sense of adventure and peace.

I was finally reconnecting with myself and had a friend by my side the entire time.

I thought about what Nicholas said the night before. He is right: I am itching to get back into Dr. Morgan's office. I don't want to waste anymore time but this weekend has separated me from therapy and speaking my truth. To grant me peace of mind, Nicholas signed us up for two long hikes Saturday and Sunday. Two different trails than the previous weekend. For a brief moment, I am distracted, but eventually, I'm hit with another wave of wanting to talk about Caden.

The next two evenings, I find myself on the back porch of our cabin, looking out at the lake. Summer just began, and the fireflies are starting to venture into the night. A few light up here and there, but my focus is on the constellations in the sky. There was a time when I could point all of them out—a moment in my life when Sophia and I would sit in my parent's backyard, looking up at the sky. I'd name each of them, providing her with a brief story about each constellation. It was my way of trying to impress her in middle school. It even became a tradition of ours until college, when our schedules surmounted sleep, and the lights of the city were too bright. But here, in the oasis of rehab, every inch of the sky is protected by the celestial body. The nearing full moon reflects brightly against the stagnant water.

I imagine this to be a place similar to where I'd want to live with Caden. I often dream about a log cabin by Lake Mackenzie with a porch where we'd both sit, drinking a cup of coffee or tea, reminiscing about our days, and just enjoying one another's company. It would be just after dinner when the sun is setting, and the stars illuminate a path to the lake. We'd have our own kayaks to roam our private portion of the water, and we'd live far enough out of the city to be one with ourselves and each other.

But with each daydream, I am reminded of the blatant fact that I am not in Maine. I am in rehab. Instead of Caden, it's Nicholas who greets me with a mug of tea, and we sit together looking at the lake. And in the silence, hot mug in hand and peace between us, I gather the courage to tell Nicholas about Caden.

The night is the first time someone stops and really listens to my side of the story. Suddenly, it isn't about addiction or cheating or whether or not I am a decent person who deserves to be loved. It's about professing my love for Caden and who I want to be for him. Between the two of us, there is no judgment because there can't be. We both fucked up our lives, and together, we are trying to figure out how to repair the pieces of our personal puzzle pieces.

THIRTY-THREE

I RUSH to the counseling center on Monday for my scheduled appointment. A nervous energy dances throughout my body as I alternate between leaning on my left and right foot as I stand in the waiting room. Every few seconds, I peek my head out into the hallway to see if Dr. Morgan is there.

Two minutes past my scheduled time, her silhouette finally emerges from the back.

"Good afternoon," I greet, jumping out of the doorway, meeting her halfway down the hall.

Her smile is bright as she comes to a halt. "Benjamin," she suppresses a laugh. "Good afternoon."

"How are you?"

She turns, and we fall in step together, heading to her office.

"I'm great," she says, her eyes crinkling in kindness.

It is the first time I see her as someone other than my therapist. Walking beside me is a mother, a wife, a friend, and a daughter. I can finally see that she is someone beyond the walls of the rehabilitation center.

Dr. Morgan opens the door and waits for me to walk over the threshold. I am welcomed by the sun captivating her office with the blinds lifted. I inhale the summer breeze that wafts in from the open window. It's a nice change from the usual air conditioning blasting cold air from the ducts. Eucalyptus oils are diffused throughout the room, a gesture meant to provide me with comfort.

I glance around the office and consider advancing on new territory. The round wooden table we always sit at appears stiff and unwelcoming. Her notepad and my stress ball are on top of the table.

I can sense her behind me, analyzing my motions and awaiting my next step.

Dust particles glisten in the sun above a cushion on the back leather couch. My smile grows, heart swelling. If I can't be basking in the sunlight outside, I want to be as close as I can.

With a pep in my step, I walk over to the couch and sink down into the cushions. I cross my ankle over my knee and smile to myself. I've been missing out on a piece of furniture that welcomes you with an overbearing comfort.

Flashing Dr. Morgan a grin, she hides her surprise and moves to collect her notepad and the stress ball. Next to the couch is a matching leather lounge chair that envelops her. She rests her notepad on the unusually large armrest and presents me with the stress ball.

"Would you still like this?"

We found on day three that adding the stress ball into my therapy helped keep my hands occupied, preventing further discomfort and distraction.

I happily accept. I don't think I need it today, but I enjoy the routine. Tossing it back and forth between my hands, I wait for her to begin the session.

"So, how was your weekend?"

"Same-sex marriage is legal," I blurt out, mid-squeeze.

"Yes," she smiles. "I watched it on Friday. How wonderful is that?"

I raise my eyebrows. Anxiety seeps into my bloodstream. I try to subconsciously suppress the tension begging to burrow in my shoulders. How can I be certain this isn't a trap?

"I have a few friends who are gay," she continues. "My husband and I actually attended a friend's wedding this weekend in honor of it."

I choke on the afternoon air, letting the rubber ball slip free.

This has to be a trap.

"Really?"

She nods, a smile on her lips. She writes a few things on my pad, which makes no sense because I haven't said a damn thing.

Excitement still tears through my skin, escaping my body and leaving behind remnants in the form of sweat on my brow.

"Do you know anyone affected by this?" Her writing stops, and her eyes connect with mine.

This is my moment.

Everything seems different: brighter, happier, cleaner. Her office is more welcoming, the couch inviting, and her smile encouraging.

I am beginning to accept myself. But can I trust her?

My moist hands cover my face, helplessly trying to wipe the sweat away. The breeze outside takes a moment to mock me, pausing its movements; the sun fills the room with a nervous warmth. I trail my hands up into my hair, trying to hide the evidence of my anxiety.

"Ben?" she questions. "You're safe here."

I try to picture her as a mother and a wife. I try to imagine what her life is like outside the office; I envision her gay friends and the kind of wedding they had.

"Me," I mumble. The word betrays and abandons me, asking for help without permission.

I retrieve the ball from my lap and squeeze it violently

with my left hand. My right reaches for the material of the couch, and I pick. I glance up to find her professional demeanor now shifting into one of endearment. The kindness she exudes makes me want to spill everything.

"Dr. Morgan?" She gives a gentle nod. "I-I'm gay." My voice pierces the humid air, louder this time. Anxiety pushes its way out of my muscles, perspiration breaking out in every crevice of my skin. I sit upright, startled at my own confession.

"And there is the puzzle piece, Ben." Her angelic words float through the air. "Your happiness matters. You deserve to live a life full of freedom and happiness. It's okay to be gay."

Tears soak my cheeks. "I'm afraid," I confess.

"Ben, this previous therapy you briefly spoke about, the therapy that seems to have negatively impacted you—it wasn't reparative therapy, was it?"

I nod.

She sucks in a breath before exhaling. Her eyes are wide, and she shifts in her seat as if she wants to wrap her arms around me.

"Ben, I am so sorry. No one should have to go through anything like that." She places her pad in her lap. "I am here to accept and help you. I want you to be happy. Together we can work through this—safely. Reparative therapy is not supported by the American Psychological Association. It's frowned upon and should be illegal. Here at Somerville Ranch, we are open and accepting of everyone. We do not discriminate. We offer world-class treatment. I promise you— and I know you hate the word promise—but I promise you we are not here to hurt you. We will not tell you that you need to change or that you can be "cured." You do not need to be cured. There is absolutely nothing wrong with you."

I curl into myself, bringing my legs up and onto the couch, hugging them tight against my frame—the couch aides in engulfing me. I try to grasp each word, hoping to collect them for safe-keeping, but the room is closing in on me. The sunlight disappears, the room growing cold, and the eucalyptus smells of mildew. Shivers erupt through me, reawakening the sweat that had just started to dry.

"I am straight. I was not born gay. Being gay is a sin," I say.

I glance around, trying to find the voice. I try to recognize the room and that god-awful smell. His satisfied, sickening smile consumes me.

"Can you repeat that, Ben?"

Confusion glazes my sight. There was never a woman with us. Her face is vaguely recognizable, but I'm still certain she isn't real. My mind splits between scenes: one filled with serene sunshine, and the other is a dungeon of damp darkness.

"Ben?" Her voice is here again. "Were you subject to shock therapy?"

My wide eyes surge. A whimper rips from my throat. Squeezing my eyes shut, I push the tears back.

"I am straight." It's as though I'm physically pulled back by his grip. "No. No. No. I'm gay. I …" I cough violently, the now dense air smothering me. "I'm … I'm … not a s-sinner."

"Benjamin, think of your wife. Think of your children. We are doing this for them."

"Shut up!" I scream, throwing the stress ball across the room. Something shatters in the distance. I look over at her shielded frame. She said she believed in me. "Don't tell me what to do!"

My skin is on fire as sweat pools through my clothes.

"You are sinning, Benjamin. Loving a man is forbidden, an abomination, and downright repulsive."

"Ben, I haven't said a word." I look up with blurry eyes. Her lips are still, but the words continue to replay loud and clear. "Ben?" Her voice shakes me. "Come back to me. I am not here to hurt you. I am here to help you. No one else is in the room."

I blink, trying to adjust to her request. Each blink is different. But every time I am thrust back into his hold. His strong, dewy hand on my arm leads me into the room. His malicious voice tries but fails to provide comfort. I feel the cold wires attach to me.

I have to get out.

I look up at the ceiling and let out a piercing scream; the sound reverberates. The buzz of the shock machine, the disturbing pictures, his voice carrying throughout the darkened room as if he is God himself. The anxiety, stress, heartache that my body carries each and every time I walk through his door soars. My skin crawls as the visions weigh me down as if he is stacking bricks onto my chest. I try to yell again.

"Stop!" My scream turns into a sob of ragged breaths. He is suffocating me, one phrase, one brick—one electric shock at a time.

A gentle hand touches my back, a hand unlike his, not threatening or unforgiving. It's delicate and kind.

"Ben, it's okay." My body sags as the pressure and weight subside at her touch. I feel weak and lightheaded. "Ben, look at me. Look at where you are. You are at Somerville Ranch. You are safe here."

Dr. Morgan sits on the couch beside me, concern etched between her eyes. Blinking, I brush aside my tears.

"I, I just—I want to love Caden." I let out a heavy sigh as if those words are the last I can speak.

Defeated, Caden's face comes to mind. His laughter warms me, and while small, I can feel a ghost of his touch. My lips turn up, but the action feels heavy—almost wrong.

"Caden, is he the partner you've spoken of?"

I force myself to maintain eye contact with Dr. Morgan. If she remains in sight, maybe she can keep Dr. Matthews out.

"He i-is, or was, but I ruined things." I try to hold on to the feeling of his touch, but the disappointment that devoured his face when we were at the park together pushes to the forefront.

Her hand rests briefly on my shoulder, giving me a slight squeeze before she returns to her chair.

"Ben, I'd like you to take your time and start from the beginning."

For the next hour and a half, I retell my story from start to finish, continuing through scheduled dinner. I speak honestly about Joshua, Sophia getting pregnant, shock therapy, meeting Caden, and everything that led me to Somerville.

Through the momentary silences, Dr. Morgan doesn't offer advice or comments, just waits for me to continue. She gives me the floor and space to tell my journey the way I saw it and how I want my future to unfold.

It's the start of my new beginning.

I MAKE my way through the rest of the night in a daze. Exhaustion sets in as I trudge through the last few hours of my schedule. It takes everything in me to not give in and retreat to the cabin for an early rest.

Though excited to reach my bed, I crawl to the cabin at a snail's pace. Before I can climb the steps of the front porch, Nick swings the door open in a greeting. I look inside to find our small table set with dinner and a slice of cake for two.

"I thought this might be necessary," he says with a warm smile. "I noticed you skipped dinner, and I wanted to celebrate."

"Why are we celebrating?" I pull out a chair, falling into the comfort of being seated. I don't want dinner and cake. Instead, I want a shower and warm sheets.

"Because you're making progress. You're becoming

comfortable with yourself. And that's important." His smile is so genuine that even my lips give a little.

I eat the meal in silence aside from the light conversation Nick offers, never once asking about therapy. After digging into the chocolate cake, I rise from my seat. Nick mirrors my movements and strides forward to pull me into a tight embrace.

"I'm sure Dr. Morgan told you about the LGBT group here. But, if you want, I'll come with you for support. You know, if you decide you want to go." I pull out of his hold and look up. His eyes are hopeful as he lifts his brows, awaiting a response.

When I first met him, his surfer vibe felt disingenuous. Never would I have assumed he'd be the single force holding me up.

I nod before leaning in and giving him another hug.

"Thank you," I whisper.

I pull away and shuffle off to the shower, ready to wash away the day's exhaustion.

THIRTY-FOUR

THE MORNING OF MY RELEASE, I anxiously sit in the cabin's living room, freshly showered with my overstuffed bag next to me. I barely slept the night before, too anxious for the light of day. There is one more session of meditation and breakfast in the dining area before I am discharged.

As I sit nervously, tapping my knee, Nicholas comes out of his room, fully dressed, offering a sad, somber smile.

"Do you uh, want tea?" he offers pathetically.

"Porch?" I question.

Nicholas nods. My restless legs jump to action before he makes it to the kitchen. I force myself to slow down, trying to take in the final moments of my temporary home.

The sun is just beginning to rise when I open the sliding glass door. Behind me, Nicholas washes our mugs from the night before and fills the kettle. Swarms of birds have abandoned their nests to fly across the orange and yellow sky.

I curl up on the Adirondack chair, letting the summer warmth heat up my skin. In just a few days, I hope I can swim with my children in the pool at my new apartment complex. A smile tugs at my lips, only to be replaced by a frown at the realization that I will no longer be kayaking with Nicholas or attempting to cook typically burnt homemade meals alongside him.

My eyes drift upward, gazing at the lake longingly. Four staff members, including the kayak instructor, are already on the lake admiring the sunrise. It's comforting to know even the workers can take advantage of the scenery from time to time.

A warm mug presses against my shoulder as Nicholas strolls up beside me on the porch. Taking it from his hands, I nestle the mug between my legs and chest, pressing closer as if it is a cold winter day.

Nicholas sits in his chair and holds his mug to his lips, allowing the steam to collect on his upper lip.

"You ready?"

I shake my head, shoulders rising and hovering forward.

It feels unfair to have the opportunity to go home before Nicholas. He is the reason I made it through rehab. He is strong enough to help someone else, yet he still has to stay five more days. Once again, he is saying goodbye to someone he trusts and confides in.

"Thank you," I whisper.

My eyes remain fixated on the staff, knowing the moment I look over at him, the tears will flow.

"Of course." His response barely takes a second to form. "You've made just as much of an impact on me, Ben. I need you to believe that." I nod. "So thank *you*." He reaches his hand out, and I meet him halfway, giving it a squeeze.

I don't know how goodbyes work in rehab. Do people promise to stay in touch and then ultimately lose touch when reality sets in? Or is it common knowledge that you don't get close to the people you meet in rehab?

We sit in silence as the sun reflects off the lake. I smile to myself. It is our first sunrise together. We've been fortunate to catch some sunsets while kayaking, but it's clear, in this moment, we've missed out every single morning.

Neither of us move or utter another word until the bell

rings. Our hands remained together, the connection wary of being broken. We want—no need to be in each other's presence, but there aren't words for the way we are feeling. My impending departure lingers as our focus rests solely on the little time we have left as roommates.

Following a serene meditation session, we venture to the dining hall for breakfast.

"When I get out, I'll come up to Maine and check out this sweet coffee shop you keep talking about." His smile is wide, but the excitement comes up short of reaching his eyes. "Maybe I can convince my sister to take the family on vacation up there."

"That sounds perfect! And of course, I'll come visit you too."

"With Caden?" He winks. "I'd love to meet him." I force out a laugh, suppressing the thoughts that nag to take over.

In the last week of therapy, when Dr. Morgan and I formulated a game plan, we decided that I should get a handle on life outside of rehab before contacting Caden. I rejected her ideas at first, wanting to run happily into his arms the moment I got back into the city, but by our last session, I understood. Running my cafe again is the least of my worries, and Caden is further down the list if I truly want to come out of this.

It isn't about Caden. I'm not getting help for him. I'm not loving myself for Caden. It is ultimately about me—with my children's well-being close behind.

"Maybe eventually. But I'd like to visit with Noah and Isabella first."

I push around the bland eggs on my plate, suddenly not so hungry. I can't guarantee Sophia will even let me take the children on a trip.

Nicholas and I have spoken extensively about visiting one another: where we'd take each other in our respective cities, what our families are like, who we would introduce each other to, the whole nine yards. We exchanged contact information the day I got my new apartment address; he promised to call the night of his release.

The two of us share something I'm not sure many other patients find during their stay. And while I'm not expecting or guaranteeing that our friendship will survive outside the walls of Somerville, I know Nicholas will always be one of the most important people to have come into my life. He is forever a shining light in my unstable journey. Even if I wish to, I can never pay him back.

After over-stretching our time at breakfast (the staff asks us to politely leave), we casually walk to the main building, ignoring the fact that Nick will be late for his next activity. As we approach the door, Nick stops and pulls me into a hug.

"Good luck, man. You've done so well. I am so proud of you. Believe in yourself, okay? That'll help everyone believe in you too." I can only nod, blinking away the tears as I rest my head on his chest.

There is a part of me that fears walking through those doors. So much has happened, so much has progressed, but it's all been in this little bubble. Now is the challenge of real world application. Everyone who knows me knew the old Benjamin Jacobson. What if they don't like the new Benjamin? What if they reject my efforts to change? What if I end up alone?

"Take care of yourself too. Call me as soon as you can," I force out.

Pulling out of the embrace, I grip his biceps and swallow the lump in my throat.

"We'll be okay," I say, my voice laced with fake confidence.

He looks up toward the sky, blinking rapidly. I let out a chuckle as a few tears escape his lashes.

Laughing pathetically at himself, he lets out a growl, quick to wipe the tears away. "Get outta here." He pushes me toward the door with a light shove, flashing a smile. "Be safe, Ben."

"You too, Nick." I pause at the door, my hand stuck on its handle. I want to say something more, but he holds up his hand and offers me a wink—making the decision to walk away first.

Serena is waiting for me on the other side. I go through the discharge process and have another physical examination, one that is seemingly easier when sober. When I am able to leave, I go to the lobby where I first said goodbye to my parents and Luke.

Before I can even blink, my arms are full of my mother. Her scent filters through my nose, and the breath I was subconsciously holding releases as her tears soak through my shirt. Glancing past her huddled form, my father and Luke both let out a laugh at my amused smile.

"I love you, honey. How are you?"

"I'm good." I grin, pulling away to look at her. "I love you."

Her face lights up with a smile. Placing a hand on my cheek, she caresses my skin. "You look happy," she states, "and healthy." She stands on her tippy toes, guiding my face down to hers, pressing a kiss to my forehead.

My dad is next, enveloping me into a bear hug. I sigh into the embrace, relieved by this wave of affection.

"I'm so proud of you, son."

I hold back tears threatening to fall at the words I have wished to hear for so many years are finally said. He is far from a bad parent, but I learned to never expect the same physical and verbal love from him as I received from my mom.

He pulls away, his palms resting on my temples. His own eyes, clouded with tears, look into mine. "I have uh done some research. And I, Ben, I love you. For you. Okay? Don't ever doubt that."

I fall into him, letting my body crumble as he holds me up.

I bury my head in the crook of his neck as my tears moisten his skin. His own sobs vibrate through the hug.

"I love you, Dad."

When the two of us separate, he reaches for my suitcase and offers his other hand to my mom. She smiles gently and hooks her hand in his. I close the distance between me and Luke as my parents walk toward the exit. Luke slings an arm around my shoulder and hugs me against his frame.

"You ready?"

I glance behind me and wave to Serena, who has a grand smile on her face. I nod to myself and then to Luke. But before he can lead me out, I yank him into a hug.

"Thank you. For absolutely everything. I'm, I'm not sure how I can ever repay you."

Luke places his hands on my shoulders, pushing me away. He studies my face, his brows wrinkling as a stern expression consumes his features.

"Ben, the fact that you are standing here—alive, seemingly happy, and healthy—that's all that matters. Don't ever try to repay me. Just please, for the love of God, don't keep secrets from me. I'm here, always. No matter what happens when we leave these doors. No matter what happens with Sophia. If you ever relapse … I'm here to support you."

With a small nod, he ushers me toward the exit.

The sentiments are soon forgotten; the ride home is filled with questions and upset at my lack of communication over the last month. My mom and dad fill me in on the minute-to-minute changes their lives have endured. Eventually, Luke veers the conversation to more serious topics: how Sophia, the children, and my business are doing.

Sophia did use the money to take the kid to Disney World two weeks into my stay; the entire family tagged along: her parents, my parents, and even Luke and Annabelle. Every last penny I offered her was spent, depleting one of my two savings accounts. I try to bury the feelings of jealousy at my exclusion and focus on what Luke is telling me.

Sophia's parents moved in to lend a hand. Annabelle stayed the first week, and my parents substituted when the other grandparents needed a break.

The cafes are thriving. The tourist season began a few weeks ago, bringing in a wave of new traffic. Word has also gotten out that I'm taking time away. The regulars are sympathetic and awaiting my return, according to Luke.

Luke doesn't offer much on Caden's end. They apparently rarely crossed paths, despite their blooming friendship prior to me going to rehab. Luke claims when they talked, it was only business. He says Caden has been looking healthier, but as per chatty baristas, Caden has been living and breathing the cafe since my departure. They told Luke that he rarely goes home and can usually be found monitoring a store or seeking refuge in my office. He has also been busy interviewing new hires and even training an assistant manager to essentially take over his role. My mind immediately jumps at the idea that he is still interested in being business partners, but I'm quickly put in place with the idea that he may just up and run when I am back.

The sudden onset of information is overwhelming. The change of schedule has me growing anxious fast. I look at the clock incessantly, imagining where I would be if I was still at the ranch. Everyone and everything outside my safe haven feels rushed and chaotic, slightly forced. I don't want to sit and have lunch with my parents. I don't want to sort out the exact location of my apartment, nor do I want to finally face Sophia after over a month of much-needed separation.

While Dr. Morgan and I set a plan and went over it ad nauseam, I didn't properly prepare for the anxiety of broken schedules and input from loved ones.

I begin to recite the plan in my head. Luke and I will spend the night with my parents, and in the morning, everyone will assist me with the move into a sober apartment complex. It is just outside Cyan City, fifteen minutes from the hustle and bustle and just over twenty minutes from my kids.

Tomorrow, I move in and get settled, and can call Sophia to set up a time and place to talk one-on-one. Together, we will draft up a schedule of when and where I can spend time with our kids. And then slowly, I can return to work—and to Caden.

TO THE DISMAY OF ANNABELLE, Luke packed up and stored all my belongings at their home. Surprise strikes me as I enter the basement to not only find my own things but the bed set Sophia and I shared.

"She wanted a new one ..." Luke mumbles, clapping a hand against my back.

I give a weak smile before moving forward to begin carrying the boxes to my parents' and Luke's cars. An hour later, we drive to the sober complex.

The complex is fairly new. The receptionist informs me that it was built a year and a half ago. They have a brand new pool and gym on the property. The residents are of varying ages; some just nineteen or twenty, and others are in their sixties. It is a regulated, dry complex—no one is allowed alcohol or drugs, and AA is on site.

Before I left rehab, Dr. Morgan set me up with a trusted new therapist who I will see for an hour every week. Already having missed two sessions with Dr. Morgan, I feel off-kilter. How is it possible to fit in a week's events into one hour? I'm not lost on the irony of my need to open up and talk about my problems now. In order to live at the sober apartment complex, I have to attend AA meetings twice a week for three months, after that, my lease is assessed as well as my sobriety.

THIRTY-FIVE

MY FIRST WEEK out of rehab involves cleaning, unpacking, and maintaining as much of my rehab schedule as possible. I keep journaling, I force myself to cook a meal three times a day, I do yoga, and I replace kayaking with running. It's crucial to keep busy. I know my schedule will ultimately change, and I will have to adapt, but the only change I can adapt to at the moment is learning to live in the silence of my new home.

I resist the urge to walk into Isabella's Coffee. The only social interaction I have aside from AA and therapy is Luke. Each day, Luke comes over for dinner. I cook for him and we decorate my place, trying to have it resemble a home. After a full week, I force him back home to spend time with Annabelle. He won't open up to me about how she is feeling, insisting I shouldn't worry about her, that I need to focus on me. I'm not ignorant, though. I know each dinner he spends with me is one more argument he has to work through when he gets home.

Nicholas even calls without fail the night he is released. It's late, well after his nieces and nephew are asleep, but the happiness and exhaustion in his voice are evident. He was nervous and terrified, but his family welcomed him with open arms. His sister, her husband, and their three children were all at the ranch to pick him up. And for the next few nights, we speak before bed, updating each other on our lives.

A week and a half after my release, Sophia and I plan for her to visit the complex. Nicholas and I spend an extra hour on the phone the night before, trying to figure out what the meeting with Sophia will look like. Though I feel comfortable on the phone, the moment I hang up, the thoughts, fears, and nightmares of what *can* happen flood my mind, leaving me restless as I pace my bedroom.

MEDITATION in the morning is the hardest it's been since my first day of rehab. After many failed attempts to calm my mind, I shower and get dressed, changing into multiple outfits. Nothing cries out, 'Hey, trust me, I'm healthy and happy. Let me see my children again.' In the end, I settle on jeans and a t-shirt. My scars scream against my tan skin.

By the time Sophia arrives, I discover there are one hundred and forty-eight steps from my bedroom to the front door if I pace six times. Running the last few steps, I quickly answer the door. Exhaustion greets me as I fall against the door frame, openly gaping at her appearance.

Sophia's makeup overcompensates for what she is desperately trying to hide. She doesn't want me to know that I've broken her. Puffy eyes, outlined with dark circles, are evident under her concealer, and the wrinkle across her forehead is now prominent. I gesture her in with a hand, unable to offer a more substantial greeting. She brushes passed without a word.

Sans permission, she gives herself a tour of the apartment, walking into the children's bedroom. She checks the bedsheets, looks in the drawers to inspect the clothing sizes— as if I have been gone for years—and rifles through the toys.

She trudges farther down the hall, footsteps halting at the base of my bedroom door. She notices the old bed set but quickly shakes it off. She isn't interested in my bedroom set up, more so interested in if someone else is living in it too. Her search continues in the kitchen, checking the food in the fridge and the pantry. She even analyzes what cleaning products I have in stock. Her investigation lasts long enough for me to boil water in the kettle, steep our tea, and cool to optimal drinking temperature.

"How did I score?" I break the silence as we both sit at the table, and her stone-cold face stares back into my own.

"Decent. You have the wrong brand of mac and cheese, you'll need to get a lot of carrots because Isabella loves them, Noah needs an easel, and Isabella will need a pair of tap shoes here."

"An easel?"

"He's very artistic. He's been taking painting classes. It started as a form of therapy, but he asked me to continue with classes." Her eyes never drop from my own—a familiar defense mechanism of hers.

"O-okay. An easel and paint. Done. But therapy?"

She grips her mug tightly, shoulders stiff. "Someone has to look after the children. It's done them well. Noah went from barely speaking to me weeks before you left to now being more open and honest with how he feels."

"So they know?"

"That we are separated? Yes."

"Soph—" She raises her eyebrow, begging me to challenge her. "How could you have that conversation without me?"

"Well, you made the decision without me. So, I started damage control. I'll be damned if I let you ruin our kids, Ben."

I twirl the tea bag string around my finger, dipping it in and out of the hot water. Sophia is still in control.

"Isabella tap dances?" I try to imagine her small frame

bobbing along to a beat. She has never been one for coordination. Even in her daycare recitals, they give her the smallest part.

"Yes. It's more of them running around and getting their energy out to music because they are still young, but she loves it. It's her form of therapy. She doesn't understand. I hear Noah and Isabella talking most nights. She sleeps in bed with him. She refuses to sleep in her bed since you left."

"And you? How are you?"

She crosses her legs, sits up straight, and takes a sip of tea. "Fine. I started filing for a divorce."

Divorce. The words feel like poison dripping from her lips.

Slouching back in my chair, I feel a violent punch to the gut. I know divorce is the end goal, but the word … the reality of it still takes my breath away.

"What are we doing about custody?"

"I'll have them throughout the week. You get them every other weekend."

"No." I shoot up from my seat, almost spilling my tea. "No, that's not fair." I lean over, elbows resting on the tablet. "I want them during the week too."

"That's unstable, Ben. They need consistency. You— you're not consistent. You could barely make it home in time for dinner. How would you get them after school, fed, ready for bed, and back to school the next day?"

"Trust me," I beg softly. "Things are different, Sophia. I am not lying when I tell you our children are the most important thing in my life. Please."

She stands up from the table, grabbing her mug as she walks to the living room. She stops at the sliding glass door that leads out to a small porch overlooking the swimming pool —the closest thing to my fantasy of the lake.

"Sophia—I need this. I've already missed too much." I join her by the window.

Her face is slender and pale in the light; a sundress sags on her fragile frame. Despite the warm temperatures, a cardigan covers her arms and shoulders.

She glances over at me, only to shut her eyes. She rolls her shoulders back and stretches her neck, taking a deep breath in before letting it out.

"Listen, yesterday my parents had to go back home. The summer daycare can only take them Mondays, Wednesdays, and Fridays. I was going to call out this Tuesday and Thursday, but if you're serious—"

"I'll watch them."

Her brows furrow, and a free hand runs through her tangled, semi-greasy hair.

"Sophia, I am their father. I can do this. Please, let me prove this to you."

She shakes her head and turns away, walking back over to the kitchen. "No, forget it. It's too soon. Noah is still angry with you. The therapist suggested starting with something familiar and easing them back in."

"So then, let's set up a time. Let's go to the park this afternoon."

"No." She sits back at the table, putting her tea down. Her head falls into her hands, her shoulder blades jutting against her cardigan. I push away the habit of massaging her neck— to calm her in whatever way I can.

"Soph," I beg. "Please."

"No, dance and art are tonight and again on Wednesday. Tuesdays and Saturdays are for tee-ball. We have a schedule we can't break."

"Then let me come watch dance. Let's go out for ice cream afterward."

"No, Ben. Look—I-I have to go." The chair screeches aggressively against the tile as she jumps from her seat.

Panicking, I rush toward her. I try but fail at stopping her as she brushes passed.

"Sophia, we need to discuss this. You need help tomorrow. Let me help," I plead.

She ignores me and opens the front door. I clench my fists, anger rising from my gut.

"Sophia!" I scream.

Her body straightens, and she freezes, her hand gripping the doorknob. Guilt fizzles and erupts inside of me. "Soph," I whisper, voice significantly lower.

Her shoulders rise and fall before she takes the last few steps out of my apartment, slamming the door behind her.

"Fuck!" I shriek. Gripping my hair, I tug at the ends and glance around my apartment helplessly.

I begin to pace. Counting each step I take, trying to force myself to think of something else. I try to stop my hands from fidgeting. I didn't anticipate her doubt. I had pictured her distraught, full of anger—but needing my help and accepting my offers.

I start to rummage through the apartment, in search of *something*, anything that can offer peace. I attempt to drink my tea. I tell myself to sit down calmly and do breathing exercises. Each attempt fails. Instead, I grab both mugs and aggressively throw them at the sink, watching them shatter to pieces. I open and slam each cabinet, knowing there isn't anything in them. There isn't even alcohol in my cleaning products or toothpaste. This is a sober location: zero tolerance, absolutely no exceptions.

I work through my checklist again: take deep breaths, meditate, yoga, dial a friend. I call Nicholas and hang up a few times.

Rummaging once more through the apartment, I search through pots and pans, only to leave the cabinets open before making my way to my bedroom. The bed set makes my stomach churn. I want to destroy it, but instead, I search through my clothes for the one thing that may be able to offer help.

At the bottom of my drawer, beneath all my t-shirts, lay his sweatshirt. I strip off the shirt I am wearing and replace it with the worn garment.

Leaving my apartment in disarray, I grab my car keys and drive toward the city. I circle the Isabella locations trying to anticipate what may happen if I walk in. I'm not ready to add work back into my schedule yet, and I'm not sure if I want my employees to know I'm back. I drive past my office, Caden's car isn't there. I drive past his apartment complex, cursing that he has underground parking. As I slow past a parking space, I decide against the idea of bombarding him at home. It isn't fair; that isn't the plan.

I make a u-turn back to my office building and park on a side street instead of in the lot. I walk into the deserted building and up to my office door, unlocking it with the keys Luke gave me back.

Caden's briefcase is on the desk chair, unzipped and filled with folders. A small sense of hope calms my nerves as my eyes catch sight of a picture frame next to the computer with a picture of me and Caden in it. It's a photograph taken the day we played hooky and spent the afternoon cuddling and kissing on the beach. His head rested on my chest as he took the photo. I wasn't looking at the camera. I was looking down at him, a smile gracing my face.

"B-ben."

The hairs on my skin stand up at the sound of his voice.

As slow as humanly possible, I turn to face him, a cheeky smile on my lips.

The man who stands before me takes my breath away. His cheeks are rosy and radiant. His hair, recently cut, is styled to perfection. His skin—he is glowing with a golden hue.

For someone who is a workaholic, he has somehow found time to enjoy the sun. And in his midst of stress, he has found time to go to the gym. Not only are his thighs defined in his jeans, but he wears a red v-neck that accentuates not only his tan but his newfound muscles.

Caden remains frozen in front of me as I analyze him. He has a coffee cup gripped in one hand and a brown paper bag in the other.

"Caden." His name falls softly from my lips. "I-I like what you did with the office." He had also rearranged all the furniture.

That breaks his trance, and he nods, sidestepping passed me.

"Yeah, uh, sorry." He places the bag on the desk before raising a hand to his hair. His shirt rises, revealing a tanned, toned stomach and a small patch of hair that continues beneath his jeans.

Swallowing loudly, I take a few steps toward him.

"Caden, you look … you look handsome."

A blush grows on his cheeks. He tries to busy himself, moving his briefcase off the chair to sit down and search through a stack of papers.

"Thank you. Um, how are you?"

"I'm okay."

He stops what he is doing and looks up at me, nodding. "Good."

"You?"

"Good. I, uh, I wasn't expecting you."

"I'm sorry. I didn't anticipate coming. Something just happened, and I—"

I watch as his face changes, already losing faith in me. Not even five minutes in, and I'm venting to him.

"I wanted something familiar." I motion my hand around.

"I thought you'd call, you know, last week."

I shake my head, and I walk over to my vacant chair stashed in the corner, taking a seat—creating space between us.

"I wasn't ready."

"So this is still on your terms?" he scoffs. "Why do you get to choose the terms of when we see each other? Did you stop to think about how that makes me feel?"

"No, I—"

"Exactly! You don't think about anyone but yourself. You can't just waltz back into my life, Ben. That isn't how this works!"

My brows narrow, and my arm begins to itch, an odd sensation that hasn't happened in weeks.

"But—but I thought we were okay?"

His shoulders slump, and he leans back against the chair.

"A warning is still nice, Ben. I have been working on my own things, you know. I am creating this life that I am happy with." He shakes his head, breathing in and then out with a loud huff. "You should have called."

"I-I'm sorry." I sigh. "I wasn't ready to see you yet. I was going to call you next week. I was going to start getting back into work. I was going to warn you and start off slow. That was the plan."

He turns back to his desk, his face falling into the palms of his hands.

"I have a whole damn plan written, and nothing is going according to the plan!" My voice rises with each word, but I try to keep myself in check. I'm slowly losing him again.

"I ..." I stand up. "T-thank you for the sweatshirt."

He lifts his head, a glimmer of hope in his eyes, but I feel my body shutting down.

"I'm sorry," I mumble, rushing to the door. I shut it behind me and ignore his defeated calls for me to return.

With a quick trip to pick up sushi and a movie, as well as a slow, contemplative drive-by of the liquor store, I make my way back to my complex. I situate myself on the couch, trying to drown out the silence. Soon the loneliness has me wishing something I never thought I would: that I was back in rehab.

THIRTY-SIX

MY PHONE SCREAMS in the silence of my darkened room. I search for it between the sheets, bringing it to my ear.

"Hello?" I croak.

Massaging the sleep from my eyes, I jerk the phone away to find it's just after five in the morning.

"Hello?" I say again.

"We need to finalize our divorce."

My skin crawls at her urgency. The hair on my body rises, sending a chill throughout my bloodstream.

"Okay."

"Now."

"Sophia, do you know what time it is?"

"I have all the papers filled out. There's an easy way, no lawyers involved, probably not even court. We just have to agree. Please just agree." Her exhaustion laces through her frantic breathing. "We can sign and send them in within an hour and then—then we wait a month or two, and it's done. I can't wait any longer."

"We need to sit and talk about this. It isn't just as simple as a signature."

"Meet me at Beanery in a half-hour."

"I'm not ending my marriage at Beanery. If it's necessary to do this right now, I'll come to you."

"No."

"Yes," I sigh. My eyes are begging to close despite the severity of the situation.

"No. The children shouldn't wake up and see you without warning."

"Sophia," I groan.

"Please. Please, just let's get coffee. I'm—I'm sorry for running out yesterday."

I rest my phone against my chest, placing my hands over my face. My middle fingers press against my sinuses, trying to stop a headache from forming. This is a mistake. She is distraught and exhausted. There has to be a better way.

But, before I know what I'm doing, I agree and am out of bed.

WE MEET at the Beanery near the edge of the city. A slower store than the ones I compete with in the city center. They only opened moments before; we are their first customers of the day. Sophia rushes in, carrying a bag filled with her laptop and already printed papers, while I sit at a table with two teas and bagels for us to share.

Without even a greeting, the papers are thrown onto the table. Her hair is in a bun that's falling out with each movement. She's in sweatpants, a ratty t-shirt, and flip-flops. It's safe to say she hasn't slept all night. If anything, she has consumed too much coffee.

"Sophia," I reach out, taking her hand in mine. Her eyes dart to me. "Relax a moment."

She inhales and eyes the food in front of her. Her hand grabs the cup, and she takes a swig, her face scrunching in reply.

"Tea? It's 6 a.m., and you order me tea?" she scream whispers.

"Well, considering the circumstances, it seems as if you don't need any more coffee. But I actually haven't had coffee in over a month."

She pauses, cup midway toward her lips to try the tea again. "What?"

"Coffee isn't allowed in rehab."

Her expression softens, and she settles in her seat. She eyes the bagel but doesn't touch it. "What other changes have you made?"

"Every morning, I meditate. Today is the first day in forty-four days that I haven't meditated first thing."

Her eyes focus on me as if she is trying to recognize the man that sits before her.

"I'm sorry," she says gently, pulling one of the bagels closer to herself and putting cream cheese on each half. "Forty-four days—that's how long you've been sober?"

"Technically fifty. I was in detox for six days before rehab accepted me."

Her mouth drops. Instead of speaking, she breathes before busying herself with the bagel again.

"Sophia?" I start. I interlace my hands and place them on the table. "I'm sorry for everything. I'm sorry for Joshua, for lying and cheating on you. I'm sorry for not telling you how terrible reparative therapy was. I'm sorry for repeating the same goddamn mistakes over again with Caden. I'm sorry I kept disappointing you." Her hands freeze, and she stares intently at the table. "Sophia, I'm so sorry I can't be in love with you."

Her eyes grow wide as she makes eye contact with me. Blinking rapidly, she tries to hold her tears in.

"I want to agree with you on the terms of our divorce. I want to grant you peace. But, you need to be reasonable with me too. You cannot keep me from our children. I know deep down that you know I'm a good father. I got lost for a little while. I wasn't comfortable with who I was, but I'm getting there. I know I don't deserve another chance, but we also made some mistakes together, so please grant me one last one. For our children."

We sit in silence for a few moments. She shuffles the papers in front of her, and once I'm about to speak once more, she screeches the chair back and excuses herself to the restroom.

The sky begins to give away to the rising sun. Yellows and burnt oranges mix in the early light as a few customers come in and out, but we still remain the only constant. A barista sends me glances every now and then, no doubt hearing our conversation. And when Sophia doesn't come out within a couple of minutes, I reach for the papers and begin to read through the documents.

The terms of the agreement are utterly different from what she discussed the day before.

She will have the children every Monday, Wednesday, and Friday, and I would have them every Tuesday and Thursday—no doubt because Noah has tee-ball. The second and fourth weekend of every month would be mine, but my weekends start on Saturday morning. With this agreement, child support wouldn't be necessary as it was quite equally split on time. However, the costs of all activities would be split. All major holidays are split in half as well. The children will remain in the Forestbrook school district instead of the school district I live in now. The house will remain hers, and she wouldn't ask for any money from my business. All in all, it seems fair in comparison to twenty-four hours beforehand.

"So?" I jump in my seat. She makes her way around the table and sits back down. Her golden hair is piled in a tight bun on the top of her head, and her face, previously moist, is now a little rosy.

"I—I agree. But this isn't what you said yesterday. What made you change your mind?"

Her eyebrows raise, and she begins rummaging through her bag. "Do you want me to change it back?" She pulls out a pen.

"No. I just—"

"Don't argue, Ben." She sighs and hands me the pen. "Please, just sign. I just want this to be done."

As I begin to sign the different papers, she reaches for the bagel and takes a bite. When I finish, I hand the papers and pen back to her.

"Also, Caden is to not see the children again until I decide it's okay. If I find out he's hanging out with you and the kids, or if he moves in, I'll bring you to court. Understood?"

I nod my head. "It's about stability, Sophia. I know that."

We sit in silence and watch the sunrise out the window as the morning rush begins. There's an unsettled peace that floats between us. It seems too simple, all too simple that I can't help feeling like this will burst at any moment.

"So, when do we start custody?" I ask as the time nears seven. Neither of us can just sit here and pretend the outside world doesn't exist.

"We can um—let's grab breakfast for them and have a talk."

"You said you did that yesterday too."

"I lied." Her shoulders drop as she finally lets down some of her guards. "I wanted to prove a point. They think you are away on a business trip. Come back with me, be the great father returning, and let's break the news. Depending on how they react, you can start today. I don't think they should spend the night yet, though. Maybe just until after Noah's tee-ball? Start slow and get them used to your apartment.

I nod and gather up our plates and empty cups.

"How about I go run to Isabella's? I'll grab you proper

coffee, get the kids their favorites, and I'll meet you at the house? That way, you can prepare them?"

She agrees and moments later, we are both in our respective cars. I drive in the opposite direction to get to the promenade. The drive doesn't make sense, I pass the other two stores to get there, but a part of me hopes to get a glimpse of Caden again.

It didn't occur to me how long it's been since I've stepped into Isabella's Coffee until the moment I cross the threshold and everything seems to stop. I'm so focused on getting what would make my children happy that I forgot about the promise to myself to take things one step at a time.

Each barista—Caden included—freezes when I open the door and walk in.

"Hey," I say awkwardly, holding my hand up in a wave.

I only recognize one staff member; the other two are brand new, oblivious to who I actually am.

Caden adjusts himself, asking the barista behind the register to go on break.

"Are you stalking me now?" His voice is low, not even a hint of sarcasm in his tone.

"No. Uh, I'm actually about to go see Noah and Isabella. I wanted to bring them treats."

Caden's face flickers, and I watch as he struggles to hide a smile. He immediately begins to mark the kids' cups and prepare cinnamon rolls. "Can I also add a green tea and a latte?"

He nods without looking up.

"Sophia and I are filing for a divorce today."

He pauses, his cheeks twitching, eyes darting up. "Really?"

"Really." I smile. "We just signed the papers. It'll be sent off this afternoon."

"Good." His lips form more of a smile before I realize he's ended the conversation. He comps my order and then starts conversing with the customer next in line.

"DADDY!" Isabella screams as I open the front door. Her arms envelop my legs, causing my hand to grip the drink tray violently to avoid spilling on her.

"Izzy, my love. How are you?"

"Mommy taked us to Disney!" She lets go of my legs and twirls around in a brand new princess nightgown.

Sophia comes around the corner and relieves me from the drinks and food. Once able, I kneel down and pull Isabella up into my arms. I give her a tight hug as she nuzzles her head into my neck.

"You'll have to tell me all about Disney, okay? I'm sorry I missed it. I miss you so much, sweetie."

As we walk into the living room, I place a few kisses on her silky hair. Noah is sitting on the couch, already devouring his hot chocolate. Sophia kneels before the coffee table and takes the cinnamon rolls out of their boxes.

Luke and Annabelle come out from the kitchen, both standing in the doorway to the living room. It feels like an intervention.

I'm relieved to find out they are only here to verify that I showed up, and they also had the lucky job of being babysitters this morning when Sophia was gone.

Luke, already dressed in a suit, walks over to me. He pulls me into a side hug, mindful of Isabella.

"It's going to be okay," he whispers with a pat on my back. "They still love you." He leans over to give Isabella a kiss on the cheek before pulling away. "I'll see you later, Princess. Can we dance again soon?" Isabella giggles into my chest and nods her head.

"Bye Prince Lukey!"

Luke blushes. My daughter is smitten with him. In just over a month, he's taken over my position.

Luke and Annabelle say their goodbyes, leaving me alone

with my family for what feels like the first time in ages. Isabella is quick to lose interest in me when she sees a hot chocolate and a cinnamon roll waiting for her. I place her on the ground, and she races over to join Noah at the coffee table. They both lean over and dig into the icing. I join the two of them on the floor, sitting next to Noah—who hasn't so much as glanced toward me.

"Hey bud, I missed you. I'm so sorry I've been gone for so long."

"You didn't even say goodbye." His green eyes pierce into my own.

Those once beautiful and charming eyes are now full of sorrow. The boy looking at me isn't a young, innocent six-year-old—he has aged into a mature, distraught big brother.

"I'm sorry, Noah. It was unexpected."

"Are you back now? For good?" I glance around the room, looking for Sophia.

She's leaning against the doorway of the living room, drinking her latte. Her eyes are watching me like a hawk, but she gives me space. If her loose-fitting cardigan the day before gave any indication to her self-destruction, the sweats she has on now only adds to the fuel. It wouldn't surprise me to find out that the bagel was one of her first meals in days.

"I'm around, yes."

"You missed tee-ball. You told me we'd do it together." I let out a sigh of relief. A few more moments before his heart is crushed again.

"I'll bring you tonight and every practice after that, okay?" His eyes instantly light up, and he jumps into my arms.

"Really?" he asks excitedly.

Tightening my grip, I'm thankful for his resilience, even if it's wearing thin.

"Really, really. I'm not going anywhere, bud."

He situates himself in my lap to finish breakfast, sharing his cinnamon roll with me. When Isabella finishes her breakfast, she tries to pull the two of us apart so she can show me her new toys, but Sophia decides it's time to break the news now.

"Isabella, Noah—Daddy and I have something we'd like to talk to you both about."

Sophia sits next to me on the floor. Noah is quick to move toward his sister, wrapping his arms around her. Together— one last time—we sit together as a family.

"Noah," I start. "Isabella, I won't be living in this house anymore."

"What do you mean?" Noah's face drops in confusion.

"Mommy and Daddy aren't going to be married anymore. We are getting what's called a divorce."

Noah shakes his head furiously at Sophia's words and holds Isabella closer. "No. No. No. No. No. Andrea's mommy and daddy got divorced, and she's really sad." His eyes grow glossy.

I look down at my arm, the scars glare up at me. I have no idea who Andrea is, but now I'm the reason my son will be heartbroken, just like her.

"Noah, honey, Mommy and Daddy need to do this. Sometimes it happens. It will be okay. We will get through this." I try to reach out and comfort him, but he pulls Isabella into his lap.

Isabella just looks at me and Sophia with a blank stare.

"Why?" he asked.

"Daddy and Mommy don't love each other anymore, honey," I say as I eye Sophia and watch as her eyes shut briefly and her chest rises. Her shoulders cave, and she starts to pick at the carpet. "Daddy doesn't love girls. Daddy loves boys." The words leave my mouth before I can comprehend my own response.

Sophia's eyes shoot over to me. We didn't discuss this, but it doesn't seem necessary to have two separate conversations.

"Will we have two daddies? Jake has two." How could I have missed that Noah has a friend with two dads?

"Possibly, one day. I may fall in love with a guy, and he could be in our life. Mommy may also fall in love with a guy, and someone new could be your other daddy too."

"Three daddies?" Noah is confused again. I let out a laugh, and Sophia remains silent. "Jake only has two daddies and two mommies."

"Oh." My face drops.

"So, we'll have two daddies and two mommies?"

"No, bud. I like men, just like Mommy."

Noah continues to look up at me with intrigue but can't seem to formulate another question.

"The good part for you two," Sophia interrupts with unexpected enthusiasm, "is that you guys get two of everything. Two homes, two Christmases, two Thanksgivings, two birthdays, and extra vacations. That's exciting, right?"

"Yay!" Isabella screams. "Presents!"

"But Santa won't know where we are!" Noah explains.

I rest my arms behind me, leaning back as I gaze over at Sophia. I never answer Santa questions. Sophia doesn't trust me to not ruin the secret.

"Santa will still bring presents here, and you'll go to Daddy's for presents too."

It breaks my heart to think she's already figured out Christmas. Instead of it being a discussion of whether we can be in the same room for the holiday, she's just decided that she'll have Christmas morning with Santa, and I get the aftermath.

"Will Santa still be watching over us from Daddy's?"

"Of course, bud. You know that Santa is always watching, no matter where you are. You should always be a good boy," I answer, and he nods.

The children remain silent after that. We don't budge, letting them take everything in on their own time. Noah just continues to look back and forth between us, as if something on our face can help him understand better.

Isabella climbs out of Noah's arms, quickly disinterested, and grabs her hot chocolate. She plops down in front of her coloring books and crayons.

"Daddy? Mommy?" Noah has his knees raised, rocking back and forth. His glistening eyes focus on the space between us, the far wall behind us, that holds a picture of the family from Noah's fifth birthday.

"Do you still love me and Izzy?"

Sophia lets out a gasp and springs forward, pulling Noah into her lap. "I love you, Noah." Her strength collapses with her words, and a sob fights its way through. She buries her face in Noah's hair. "Daddy loves you too."

"Noah, our love for you and Isabella will never change. Ever," I promise, connecting my eyes with his while Sophia continues to smother him.

After a few minutes, Noah breaks from Sophia's bear hug and excuses himself to go watch television. Reluctantly, we let him. I'm not prepared to invite him to spend the day with me yet. I'm not ready to hear a 'no' slip past his lips.

"Follow me," Sophia mutters between her teeth. Her sweet, caring voice vanishes the moment Noah turns on the television.

The two of us walk up the stairs to the second floor. Out of all the times, I walked these steps, all the memories this home carries, I can only think of the last night I spent here— the night I took Sophia's heart in my hands, gave her hope, and shattered it into minuscule pieces.

She leads us to the bedroom. I immediately stop in my tracks. She's destroyed all traces of familiarity. She pushes me into the room and slams the door. I'm barely able to focus on her anger with all our memories stripped away.

While I anticipated the redecoration in terms of furniture, I didn't anticipate *this*. A white queen size bedroom set, complete with a new dresser, vanity, bed frame, and night tables, fill the room. The white walls are freshly painted, covering up Noah's crayon phase and the scuffs from moving furniture throughout the years. The wedding shrine we had created above our bed frame is gone. All the family photographs that included me no longer exist. They were replaced with photographs of her and the children, interwoven with other artwork. The once blackout curtains we had are now replaced with stunning white lace curtains that flow, capturing the sunshine, making the room brighter than it ever was. And the bed is suffocated with king-size down comforter.

"Are you even listening?!" Her scream cuts through the air. "You told our children you're gay." She begins to pace.

I sidestep her, so she has space. "I am, Sophia. I am gay."

"But you thought *now*, you thought *today*, was the day to tell them?" She spins on her heels to face me. "Without even discussing it with me?"

"What is there to discuss? I am gay. I can't hide that anymore. The reason I went away was so I didn't have to hide."

"They aren't ready. They don't understand."

"So, we explain it to them."

"Let's have some ground rules, shall we?" She closes the distance between us, fisting my t-shirt. "You will not introduce Caden or any man for that matter until it is approved by me. You will not live with another man until I approve. You will not be engaged or married to another man until I approve. Are we clear?"

"You're being ridiculous, Soph. Of course, I know to be careful when it comes to introducing a potential partner. But I'll be in control of when."

"No." She lets go of me with a shove and crosses her arms.

"Sophia, are you—are you uncomfortable with me being gay?"

Her eyes dart to the floor. "Get out!"

An obnoxious laugh rolls off my tongue. My blood is boiling with rage. "Are you fucking kidding me?" My tone has her looking directly at me. I shiver at her fiery eyes. They are the ones that haunt me in my nightmares. The same looks she gave me when I shoved her.

Sophia loathes me.

"Benjamin," her voice is laced with contempt. "Get the fuck out of my house." I take a few steps backward toward the bedroom door.

"I'm taking the kids for the day. They'll be back after tee-ball."

Her mouth opens, ready to engage in a new round of fire, but it instantly shuts when I lift my eyebrow.

She sits down on her bed in defeat; the comforter wraps around her as it fluffs up at her weight.

"His tee-ball gear is in his closet. He likes wearing those red gym shorts and that damn Captain America t-shirt you love so much. He's anal about it. Practice is at 4:30 at the town park. Don't be late. Have dinner with them and then bring them home."

"Thank you," I whisper.

My hand connects with the door handle, and I silently slide out of the room, catching a brief moment of her collapsing back on the bed, covering her face with her hands.

After gathering Noah's gear, the next task is to convince the children to spend the day with me. Isabella readily agrees. Her coloring book shuts, and her shoes are on faster than Noah can respond. He needs a bit more convincing. Noah has a checklist of everything he needs for tee-ball, down to what he does beforehand to what he eats for dinner afterward. Sophia is wrong. He isn't just particular about the clothing he wears.

I'm able to talk him into coming with me, but the real struggle starts when each activity I mention is answered with a prompt "no." I try to keep within Sophia's boundaries by not bringing them back to my apartment until we speak about it in detail, but swimming flies out of my mouth faster than I can comprehend. And when Noah says yes, I throw caution out the door.

The car ride is filled with Isabella's voice, chatting about the tea parties she's had with Luke and her tap dancing classes. It is evident that Luke and Annabelle spent their free time with my family now. Luke turns into a prince at least three times a week since I left. Something he very clearly forgot to mention.

Noah is silent, only offering corrections to Isabella's stories. Even his critical eye of the apartment complex doesn't have him speaking. His reaction is similar to Sophia's—taking it upon himself to walk room to room to analyze the place.

He spends most of the time critiquing the room he shares with Isabella. Isabella is quick to check out her two new dolls and stroller I purchased. She squeezes both dolls into the stroller, not able to decide which is best, and straps them in before venturing around the apartment.

"I was thinking after we swim, we could run to the store and buy you an easel and Isabella some tap shoes?"

Noah glances over while he rummages through his closet. "A new mitt and baseball too?"

"Of course." I honestly can't believe I forgot that in the original round of shopping.

He studies me for a moment before nodding. Jumping up, he walks over to his dresser. "Izzy, time to swim!" he yells, the sudden volume causing me to jump.

With their resilience, I'm able to spend the day with my children as if no time has passed.

When it is time, we gather in the car and drive to Forestbrook park. The baseball field is on the opposite side of the parking lot, where I attempted suicide. Just seeing the lot and the street lamp—knowing that just over a month ago I was ready to end it all and now I'm driving to tee-ball—leaves me unsettled.

I momentarily lose track of the conversation we are having in the car as I try to recognize the man I am now to the man I was. I feel like the days are passing faster than I can fathom. Almost like the pace of my life is moving too fast for me to spiral, but what happens when things slow down? When life becomes *normal* again? Will I be able to maintain this person or will I be haunted by my inner demon?

Pulling into a parking space, I see children Noah's age all gathered around Luke. He is dressed in gym shorts and a t-shirt, sporting a Red Sox cap.

"Why is Luke here?" I look to the backseat, turning off the car.

Noah is practically out of the back door. We had purchased him a new mitt and baseball like promised, and he is more than eager to show them off.

"He's the assistant coach, Daddy!" Noah laughs and rolls his eyes at my question.

He bolts to his friends while Isabella and I take our time walking up the small hill to meet Luke.

"Hey guys!" he greets. The children begin to scatter when their assistant coach's attention turns to me.

"Failed to mention this gig." I lightly laugh as I put Noah's water bottle on the bench.

Noah's friends are already surrounding him, checking out his new mitt. Isabella wanders off, joining the little girl digging in a dirt pile.

"Noah was excited about tee-ball until he realized you weren't coming back in time. He was terrified to do it alone, so I went with Sophia the first time. I talked to the coach, and he asked if I wanted to help out. So here I am, weeks later, an assistant coach. Who would have known?" He shrugs his shoulders as if stepping up into a father position isn't a big deal.

Luke looks out at the kids now gathering around a guy who appears to be the actual coach. The smile that graces his face is enough for me to know that he found his calling. He was always playing sports when we were in school and always wanted to coach—but when he had his own children.

"Thank you," I say softly. I reach out and pull him into a hug. "They love you. They are so lucky to have you as their uncle."

We pull away, but Luke keeps his arm wrapped around my shoulders.

"I love them too. I've spent so much time with them recently, I feel like they are my own. And Noah—he's grown so much. I'm trying to keep him young."

I nod and give him a dismal smile. I gently push him off me with a laugh. "Go do your job, Coach." Winking, I walk away and find a spot on the bleachers amongst the other parents.

LUKE JOINS us for dinner afterward. Apparently, a pizza joint in town is the place to be. Noah says we have to order the pepperoni pizza with cheese garlic knots—and he is allowed one soda of his choice. He isn't entirely happy that Sophia isn't joining us, it is part of his routine, but he gives up the argument when his soda arrives at the table.

Halfway through our dinner, where the conversation has been dominated by Noah catching me up on tee-ball, he interrupts himself.

"Boys can't like boys, Daddy."

I choke on the pizza. The family in the booth behind us stops talking as I cough, gasping for air. Luke offers me water, patting my back. Tears stream down my cheeks as I rack my brain for a response and a desperate plea to breathe. Through my blurry vision, Noah and Isabella look at me puzzled.

"Are you okay, Daddy?" Isabella asks.

When I manage to swallow the pizza, I wipe my eyes with a clean napkin and take a few gulps of water.

"Noah," I breathe, trying to calm myself. "What do you mean?"

He glances around the restaurant, and I follow his gaze. Most of his team joined us at the same eatery. Almost every table is filled with a mother and father. And if there is only one parent, it's the father. While Luke and I aren't a couple, we are the only table with two men.

"Everyone has a mommy and daddy. Mommies and daddies love each other. Daddies and daddies don't?" His confidence dwindles when he questions his own logic.

"Noah, did I ever tell you that I have a friend who has two daddies?" I peer over at Luke with my own puzzled look.

Noah shakes his head, taking a big bite of pizza as if this is a normal conversation.

"Well, I work with a friend who is pretty similar to you. When he was just a little older than you, his mommy and daddy got divorced. And his daddy fell in love with another man, who also became a daddy to him. We can't control who we fall in love with, Noah. Anyone can love anyone."

"Why are there more mommies and daddies? Can mommies love mommies?"

"They can," I offer, trying to regain my grip on this conversation. "There are plenty of two mommy families out there."

"Do I have another daddy now?"

I shake my head and try to continue eating, pretending this isn't a big disruption despite some parents watching this discussion unfold.

"Not yet, bud. But I'll make sure when you do that he is really special and fun, okay?"

He contemplates my answer and takes a few bites of pizza. Izzy has barely glanced up after I stopped coughing. She is happily drawing on the placement with the crayons provided. Her picture is covered with her free hand as she scribbles away.

"Will you still love us if you love another daddy?"

"Of course. I have more than enough love to go around."

He nods his head. I eagerly await another question, but he starts up a new conversation in whispers with Isabella. Just like that, it's over—possibly leaving me more unsettled.

As we finish off our meals, Noah helps Isabella color, and we decide to call it a night. It isn't until I bring the kids to Sophia's doorstep that Isabella hands me the placemat. She insisted on bringing it home, and even after a few attempts on the way out of the restaurant, she wouldn't let me see it.

"Here, Daddy, I love you," she says, hugging my legs as Sophia opens the door. Noah gives me a hug around the waist before he runs off inside; Izzy follows in suit.

"I love you both," I yell.

"I'll let you know about Thursday," Sophia spits, shutting the door as soon as her words escape, leaving no room to argue.

Underneath the porch light, the picture is illuminated. There are four stick figures standing in some very tall grass. Noah and Isabella stand in the middle of the page, and on either side of them are two daddies. Noah had written, "Daddy, Noah, Isabella, Daddy?" above our figures.

With a sharp inhale, I look up at the sky, trying to blink away the onset of tears. Despite how parenting seems to be going at the moment, Sophia and I have raised our kids well.

When I get home, to the apartment now in disarray, I hang the photo front and center on the bare refrigerator.

Everything is going to be okay.

THIRTY-SEVEN

THROUGHOUT THE REST of the week, I stay away from Isabella's Coffee. I focus on getting my own schedule down. I put time and energy into figuring out the direction I want to take the cafes in. I think about what I want from Caden and what I can do to get him back. And most importantly, I focus on spending Thursday with my children and ensuring they have a peaceful first night with me.

It took a lot of pleading with Sophia, but once she agreed, it also took a lot of convincing the children to give a new location a try. After cooking their favorite meal, watching a movie, and eating dessert, I read them one too many books before they peacefully fall asleep. Even after a seamlessly flawless evening, both of them end up joining me in bed halfway through the night. I'd be lying if I say that I'm not in love with providing them comfort. When I drop them off at daycare Friday morning, they ask when they can sleepover again, making me feel pretty confident that I can do this. The next step is having them for an entire weekend.

Sophia keeps her words to a minimum. She filed for a divorce that Tuesday but didn't tell me until Thursday. She never apologizes for her discrimination against me, and I proceed not to tell her about the conversation Noah and I had over pizza. We keep things to a basic greeting and an update on the kids—leaving the heavy air to weight between us.

The following Saturday, I gain the courage to call Caden. After a few pep talks, I pick up the phone and dial. My stomach sinks as it goes directly to voicemail after one ring. He isn't busy; he's actively choosing to ignore me.

After pacing my apartment, rummaging the cabinets for the liquid that can't be found, and trying to convince myself that it isn't anything personal, I get ready for bed.

It isn't until I am lying in bed, about to turn the light off, that the phone rings.

"Hey," I answer, after letting it ring twice, refusing to seem overzealous.

"Hi, I um, I'm sorry about before."

"It's okay. I just wanted to hear your voice."

I initially called to tell him I wanted to come back to work. I was going to approach this professionally before I tried to get personal again. But as his voice drifts through the speaker, my body warms and swells. My defenses melt.

"Can I ..." he pauses. I can hear his unsteady breathing, the hesitance in his voice, and if I concentrate hard enough, the sound of wheels spinning in his mind. "Can I see you? Can I come over?"

I'm overwhelmed by the grin that takes over. Pulling the phone away from my ear, I realize it is just nearing nine.

"T-tonight?"

"Yes."

"Please," I breathe.

I tell him my new address, and he promises he is on his way. Before he hangs up the phone, I hear the elevator ding in the background.

When the call ends, I jump out of bed as fast as I can. I— I'm not ready for this. I haven't shaved in a few days. I haven't showered since Thursday. There are dishes in the sink that I planned to wash in the morning.

Taking the quickest shower of my life, I decide to skip the shave, hoping he likes scruffier me. Thankful for the dish-washer I haven't used yet, I throw all the dishes inside. Just as I put the kettle on to make us some tea, a knock at the door sounds.

I quickly run to the bathroom to check my hair—half dry, half a mess; I make a mental note that I desperately need to get a haircut in the near future. I adjust my v-neck and jeans, hoping to conceal the fact that I wasn't just in bed fifteen minutes prior.

When he knocks, I race to open it.

He stands there in the dim stoop light, a smile on his face. He recently trimmed his hair and is freshly shaven, standing before me in a t-shirt that is too tight.

"Hi," I breathe, leaning against the door. My body grows weak just at the sight of him.

He lifts the plastic bag in his hand. "Mint chocolate chip ice cream?"

I laugh, thankful for the break in tension. I take the bag and move away from the door.

Caden walks in, glancing around the apartment without an ounce of scrutiny. I shut the door and bring the plastic bag into the kitchen.

When I turn to speak, he is directly behind me, cornering me against the counter. Breathing heavily, I can feel each and every hair on my body bolt upright. His fingertips come to caress my cheeks, rubbing over my stubble. His eyes light up. It's as if time has slowed, and the world is about to play a cruel joke on me.

His hips graze mine when he takes a step forward. I close my eyes, trying to focus on something other than his body. I'll be damned if I let anything ruin this. Warm and moist, his lips touch mine, hot breaths fill the cavern of my mouth.

As his lips press to mine, his right hand trails up my skin and tangles in my damp hair. When the hand on my cheek creeps to my neck, I gain the courage to place a hand on his hip, tugging him completely against me.

I swallow his moan.

This has to be a dream.

His tongue traces my lips, and he applies more pressure to the back of my head, holding us together, steady.

The kettle screams in the background. Suddenly, a rush of cold air flies between us. Caden takes a few steps back, leaning against the kitchen island. His cheeks are rosy as his hand touches his lips. He looks just as stunned as I feel.

Reaching for the kettle, I switch the burner off and turn back around. I'm afraid of what is to come. Will he run off? Did he make a mistake?

"C-caden—" He motions for me to be quiet, taking a few steps to the side.

"Bedroom?" His voice is low, eyes shifting to the hallway.

I stumble over my feet, trying to move as fast I can. A new wave of confidence rushes through me as I grip his hand in mine and lead him through the apartment. He closes the bedroom door behind him, quick to flip us, so my back is pressed up against it.

The tables are turned this time, and I am more than ready to give up control.

TANGLED IN THE SHEETS, our bodies stuck together like glue, Caden begins to speak.

After making love twice, my body is ready to shut down, but Caden is renewed and energized. He starts asking about everything that has happened since rehab: what I did there, how many days I've been sober, if I made any friends, what seeing my kids was like, and how Sophia is reacting. At one point, we have to sit up because my eyes are beginning to close.

Following the questions, he retreats to the kitchen to find my ice cream stash because the ice cream he brought melted. He returns with two bowls for us to devour as he continues with more questions.

As the sun rises, we make love one more time before drifting off into a deep sleep. He rests his head on my chest, my arm holding him tight against me.

When I wake up late that afternoon, Caden is still fast asleep. Reluctantly, I force myself out of his arms and decide to take a quick shower. As soon as my shampoo rinses from my hair, the curtain moves. Caden's hands rest on my hip bones, his chest pressing up against my back. His lips place butterfly kisses along my shoulder blades.

Leaning my head back onto his shoulder, I let out a soft moan.

"Good afternoon." His voice floats through the shower.

"We'll never get out of here now."

He lets out a soft laugh. "Too bad for you. I'm starving." He flips us around, so he is now underneath the water. A smirk graces his lips. He grabs the shampoo and starts to seductively wash himself, eyeing me the entire time.

It takes all my strength not to pull him into me and make love to him as the water drips over his newly chiseled body. While I showered him with love the night before, I hadn't appreciated every single inch of him yet.

He rinses and gives me a wink, shutting off the water.

"Let's eat!"

Instead of cooking an elaborate meal like I intended to, we both get dressed in sweats and settle on toasting bagels. As I am spreading the cream cheese, I catch Caden studying the picture Isabella drew. He traces the stick figure of the daddy with a question mark. A smile graces his lips, oblivious to my eyes watching him. As he turns away, I focus back on the bagels.

"I love you." His words are gentle and soft as he places a kiss on my cheek.

The kettle interrupts us, and Caden begins to search through cabinets.

"There is no coffee. Tea okay?" I open the cabinet with tea, providing him with a few different options. His hesitance is quickly covered.

"Tea's perfect."

We eat outside on the porch. Families are already screaming and laughing in the pool as it's nearly three in the afternoon. We sit in silence, listening to the excitement. I find myself admiring the way Caden watches the families. His smile grows each time a kid shows their parent some new trick they can do.

"Caden?" Breaking his gaze, he looks over at me. "Where do you imagine yourself five years from now?"

He squints and places his empty plate on the small table in front of us. He positions himself sideways in his chair to face me.

"There's a beautiful log cabin about an hour outside of the city that overlooks Lake Mackenzie. It's secluded and out in the country with a long dirt driveway as the house sits just yards away from its own private canal on the lake. There are no neighbors in sight, and currently, it's rented as a vacation home. I've spoken to the owners about buying it from them, though. I'd be married to a man, in a healthy relationship, where we are both loved and supported. We would have three beautiful children—I'm hoping for girls by a surrogate. We'd go ice-skating on the lake in the winter and have cozy nights by the fireplace. In the summer, we'd swim and kayak, and I'd bring the kids fishing like my father always did with me. We'd have campfires and catch an endless amount of fireflies." He gets lost in his thoughts, a smile remaining secure on his face. The glimmer in his eyes is the brightest I've ever seen.

"My family vacationed in a cabin once, up on the border of Canada when I was ten," he continues. "Since then, I wanted that life to be my reality. So, a few months ago, before I took the job at Isabella's, I started talking to the owners of the cabin here. I started figuring out what I'd have to do in order to afford it. Another hesitance of leaving Beanery's security. Recently, my picture changed," he looks over at me, his smile growing as does his confidence, "only slightly. Now, Noah and Isabella are running around the backyard, playing with our little girls, taking their younger sisters under their wings as the two of us sit, happily married, on the back porch watching them. We are both partners in Isabella's Coffee, having even opened up a shop in the small village near the cabin. Our main focus though would be on spending time with our family and the life we created together."

My vision blurs as he finishes speaking. This man has visions of our life together beyond our next date. He has confidence in me, confidence that I'll get through this, that I'll be the dad he'd willingly choose for his children, and the confidence that our relationship will end in marriage—all while I have been debating whether or not Caden would even give me a second chance.

"And you?" His words are soft, his hand reaching out.

I lace our fingers together, looking over at the swimming pool. I truly try to imagine my life five years from now.

Tears involuntarily escape, creating paths down my cheeks. I squeeze his hand and bring my eyes back to his bright hazel ones. Lifting his knuckles to my lips, I kiss them gently, one by one.

I can't remember the last time someone asked me about my dreams for the future. But at this moment, I am certain anything is possible.

I stand, pulling him up with me. I rest my hands on his hips and lean in, pressing a kiss to his forehead.

"I love you," I breathe into him, connecting our lips.

Happiness isn't about maintaining perfection. It isn't about the stunning home, the cookie-cutter family, or the perfect job. Nor is it underneath the whiskey; it isn't in the burn at the back of my throat as it soothes my pain into temporary peace. Happiness is in the wave of comfort, in the genuine smile found when loving someone without obligation, in giving without needing a reason to. Above all, happiness is honoring myself, accepting imperfections and flaws as a part of my being, and knowing at the end of the day, if I have myself— the rest will follow.

ALSO BY CHELSEA LAUREN

Simply An Enigma

"You Matter, Marley Mae" and "Happy Ex-Mas" from *Winter Neverland: An Anthology*

ACKNOWLEDGMENTS

Without these incredible people below, Benjamin's story wouldn't have been possible. But equally, without some of these people, I may not be here today. So before I thank them, I'd like to take a moment to speak on mental health.

For those who are suffering, have suffered, or may suffer in the future: I want you to know how grateful I am that you are alive. Benjamin believed that suicide would be the answer. I once thought that suicide could have been the answer too.

But, suicide is never the answer. Mental illness is complicated, messy, and difficult. We all struggle differently. One person's methods may not be what helps you get through the fight. One thing that does help, though, is communication. Having a person in your life that you can open up to, whether that be a friend, family member, someone on the internet, or a therapist. When you're ready, reach out a hand. I promise you someone will grasp on tight and help you through it. It won't always be easy. There will be bumps and roadblocks to get through. Maybe your first or second therapist isn't the one for you, and you have to continue the search, but I promise it can get better. The person you'll find at the end of the fight—the person standing in the light at the end of the tunnel—will be the best version of you. The strongest, most powerful version you're capable of will be so grateful you asked for help and lived to tell your story.

You Matter.
You Always Will.

Sometimes we just need a helping hand. And if you believe there isn't anyone around you who can help or understand what you're going through, let me be the one to find the help for you. I can always be contacted at chelsealaurenauthor@gmail.com or representpublishing@gmail.com. Or check out To Write Love On Her Arms at twloha.com. This organization kept me above water until I was ready to ask for help.

You are not alone. Not now, not ever. I believe in you.

So thank you to my support team, those who were with me in my darkest days. You know who you are, and I'm eternally grateful I am now able to live my dream and show you my successes. For those new to my story, thank you for being here with me and continuing this journey.

Michelle, you came a brilliant asset to Ben's life, always able to offer different solutions to his problems. You're my ultimate cheerleader. I always know when I need motivation, you're right around the corner. You're the one I want standing next to me when all my dreams come true. I love you, always and forever.

Becky, we've accomplished a pretty stellar unwritten bucket list, and you've been my rock through it all. Never in a million years would I have thought you'd be my editor, but it all fell into place. We've had our ups and downs, but thank you for your honesty and for dealing with my failure to take feedback. Most of all, thank you for always being you. I love you.

Mom and Mike, without your support to follow my dreams, I might not have believed that I could turn this into a career. Thank you for believing in me and supporting me when I needed help. Thank you for not nagging me to chase a "real" career, knowing that I could make wise decisions on my own and I'd do what I could to survive. I love you both!

Ashley, thank you for calming my panic in the final few weeks. Your suggestions only made the story stronger! Thank you for always believing in me. Thank you for reminding me of the reasons I write. I love you!

Kris, thank you for giving me two of the greatest nieces in the world. Being an aunt only motivates me to be the best person I can for Mackenzie and Mia. And thank you for your constant love and support. I love you!

Tom, thank you for believing in me and picking me up when I'm down. Having been through my worst moments, you came back around for my best. You are such an inspiration to me. Over the final weeks of this book, you became my crutch, checking in multiple times a day just to make sure I was okay. Thank you. I love you. Don't ever change.

EB, if you've picked this up somehow, somewhere, and have gotten to the end, thank you. Without you coming into my life, I wouldn't have had the inspiration for this story. The stories don't align, but I hope I didn't encroach. May all your dreams come true.

Brittany, we met through my first edition of this book and I am forever grateful for our friendship. Thank you for your continuous writing help, graphic designs, work with Represent Publishing, and being an incredible friend! I love that we wrote a book together, and I hope it isn't our last. I love you!

Kevin, I didn't know you when I wrote the first published edition of this book, but your support for my writing and your belief in my editing company mean the world to me. I can't wait for forever with you. I love you!

While this book takes place in Maine, Lake Mackenzie is based off Lake Michigan in Chicago and the surrounding park has bits and pieces of Australia. A lot of my inspiration was taken from my travels through Australia. Thank you to each and every person I met, became friends with, and especially those who read my novel. Thank you, Gin Palace in Melbourne, for being the inspiration behind Gin and Grin and to Cronulla Beach in New South Wales, where I spent a lot of time contemplating my life and this novel. My year in Australia benefited this novel more than I could have dreamed.

LGBTQIAP+ Community: You are human, you are loved, you are not abnormal. There is absolutely nothing wrong with you. You deserve to be loved and to find happiness even in the crazy, messed-up world we live in. Reparative therapy is not supported by the American Psychological Association. It is unconstitutional, and if we work together, we can make it illegal in this country. Don't ever try to let anyone say you aren't good enough. You deserve to be your true self. I am your ally. I will continue to fight for you. Promise me, you'll continue to fight for yourself too.

Love will always conquer hate.

ABOUT THE AUTHOR

Chelsea Lauren is the author of *Underneath the Whiskey* and *Simply an Enigma*, and two short stories in *Winter Neverland: An Anthology*.

She's an upstate NY native, establishing new roots in her hometown with her partner and St. Berdoodle, Kaiya. Chelsea has been writing ever since she had vivid dreams in middle school. The only cure was to write them down, and only then, did Chelsea realize she could become an author.

Chelsea is the founder of Represent Publishing, a self-publishing company dedicated to helping authors strengthen their writing, edit, and publish their novels. Her passion lies in helping others accomplish their dreams.

When Chelsea isn't writing or working on her business, you can find her devouring books, snuggling with her pup, camping, or having game nights with her friends.

www.ingramcontent.com/pod-product-compliance
Lightning Source LLC
Chambersburg PA
CBHW051604100726
47898CB00001B/217